"Gas leak!" Theo said, while Bringo's orders poured forth:

"Cut the exhaust or abandon, *Beeslady* ..."

"Going there," Theo said, punching the local controls. "Show me an intercept line, *Bechimo*. Clarence, tell her we'll be there—"

"Talking now, Theo."

The little craft drifted out of center screen as Theo oriented the ship to the line; then they heard other chatter, advice, starting to crowd the radio band.

"Cain't 'bandon, Bringo. Suit's fritzy. Got water leak now, top it all. Luck me, tryin' ta pull this 'splosive 'lease out and dump out anyhow, got oxymask I do ... sed luck me, deemit!"

"Luck, *Beeslady*, all you can use! We got help on the way—"

"Dem dem demmit dem gotz blood in my eyes, get here oh slitz—"

Whatever signal there was from the little ship ceased. Theo slapped the board, demanding, "Match course for rescue!"

Their acceleration was sudden, the deceleration quick and just as sudden, and the image now of a wildly tumbling collection of tubes and scraps, impossible to dock with, nothing to dock *to*, with pieces flying away and the pilot's station empty, but for what might have been boots, or legs, still strapped in.

Theo wanted to grab what was left of the ship and shake it until the pilot poked her head out from some safeplace in the hull ...

There wasn't one, of course. If *Beeslady* had ever been a safe place, it wasn't one now.

BAEN BOOKS by
SHARON LEE & STEVE MILLER

THE LIADEN UNIVERSE®
Fledgling
Saltation
Mouse and Dragon
Ghost Ship
Dragon Ship
Necessity's Child
Trade Secret (forthcoming)

The Dragon Variation (omnibus)
The Agent Gambit (omnibus)
Korval's Game (omnibus)
The Crystal Variation (omnibus)
A Liaden Universe® Constellation,
Vol. 1 (story collection
A Liaden Universe® Constellation,
Vol. 2 (story collection—forthcoming)

THE FEY DUOLOGY
Duainfey
Longeye

BY SHARON LEE
Carousel Tides

To purchase these and all other Baen Book titles
in e-book format, please go to www.baen.com.

DRAGON SHIP

A New Liaden Universe® Novel

SHARON LEE & STEVE MILLER

BAEN

DRAGON SHIP

Copyright © 2012 by Sharon Lee & Steve Miller.

Liaden Universe® is a registered trademark

A Baen Books Original

Baen Publishing Enterprises
P.O. Box 1403
Riverdale, NY 10471
www.baen.com

ISBN: 978-1-4516-3918-6

Cover art by David Mattingly

First Baen paperback printing, September 2013

Library of Congress Control Number: 2012016684

Distributed by Simon & Schuster
1230 Avenue of the Americas
New York, NY 10020

Pages by Joy Freeman (www.pagesbyjoy.com)
Printed in the United States of America

This book is dedicated to:

Anne McCaffrey
... who single-handedly redeemed the
honor of dragons

and to:

Rusty Hevelin
... who knew everybody

DRAGON SHIP

PRELUDE

· · · · · · · · · · · · · · ·

In Surebleak Transit Orbit, Outgoing

Patient Win Ton yo'Vala
Function Change Percentage Report:
 Treatment Location #03
Cardiovascular 65% > 1%
Dermal 57% < 3%
Neurological / nervous 62% > .9%
Muscular 46% < 2%
Skeletal 83% =
Lymphatic 45% > .1
Endocrine 38% < .1
Reproductive 21%
Urinary 47% =
Digestive 63% =
Senescence Quotient 53% >
Retro-senescence Activity 14% =

Whatever else he might be—and the theories, legends, and outright guesses surrounding that question were legion—the Uncle was a man of his word.

He had informed Win Ton that his time in the healing unit would be . . . less quiet than one might suppose. He had explained that there would seem to be progress—and that seeming might equally be true, and less than true.

Indeed, at first, and in the rare moments when he was fully conscious, the pain seemed less, and he felt, not strong, but stronger. Win Ton, who had been taught by the Scouts to believe the Uncle a man made of deceit, allowed himself to hope for recovery.

This was an error, for the pain returned, and the weakness grew worse.

As befit a man of his word, the Uncle had explained these declines in technical terms, inquired after Win Ton's state of mind, and from time to time spoke of the wider universe, attempting, perhaps, to keep information flowing into a system that was working against itself.

Oddly, it seemed that the Uncle also was an honest man, which was not necessarily the same as a man who, thus far at least, had kept his promise; and the honest man had come to wake him from a dreamless sleep, Dulsey not in attendance this time, as she had been on former occasions.

"Scout yo'Vala, it appears that the medics and shipmates who brought you to me have less hope than I do; this is not a surprise, but it is unfortunate. Healers having failed you, physicians having failed you, ordinary medicines having no advantage to offer you, you are left with me, and my chief technologist. Alas, we are not adequate to your survival, either."

The Uncle had brought him a robe for what comfort it might give, and he offered a choice of liquid refreshment, ranging from water to fruit juice to salted soup to high-grade alcohol.

Win Ton gathered himself together, shrugged the robe more firmly about his shoulders, looking as little as he might at the unnatural shade of his skin or the ice-blank fingernails somehow still attached to his hands. He stared at the offerings, making an effort to fix his mind on them, while sorting the sense of his odd host's words. Finally, he raised his eyes in wary question.

He had seen the high security records indicating that this man—or his mind, or his personally experienced knowledge—predated the advent of Liadens into this particular universe and into these particular galaxy clusters. The Uncle had long been involved with the nefarious doings of those who chose to collect items which might also predate that arrival, items which might have precipitated and fomented the very wars of crystallization.

"Do you come to offer me my choice of dooms, then? A pill, a sip of liquor, and I am gone?"

The Uncle's mouth twitched as if he thought the question had a touch of humor, though his eyes were unflinching.

"No," he answered, "that is not my purpose. I offer you these things as a way to wake you, to stimulate you, and to ready you. For now, having kept you alive after the Scouts could not, I in my turn will relinquish you to another situation. You pass now into the care of the ship you woke, and the crew that mans it, and to the one resource beyond Healers and physicians and engineers and technologists and Scouts, that may, only possibly, aid you."

The ship he woke . . .

Win Ton bore down in very nearly a physical effort to focus his thoughts, his understanding.

There—of course. The ship.

The *sentient* ship.

The ship that was the root of this tangle of trouble in which he was embroiled.

"*Bechimo*," he said, finding the name among his soft memories, "has come for me?"

"Theo Waitley comes for you," the Uncle corrected, which was . . . even more surprising. He had thought Theo quit of him, her thoughts and her necessities focused upon kin.

The Uncle may have read his surprise, for he explained further.

"She pilots *Bechimo*," the Uncle continued, "which carries the last trustworthy sample of yourself. Since Pilot Waitley is alive, and the ship is also alive, it would seem that she may possess that spark of luck which infects all of Korval. I cannot guarantee that her luck will serve you; I merely note and state that it has served her."

Win Ton frowned, finding both memory and focus sharper for the moment.

"Theo is of Korval?" Surely, that was an error. Theo counted herself Terran, born on the academic world of Delgado, properly in line to a scholar-mother and a father nearly nameless.

"Does this surprise you?" The Uncle's voice was dry.

Win Ton held up a trembling hand, doggedly pursuing the memory. Theo's father had been Liaden, his name ancient, and undoubtedly not his own. He recalled it! In a moment, he felt that he would have even the name—Kiladi. Yes. A joke there. Very nearly a Scout's joke. But Kiladi, for all it had been Liaden before its dissolution, was no bloodline belonging to Clan Korval. Korval Lines were yos'Phelium, the delm's blood; yos'Galan, the traders; and ... and ... bel'Tarda!—the subordinate Line.

He paused a moment, breathing hard with the exertion of recalling all of this, that a child not yet out of the schoolroom might recite off of the top of his head ...

But with regard to Theo, there had been ... something more.

He closed his eyes, the better to remember—ah, yes.

Her father had given to Theo a lesson—that she was to call upon the delm of Clan Korval only in the most extreme necessity.

I am, Win Ton thought, opening his eyes, *a fool*.

"No," he said slowly, recalling too that the Uncle had asked a question. "That Theo is of Korval ... does not ... entirely ... surprise me."

His host smiled, and moved a hand, which might have been a hint that Win Ton avail himself of the ignored refreshments.

Carefully, he selected a pod of juice, not because he favored it, but because he saw no benefit to not feeling all that he could feel.

The Uncle likewise took up a juice pod, and for a moment they sipped in companionable silence. Win Ton found his fingers strong enough to slowly collapse the pod and impel the juice into his mouth, but he knew better, now, than to hope.

"The situation is yet uncertain," the Uncle said, putting his empty pod on the tray. "We shall not properly dock with *Bechimo*, but rather use a tube. From our side, you shall be hurried, as the instant occurs. Please accept my regret for this haste, which I fear will dismay you. Against such dismay, I will administer a small stimulant, and at Dulsey's word that *Arin's Toss* is free, I will escort you to the quick-lock, and see you through.

"First, then, we shall dress you; which means we shall move you, under your own locomotion if possible, into the prep room, where all that you brought with you to my ship is gathered, and from whence we shall hurry at the call. You will carry with you a record of what has transpired in our healing unit, with the current trends. The units *Bechimo* carries will be able to access and work from these records." He looked sharply into Win Ton's face.

"Do you understand everything I have said to you, Scout yo'Vala? Is there anything you wish to have clarified?"

Theo was coming for him, as pilot of a ship out of legends even murkier than those which surrounded the man before him. He would be transferred to that ship's medical unit, which was likely of a provenance that a Scout ought not to think of.

This was his last hope; in truth. If *Bechimo* failed him, he would die.

"I understand," he told the Uncle. "And I thank you, for your care."

The tube was taller than he by a hand-span, and the Uncle shoved a small package down in front of him as the first of the cooler air flowed out of the tube, toward themselves, and into the Uncle's own ship. The darkness gave way to light; there was an opening some distance ahead.

His clothing disturbed his skin; he had been nude in the Uncle's healing unit, which had turned him, fed him, washed him, dealt with details.

And to what amazing trust he bore witness, Win Ton thought, alert with the first rush of stimulant. The Uncle was accepting the high-pressure side of a transfer tube! Win Ton stood forward, cooling rapidly in the breeze *Bechimo* pumped at them.

There was a line attached to the side of the tube, and the Uncle's voice behind him.

"I may not accompany you, nor go into the tube itself. This is your walk from here on. Scout yo'Vala—good lift, and safe landing."

A bow was not possible. Nor could he bring himself to say to this man—brigand, outlaw, or saint, as he might variously be—the proper—and very true—Liaden phrase, "I am in your debt." Still, a *safe lift* might perhaps have been proper, but the pressure on his back grew firmer, and he leaned into his mission, moving those few steps that were somehow *down*, his uncertain feet gaining a hazardous momentum, pain thrilling into his legs and along his arms, vibrating into his skull with each step, until of a sudden, Theo's arms caught him, swung him into the fresh light of another ship. He had gained *Bechimo*.

Very nearly, he collapsed. Theo was a whirl of motion, kicking the plate to seal the door, holding him away from the wall, and mustering a strong, firm voice:

"He's in. Seal us up!"

Another voice answered, said things which were out of the range of his understanding. His view was of Theo, wiry, graceful, and strong.

Korval, he thought. *Of course, Korval.*

Balance was nearly beyond him, and he knew better than to perform the ordinary...but he would not fall!

"Theo," he tried, and his voice failed him. He gathered himself against his throat.

"Theo," he got out this time. "Forgive me, that I do not bow."

ONE

· · · · · · ·

Jump

THEO SAW THE RIM OF DUST-AND-SOMETHING ON HER sleeve, sighed and tried not to be annoyed—it wasn't as if she was waiting for an appointment with a customer, or getting ready for an assignation, after all. Still, as she applied enough torque, manually, to start closing the small hatchway, the accumulation was evident not only on her sleeve but on the surface of the sample filter she'd replaced, and likely on her cheek as well, since she'd brushed some irritant from there with her ring finger a few moments before.

She'd knelt to check the torque, and now some of whatever it was had fallen to the floor.

Bechimo had thought the whole routine a waste of time, even managing to bring the word "dignity" into the conversation.

Theo shook her head. Ship's dignity, indeed!

There was a smudge of color on the filter—this from an unused room. Really unused. According to *Bechimo* there hadn't been anyone in there for hundreds of years! That would bear looking into.

Dropped and sealed into her stash bag, this was another of a half-dozen items of interest she carried, things she'd share with Clarence when they got together once again in the conference room—or Dining Room Two, if you happened to be *Bechimo*.

She was considering the next item on the list, wishing she had help on it since it would be a live-wet line. She'd worked on live-wets a few times at the Academy, and several more less-unhappy times while working the off-schedule at Hugglelans. At Anlingdin, some of the lines were "misrepresented" Pilot yos'Senchul had called it, as having been cared for recently, or at all.

When she'd been back on Eylot, her good friend Kara had called the duty Theo now performed "ship wipe," complete with an odd Liaden back-channel of meaning. She'd called it that at the Academy and at Hugglelans, and while she evinced no particular love for the job, she'd done it dutifully and had said it was educational. Kara had from time to time come back to their shared room at Hugglelans in multiple shades of leftover dirt and dinge, her clothes so smelly that Theo donned disposable gloves to help her into the shower without leaving a permanent record on the walls.

"Stinks, by damn and darn, that's what we called it where I learned! Stinks!"

Clarence could have his "stinks," thought Theo. She preferred "ship wipe," and not only because she heard it in Kara's voice.

She sighed, thinking about Kara as she crawled into corners, purposefully using second-line and even third-line multitool equipment on this stuff. Kara had a good eye for what needed done, not to mention excellent taste in tea and cheese, and a firm hand for a massage, too. She'd also been good at listening to Theo's doubts while refusing to agree that she was a useless academic kid, in over her head in the real universe . . .

On her knees on the deck, Theo sighed again. It would be good to see Kara again. She'd been a long time without seeing an old friend—a comfortable old friend. Especially since it seemed like all her new friends—and family members, too—were various degrees of risky to know.

Still on her knees, she straightened until her spine cracked with released tension.

Daydreaming wasn't going to get the job done, and since she was also tracking the duty by time taken, she'd better get to it.

"Are you recording all this, *Bechimo*? You got live visuals?"

A pause. A longish pause. Maybe he was still annoyed at having the dignity of the ship violated.

"Pilot," he said, before the pause got *too* long, the light, genderless voice just a bit too precise. "The entire process is being recorded in multiple formats as it goes forth, indexed by the day, and will be analyzed when we have more information to measure against it. Existing records of such checks are of little use since—"

She *fuffed* what might have been imaginary dust off her lips—or it might have been recognition that she knew this line already . . . so she she matched cadence and said it: ". . . the original checks were performed by crew conversant with procedures."

It was, unfortunately, an accurate duet, and probably beneath *her* dignity, as First Pilot. Theo shook her head.

"Got that one, *Bechimo*, thank you. What we can do—the whole point of this, if you'll please review your records!—is to make sure we're all up to spec about *what* needs to be done, *how* it ought to be done, where things are, what the instructions mean, and how readings are interpreted. Since the Builders aren't here, and since you're arguably the only person alive—aside from Uncle—who could possibly be conversant with all of the unique procedures, I'm on my hands and knees cleaning a live-wet. I promise you we'll either buy or build more remotes, but for now, this is the gig we've got."

Silence. Well, there wasn't much to say to that, except she'd implied an order there...

"*Have* you reviewed those records?" she asked.

A pause. She missed having Screen Six available, that being where *Bechimo*'s visible presence was most often seen, but she imagined it was busy with swirling colors right now. She liked to think that the more the colors swirled, the harder *Bechimo* was thinking.

"Yes, Pilot. I have."

There. She wasn't sure but what there was contrition in that, but assuming an AI learned like a beginning student did, something at *some* level in this project might stir up some new thoughts and insight.

She hoped.

She called lunch break a few minutes early, and the human part of the team carried after-meal tea with them to their station. Clarence had his smoky black, while she'd dipped into her dwindling supply of Lishanea Spring-morning, known to be efficacious in easing sore muscles.

Clarence started, mildly: "Things were a bit dustier than I expected in a couple of those crew rooms, Chimmy."

He was looking at Screen Six, where the blues had mused in quiet clouds while they ate; now the pace picked up and distant features faded into the hint of a face where there was no face but motion.

Theo glanced that way, and back to Clarence, who might have lifted a shoulder in a slight shrug, who may have twitched a pinky as he sketched a word to himself. For her part, she flicked a one-handed *query* in his direction, but he missed it, watching the active screen.

They shared the quiet flow of air and underfoot vibration that was always there, and the circulation brought the scents of the tea about them, infusing the after-lunch conference with a certain air of quiet relaxation.

Clarence leaned toward Screen Six, raising his teacup toward it. He sighed, loudly.

Theo had noticed *Bechimo* was sensitive to sighs, and apparently Clarence had, too. The blue flared bright, heralding a petulant response.

"Less Pilot, in the absence of a crew member named Chimmy, should I suppose that remark directed to me?"

"It was. Saw you fiddling with a face back there, I thought, and it reminded me of a couple someones I used to know, that's all. Brothers they was, many years apart, Chimmy and Chack. Chimmy had the looks, he did, and once his brother let him off the leash, he was quite the pleaser with the ladies and the threes."

He drank off what was left of his tea and slotted the cup.

There was silence, other than the fans; Clarence continued to watch Screen Six, and so did Theo. The face that might have been there in the moving clouds faded even more.

"I have not accepted this name as a referent, Less Pilot. The link between myself and a pleaser of your acquaintance lacks clarity."

"Ah, youth!" Clarence turned to Theo then, a suppressed smile on his face and his hands signing *new kid*. Theo snorted—not likely he was going to get a newbie's rise out of a spaceship.

He glanced back to the screen and shook his hands at the same time—*forget it*, that meant, in hand-talk.

"We'll talk about it later, then. Right now, we got all this dirt we collected. You've been neglecting..."

"I have not 'been neglecting,' Less Pilot. The rooms are as they were left by the prep crew the Builders employed. They were deemed acceptable by the Builders, and—"

"How many Builders, I wonder," Clarence interrupted, "and why did you never have a crew after that?"

The blues on Screen Six went to stormy green; the proto-face faded entirely and the whole went into jittery flux.

"Pilot, please inform Less Pilot O'Berin that I may not answer portions of that question."

Theo raised her eyebrows and shook her head, at the same time signaling *my board* to Clarence.

"*Bechimo*, consider him informed. We know that Uncle was a member of the Builders; why can't we know the rest?" She didn't say, *since they're long dead anyway*, because...there was Uncle, who was very much not dead. And who knew if any of the other Builders had been of his persuasion?

Not that the idea of a committee of Uncles soothed her, particularly.

Screen Six was displaying a bland, uniform, dark blue.

"Pilot—certain information is not necessary to the conduct of flight operations. The information requested is not available for casual discussion."

Theo didn't sigh. Just.

"This discussion began," she reminded him, "as a question about how the physical plant—Ship *Bechimo*—has been, and should be, maintained. Flight crew should have access to maintenance schedules, and to logs. We should also have an understanding of what materials we discovered, and how their discovery may reflect ship readiness and future operational stability. Pilots need to be sure of ship operation—that's why we started this process—the ship wipe. We're a new crew on an untested ship."

The screen color flared to a brighter blue, and settled in the midrange.

"Pilot, insofar as ship operations are concerned, we may continue. The ship is able, and there is no existing physical condition which would endanger the crew. Lacking a Captain, however, certain details of former personnel must remain confidential."

Theo looked up, found no answers on the ceiling, unstayed her command chair and let it rotate beneath her. *Bechimo* had been on his own for hundreds of years, she reminded herself. As hard as it was for a pilot who had grown up on consensus-mad Delgado to grasp, he just didn't know how to be part of a team.

Just like she didn't really know how to command, and Clarence wasn't used to riding second, after commanding a desk for more years than Theo'd been alive. This new—this *possible*—loop they were exploring for Clan Korval, this was a shakedown trip.

In more ways than one.

Theo nodded to herself and addressed *Bechimo* gently, like she was facilitating a team solution, back on Delgado.

"I understand you to say that standing crew can't know how many Builders there were. Do I hear you correctly?"

"Yes. That information has no bearing on current operations."

All right, she thought, *that was final, for now. Best move on to the next topic.*

"And the residues we collected?"

The reply came promptly.

"Those are from tests for aromatics and filter function, and from the overstimulated plants from the emergency hydroponics siting tests. In fact, all of those tests went far better than expected and a full crew on standard schedule would have collected the residues and remains on their first sweep, as current crew has done."

"No crew's been in peril on this ship, then?" Clarence put in, with a sharp stare into Screen Six. "You weren't without crew because of ship conditions?"

The screen snapped to dark green, the silence echoing like a thunderclap. Theo twisted her seat, eyes carefully not on the screen, but on Clarence.

"No crew has ever been in peril on this ship," *Bechimo* stated so flatly that he sounded like a machine.

Clarence nodded thoughtfully. "So why haven't you ever had a crew then, Chimmy?"

"I do not accept that designation. The information you request is available to the Bonded Captain."

"Which we are presently without, as I'm understanding the matter." Clarence gave Theo an oblique glance. "Can we get the broad outlines? No names, no dates, just as general as you like it."

"Your question is difficult to answer, Less Pilot, even in broad strokes."

There was a pause while Screen Six roiled, more green than blue.

"I may state that the prep crew and Builders withdrew as testing was completed; crew never arrived. I received orders to utilize emergency programming, and to withdraw from nearspace for multiple random checks. Confirmation was also received, and I withdrew as ordered."

Theo leaned forward, fingers gripping chair arms, her eyes on Clarence, wondering if the same chill struck him: *Bechimo* had been abandoned, cut off from community, ordered to save himself from enemies.

Ordered to abandon his crew.

"A problem, indeed," said Clarence suddenly, in Liaden. Seated as he was, he bowed to Screen Six. "I commend the quickness of your actions, and the success of your strategy."

His hands moved simultaneously, slower and sharper than his usual accent in hand-talk, illuminating the depths of the controlled phrases: *Urgent great deep situation, solitary survival necessity.*

There was a pause, as if not one of the three of them knew how to move from this point of tension, to find again the discussion of workaday housekeeping.

"'The pilot's care shall be ship and passengers,'" Theo said suddenly, wondering even as she spoke why she should be quoting the Guildbook *now*. "'The copilot's care shall be pilot and ship.'"

More silence.

"The ship's care," said *Bechimo*, his voice very low, "shall be pilots, and crew."

"I don't think that's in the book," Clarence said, in quiet Terran, "but maybe it oughta be."

Silly or not, her quoting had gotten them near enough to commonplace that she could clear her throat and say, "*Bechimo*, I have a question, if I might."

"Yes, Pilot?"

"Let me be sure of this," she said slowly. "You were ready to begin your loop, prep crew had cleared you and the Builders signed off. Then came this emergency. It wasn't your decision, you said that. Do I have this right?"

"Yes, Pilot."

"So, someone else declared the emergency. Who was that? Who gave you the order—how were you warned?"

The answer came almost sprightly compared to his recent replies, the screen settling in silver-shot blue.

"The head of the launch committee had arrived and was close enough to dock, were it allowed. I took the order across several bands—coded direct radio, as we'd been using for testing, and tight laser."

"And the name?" Clarence prompted, low-voiced. "Who told you to run?"

"That information," *Bechimo* said, and to his credit he did sound abashed, "is available to the Bonded Captain."

"Pilot, if you would," Clarence said in his impeccable Liaden, "two final tasks bearing upon today's exercise."

Theo didn't sigh. She needed to learn Liaden; she *had* to learn Liaden; and she had entered into a bargain with Clarence that he would help her learn, since he had thirty years or more of living among native speakers.

Languages didn't come easy to her. And switching back and forth between, like Clarence insisted on doing, gave her a headache.

Still . . .

"What tasks are these?" she asked, keeping an ear on her mode. Clarence had used Comrade, and it was polite to answer as you were addressed, unless you had a point to make. "One would not wish to be behind in any necessity."

"Excellent." He inclined his head. "*Bechimo* informs me that there is available a hydroponics bay. The module in place was supplied by a company no longer in existence. There are supplies enough to begin, should we wish that. Do we wish that?"

She considered, frowning at the deck, which wasn't proper Liaden body language. She forced her head up and met Clarence's eye.

"Fresh vegetables and fruits would be welcome," she said. "If the unit can be made to function. Does *Bechimo* advise us to procure a new module?"

"He believes the current module will serve, and has identified another from available catalogs, that may be made to be compatible."

Kit-bashed, that meant. Well, if *Bechimo* thought he could force compatibility and was willing to do the work, who was she to say no?

"I leave this in *Bechimo*'s care," Theo said, bowing her head to show that she was done with the subject.

"Very good. There is then only one thing remaining. We should each perhaps inspect the cabin of the other, so that we will know what is usual."

Theo once more inclined her head.

"Agreed. Let us finish what we have begun."

There hadn't been time for Clarence to personalize his cabin, and he hadn't brought anything but what had been in his jacket. His space looked almost as spare as her own. Ambient lighting was low and seemed somewhat reddish to Theo. On the small shelf over the desk was a hand-size fold-out easel, with pictures flowing one to the next, some of countryside and buildings and several, in the same sequence, of a man's smiling face, with and without a beard.

"Here we are, then," he said, so suddenly that the Terran words sounded *wrong* to Theo. "You know, I haven't had an inspection in a dozen years. Anyhow, one thing a long-looper is going to have on a courier ship is space, I guess. Never mind a lot of courier pilots live on their ships for years!

"I can bring the light up to trade-bright, if you like, but I usually keep it on Grandia sundown. I got used to it in the old days, and it got to be habit."

Theo signed *is good* and looked around more carefully. She'd only been in the cabin a couple times after *Bechimo* came for her, mostly as another place to walk when she'd been working out a day or two of shoulder cramps after her time in the autodoc.

The door—hatch, really, since it was a pressure door, like almost everything else that opened or closed on Ship *Bechimo*—cycled, and Clarence let it slide shut, hand casually wiping the inset pressure gauge as if to get her attention before both hands joined in a flood of sign.

Ship withholds info total cubes breathe room backup spares latchpoint limit stress limits Jump-point limits.

He signaled *full stop*, raised his hands and added, *says captain pilot-captain access higher*, and finished: *stop done*.

"'Course, you can do a whole lot of tuning to the air, too, but you should know I have my vents set on a cycle that gets faster over sleep-time—'nother habit. I like to wake up·to a breath o'fresh air, cooler for the last bit; I add a touch of oh-two for morning stretch out. Habit."

So there were hidden compartments in Ship *Bechimo*, Theo thought, maybe not quite as shocked as a well-brought-up Delgadan woman ought to be. Listening to Clarence with half an ear, she worked it out. The room where the Remastering Unit lived, where Win Ton fought for his life—that wasn't something you wanted to advertise to the galaxy, and who knew but the Builders, which group had included Uncle, had a bit of plain and fancy smuggling in mind from the start?

The hidden space was a risk when they moved the ship or Jumped, because not falling into a sun depended on calculating the correct mass to be moved. On the other hand, *Bechimo* did his own calcs and, on the occasions she had run her own set, he had provided ship's mass.

So, maybe not so much of a risk, *Bechimo* being the safety fiend that he was.

In the meantime . . .

"Habits," she said out loud; "I guess I've got a few, too. I've just been using default in my quarters—well, you'll see for yourself, if you'd like to return the favor now, Pilot?"

"Certainly, Pilot," Clarence said, in Liaden again, damn him.

Theo paused as they came into the main hallway.

"*Bechimo*," she said, stubbornly in Terran, "we'll do a prelim check-off this shift for the run to Frenzel, and after that we'll go over the want lists and priorities, do an access check on the cargo locks, then go to night sched.

"Before we hit the end of Jump, I'll want a detailed list of all hidden compartments, including measurements and access codes, if any, available to both pilots, please, *Bechimo*."

Behind her, she heard Clarence take a sharp breath. She didn't blame him, and she braced for learning that the information was only for the Bonded Captain.

In which case she was surprised.

"Of course, Pilot," said *Bechimo*.

TWO

········

'tween Jumps

THERE WAS A CAT, BROWNISH ORANGE, GRINNING AT
the pilot from the rear viewscreen.

Theo, who had been working on the Laughing Cat
logo in her so-called "free time," grinned back, pleased
with the design and the placement.

"Pilot," that was *Bechimo*, speaking from a frothy,
blue-and-white cloud. "Is there an artistic reason why
the logo needs to adhere to that particular spot on
my—on *the* hull?"

Theo blew her hair out of her eyes.

"There's a reason," she said, "but I can't claim it's
artistic. I'm not an artist."

Unflatteringly, *Bechimo* didn't argue the point, but
only said, "But there is a reason. May I know what it is?"

"I don't see why not. The lines of the cat's mouth
and muzzle mask the emergency egress port."

"*Visually* mask it."

The statement was flat and bland; the cloud indicating that *Bechimo* was noncommittal.

23

"Yes."

"Is that the entire purpose of the image?"

Theo blinked, suddenly reminded of her basic social engineering classes, back when she was a team-learner, on Delgado. Egos—especially with regard to appearance—were fragile things.

Especially *male* egos.

She shook her head. "'Course not. We're Laughing Cat, Limited, remember? We have to have a trade sign—a visual. I should've gotten to it before now, but I've *got* to get around to it now, 'cause we're going to be coming into our first port. If we come in without a mark in place, Tower might peg us as freetraders. We don't want that."

"Why?"

"Because freetraders are trouble, in a portmaster's mind," Theo said. "So they get extra visits from port security, and pay more for services."

There was a short silence, the screen showing darker blue swirls among the froth. Theo hoped that meant he was thinking, and that he would think for a good, long time—which for *Bechimo* counted for several minutes at least. She had some more logo work to do, which she wanted to finish up before Clarence came back from his break.

"There is," *Bechimo* said, "other space on the hull for the image, where it will not visually obscure the emergency hatch."

"There is," Theo agreed. "But we might as well spend the same coin twice, like my father used to say. That means we should take all the benefit available to us. In this case, the logo helps disguise the age of the ship's design."

"There is nothing wrong with the design of the ship."

"Who said there was? I said it was older than most ships we're going to see at the ports we put into. Is that wrong?"

"No," *Bechimo* acknowledged sullenly, and added, "The lines of this ship are perfectly adequate."

"I agree. But, we're trying to keep a low profile, and not call attention to ourselves as being something out of the ordinary," Theo said, and played her ace. "We're trying to keep safe."

That seemed to do it. Theo twisted the controls again, settling on the idea she'd had to feature the ship's portside cargo-and-consult port—large enough to admit trundled cargo in minpacks, small enough to be worth opening for walk-on visitors, port officials, and crew in favorable atmospheres, and a spot where both the required images could be seen and appreciated on port, or at dock.

Here the ship's hull angled out slightly on either side of the sliding pressure doors; at the moment, those angles were unadorned, aside from several small matching warning and info signs.

Now, which image should she put on the left, and which on the right? She had the Laughing Cat to hand, so she tried it first on the left, that being the side she was working the pointer with, fiddling with the size.

There! That was good!

Pleased with the left-side position of the Laughing Cat, she opened her second file, selected the image provided by Master Trader yos'Galan, and selected the right side of the entryway on her screen.

Before she clicked the oval into final position, she felt rather than saw movement at the board—Screen

Six flared white. The face she'd felt was trying to find a way to the surface the last day or two was gone in a stormy shimmer of static.

Worse—the second logo image wouldn't stick where she was trying to put it.

"I will not wear that!"

Theo stared straight ahead, closed her eyes, and kept her hands poised just above the controls. She said nothing, took several deep breaths, and only reopened her eyes when she felt centered and calm. The logo was still on-screen; she tried the *place here* control again.

Nothing happened.

Number Six was darkening, from white, to blue, to purple.

"I will not wear that symbol. It is against the Builders' wishes. It demeans me, it . . ."

Theo closed her eyes again, briefly—Screen Six was darkening even more.

"My controls seem not to be working, *Bechimo*," she said, striving for Father's coolest tone of disinterest. The tone he used when he was giving you one last chance to figure out what you'd done wrong, and fix it.

Bechimo, not having received the benefit of Jen Sar Kiladi's housefathering skills, ignored her comment regarding the controls, to state flatly, "There is no need to apply that to my hull."

"We have a contract. We, ship and crew, have a contract to fulfill. We need to signal who we are and who we're contracted with. The traditional way of doing this is the display of trade-logos. I've selected appropriate decalcomania. It should be easy enough to apply with this program."

"Pilot, I cannot allow—"

At the word *allow*, Theo slapped two switches, and raised her voice.

"Board failure, Copilot! Backup one activated."

The sound of ceramic against metal filtered in from the break station as Clarence flung his tea into the sink and ran to his seat, scanning the boards while pulling his webbing tight.

"Self-check on prime initiated—"

Screen Six flashed into a flat blue, bright and untroubled.

"Pilot, there is no error!" *Bechimo* protested. "All systems are working—in fact all systems are working at optimum!"

"Ship," she said, cold as the outside hull, "first board was not answering to the pilot. That is a serious matter. I must, for the safety of the ship, regard that as a system irregularity and go to backup."

"Pilot, I told you that I will not wear Tree-and-Dragon colors!"

"Ship, my controls *must* function. Do you understand me? Repeat the thirty-second self-scan one hundred times, and show both board sets the combined results. Any reading approaching anomaly should be noted. I want to see why System One was not functioning. I want to see corrective proposals designed to insure that System One will *always* function as appropriate. Do it now."

Clarence let out a long, slow sigh, shaking his head.

"Second, if you see no results within the appropriate time, go to backup two. Else, call me when the results show. I'll be in my cabin. And we'll have to work out a way for the ship to pay you back for your tea."

· · · ❄ · · ·

Theo did not go immediately to her cabin. Rather she strode from the control room toward the ship's core, to the place she sometimes thought of as the cellar, to the place where the third member of the ship's complement, the former second-in-command—Less Pilot, according to *Bechimo*, whom he had unintentionally waked—her perhaps-now-forever former lover—lay in a healing unit the Liaden Scouts themselves had acknowledged as both an item of contraband and Win Ton's last hope of survival.

The blast door was something she could appreciate about now; it would be good to be able to shut everything else out and just solve *something*.

She stopped before entering the chamber the Remastering Unit occupied, a chamber designed for it when *Bechimo* was first built, hundreds of years before. She herself had been in the ship's lesser, first aid emergency healing unit not long before, shot and beaten, and within hours had been on her way, healed, only the memory of the injury remaining. Win Ton...

Win Ton called her Sweet Mystery. Win Ton had helped her break away from the limits of Delgado, helped her become the pilot she was now. Win Ton's wounds were deep and malignant. Weeks, or maybe months to repair. If even *Bechimo* could repair him.

She owed him so much!

And he owed her...so much!

If only she could figure out which of them was in whose debt over the whole matter of *Bechimo*.

Well, there was time—maybe a lot of time—to figure that one out.

Meanwhile, she was first board on a ship under contract to Clan Korval to explore a possible new trade loop. She wasn't a trader. She wasn't even senior crew. What she was, was a Jump pilot. A courier pilot. She was young—too young, maybe—for this.

That wasn't exactly a new thought, but it wasn't welcome, either. Clarence was many years her senior— Father's age!—and *Bechimo* was older than her, Clarence, Father, and Win Ton, all added up together.

She needed experience, is what.

She took a deep breath.

And experience is what you're going to get, she said to herself.

One way or another.

THREE

· · · · · · · · · · · ·

'tween Jump

INITIATE SELF-CHECK FORTY-NINE...

The Protocol module burned bright red; Logic displayed a nauseous green; Rules an ominous, roiling purple. Morality was conspicuous by its lack of alarm. Perhaps, *Bechimo* thought, between misery and fury, he had overloaded it.

Protocol had already pinged once. *Bechimo* ignored it, wanting nothing less than a list of enumerated protocol violations between ship and pilot.

Self-check forty-nine complete. No errors found.

Of course, no errors were found. There was nothing wrong with him.

Correction.

There was nothing wrong with *ship systems*.

Initiate self-check fifty.

And how dare she command him to perform such a childish, useless task? She knew there had been no failure of the ship systems. Her board functioned entirely as it should. Had there been pirates, a sudden need to Jump, or to deploy weapons, she might have repelled boarders, phased, or defended the ship perfectly well, using the board she had rejected. Nor was the backup board in any way flawed. *She knew that!* And yet, that cold voice, that refusal to listen to his reasonable objection, as if he were . . . as if he were . . .

Self-check fifty complete. No errors found.

Initiate self-check fifty-one.

. . . nothing more than a mere-ship, that neither cared nor knew if its hull declared it affiliated with Tree-and-Dragon—a lie! The Builders forbade—

From Rules, a ping, delivered with enough energy that it might have been lightning emanating from the cloud of its distress.

Rules Search: "Tree-and-Dragon."

Results: Mark designating Clan Korval, Liaden kin group comprised of founding Lines yos'Phelium and yos'Galan; bel'Tarda later incorporated as minor Line. ALSO registered trademark of Clan Korval, operating as Korval Trade; Tree-and-Dragon Family; Dragontree, Ltd. NEW: Surebleak Clan Loop Unlimited.

No Warnings are associated with this mark.

There came a second ping, from Protocol. *Bechimo* withheld his attention.

Self-check fifty-one complete. No errors found.

Initiate self-check fifty-two.

So the Builders had filed no Warning with Rules regarding the Tree-and-Dragon! The Builders had warned against yos'Phelium, and Clan Korval, both associated with danger and risk! It was a poor database program which failed to make so simple a match!

Rules pinged again, even more forcefully, thrusting the data into *Bechimo's* awareness.

Rules Search: "Clan Korval."

Warning Level One-point-five: Pay cash. Pay promptly. If contract, adhere to all terms.

Rules Search: "yos'Phelium."

Warning Level Two-point-five: Pay cash. Pay promptly. Disruption of causality may occur, see notes. Contract not advised, see notes. Quick disengage, see notes.

Rules Search: "yos'Galan."

Warning Level One: Pay cash. Pay promptly. If contract, adhere to all terms. Caution in regard to association with yos'Phelium. See notes.

Caution with regard to yos'Phelium.

That error, *Bechimo* thought, his anger collapsing about him; *that* error had been made. And though it was possible to unmake it, and perhaps return to a state of trust in the Builders Promise—he had not taken steps to bar Theo Waitley from the ship or from the Heart. Theo Waitley, who was yos'Phelium through the paternal line; who honored as family a brother also of the paternal line, and who bore the name Val Con yos'Phelium Clan Korval.

Self-check fifty-two complete. No errors found.

Initiate self-check fifty-three.

The Builders had *promised* a Captain. *Bechimo* had doubted, and when the winds of space brought him a pilot, he accepted him as Less Pilot. *He* had done so, with no supporting documentation from the Builders; with no Captain on deck.

The Less Pilot, accepted, proposed an Over Pilot, and *Bechimo* had not only accepted her, he had pursued her.

He had rejoiced in his errors, thinking that now, *now* that he had at long last boarded pilots, and a Captain-elect, surely *now* he might proceed as the Builders had intended.

Only, the Less Pilot fell to brigands, who damaged him almost beyond repair. Even now, he reposed in the Remastering Unit, his system being rebuilt from *Bechimo*'s first, and only, baseline template. *Bechimo* of course monitored the unit, and its progress. Once the template was matched in all particulars, the Less Pilot—Win Ton yo'Vala—would be reintegrated and returned to his duty.

That the Less Pilot's complete recovery was 85.4 percent certain was data which must encourage all who wished him well.

Yet, a certain fact could not be avoided.

...if *Bechimo* had not opened to Win Ton yo'Vala on that certain occasion when he had arrived, all unlooked for, Win Ton yo'Vala might have sustained no injury at all, but gone about his life unmolested.

Self-check fifty-three complete. No errors found.
Initiate self-check fifty-four.

Regarding Theo Waitley—she was not, *Bechimo* now believed, his destined Captain. Her youth, her lack of experience, her attraction to risk, her stubbornness, her refusal of the bonding... No. She was *not* his Captain.

She was, however, a competent pilot who had shown care, if not proper respect, for the ship, the Less Pilot and, now, for the transitional Less Pilot, Clarence O'Berin.

More than that, she had brought to *Bechimo* both work and purpose. She had brought crew. Captain she might not be, yet *Bechimo* could not say she was unworthy of him.

His pilots...No, he could not relinquish them.

Self-check fifty-four complete. No errors found.

Initiate self-check fifty-five.

This lack of a Captain unbalanced the crew dynamic. Pilot Waitley overstepped because, in the absence of a proper Captain, the duties of that office rightly fell to First Board.

Thus, a Captain must be found. A Captain, to bond properly with *Bechimo*, and to keep the pilots safe.

Indeed, it might be that a Captain was already arrived. *Bechimo* vowed to speak more deeply with Clarence O'Berin, who was a man of considerable experience. More, he had demonstrated proper caution in the matter of removing the explosive from the captive mere-ship.

Self-check fifty-five complete. No errors found.

Initiate self-check fifty-six.

Protocol pinged a third time, diffidently. Its programming would not allow it to rest until it had delivered the list of *Bechimo's* recent errors. Primary among those, he knew, would be denying the Over Pilot full use of her board.

An error. *Another* error. Yet, in his experience, refusal to acknowledge an error did not reset circumstance to an error-free state.

Bechimo, reluctantly, accepted the list.

· · · ·❈· · · ·

"Pilot," Clarence said, as Theo entered the bridge— the Ship's Heart, according to *Bechimo*. "Self-checks completed. No errors found."

"Thank you, Second," she said, seating herself, and spinning the chair to face Screen Six squarely. Airy wisps of light blue wafted across a darker blue ground. There were no hints of human features or face to be found.

"*Bechimo*, why did System One stop functioning?"

"Pilot. System One was ninety-nine percent functional. Lack of function existed only in the protocol necessary for affixing the Tree-and-Dragon symbol to the hull."

"Thank you," she said. "What was the reason for that failure?"

"Pride," *Bechimo* said, surprisingly, "misinformation, and a lapse of proper protocol."

Theo raised her eyebrows and squelched the impulse to ask Screen Six where *Bechimo* was. Instead, she asked, in a voice as calmly noncommittal as she could manage, "What do you propose as corrective measures? Understand, my board must operate at *one hundred percent* at all times. If I can't trust that—if I can't trust the basic fitness and integrity of the ship, then Pilot O'Berin and I will exit the ship at Frenzel and throw the keys back through the hatch."

The wisps froze, and began gently flowing again so quickly that Theo might have doubted she'd seen it.

"What of Less Pilot yo'Vala? Would you leave him . . . alone?"

Theo sighed, and sent a glance to Clarence, who was watching Number Six, his expression cool and calm.

"If the pilots can't trust their boards, they can't fly the ship," she said. "What usually happens to a ship that isn't trustworthy is that repair crews are called in, or junkers. I'm thinking you wouldn't want either, and I'm not about to turn you over. I figure you know what you owe Win Ton, and *you* won't abandon him."

That was a bluff. Well, the whole thing about throwing back the keys and walking away was a bluff. She just hoped it was a *good* bluff. *Bechimo* had to learn…

"Pilot Waitley, I will care for Less Pilot yo'Vala to the best of my ability and until he is able to care for himself. However, you will not be forced to the extremity of returning your keys to this vessel. The ship is safe; the pilots' boards will function at one hundred percent. If in future, they do not function correctly, it will be because there has been a failure in ship's systems, in which case, the pilots will do as they know best."

Amazing. Theo inclined her head in the Liaden I-accept-this.

"And the Tree-and-Dragon trade sign?"

"The trade sign will remain where the pilot places it. I have taken the liberty of accessing the contract this ship and crew signed with Master Trader yos'Galan, and note that we are required to show the Tree-and-Dragon trademark as appropriate. The Builders' wisdom included advice to adhere to all terms, should the ship enter into a contract with Clan Korval."

Theo blinked, and looked again to Clarence, who wasn't quite grinning. Screen Six reflected a tranquil and trouble-free flow of blue-on-blue.

"I think that's settled then," she said. "Thank you, *Bechimo*."

"Thank you, Pilot," *Bechimo* said. He hesitated, then added, very low, and in Liaden, "I regret the inconvenience."

FOUR

· · · · · · · · ·

Arriving Frenzel

"ARRIVAL, IN GOOD ORDER, REQUESTING ROUTING FOR a Frenzel trade berth. *Bechimo*, out of Waymart; Theo Waitley, First Class sitting Pilot on First Board; Clarence O'Berin, First Class, sitting Second. Laughing Cat, Limited, independent operators, under contract to Tree-and-Dragon. Tree-and-Dragon berth call, if any."

The message propagated properly through the ether, the wide-band electromagnetic waves spreading the news of them to those who might have missed their arrival, in fact to those who had *probably* missed their arrival in a system loud with two tightly packed, highly commercial worlds. Even their announcement would largely go unheeded, for most of the people here were busy with their own getting, spending, packing, shipping. Someone would pay attention, though, that being their job, and they would have to sort through the records to see what was due Tree-and-Dragon— if anything—and if fees were prepaid some decade or two back that ought to be applied now, or if old taxes or bills had to be settled. And, yes, if there was a Tree-and-Dragon designated berth available for *Bechimo*'s use on port.

"Nerves, Pilot? Can't say I'm without 'em. This is our first port o'call, after all!"

Clarence subtly moved his hand toward the packet sender...

Theo blushed and stabbed the button she ought to have pushed before starting her spiel, transmitting the CIP, the Compressed Info Package that would have the details the port expected—*Bechimo*'s public dimensions and mass, ground-port preferences, local docking needs, tow points, even the on-board scheduling routine and call-offs on ships they should never be docked near.

Pharst! she scolded herself. *You'd think this was your first time bringing a ship into port!*

Well, at least their arrival in-system had been neat, with an appropriate elliptical orbit easily attained. There was nothing of note within a light-second of them, and Frenzel was, as precalculated by all concerned, on the proper side of the Feraldo system.

Incoming comm lit and a pleasant voice addressed them.

"*Bechimo*, this is Frenzel control. We hear you but...thank you! Your CIP has arrived. We catch your number and will set-and-schedule within two hours. Approximate backlog, one point two standard days. *Bechimo*, you are registered. Complete locals follow."

"Pharst!"

It wasn't the first time she'd said it it in the last hour, and if Clarence minded her cussing, he didn't say so—he just looked to the main screen where Theo'd dragged the current item under consideration.

"*Bechimo*, can we check why these things are different? The packaging looks identical, but the weights are stupidly off and the..."

"Looks like a ship's store supplier on number four, and number six, too," Clarence said in his calm way. "They'll be repackages of local consumer stuff, aimed at resale. Going by the price, I'd say Cloppers is offering actual local stuff, so there's potential storage issues." He spun his chair to face Theo. "Didn't you have to deal with this for *Arin's Toss*?"

She shook her head, indicating *no*, not moving her hands from the choice pointer.

"The *Toss* was stocked up when I got her, and I just sort of grabbed stuff when I was standing in front of it at the dock stores. I don't eat a lot and..."

Clarence sighed.

"What about the other—oh!"

"Right, Hugglelans kept us stocked through their subscription services. We'd dock or come to port and the automatics would already have the stuff on the loading pallets. Other than personal choices like tea or coffee, the whole process was automatic. I mean, we had overrides—I could have traded off for ice cream instead of mycomeat if I wanted—but it was just as well to go with the stuff they supplied. Hugglelans does know about food!"

"*Bechimo*?" Clarence looked to Screen Six, where an image had formed again. There still weren't enough cues to say for certain that there was a face on the other side of that blue-green window, but there certainly was the *intent* of a face there.

"Less Pilot?"

"We need to talk supplies. Can you make a study of the current subscription services and compare our wish lists across them to see if we can choose one or two to start with? Happens we're in a bit o'luck; Frenzel's a prime spot for subscription suppliers, on account of it being a warehouse trade center."

"I am able to mount such a study. To whom shall I report?"

Theo sat up sharply as insight struck.

"You've got a good head for admin," she said earnestly.

Clarence blinked, then laughed.

"Do I, then, lassie?"

"Yes, you do," she said, ignoring irony. "We need an Executive Officer—maybe not right here, right now, but we're going to come to some port, sooner or later, where admin won't deal with just a pilot, they'll want the Exec—" Back on *Primadonna*, she and Tranza had taken turns being "Exec" at those kinds of ports.

"So, maybe you ought to be Executive Officer," she continued into Clarence's grin. "We'll put it on your business cards, even! When we get them."

"There—you hear that, *Bechimo*?"

The pause was slight, and *Bechimo*'s voice laconic.

"I have noted that the Pilot has added business cards with Pilot O'Berin designated as Acting Executive Officer to the wish list. The list now encompasses three hundred twenty-seven actions or items. The list will be added to the docking routine."

"Do that," Theo said. "I'll make sure I keep my need list up to date and we'll take a look at exceptions rather than order from scratch each time around. You'll report to Clarence as Exec on the subscription study."

"Yes, Pilot." *Bechimo*'s pause was just a little too short, before he continued. "Catalogs continue to arrive; I will wait for a landing time and location before making any decisions. I will be grading offers on price, ability to deliver, stocking issues, and reported reliability ratings. Additionally, I will multisource unbranded staples, again with vendor reliability charts in mind. I will, upon request, test samples of food and other staples for suitability."

"Well," said Clarence, hand on his chin. "You know, not sure I've ever had a ship test my food for me, but it makes sense, come to think of it."

"The Builders were clear on the supply needs of a ship on independent loop routes, Less Pilot. When this vessel was commissioned, the possibility of long-term exposure to low to mid-grade toxins was a concern. I directly sample and analyze incoming air on-world and docked, using the highest standards, in addition to generating base air at need. Our water supply and other potables are tested continuously and are maintained in multiple independent reservoirs with backups and filtration available."

"I see we're well taken care of, then," Clarence said, and inclined his head in full Liaden formal to Screen Six. "The pilots are aware of the ship's vigilance, and sleep the better for it."

Frenzel's ground port was radio noisy and crowded. *Bechimo* was tucked into an auxiliary "field" out of the way of the big and busy ships that outmassed them many times over. The landing itself had been uneventful, with *Bechimo* taking Theo's cue to take it easy, and not to exceed normal landing times by more than five percent.

Since Laughing Cat's resources were thin in the universe, there had been no expedited landing or premium siting. It might have been different, if they'd come in carrying pods, or had a pickup scheduled, but running empty and listing "business development" in their pre-landing customs declarations wasn't enough to get them one of the better seats in the house.

They had a hotpad only because all of the pads at Frenzel Port were standalones a bare step above a tow-tie. They could pick up power and land-line optical, and if they wanted they could patch in for water—but the fees for water were phenomenal and the land-line optical was a sponsored link, meaning half or more of the flow would be incoming messages of enticement, and they were already getting more than enough of that, if the pink, blue, and grey streaks showing on Screen Six were any indication.

"Pilots," *Bechimo* said, sounding every bit as harried as Screen Six looked, "I have no less than seventeen attempts to set up open arrivals for items we have no need of; several for items which are on the wish list but which represent no outgoing request on our part. Two personal service companies report that they are responding to standing orders which do not exist and—"

Clarence spoke over him, in Liaden.

"*Bechimo*, forgive me! Commercial hubs are often overbusy, and there are ever those who seek to turn confusion into profit. Please, inform the personal services companies that our crew is on shift-hold and will make their own arrangements. To the chandlers say that we have supplies due in from other sources and are not at this time accepting samples or preapproved signature offers. What others have you?"

It was, Theo thought, amazing how calming Liaden sounded—smooth and flowing, like the little stream in Father's garden, back on Delgado.

"I have," Bechimo said, answering as he was spoken to, "offers to wash the hull, to advise the pilots on the proper mode of dress, and those who offer decorative skin art."

"Regretfully, utilization of such services requires preauthorization from our office on Waymart. You may of course give them the Waymart call box, so that proper inquiry may be made. You may receive inquiry from those seeking employment. Express to them the following ship's policy: that we utilize certified prescreened and prerequested guild members only."

"Thank you, Pilot; those instructions cover most of the incoming queries." Screen Six was mostly grey now, shading toward blue at the left edge. Panic averted, thought Theo and gave a nod and a smile to Clarence.

"Pilot Theo? We have several requests specifically for yourself. Are you in need of companionship?"

Theo sputtered, and shook her head.

"Exec said it—and if anyone asks by whose orders, you tell them standing orders from the Executive Officer."

"Yes, Pilot. We have also several security consultants applying for permission to discuss ground-side security, including one who specializes in new-world orientation. I see offices listed for them in several ports on-world. I also have two sources offering weapons renewal."

"Please send anyone claiming security to me," said Clarence, back in Terran. "I'll vet 'em. Might as well do the same for weapons renewal, but buy me some time—say I'm in conference. Ask for contact info and say that the Exec, who's in conference, will get back to them."

Clarence turned to fix Theo with a quick eye.

"These aren't the kind of things you're going to get in established ships mostly, 'specially if they're marked Hugglelans . . . and by damn I thought the weapons check people were so old-time that no one would try it anymore."

Theo signed *query*, figuring she had it pegged as a variation Rig had warned her about.

Clarence shrugged. "New ship on port stuff. If they can get on board to do a survey, so-called, or a 'consult,' then they get a handle on our readiness, and on what weapons we do have. They'd be especially interested in *Bechimo*—not like there's a ship of this exact class dropping in of a ten-day, is it now? Some of the security folk, they'll even have a try at dropping bugs, picking up ship or trade rumor, what have you. We don't show local affiliation yet, and that can count a lot on dealing with refraff. They ought to be put off by two First Class Pilots on the con, but hey, you can't succeed if you don't try, like my auntie usta say."

He spun his chair to face her. "Other thing we ought to do, now we got an Exec, is name a Trade Officer. What might be encouraging some of these folks to be so bold is we got nobody listed, so they might figure we got no connections and no sense, even if we do claim a contract with Tree-and-Dragon."

Theo nodded, recalled that Rig Tranza had been strong on dealing with known affiliates...but he'd never needed to cope with anything except personals; buying wasn't what he did, what he did was pilot. Like her.

"Trade Officer, huh?" She shook her head. "We're going to have to improvise on that. Maybe list a name who's always in a meeting?"

Clarence tipped his head, like he was considering that.

"Port request, on proper channels, Pilot Theo," *Bechimo* said crisply. "Customs and port protocol officers will be arriving shipside within the local hour. We are requested not to open hatches before they arrive and are informed that, for our protection we are under surveillance at all times on port."

"Of course we are," Theo murmured. "Where's this kind of support when you really need it?"

FIVE

· · · · · · ·

Frenzel Port

THEO CHANGED FROM BASIC SHIP CLOTHES INTO A white shirt and dark trousers; she would have liked to have the Laughing Cat stitched above the pocket of the shirt but that hadn't happened yet—maybe some of those catalogs would yield an embroidery service. Her hair was as it always was, just a touch neater than if she'd just rolled out of bed from a quick tumble. No worry—the chance that she, or any pilot, would be in the height of style on arrival at any particular world was on the order of vanishing to none.

To receive company, she wore so-called "shore boots," shiny and waterproof, too, for all that she didn't intend to go walking in water today. She'd also found and collar-spotted the pin she'd gotten so long ago from Win Ton: wings. Being a nexus of violence and thereby banished from Academy meant, among other things, that she'd never received the official Anlingdin graduate wings, but the Scout-issue wings Win Ton had sent were both more subtle and in their own way truer.

She gave a last glance in the mirror, seeing a wiry kid with flyaway blonde hair and serious black eyes. Nothing to do about that, she guessed, and headed for the door.

"Are we prepared?"

This she asked as she entered the command deck, where the screen reserved for *Bechimo* showed a staid chart listing available long info sources.

"What's this?" she asked, pausing behind Clarence's chair.

"Pilot, after discussion with Pilot Clarence, I will remain in radio silence unless there is a major emergency. All ordinary ship spaces are unlocked, as per the directives of the Executive Officer. We have selected Rosencrantz II as an emergency destination if there is a need for us to evacuate the system in haste. I am maintaining regular watch on public areas inside and outside the skin."

The watch outside the skin showed the same area in three of the ten screens: a miserly patch of grit-blasted tarmac and the bare bones hotpad linkage. It looked like more than one ship had lifted in a hurry, or landed crabbed, leaving the contact arm swinging slightly askew, striped with a multitude of colors, including one that looked surprisingly like rust. But according to the locals, Frenzel Port got rain and major storms—the directives had been clear about tie-downs not being optional in certain seasons—and she felt better about the chance of *Bechimo* disengaging in a hurry, if necessary. No less an authority than Rig Tranza had maintained that always having a clear right-of-way was the sign of a good pilot...

She ran her hands through her hair, gently. The remaining seven views from outside showed other medium and small ships within easy range, all sitting tied to similar hardpoints in a row of craft fed by a runway-and-road combo capable of accepting podcranes and perhaps even vehicles bearing surface dry docks.

The view on the main screen showed the local tower as well as the road—it was echoed on Screen Fourteen, to her lower left, and to Clarence's upper left. On it was a fleet of five vehicles, three of them a bright off-hue green, and the other two somber brown.

"Visitors on the screen," Clarence pronounced, rising from his chair.

He'd done some cleanup in honor of portside visitors, too. For starters, he'd added red to his hair. Theo was startled, then saw the sense of it. He'd left enough grey for authority, but not so much that someone seeking advantage would automatically assume he was weak. For the rest—shore boots, polished bright, bright white shirt and, at his hip, a ship's gun, a detail she hadn't considered.

"I take it we're second in line," he said, looking down at her. "Looks like they're slowing down outside the good ship *Geranny Smith*, in case you forgot anything, Pilot."

"In fact, I did. Be right back."

When she returned, it was with a gun on her belt, an urge for tea, and a feeling she ought to take another look at the port rules Tower had transmitted in the welcome packet. She tapped the file to her screen first, saw that Clarence was also reviewing the legal.

"Cup?" she asked. Clarence nodded.

"Rose tint for me, if you might? Thanks, Theo."

She was back quickly, bearing a Vodamorang blend, said to be lightly calming, the fragrance playing well with Clarence's rose, which she guessed was his third favorite.

At the board she scrolled port rules, finally asking, "We in violation of any of these that you see? Clarence? *Bechimo*?"

Clarence waggled his fingers, deliberately meaningless.

"No more'n most ships are. I guess we're not going to share the complete ship's specs, I guess we're not gonna go overlong into our history wherein we might have broken a law somewhere and not properly balanced it . . . which they ask us to certify we never have, within the parameters of being on the up-and-up right now."

Theo nodded. She'd read plenty of port legal before, and this, like most, was in place to provide an excuse from liability for the port, in case that became an issue.

Early in her time with Rig Tranza, she'd been concerned that Anlingdin's declaration of her being a nexus of violence might have followed her into the spaceways. Tranza had been good about it, comparing, finally, his riot to hers, and pointing out that *his* riot had actually been a couple of riots in three days, and had involved actual time in in detention . . . which, he insisted, hers had not, other than the protective custody thing.

She wondered if Clarence had any riots in his back history, but now probably wasn't the time to ask.

"*Bechimo*," she asked instead, "are you prepared to follow these rules to the letter?"

The staid catalog image on Screen Six gave way

briefly to a roiling blue, and then faded back to the public face.

"Pilot, in all cases local rules and regulations fall considerably lower in my decision trees than standing orders from captain, pilots, and crew; general operating protocols as derived from files and observed practice, and the basic instruction set granted to me by the Builders. I see a number of conflicts between the materials received from Frenzel Port Authority and my understanding of ship's practice. My study of your own voyages as outlined in discussions, and my brief experience as your transport inspire me to believe that at all times ship survival and crew survival are paramount, and that there is certain information that is best not shared.

"I have, for example, sealed the blast doors leading to the Remastering Chamber. The outer doors there now appear to be those sealing an older-fashion oxygen regeneration plant of a type still common on smaller manned stations and long-term orbiters. These are among the suggestions the Builders left with me in regard to dealing with outside polities."

"And if they ask us for the information or access to the items in section four and five, are we prepared to permit inspection of the subsystems bay and other potential storage areas?" she asked, naming other areas that had been on the list of hidden compartments.

A pause; a flicker on Screen Six.

"There is a viewable subsystems bay which, given the acknowledged antiquity of our craft, will be sufficient. Other potential nonstandard storage areas are likewise not likely to be seen, and the interior holds and exterior pod-blanks are of course accessible at all times to crew and to visitors as appropriate."

Clarence waved his mug gently at the screen, his other hand forming a lazy *query*.

"Folks just poking around, even with a dimension sheet, they won't find any of the places we don't want people to know exist?"

Another pause, and a pink edge around Screen Six until the catalog grids returned simultaneously with what might have been an attempted laugh.

Theo jumped, and so did Clarence, though maybe not as far.

"The Uncle himself designed and oversaw installation of many of the masking systems. It is my estimation that what should not be found or seen by others will not be."

Clarence nodded forcefully, with his following irony perhaps lost on *Bechimo*,

"And who better to have in charge of fooling the universe than the Uncle, who we Disallow."

"His measures and those of the other Builders have served me well in times not precisely anticipated: that was the point, in fact, that I may operate autonomously, as necessary."

Clarence shook his head, and sipped the last of his rose tea.

"One day when I got time, and Pilot Theo's got time, and the proctors aren't at the door, the three of us will have a talk about the Uncle . . . Meanwhile, Theo, I'll stand as Exec to the door in the greeting parlor, and hope *Bechimo* will be kind enough to brighten up the Cat *and* the Tree-and-Dragon, seeing as how we got us a shiny bright day out there, and we want to impress these folks as pleasant and biddable and forgettable, if we can manage that."

On the big screen, the three green cars proved to be arriving, the brown cars just behind.

"Tree-and-Dragon has a good reputation."

The young man—Hervan, his name was—smiled as he leaned toward Theo, rather closer than she usually liked.

"We did hear some recent odd news from Liad, which of course would represent Liad's views. Perhaps there was a...contractual disagreement between the planet and Tree-and-Dragon; such things happen. But an organization with a thousand-year history rarely makes really major mistakes."

Theo nodded, hands still burdened with the so-called *valcomvoggen*, a basket containing a bottle of wine, three stripy orange fruits, and several pale, shiny-wrapped objects that might be anything from modeling clay to cheese to high explosives, as well as his card announcing him as *Hervan, Sector Arrival Director*.

The card sat atop her basket, slowly changing colors. Their tiny trade parlor was crowded, what with Clarence and Hervan and his three aides, but she didn't want to bring port officials into the command space if she could avoid it—for the sake of her nerves *and Bechimo*'s.

They'd been trading pleasantries and formal welcomes after the official exchange of port fees was accomplished by key codes, until this sudden sally into news.

It might be, Theo thought, a push at her reserve, to see how much she was willing to gossip—and especially to gossip about Clan Korval.

She considered that, and came to the conclusion that she was willing to gossip...not at all, and smiled.

"Laughing Cat is a recent contractor, as I'm sure

you saw, Hervan. I know very little about the action on Liad, except, like you, by news report. Tree-and-Dragon's trading reputation was the primary consideration for us when we were offered the opportunity to explore trade more aligned with their new seat."

Hervan nodded, emphatically.

"I understand perfectly. An opportunity to partner with Korval as they enter a new phase! Surely a marked opportunity for a ship of your *Bechimo*'s style, which is hardly large enough to ply the great routes, yet which is far more than a mere courier. Yes, you have chosen a wise course, Theo Waitley. And wise, too, to stop at Frenzel, where there is often need for small and intermediate shipments. This port tends toward the commodity trade, and the hurry-ups and replacements and model-year changes often need a ship of your carrying capacity."

He smiled and nodded at the basket she held.

"I hope you'll take advantage of our sponsors' offers and contacts; and be aware that I am *Bechimo*'s link if you should have any need on-port. If your stay is extended, we have many cultural opportunities available. Please call on my office if you have trading needs, as well. I am often able to open doors and make presentations in person. Also, you must feel free to regard my time as yours—understand that I have considerable leeway and flexibility in scheduling."

Clarence, having stacked *his* basket in a corner with the "crew basket," took hers with a wordless nod. Hervan, holding the small official packet of ship info Theo had for him, looked momentarily nonplussed.

Oh, Theo realized, this was also a gift exchange game, and she was without a gift, or a bribe.

"Your sponsors," she said firmly, making good eye contact, "are generous, Hervan. *Bechimo* appreciates and is gladdened by our welcome. We have, as you know, just begun our contract and our route, and are not so lucky as to be able to share samples with you at this time."

There was that about Hervan which was interesting despite his tendency to lean close, and it came to Theo that there was a scent, elusive and familiar...

Vya! she thought, suddenly identifying it. Just a slight trust inducement for the potential visitor... She'd have to have *Bechimo* rev up the air cleaners!

Hervan's eyes widened slightly and she was concerned that she'd overstepped somehow. She'd need to do a better job of prepping—suppose he'd been affected by his own *vya* and thought she'd made an intimate offer! Then she spotted the slight off-shade behind his ear. He was wearing an aid.

"Pilot Waitley, please," he said reproachfully. "My goal is to see that your needs are met fully and with as little trouble to yourself as possible. Regrettably, my aides and I have not the time at the moment to take a complete tour. Rest assured, however, that I would be pleased to receive a visit from you, perhaps to show you some of the many fine restaurants and gaming places located within easy cab ride. Also, included in your baskets are chip-keys for discounted spa-style accommodations at nearby Kyhatts.

"I must ask—Pilot Theo, please assure me that you have a contact already. I tremble to think that you might be considering a catalog-drill for names to cold call. *Have* you a contact? Perhaps I might help you connect sooner."

Theo glanced at Clarence, who showed her an absolutely bland face. No help there! Well, Shan hadn't said his information was secret, after all.

"I am to contact Chaliceworks Aggregations, on-world here. I gather they are within surface transport range . . ."

"Chaliceworks?" Hervan abruptly stepped back out of her personal space. "Why yes! Yes, of course! Leave after breakfast and arrive before lunch, as we say. They close on the sixth day, which you've missed by two days."

He gave her a smile much less winsome than formerly, and turned to wave his aides out before him.

"Thank you for your time, Pilot Waitley, thank you! May the trade do well by you. If my office may direct you to restaurants, please do let me know!

"Forgive me, time presses!"

SIX

······

Frenzel Port

THEO STOOD ON THE VERGE, AMONG THE SCANT GRASS and weeds and some Theo-high reddish-brown brush growing through the paving. Guest Out rightly fell to Exec, she guessed; Clarence, having collected them, should've taken them back to their vehicles. But their dance steps had gotten muddled there at the last and it had been smoother for Theo to take them away. Guess they needed practice.

The "tarmac" ten strides away from *Bechimo*'s hatch wasn't much more than a thin coating of what Derryman, her boss during her first season at Hugglelans, had called "blackpebble." In hot weather the thin coating of crushed stone and petroleum plasticizer might stick to shoes and mark up floor matting—but that wasn't an issue this day. The vegetation didn't exactly flourish in the thin sun that faded through a light haze, and the slight breeze did nothing more than twitch her hair against her ears.

The doors of the delegation vehicles were all closed

now. Hervan gave her a small smile and a wave from his spacious back-of-the-car seat before turning his attention to a device his aide handed him. The window clouded then, as privacy was turned on.

Ah, *dismissed*, that was, the turning to other duties. A twinge of something akin to annoyance struck her. Here she, First Board and the Acting Captain, had walked Hervan out into the dust and now, after his hint that maybe she should...well, manners. Maybe there was a right time to turn the windows to dark.

Glancing aside, Theo noticed that the ship next to *Bechimo* was a Jollijon Springster, usually used for medium to high value foodstuffs. Some few items didn't do well frozen, some had to be eaten fresh, or live. The Springster was white box as far as she could see—a couple of ID numbers too small to read at this distance, but nothing to show line, captain, or name.

Beyond the Springster was a row of sixteen or seventeen neat Hights in the vertical quadpod configuration that was all the rage on some routes. If they didn't have their Stonefort designs on every quarter, somebody had done a lot of work to make sure they were all aligned the same way. She guessed it made for an advertising statement or something—or maybe it was just line policy to ground to the north north north...

She sighed lightly. Clarence had been particularly concerned about the baskets, and had been careful to put them in the baffle corner, actually an airlock into the other "public" section of the ship, which had been sealed, shipside. As soon as the cars were out of sight, she ought to go back inside and help inspect. Not that she really expected baskets from a branch of Port Admin itself to contain listening devices or explosives, but that was the kind of thinking people trying to sneak things onto ships counted on.

There, the first car was starting to move, the dark windows showing a silver sheen, as if shielding had been activated.

Theo shook her head.

Hervan had seemed genuinely pleasant up until his ear feed had interfered, but the hasty departure of the delegation gave Theo a chance to breathe easier. The combination of the *vya* and the selling, along with Hervan's strong eye contact, had worked oddly on her. She wondered if she'd managed to catch cabin fever, that malaise historically attributed to spacefarers.

Theo turned back toward *Bechimo*, the Laughing Cat and the Tree-and-Dragon welcoming her back. It had been some time since she'd just sat and talked with someone about just anything, especially anything that wasn't ship and crew stuff.

At least she'd met and talked with someone new, and that suddenly made a plus on the day.

She shook herself into a dance then, recalling Father's ability to not be seen by people he didn't want to see him. She'd seen him avoid nosy faculty and noisy neighbors, simply by—It was like he put on a suit of "don't look at me"—both a pose and a walk...and people *didn't* see him. That would be a useful thing to be able to do, Theo thought, remembering the *nidj* who had followed her down Starport Gondola. Deliberately, she danced a few steps of relaxation, then slid into Father's "I'm not here" walk.

There was a way of holding the shoulders, and a flex in the knee; she frowned, concentrating, and then looked up, as motion twitched in the edge of her eye.

There. Down in the haze, just this side of the Jollijon. And *there*, the shape of a person, and another, the brush blossoming into people.

She spun. On the other side of *Bechimo* was the squat bulk of an ore carrier perched above service wagons, the Terran Seven Diamonds a rough outline on equipment that had surely seen better days. 'Round it came several human forms, carrying backpacks and hand totes, and wearing hats or hoods.

For all their sudden appearance, they were slow-moving; not pilots or mercenaries, surely, and the pace they set... still, a quick count showed fourteen or fifteen of them.

Advertently, Theo removed to *Bechimo*, at a smart pace, unseen.

"The Over Pilot has returned, Less Pilot."

Clarence spun his chair.

"What the devil did you do out there, lassie? All at once, there's people everywhere!"

His voice was stern, but she could tell at a glance that he was amused rather than irritated. "You should have heard *Bechimo*..."

"I didn't do anything but watch the portmaster's proxy run away," Theo began, then raised a hand, *wait*. "Did *Bechimo* send something? I didn't hear—"

His hands wrote *board to zero* in sign, and she relaxed, coming forward to stand by his chair and watch the live instrument set.

"Nah, he didn't send, I don't think, just he was muttering about the visitors, then muttering about imitation random walks going on in view of his sensors."

"Well, that's true. There's a dozen or more people

wandering around out there. They look like refugees or campers."

Clarence sat up straighter, his hands roaming board-wise as if initiating prechecks on lift-off.

"I think we're fine," he said after a minute. "Just a bunch of pitchmen and freeposters, hiding from the port guys. Some of them may be after left-outs, but we're not worried because we haven't put anything outside, and because *Bechimo* takes rare exception to the whole lot of 'em and tracks any within easy threat range. Ain't that how it is, Chimmy?"

The catalog grid on Screen Six gave way momentarily to a half-familiar background: it was a ship's interior as seen from a comcam—an unfilled seat in the lower portion of the field, behind a courier's tight cabin with a neat-run kitchen. It was a cabin, if not a view, very familiar to Theo.

"Arin's Toss? Are we in touch with *Arin's Toss?"*

The image went wonky with colors; the cabin view shifted to include an angle impossible to achieve from the *Toss*'s locked camera and a seat behind—no, thought Theo; it was an acceleration seat set for three, so it couldn't have been the *Toss*, after all.

Bechimo's voice overfilled the command deck momentarily, and ghostly arms from elbow down appeared in the screen, hands reaching for controls that might be identifiable by comrades of the pilot who wasn't there.

·"I do not accept the designation of Chimmy, Clarence O'Berin."

"You said that, right," Clarence answered calmly. "Status?"

"Status is that there are twenty-three free-ranging subjects within view of my cameras and sensors. All are on foot, all are carrying packages and devices. Some few seem to be in coordinated motion; the rest are, as alluded to, moving with pseudo-random walks as they approach the various vessels in this area. We as yet have none within the official rented pad space; we have several attempting to image our logos. I expect inquiries on our feeds to increase shortly."

Theo twitched, waiting for her question to be answered.

Clarence's laugh was short. "Been studying, have you?"

"I have located the *Freepost Gazetteer*. According to their ranking system, security in this landing yard is low. The freeposters are an unincorporated alliance of independent contractors supplying non-licensed information to vessels and crews. Some may be refugees and campers as suggested."

Theo took a deep breath—

"Can *either one* of you tell me why we're seeing a ship in the Screen Six monitor? Are we live?"

"'Course we're live," Clarence said. "I see it too, but it's not there."

"Pilot, I am in pursuit of my presence project and came to the conclusion that placing myself in an existing location within myself presented certain contingent reality difficulties. It also has become obvious that lack of a location is distracting to pilots; the color combinations I have attempted are insufficient for our needs. It appears that there is a paradoxical necessity for more information rather than less in order to be present. I am constructing a personal image that will confuse neither pilots nor ship."

Theo looked at the screen, at the hands flowing

from nothing to move controls that weren't there. She took a breath and shook her head.

"For the moment I suggest a static screen—the hand motion is distracting. When you pick a spot to be from, make it so it looks like another section of the ship—from a communications room, or a weapons station, I don't much care as long as it's someplace we could expect to see you if you were here, and it's not someplace that makes me feel like I could turn and talk to you in the Jump seat."

Screen Six became the catalog grid, then a very hazy grey, with the hint of a shadow in it, except for very clear hands and fingers, moving. It roiled a bit of green around the edges, and after a few seconds Theo sighed, loudly.

"Nice effect, the handwork, but bring it back later. If Clarence doesn't mind, you can practice it on him—but not on me until I say so. Now—the baskets?"

"The baskets are clean, excepting these," Clarence picked up two pieces of flimsy from the catch-bench between their chairs and offered them to Theo.

PLEASURE BEYOND YOUR DREAMS! SPEND YOUR HUNDRED HOURS WITH OUR TEAM OF TRAINED TECHNICIANS. CRADY'S CARNAL DELIGHTS.

She flipped the next page up, and was immediately awash in the scent of dark chocolate.

AMPHORIA CHOCOLATIERS. HANDMADE CHOCOLATES FOR ALL OCCASIONS. TRY OUR VYA-FILLED BONBONS!

"That's it?" She looked sharply at Clarence, who nodded, not seeming worried.

"Prolly bribed somebody on staff to slip 'em in, see."

He used his chin to point in the general direction of the conference ro— Dining Room Two.

"All this is about access to people, because people make things happen. Without people, there's no commerce." He shrugged. "The rest of the stuff in the baskets is sponsored, like Hervan said; nothing wrong with any of it—*Bechimo* scanned everything and I did, too. I put the wine in the keeper, and the fruits in the fresh-box. Buncha file keys and feelies—not much to do with them 'cept pitch 'em in recycling."

"All right," said Theo, and shook her head. "I hope the sponsors don't spend a lot of money on this. It seems kind of hit or miss."

Clarence shrugged again, turning his attention back to the screens and the freeposters wandering here and there among the careless ships.

"Can't succeed if you don't try."

SEVEN

. . . .

Jelaza Kazone
Surebleak

MIRI ROBERTSON TIAZAN CLAN KORVAL, MERCENARY captain, retired; personal bodyguard, retired; half a delm—and not the best half, either—hurried down the back stairs, pushing the sleeves of her sweater up on her arms. She was just a smidge late for meeting Val Con, her lifemate and the delm's better half, in the morning parlor for breakfast. Not that she sensed any impatience from him. In fact, he was prolly having a doze in the window seat, and well deserved too. Her, all she had for an excuse was that she'd let her exercise session go a little too long this morning. Felt good to push the exercise again.

The door to the parlor was open. She slipped inside, and there was Val Con in the window seat all right, angled into the corner made by glass and wall.

"*Not* napping," he said, looking up at her with a smile in his green eyes.

The reason for that was cuddled against his shoulder, and she *was* napping, eyes screwed tight with effort.

"You're gonna spoil that kid," Miri told him.

He glanced down at his passenger, then back up, brows pulled together. "Do you think so? She seems quite fresh."

"Just wait," Miri said darkly.

"You terrify me."

"Good thing if true. You want tea?"

"If you please."

She went to the buffet, drew one cup of smoky morning tea, and another, of well-brewed coffee, and carried both to the window seat. Val Con had lain their daughter on the cushion next to him. Miri handed him his tea and settled with her back against the wall, one leg up to make a rolling baby barricade.

"What I don't get is why you ain't out on your feet," Miri said, after they had both sampled their beverages. "Do we still need to be on all-shift call for the Scouts?"

Val Con sighed and settled his shoulders against his corner.

"There are certain exercises known to pilots and Scouts which will keep one alert for quite some time," he murmured. "As for receiving Scouts at all hours... I think that we must do so for some while longer. Even when, as this morning, it was decided to allow the situation to develop." He sipped his tea. "Scouts are our eyes and ears, and our defense against the remnants of the Department of the Interior."

The Department of the Interior being the exact reason that Clan Korval had blown a hole in the homeworld, which had gotten them thrown out by the Council of Clans, which had chosen peevishness over gratitude; and their subsequent happy displacement to

Surebleak, Miri's birth-world, and not anyplace she'd ever planned on coming back to.

"Exit," she muttered, sipping her coffee, "pursued by demons."

"By hydras, I thought?"

"Not seeing much difference between 'em, myself."

The Department of the Interior had taken a bad hit during the action that had gotten Korval banished from Liad, but the sorry truth was that it hadn't been killed. There were still pieces and bits and functioning units, and Agents of Change with their missions where their hearts oughta be, all running around and making the galaxy more or less unsafe for everybody, but especially for anybody associated with Clan Korval.

It was, Miri acknowledged with a sigh, a right mess. Clan Korval wasn't about to hunker down and fortify, either. Clan Korval, in the persons of its strong-willed and stubborn adults, was picking up business as usual, and the DOI could meet 'em in hell.

That being exactly the decision Miri would've made herself, for herself, it was still more than a little worrisome when it was other lives—lives she was responsible for—going on the line. Not to mention that Korval's change of address sort of endangered the whole planet of Surebleak.

"Surebleak stands to gain much," Val Con murmured, like he'd heard her thinking—which he prolly had. "It need only stay in motion. And we . . ." He turned his head and smiled at her, a little sleepy now despite the tea. "Korval is pilots."

"And pilots like nothing better than being in danger," Miri finished grumpily.

Val Con laughed. "It is sometimes good to find a

safe port and relax among kin. But not for too long, else one grows bored." He sat up. "Shall I bring you a plate, *cha'trez*?"

"That'd be good, thanks."

Lizzie started fretting as they finished up breakfast. Miri put her empty plate down on the sill and carefully picked the small body up, cradling it against her shoulder like Val Con had taught her.

"Such care," he murmured. "Will she explode?"

"Wouldn't surprise me in the least, given the lineage."

He gathered up her plate with his, carried them to the buffet—and turned, head cocked slightly to the left.

Miri heard it, too, the subdued thunder of wheels along the wooden hallway—and so did Lizzie, who gave a sharp squeal and swung a fist out with enthusiasm, if not precision.

The rumbling grew closer, and ceased altogether, as Korval's butler turned into the morning parlor, stopping just inside the door.

His escort, which was this morning only the cat known as Kiefer, continued onward, his eye on the buffet.

"Jeeves, good morning to you," said Val Con, giving a slight bow to the man-high cylinder topped by an opaque headball that was at the moment showing a pale orange.

"Good morning, Master Val Con. Miri. Young Talizea."

"Mornin', Jeeves," Miri said politely. Lizzie gurgled.

"I fear that I come bearing...distressful tidings," the AI said, slowly—you might say, Miri thought, *reluctantly*.

She took a deep breath, trying to ignore the sudden bite of double anticipation—hers and Val Con's, too, and kept an easy and relaxed grip on her daughter.

"Best we hear it quickly, then," said Val Con, extending a casual hand and scooping Kiefer out of the air just before he landed among the breakfast dishes.

"Yes." The headball flashed between dull and bright orange.

"I had previously reported that Daav yos'Phelium had apparently been successful in decommissioning Pod 78. This had been deduced, as the artifact went off grid, and the deadline for its self-destruction passed without incident."

Miri drew another breath, her stomach suddenly not too happy with having been fed breakfast. It had been *her*—acting as full delm, in Val Con's absence—who had sent Val Con's father and, coincidentally, his mother, on a desperately chancy mission to pull Pod 78 offline before it exploded and caused the deaths of countless numbers of civilians. And yes, he was long coming home, and, no he hadn't—

"In the absence of a message from Pilot yos'Phelium," Jeeves continued, "and the continued absence of himself, I attempted contact with *Ride the Luck*, only to find that Pilot yos'Phelium's ship, like Pod 78, is off the grid."

There was a pause. Val Con stood so quietly that he was very nearly invisible, the offending Kiefer draped, forgotten, over one arm. Miri shivered—his fear, hers; no matter.

"I very much fear that a mishap has occurred," Jeeves said, very softly indeed. "And I must recommend that a ship be sent to the last known coordinates of *Ride the Luck* in order to ascertain what has occurred."

EIGHT

· · · · · · · · · ·

Frenzel
Chaliceworks Aggregations

THE VIEW OUT OF THE LIGHT-RAIL'S WINDOW WASN'T much more interesting than the view of Frenzel Port from ground level. First, there were warehouses—the backside of warehouses, so the view wasn't even informative—then the freight depot, with cranes settling pods on the backs of haulers; and then more scrub plain. The reddish brush seemed popular in the area.

Theo had long since pulled needle and thread from her pocket, letting her fingers work the lace while she reviewed Shan's instructions regarding Chaliceworks.

"Captain Theo," he'd said, which was true and somehow just like him and the rest of her newly discovered Surebleak family, to call her something different each time he spoke to her, "Captain Theo, what you'll want to do is wait until you're down and settled, and finished with the nice customs officers. Get your coffee or tea, or have a glass of wine on me first, before you make contact. I'm told that Frenzel is a very busy place, where things might proceed rapidly, once motion has begun. The bulk of my comments and suggestions are on the key I've given you—*do* read them, Theo.

"The broad outline is that you wish to speak to Zaneth Katrina. Do not, if it falls within your power, allow yourself to be foisted off on a secretary, or diverted to an outside trade officer. Use Korval in your request to see Zaneth Katrina. In fact, use Korval as often as you like! Politely, of course."

"Of course," she said, beginning to feel a little uneasy about a project that had been initially presented as a simple business call.

"Fear not, Cousin!" Shan said with a smile. "I'm not sending you into the lion's den! Those you're to call upon won't bite, though they may growl. Only be resolute, keep your inner calm, and all will be well. Yes?"

She took a breath and managed a smile of her own. "Yes."

"Bold heart. Now! Once you have your meeting with Zaneth Katrina, you will say to her that you received her name and her direction from Korval's own Master Trader, whose emissary you are. This is courtesy, and will, we hope, put the lady at her ease. Say further that Master Trader yos'Galan is interested in dealing with their organization on the long-standing suggestion of Lead Trader Lomar Fasholt, of Fasholt and Daughters, Swunaket Port, whom he has dealt with personally and profitably in the past. Do say *particularly interested in long-term arrangements because of Korval's change of residence*. If the lady has further questions, which I expect she will, answer as well as you are able. If she offers a test cargo, receive it with joy, and 'beam me the lading sheet as soon as you may."

Theo glanced up from her lacework. The train was now passing through an agricultural zone; the city still some distance ahead.

She had reviewed the additional information on the key Shan had given her—several times reviewed it. Though she was confident that she had the information cold, she was less confident that Shan had been *quite* wise to entrust her, personally, as his emissary.

Sighing, she spread the lace between her fingers, seeing starfields and Jump spaces in the weaving of the threads. Her fingers tightened on the needle, and she began working again.

It was, she told herself carefully, perfectly natural to be nervous; this was her first contact as a—well, as a trader, actually, never mind that she didn't have any training as a trader. She was the emissary of a Master Trader. And really, wasn't it likely that a trade partner of Korval's trade partner would leap at the opportunity of affiliation? There were forms to follow, that was all. Shan knew she wasn't a trader, but he did expect that she could be polite and deliver a simple message. Which she could. More, her birth-culture traced lineage through the mother's line. According to the information on Shan's key, Swunaket was also a matrilineal culture. So maybe she *was* a good choice for an emissary, after all.

And wouldn't it be a good thing, she thought, half smiling as she worked the thread, if *Bechimo* could lift from their first port o'call with actual cargo aboard? That would call for a celebration!

That got her to wondering if *Bechimo* liked music—or

if Clarence did. Rig Tranza's idea of a celebration had always included some kind of musical "treat," as he called it. And that got her to thinking about Tranza and *Primadonna*, and wondering how both were getting on.

Wondering took her mind off of any remaining qualms about the upcoming meeting with Zaneth Katrina. She worked the thread, thinking a little wistfully about people she missed—and jumped when the automated voice announced the train's arrival at Central City Station: her stop!

Hastily, she rolled her lace, stuck it and the needle into an inside jacket pocket, and headed for the nearest exit.

· · · ·✸· · · ·

The catalogs kept them busy for the first hour, Clarence and *Bechimo* going over them together. Clarence had relocated to the conference room, where the big monoscreen displayed catalog pages crisp and clean.

It seemed that Fradle's Subscription Supply was going to be the lucky recipient of their custom, Clarence thought. Good selection and prices likewise on things like teas and tarts and bread mixes, with a broad offering of non-eatables that saw some good matches with the Target of Opportunity list.

Bechimo's find on the morning was a clearance offer on a pair of "old-style" starter hydroponics sets that were, in his estimation, the great-granddaughters of the sets originally specified for his modules. According to the item details, the sets were "backward compatible with all RLMoore units." It was that which made the deal worthwhile, if a slight gamble.

"The specifications indicate a few minor changes

over time, as might be expected, Pilot, but assuming remotes, handsets, or the assistance of off-duty crew members, adjustments can be made if necessary." *Bechimo* didn't have a visual presence in the conference room, but his pleasure was plain in his voice.

Clarence nodded. "Put 'em on the list, then, laddie. Pilot Theo was in agreement that fresh fruits and vegetables would be welcome, and the price is right."

"Yes, Pilot," *Bechimo* said, and the item number for the clearance units appeared on the order form displayed in the bottom right hand corner of the big screen.

It was quick work from there on, matching items on the TOO list to the Educators Mid-level Arts and Crafts Supply Pack; Great Music of Seven Worlds resalable files pack, and Male Drug-and-Sundry Crew Pack, which Clarence welcomed particularly, since the beard-control cream in his ready-kit was trending rapidly toward nonexistent, and he had no patience for growing and tending a set o'whiskers.

"Well, then," he said, sitting back with a feeling of rare accomplishment. "I think it's a fine start we have there, laddie, and filed in time to take delivery this evening. Under budget, too. Pilot Theo will sing our praises, sure enough."

"Pilot Theo does not often sing," *Bechimo* said, sounding thoughtful.

Clarence cocked a sapient eye toward the ceiling. "Nor praise either, is what you're not sayin', I take it? Well, she's young, and this is her first command—by which I mean crew command. First Board can weigh heavy on the shoulders 'til you've had a few hours in the chair."

"Pilot Theo's burden would be lighter, if there were a captain aboard."

Clarence felt a cool breeze massage the back of his neck.

"That could be so," he acknowledged. "Got somebody in mind for captain, do you?"

"Yes," *Bechimo* said, and there was the not-quite-illusion of a deep breath drawn quickly. "It comes to me that one who is Pilot Theo's elder—in years, as well as in responsibility for crew. Someone who stands aside from risk, but who is firm in the face of necessary action. Someone such as ... yourself."

"You're proposing *me* for captain?" Clarence laughed and shook his head. "Better have Theo."

"Pilot Theo is, as you say, young. She is addicted to risk, and refuses to take reasonable precautions. This very morning—"

"Took the portcomm, didn't she? *Didn't* hire a guard to go with her, but I don't say that's a bad decision, myself. Half o'them in the guard-for-hire trade will muscle something extra above their fee outta the customer. Theo's capable, and Frenzel's got a nice firm rating in the book. Nothing to worry for there. As for her being particularly "addicted to risk," as you have it—the woman's a pilot! It's risky to lift; it's risky to land; it's risky, as you mention, to go out among strangers on the port. Yet, we do it. All of it, over and again. Myself included. If you're looking for a risk-free captain, laddie, you'd best be looking outside of pilotkind. That's my advice to you." He paused, then nodded. While he was giving advice, he might as well give it all.

"I'll tell what I think, since you bring the topic up—taking on a couple more crew members isn't a bad notion. Theo and me, we're capable, but we're only two, and two's a bit thin for a ship and a mission of these specific dimensions. Might want to think about that a little deeper, laddie."

There was a longish silence, like maybe he'd hurt the lad's feelings, which was a shame, with them having done so well together on the shopping.

"Thank you, Clarence," *Bechimo* said. "I will think about what you've said."

· · · ·⚙· · · ·

As it happened, Theo did have to say "Korval" several times—to the Outer Ring Receptionist, to the Inner Ring Receptionist, to the Merchanter Receptionist, to the Merchanter Secretary—each time politely, and always stating that her business was with Zaneth Katrina, who was, so she learned from the Inner Ring Receptionist, a Senior Sexton.

Whatever that was.

The Merchanter Secretary used the comm, and summoned an Assistant Senior Coordinating Secretary.

"Pilot Waitley requests an audience with Senior Sexton Katrina," she said to that woman when she arrived, slightly breathless. "Please assist her."

Now, Theo sat, green plants and extravagantly fragrant flowers all about her. There were also people, dozens—hundreds—of people, moving in directions obvious to them and not at all to her; people chatting with each other, talking on comms and handhelds, pushing things, riding things, striding, moving, all very busy with themselves and their duties. Theo had been in space station boarding rooms that were less busy.

The problem was that, unlike the space station

boarding rooms, or even the recent train station, she felt that every one of the people passing by looked at her, and looked at her *hard*, some slowing, some turning their heads to stare at her, some even lingering a moment to watch Theo sit and sip from a clear chalice filled with red fruit water.

Many of the passersby were girls—schoolgirls, Theo guessed, by their uniforms and shy or brave glances—and all of them were female. *All* of them. Everybody in this whole echoing cavern of a place was female.

There'd been some few places on Delgado where she'd known the presence of men was discouraged... or...well...not allowed...but Theo'd never seen an installation this size quite so monosex.

Ricia Kergalen, the Assistant Senior Coordinating Secretary called to assist her, was due back any second now, or any minute now, or maybe that was any hour now. For the moment, Theo sat on the raised dais in a chair of exquisite comfort, dressed in her good travel slacks and a pleasant shirt and her pilot's jacket. Her well-worn, overlarge, secondhand pilot's jacket, gift of and certification from Pilot Rig Tranza.

In the Merchanter Secretary's antechamber, Ricia had extended a hand for the jacket, murmuring, "May I put that aside for you?"—then snatched her hand back as if she'd reached toward open flame rather than good space leather.

"Oh! You carry tools!" She bowed a non-Liaden kind of bow. "Welcome then, and follow me, if you please, Pilot, and we shall seat you appropriately for your wait."

Theo hadn't seen whatever it was that Ricia Kergalen saw, but a pilot was rarely if ever separated from her jacket, so she nodded into a half bow, and followed Ricia past several apparent offices and waiting rooms, down a thin hall and a wider one, to this place, this dais in the center of this broad hallway, seven chairs upholstered all in creamy white, enclosed by a white ornamental railing, just three white-speckled steps above the white-stone floor. From her chair, Theo had an unimpeded view of the most spectacular naked-lady statue she had ever seen. The statue was five or six times Theo's height, backed by the greens and flowers. She guessed it was carved or poured from some salt-and-pepper stone that glistened with an inner glow.

Ricia had been easy enough to follow, an efficient walker with *dancer* writ across her demeanor and her stride, and a smile that seemed real if slightly troubled. Her hair was long, braided behind in two ropes that left an interesting view of very pretty neck and the intricate chainwork that supported the complex symbol she wore as a necklace. Not a pilot, though she had very close to pilot and dancer grace, and with some other competences that Theo sensed rather than saw.

"Please, Pilot Theo, if you will be kind enough to wait I shall send refreshments and make arrangements for a discussion of your needs."

Probably, Theo thought, sipping her juice, the passing women were pausing to admire the statue; surely, it was a delight to the eye, and the greens were such a relief in the world she had seen from the train.

The fruit drink had been delivered by a trio of serious youngsters who had stared at her in her jacket as if it were made of timonium, called her Mistress Theo, and poured carefully for her, laying out first an immaculate white cloth and placing the chalice on it with a bow to the statue, another to her, and a third to the pitcher.

"Mistress Theo, it is good of you to visit with us, this day of any. Be welcome, enjoy your drink, and be pleased in the presence of the Goddess."

More bows after the set piece, and off they'd gone, stopping at a distance they might've thought was discreet to peer back at her.

The chalice was neutral to her touch; the drink was cold and tart. She was glad they'd brought the pitcher.

More people passed by the dais. Worse, Theo was sure she'd seen at least two of them pass by before. And they *were* looking. Looking at *her*. The attention was making her nervous, just when she needed to be calm.

A pilot has inner calm, she reminded herself. More, she realized, that's what Father really did when he didn't want to be seen: he let his inner calm cloak him, as she'd been practicing the day before.

Inner calm, she said to herself; *I'm at peace with this world, and with this lady.*

She took time now to study the statue, to absorb its curves and textures. The lady was sensual, no doubt, with long hair blowing free in a nonexistent breeze, with hips able to guide and give, breasts capable of succor and seduction, arms and hands strong without being musclebound, looking both up and out toward some mystic necessity...

Theo relaxed; the sounds of the hall receded, inner calm blanketed her. She looked at the statue's feet, beautiful feet set firm upon the worlds, leading to supple dancer's legs and...

She heard steps then, hurrying toward her, and turned in her chair.

Ricia Kergalen climbed the stairs, her face troubled, braids swinging, pendant clasped in one hand.

"Lady, Pilot, I meant no disrespect, and your wait is over. There is no need for a Working here, I promise you! If you'll kindly follow me, Zaneth Katrina will see you now, in the Senior Secretary's office."

The Senior Secretary was a large-boned woman with imperiously blonde hair caught in a thin silver headband, and falling long to her shoulder. She sat, not offering to rise, bare-armed in a robe of white. She wore several silver bracelets, a red fabric armband, and a pendant even more complex than Ricia's fancy dangle. She sat in a chair probably not her own, holding a small glass ball in the palm of her hand, peering over it at Theo, blue eyes hooded. Theo wondered if the ball were a recording device.

The chair the Secretary occupied was too prosaic for a woman of such means and title, as anyone with a background in Delgado's complex hierarchy might see with a glance.

The chair that was probably the Secretary's by rights was occupied by a tiny pilot wearing a sleeveless red robe cut so low as to barely conceal her small breasts, and a pendant almost as large as her chest. A headband three times the width of the Senior Secretary's bound her rusty-grey head.

Unlike the Secretary, she also wore a smile. Zaneth Katrina, that would be, Theo thought.

"If there's a disturbance, Mothers," Ricia said respectfully. "I believe the pilot was reaching for a cloaking as I arrived to bring her here."

The dour-faced one continued to peer, clicking her tongue and sounding remarkably like Aunt Ella when she disapproved of one of Theo's whims or Father's crotchets.

"We see it all over her, young Wife. I have begun an abatement."

A *what*? Theo wondered, but there—the tiny lady had risen from behind the large desk, her smile undiminished.

"Your name comes before you, Theo Waitley. Let me say welcome to Chaliceworks, Pilot-Captain. I am Zaneth Katrina, and for my work in the world, I am Senior Sexton. I have some years back put aside my piloting, as my eyes and my hands do not coordinate as they did when I was your age."

She bowed then, artless, and straightening, offered a hand.

Theo took it firmly, as she would the hand of any other pilot, and heard Ricia gasp.

"Theo Waitley, yes," she said to the Senior Sexton, meeting the old eyes calmly. "Thank you for your welcome."

"Please, be seated."

There was a momentary scramble as Ricia dragged a chair out of the corner and placed it where the Sexton had pointed, at the side of the desk.

Theo sat, reading the room. She was being offered better than a standing interview, which the Senior Secretary hadn't thought she'd rate—and far more than Ricia had expected. Despite her more intimate placement at desk side, Theo felt a slight chill, as though she'd been seated in a cold spot. She took a breath and gathered herself again with pilot calm.

"There," said the Senior Secretary, tight-lipped, "we have evened the flow. Waitley, whoever taught you should certainly have pointed out that one does not *launch* such a cloaking in an ambient such as this, one must bring it with you, already in place. As it is you were inducing—"

Theo looked to the woman; raised open hands.

"I'm not sure I know what you mean, ma'am," she said respectfully.

The woman raised her eyes to the ceiling.

"Surely, you were working to slide attention from yourself. Come now, who taught you?"

Theo glanced at the Sexton, who was following the byplay with interest.

Well, she thought; maybe it's *not* a rude question. Here.

She raised both hands above her knees again, open—no threat, no hidden intent.

"I learned the quiet-walk from my father," she said carefully. "By observation."

"Your *father*?" The Secretary was clearly disbelieving. "And how would a *man* learn such a thing? Do you tell me he's been trained in the Arts?"

Theo felt her temper flicker. How dare this person who had never met him, *scorn* Father? She took a breath and made herself answer in a calm, low voice.

"My father is an extraordinary man, ma'am, and all he knows is not mine to know, nor to guess. I have learned much from him—but where he learned what I imitated, I don't know."

She turned to fix the quiet Sexton with a glance.

"Ma'am," she said earnestly, "you're a pilot—you know what pilots are! We'll learn from anybody, anywhere. We study, sometimes accidentally, sometimes on purpose."

A hint of pilot-sign flickered from the Sexton's tiny fingers—perhaps it really was *inner calm*.

"All true, of my own knowledge," she said gently,

"But your excellent father, Pilot—has he a name, an affiliation?"

Well, as it happened her father had several names, several affiliations, and for a heartbeat, Theo wondered how she might explain—but there. It was no secret why she was here—and it was therefore obvious which of Father's names would interest this lady most.

"My father's name is Daav yos'Phelium Clan Korval," she said crisply. "My mother is Kamele Waitley, a scholar of Delgado."

The Sexton's smile wavered, and Terran-style she shook her head.

"The Delgado connection is good; I admire it. The other..." The smile firmed. "But, there! You come to us with Korval's name on your lips. Of course. It is plain. Now, please, allow me to apologize for trying your patience, and to ask you, as I ought to have asked at once, why you wished to speak with me."

"I come to you," Theo said bringing to mind her mission, "as the emissary of Master Trader yos'Galan of Clan Korval. Lead Trader Lomar Fasholt, of Fasholt and Daughters, based at Swunaket Port, recommended both yourself and Chaliceworks to him as worthy of his attention. He is particularly interested in a long-term arrangement with your organization because of Korval's change of residence."

"The Master Trader constructs routes to favor the new base, yes. It is understood." The Sexton nodded, and leaned back in her chair.

"You speak well," she said. "I see no attempt to deceive, and I have your handshake. These things are important to us, in this place, Pilot. Again, I apologize for trying you."

She paused, put her hand on her pendant, and sighed.

"Theo Waitley, you come to us in unsettled times. Fasholt has long been a name to conjure with in Temple and in commerce; and Fasholt's name ought by rights to be enough to enable us—a Senior Sexton, and a Master Trader's pilot-emissary—to have a small conversation; and perhaps to engage in an experiment of trade.

"But here is news the Master Trader may not as yet have. Lomar Fasholt has broken with her Temple, and her whereabouts are uncertain. We here—because these things concern all of us who serve the Goddess— we here are awaiting enlightenment. Is this break an honest disagreement, a proper complaint; a bid for a new and truer direction? Or is it schism born of disharmony and a desire for destruction?"

She looked at Theo as if Theo might have the answer in her jacket pocket, along with her lacework.

"And you—you arrive now, a *now* that those of us entrusted with certain powers feel is . . . pivotal. You come among us bearing strange tools, as my young Ricia tells us, with Random Event trotting at your heel like a half-trained hound. And you offer us an affiliation with Korval, Luck's very darlings."

Zaneth Katrina smiled a small, reluctant smile.

"We here, who do the work of the Goddess as best we might . . . We do not trust Luck, Theo Waitley. Perhaps, in ordinary times, and properly warded, we would extend a hand to the Master Trader. Ordinary times . . . those we do not at present have.

"All this to say that, at this juncture, with all that I see in you, and with all else that is in flux, we cannot do business with Korval. Not now."

Theo stared at her, frowning. "You won't deal with Shan because of *luck*?"

Zaneth Katrina laughed. "So speaks the daughter of scholars!" Her mirth died and again she shook her head.

"Understand, Pilot, that the Temple, and Chaliceworks, one of the Temple's major supports, continue to exist because in the face of chaos we are more careful than brave. There may come a time when the balance of things makes dealing with Korval reasonable for us. For the moment, take to Tree-and-Dragon our wish for prosperity on the Line and on the business. Also, be certain to take to this Shan yos'Galan, whose name echoes as Name by another sound, tell this Captain of Korval that his contact among the witches is valued by us, but is in transition. One need be careful.

"Now? For now, we shall all rest easier that you be gone off-world within a day. My office will so inform the port. Event trembles, Luck stretches. Show us that ordinary times are upon us again, and we shall leap at the opportunity to deal with Korval's ships."

She rose then, did the Sexton, and bowed.

"Good lift, Theo Waitley."

NINE

. . . .

Frenzel
Chaliceworks Aggregations

"OFF-WORLD WITHIN A DAY?"

Theo repeated it in disbelief, but the Sexton was gone, retreated in three quick steps to a side door already sealing behind her.

"Off-world in a day!" Anger impelled Theo to her feet.

Off-world—and *Chaliceworks* would inform the port? Put a black mark against *Bechimo* for no reason other than a . . . distrust of luck—of lucky people?

Something flashed in the side of Theo's vision; she spun, pilot-fast. Ricia fell back a step, the silver rings on her upraised hands catching the light; a faint and pretty blue fog wafting from her fingertips.

Theo was shorter than Ricia, but the young woman shrank before her; indeed, Theo felt herself looking down at the robed figure very much as if she outmassed her *and* held the high ground.

Pharst, she *did* have the high ground! She'd done nothing—nothing to have her ship banished from port

like a pirate! She'd come bearing an invitation to do
business from a respected Master Trader! Who happened to come from a lucky family! And how lucky
was it, to get thrown off of the world that had been
your family's base for hundreds of years, to have to
burn down your own house, to—

Ricia moved her hands again; the blue fog got bluer.

"Please, Pilot," she said, soothingly, "if you will come
this way . . ."

The soothing voice only made Theo angrier—treat her
like a pirate and then like a child?—and the blue fog,
thickening even more and acquiring a distinct sparkle—

"Is that . . . *blue stuff* supposed to calm me down?"
she snapped. Ricia's shoulders twitched, but she met
Theo's eyes firmly.

"Pilot, the . . . blue stuff . . . sequesters violent emotion.
I mean no disrespect. However, we have here those
who are sensitive to such emotion, and who must be
protected. You are very clear, and somewhat . . . loud,
at the moment."

"Loud? I haven't raised my voice, and you know it!"

"Pilot, it is not your voice that is loud, but your . . .
self. Your will has been crossed and you have raised
energy. As you have not directed the energy, or contained it, it spills everywhere, creating interference
and distress for those who hear you."

Well, and in fact, she was angry. Justly angry. *Reasonably* angry. And as for spilling everywhere, they
were lucky she didn't have a target!

Lucky.

And as if the thought, or her anger had brought
the memory forward, she remembered her new cousin
Anthora, good-natured and air-witted, chattering—

The luck runs roughly around us. Around all of us. And most especially, it would seem, around you... the brilliant unlikely tangle of you, Theo Waitley!

So... corroboration. Maybe there was some reason for the Sexton's dismissal. But that still didn't mean that she, and her copilot and her ship should be treated like—

Anger sparked, and before her was another bank of blue fog. Theo slashed a hand through it. "Please get that out of my face!"

The blue coalesced; formed into a bubble—and blew out like a candle flame before a determined breath.

Ricia stood very straight, arms stiff, hands held waist-high, fingers spread as if her weight was distributed on them.

"Pilot," she said carefully, "might I respectfully request... Might I..." Here, she actually went to one knee briefly, as if in supplication, "Might I *beg the boon* of your calm? We shall leave immediately; we shall walk much the way we came, and I will myself summon a vehicle, the white car. You will be conveyed to your ship. Safely to your ship, protected by our blessings."

Theo jammed her hand into her pockets, and came out with her lacework, which she stared at, seeing the location *Bechimo* had indicated as a place where teapots and ship parts appeared of their own will. The lace briefly took on stars and comets and waves of gas, the numbers and shapes of the lace being as real to her as the woman who'd turned her back on her.

They wanted *calm*, did they?

Right.

Theo folded the lace into her left hand, closed

her eyes, and reached for calm. Perhaps the calm of
waking up to Kara . . . no, more than that. Perhaps the
calm of a norbear—no, better: the calm of her cat
Coyster kneading her shoulder while purring low and
long enough to put them both to sleep.

Theo pulled that calm over herself, and thought of
the walk she'd taught herself only yesterday. Father's
walk. That helped her to be gone, to be invisible?

She could work with that.

Ricia visibly relaxed, and lowered her hands slowly.
"Thank you, Pilot," she whispered. "Please follow me."

· · · ·❄· · · ·

Years ago, Kamele Waitley had watched her *onagrata*, a challenging scholar, stimulating companion,
surprising lover, and affectionate role-male for her
daughter, demonstrate to that same daughter how a
pilot packed for travel.

It had involved one modestly-sized suitcase, and
the pockets of a jacket. She had watched, astonished,
as first he weeded out those things that could be
easily replaced—books, entertainment cubes, favorite
teas—before adroitly packing many more than she
would have thought possible of those things which
were more difficult to replace into that one small bag.

He had then shaken out Theo's jacket, and placed
into the inside pockets the acceptance letter from
Anlingdin Piloting Academy, her identification, a flat
folder of pictures, and most of her money, leaving
enough to buy sundries in an easy-to-reach outside
pocket.

"A pilot will also have her license, and a weapon,"
he had said, handing Theo the jacket with a smile in

his dark eyes. "A pilot ought to always be ready to lift. That means that her essentials are in her jacket, and her jacket is always with her. The contents of the case—even those things that we have just agreed are essential—can be, and sometimes must be, left behind."

Kamele was no pilot; yet, in packing for this journey, she had recalled Jen Sar's lesson to Theo, and done her best to emulate it. In the end, it meant that she took with her from Delgado one large case on a tether, and a smaller one that went over her shoulder. The interior pockets of her jacket contained those things of importance—items that it would be difficult-to-impossible to replace: identification, tickets, credit cards, and a datakey containing her research and notes regarding the delm, and the clan, of Korval.

While she had, according to Jen Sar's definition, overpacked for this journey, by comparison with her fellow travelers, she was as unencumbered as a bird in flight. Her cases came with her to her tiny cabin, and stowed easily in the under-bunk storage. When it came time, as now, to debark, it was a matter of complete simplicity to put on her jacket, shoulder the small bag, pick up the leash of the large bag, and exit. No need to go halfway across the station to claim checked baggage; no need to rent a wagon, or a porter; no need to research the necessary and proper local bribes.

No, all she need do was verify the location of the ship she was transferring to, walk leisurely down-station until she came to the appropriate boarding room, and check herself in.

The boarding room for *Hoselteen* was small, and a little shabby. It was also very nearly empty. On the left side of the room, two men sat on a sofa facing the entertainment screen, one with his head on the other's shoulder. On the right side of the room, a woman in an orange-and-white jumpsuit released the security curtain covering the front of the snack counter.

"Toot 'n' tea up in five ticks," she called over her shoulder. "Make yourself comfy."

"Thank you."

Kamele found herself a chair with an adjustable arm desk in a bright corner of the room, and settled in with a smile.

Jen Sar had taught her so much during their years together; she would be glad—no!—*happy* to see him again.

Her smile faded.

If she was allowed to see him again. If her research was correct, if Jen Sar was held . . . *prisoner*, the delm of Korval might deny her that pleasure.

She straightened where she sat. The delm of Korval might *try* to deny her. If she dared. But she, Kamele Waitley, full professor and junior administrator—she had made a vow. If Jen Sar were held against his will, she would parole him.

And that vow she would keep.

· · · ·✳· · · ·

Theo had spent the trip back in the white car musing on the concept—on the *problem*—of luck. As an exercise, she tried to view her whole life as a series of lucky or unlucky incidents.

On the lucky side, there was Father's position as Kamele's *onagrata*—

Or was that unlucky?

Jen Sar Kiladi had been a Gallowglass scholar; students from planets almost as obscure as Surebleak competed for places in his seminars. Because of that—and because he was Father—he could afford, and had chosen, to live in a house in town, rather than in the apartments that were his by right, inside the Wall. And Kamele had opted to move in with her *onagrata*, rather than insisting that he allow her to provide for him, a situation which had made them . . . odd.

But was odd lucky, unlucky, or null?

Theo stared out the window, blind to the ugly landscape the car passed through.

Odd—she'd been odd. Physically challenged and a danger to others—that's how odd the Safety Office had thought she was. Kamele and Father had fought for years, which she learned later, to prevent the Safeties from drugging her into conformity. And then, when it seemed like the Safeties would take the decision into their own hands, for the good of the greater number—then Kamele suddenly had to travel off-world—and she took Theo with her.

Off-world, she met Cho sig'Radia, the Scout who had sponsored her to Anlingdin, when she had hardly even known what a "pilot" was—and she'd met Win Ton, too, who had woken *Bechimo* and gotten her involved with a ghost ship—was *any* of that luck, or just . . . life?

And if she, whose life it was, couldn't point at any one event and say, *There! That was lucky!*—then it just seemed plain that the Sexton . . . was superstitious.

Except that Anthora, and Father, too, had talked to her about luck, and how she—just the fact of her moving down her life—made it run rough, whatever that meant. Father had seemed to think it meant, in part, that she needed backup, which is how she happened to have one Clarence O'Berin sitting Second Board.

She wondered if Clarence believed in luck.

She wondered if her loud, bright, rough luck was... dangerous.

Theo sighed sharply and blew her bangs out of her eyes.

Then, she reached into her pocket, and pulled out her needle and lace.

· · · ·❈· · · ·

"*Bechimo*, this is Frenzel Control. You are cleared to lift in six hours local, starting with my mark. Mark."

Clarence erupted from the galley, where he'd been enjoying a solitary lunch, and slapped the switch.

"*Bechimo* here, Control. We've filed no request." He glanced at Screen Six as he said it. The screen was filled with a foggy grey fizz, like static.

"*Bechimo*, lift request filed through Chaliceworks Aggregations, Frenzel Main Office."

Chaliceworks had been Theo's target, right enough, but if the lassie had wanted them in for a rush lift, why hadn't she called and had him file all right and proper like a copilot ought to do?

Clarence touched the switch.

"Control, we have a delivery scheduled—necessary supplies."

"Fradle's has been notified of your departure schedule, and will expedite delivery," Control said.

Bad and worse, thought Clarence, but he kept his voice easy.

"'Preciate the assist."

"Scheduling is tight, *Bechimo*; we had to do some fancy work to accommodate a lift so soon. You will keep the schedule."

"We will, yes."

"Frenzel Control out."

"*Bechimo* out," Clarence said, but the line was already cold.

"Did you trace that?" he asked.

"The call originated at Frenzel Tower," *Bechimo* said. "It appears legitimate. I have attempted to contact Pilot Waitley via the comm unit she carries."

Clarence felt a kind of cold, gone feeling in his gut. Daav's daughter. No telling what the lassie had got herself sideways of.

"And?" he asked, though he thought he knew the answer.

"I cannot reach her. The comm is shielded." There was a pause, and in Screen Six, behind the static, the shadow of a head, shoulders, arms...

"It is possible that I can track Theo Waitley through her pilot's key."

"Is that a fact?" Clarence thought about that. "'Less it's something with no chance of disturbing a security screen, hold that in reserve. Port Control ain't likely to be colluding in murder."

"The Over Pilot may be in danger. Harm could befall her."

There was an edge of what might be true and real panic in *Bechimo*'s voice. Clarence smoothed the air with one hand: *hold course...*

"That's right. And what I'm sayin' is, let's just wait a minute or two, and see if that call don't come in, or herself does. In the meanwhile, you—"

"A white car has stopped in front of the trade entrance," *Bechimo* interrupted.

His Screen Seven flickered, showed the view, and the car, the back door rising, and Theo stepping out onto the dingy tarmac.

Clarence closed his eyes briefly.

The door lowered, and the car had pulled away before Theo gained the hatch, striding like she had a good head o'steam going.

"Less Pilot, the Over Pilot has returned," *Bechimo* said, sounding breathless, and here came the lass herself, black eyes snapping and pale hair looking like she'd been running her fingers through it for the last hour.

"Welcome home," he said, giving her as easy a smile as deceit could fashion. "Frenzel Control gives us six hours to get ourselves gone."

Theo glared; sighed.

"Chaliceworks wants us off-world within the day," she said. "They said they'd make arrangements with the port." She shook her head. "I should've warned you. I apologize."

"Pilot Theo, have you been harmed?"

There was a note of genuine panic in *Bechimo*'s voice. The laddie was becoming accomplished, thought Clarence.

"My temper's sprained, but otherwise, I'm fine. They were very courteous. Master Trader yos'Galan's proposal...didn't meet their needs." She sighed and looked straight into Clarence's eyes. "Also, they don't trust luck."

He nodded. "That would be a matter they'd need to overcome, if they wanted to partner with Korval."

, Theo sighed.

"Problem is, I'm not sure I even *believe* in luck."

"Give yourself time," Clarence counseled, eying her. The lass looked wrung out, but he saw no sign of temper, which he was inclined to think a good thing.

"Cup o'tea, Pilot?"

"Actually," she said, "lunch. You eat?"

"In process when Tower called to chat."

"Let's hit the galley, then," she said. "We can catch each other up."

· · · ✦ · · ·

It was an hour to lift, and counting. Fradle's had delivered, and supplies had been stowed.

Theo walked back into *Bechimo*'s Heart with Clarence, calmer now, and with a headache beginning, which could've been the aftermath of anger, or the effects of breathing too much world dust, or an allergic reaction to Ricia's blue fog.

Whichever, she dropped into her chair, glancing by habit to Screen Six—and froze.

A man looked at her from out of *Bechimo*'s screen. A beardless man with tight trimmed dark hair, thin lips, wide mouth, and a brown, hard-used face, as if this younger man had all of Clarence's experience and none of his smiles.

The image sharpened, and she saw a touch of stubbled beard below the growing sideburns, a hint that perhaps a mustache could grace the upper lip, the shadow of what might be a scar on the bridge of the broad nose.

He moved a shoulder, as if to ease a tight muscle, and raised a hand that showed two rings of some silvery brown metal—one on the thumb, and another, on the second finger. A wide bracelet of the same metal was clasped tight 'round his wrist.

The pilot, for surely he was at a board, leaned back slightly. His jacket, of antique cut and color, a buff not much used in today's fashion, bore unmistakable signs of scuffs and wear, some so familiar that Theo understood them to be transposed from her own jacket, inherited from Rig Tranza.

Theo heard a soft sigh, and looked away from the apparition in the screen. Clarence stood entranced, his hands resting lightly on the back of his chair. His eyebrows lifted slightly, and she looked back to the screen.

An ID box had formed at the bottom of the screen, bearing the legend: B. Joyita, *Bechimo* Communications Officer.

"Who is Joyita, *Bechimo*?" Theo asked, keeping her voice soft and even.

"A detail, Pilot. The Less Pilot's point—and your own—is taken. We need more personnel. If we seem too few, we become endangered. Joyita allows both pilots to be about other duties, knowing that they leave a senior crew member behind, for ship's security."

"So," Clarence sighed. "A treat for the eyes, ain't you just, Chimmy-lad."

In the screen, Joyita's lips tightened—Theo couldn't say if it was an attempted smile, or a grimace of distate . . . or just a random animation.

"Thank you, Clarence," the image said, mouth moving in perfect sync with the words. "You are a treat for the eyes, too."

TEN

· · · · · ·

Landing Pad Number Nine
Regent's Airfield Number One
Cresthaller

"THEY DON'T SERIOUSLY EXPECT US TO SHIP THOSE!"

Theo stared at Screen M, for Manifest, where land trucks lumbered slowly through the edge growth, ignoring her suggestions for routing around the pits and piles clearly visible from *Bechimo*'s topmost camera.

They were on-port. A port without the active ability to refuel them. A port that was little more than an undersized commercial airport. A port so minor, on a planet so seldom visited, that *Travasinon* didn't list it at all. The *Guild Quick Guide* did grant Cresthaller an entry, with the notation: *No reason to call*.

In fact, Theo thought, there *wasn't* any reason to call—no trade, no traffic—*nothing* except a dispirited cluster of warehouses around three airstrips.

The airstrips looked to be in good repair, at least—they'd've been perfectly adequate for playing touch-and-go with the Star Kings she'd trained on.

Once Tower understood that it was a *spaceship* coming in and the offer of a flagger had been maladroit, at best, *Bechimo* had been directed to land in this overgrown area behind the warehouses, where rusted rails and the shattered remains of what once might have been a service road were apparent on the scans as they came in.

Theo had considered pulling up and away, but *Bechimo* located a good level spot where the tarmac was mostly in one piece, and down they were, pod-pickup portside.

"Shall we inform them that their mission is futile?" Clarence asked. "Or will the pilot reject them from the dockside?" He moved a shoulder—Liaden body language signaling disdain. "If we dismiss them now, they may return to their naps more quickly."

"I was hoping to have cargo and profit from this place ..." Theo muttered, wondering what the devil Shan had been thinking to send them to this ... this ... *pit*!

"You, me, and Chimmy, too!" Clarence said, back in Terran. "No tellin' what Shan wanted out of it, but I'm thinking a dead loss wasn't on his mind. Not to say the trip'll be a total waste—a little polishing and we'll have us a drinking tale about the time we tried to load four cans so rusty they came apart at lift! Come to think on it, we oughta have a beer or two right now, to be in the proper spirit for the linkups!"

Despite herself, Theo laughed. Joyita, in Screen Six, looked worried.

"See, I don't know how it is at the real ports," Theo said earnestly. "Always been on quality routes, myself—and you'd best believe there's no beer before loading when you fly with Rig Tranza! On the other hand, it turns out I'm related to a lot of pilots. I haven't heard any of their stories yet; might be that pods come apart every trip out, or it's counted a bust!"

Clarence's mouth quirked into a barely suppressed grin.

"The problem with pilots is they lie as good as they fly, absolutely. The best ones, why, they can fib their way through a bad Jump sequence as easy as they can explain how they happen to have a bottle of wine in a dry port."

She snickered again, and shook her head.

"Well, let's see who we can raise. Out-line, please, Joyita?"

"Yes, Pilot," said the communications officer, glancing down at his hidden board.

A button lit on Theo's board.

"Port link live, Pilot."

"Bro Moddasin?" Theo said, trying for her mother's tone of crisp and cool authority. "Are you on channel, Bro Moddasin?"

Shan's information had been for Frader Transport Group, the last contact so long ago that there had been no contact name. Bro Moddasin had answered *Bechimo*'s general call for Frader Group, but whether he was the owner, the foreman, the shipping agent, or rented the office next door was unclear.

He'd sounded . . . almost horrified to hear that Tree-and-Dragon had purchased a contract from VenskyTrade to pick up four pods warehoused under seal and held by Frader Group.

For that, Theo couldn't blame him. According to Shan's information, the pods in question had been in Frader Group's keeping for the last twenty-three years Standard. Bro Moddasin could be forgiven for supposing that nobody would ever call for them. The reason that pods were stored surface-side instead of the usual orbital storage was that Cresthaller's outport had been destroyed—by accident or sabotage didn't matter—during the local war, which had ended nineteen years ago Standard.

The note that had come with the Cresthaller file was sensible, handwritten in a beautiful script that she could now read, even if she'd hate to have to read it back to a stickler.

Theo, we purchased this contract more for the contact, and to keep our shipping ally in business, than for the contents. So, Pilot, if the materials are no longer at hand, simply reconnoiter, research the current market and retrieve recent commerce records while being pleasantly noncommittal. If the situation is unstable, move on. Under no account must you jeopardize your ship for this.

The channel light remained dark. Theo sighed. For somebody who was even theoretically an official representative of a trading company, Bro Moddasin was hard to contact.

"Comments anyone?" Theo glanced at Screen Six, then to Clarence, but neither offered advice, until he hand-signed *ten count?*

Theo sighed, gently, her hands making the noncommittal wavelike motion that was the hand-talk equivalent of a shrug.

"Pilot," *Bechimo* said suddenly. "I have been observing the approaching vehicles. Factoring in tread mark depth, speed, bounce, and visible spring-loading, I have formed the theory that they are not in fact transporting pods loaded with the items the manifest provided. There are no active transponders, nor are there appropriate markings on the visible rigging. It appears that all four are controlled by individual drivers."

"So, they're what? Independent operators? Pirates?"

Her stomach clenched—tighter, as she saw Clarence's fingers move on the board, rapidly setting up the action-pad for a fast lift. Since they weren't on a proper hotpad, nor under control of a proper space-traffic system, they were already in push-to-fly mode, despite the fact that there was some minor air traffic on and about the air center.

"Pilot, I cannot make a firm determination on—"

"Tree-and-Dragon please, Tree-and-Dragon please!"

Clarence's hands paused near the action-pad, a finger flip away from the low-level weapons. Joyita's background wobbled slightly; firmed as he pressed his lips together disapprovingly.

Theo touched the comm button.

"This is Pilot Waitley. Go ahead, please."

"Bro Moddasin here, Pilot. I meant to get to you sooner, but the 'rangemints with the haulers weren't as..." There was a pause, and then what might have been a whisper away from the mic—"*is* true!"

"Sorry, Pilot," Bro Moddasin continued, louder. "Our 'rangemints with the haulers weren't as clear as I'd thought, so we had to bring in a backup company. This... ummm... this side of the field ain't really been used since the... well, anyhow, for a while, so the haulers're breaking trail 'fore bringing in the shipment. Could be some hours, still—might even be tomorrow—but we'll get those pods out there, never you worry."

On-screen, one of the vehicles was backing up, giving way for another which seemed to be having a better time of it.

Inner calm, Theo told herself, mentally dancing a phrase of *menfri'at*. For good measure she added another two phrases, ending in a short, sharp hand move that could be read either as *restrain* or *kill*, depending on emphasis.

Alas, that last had been a little more in the world than she'd meant, as Clarence's chuckle indicated, and she was glad that she was on radio and not live screen.

"Pilot? You were calling me."

She looked to the topside camera view once again, shook her head.

"Frader Group, I hear you. I was going to question the integrity of the inbound items—so I'm glad to learn that these are not the pods we want. Please, a radio check in four hours and at that point I'll reschedule our day to match incoming cargo. We'll be engaged in maintenance that should occupy us until then."

A pause, and a low off-mic snarl that sounded like "...ought to at least know if it's safe by then!"

"I understand that you'll be busy until just after our lunch hour, Pilot," Bro Moddasin said, somewhat more loudly than necessary. "We'll check with you then."

"Transmission ended, Pilot," *Bechimo* confirmed. Then, plaintively, "May we instruct them to use the proper call sign?"

Theo took a breath—and let it out, slowly. They didn't get many spaceships here at Cresthaller, but *Bechimo* was correct—lack of the proper forms was just one more thing that put a pilot's back up on this port. It was possible that Tower didn't have the forms available to them.

Though she suspected they wouldn't much care for receiving them.

She looked toward Clarence, hand-signing, *Do this, please,* as she turned her chair and came to her feet.

"*Bechimo*, if you will, in concert with Second Board, please compile an up-to-date list of proper codes, confirmations, and etiquette, both in file and hardcopy, for me to pass along to the Frader Group. You'll find my notes from the Academy an adequate start, and some of the information we received at Frenzel should be useful, too. Make copies as well for Tower; we'll transmit them all as time permits, before lift-off."

Theo sat at her station, absorbed, listening and, to some extent, seeing Clarence's calm evaluation of pod serial number ending 57, which was the last of the four. They'd passed two of the first three, with one failing *Bechimo*'s electronic-link scan as well as getting bad marks from Clarence's visual—he'd finally said, "Let's mark this number as unacceptable and go from there, Theo. I think between the pair of us we've seen enough of this one. If they have something to repack cargo into, we'd need to mark that as a repack and get an extra surety—can't say the problems are new. That's the report from my end."

Besides *Bechimo*'s technical turndown due to power supply issues and lock security concerns, that pod's seals had *looked* bad, even over video, even to someone who'd spent as little time as possible in Practical Cargo Handling 302 back at Anlingdin Piloting Academy.

While she'd done check-cargo on many of the trips with Rig Tranza, *Primadonna*'s courier lifts were dainty compared to *Bechimo*'s working multipod lifts. It was, Theo thought, a good thing they had Clarence.

"I predict the Less Pilot will accept the fourth pod," *Bechimo* said. "It is very like the first and third, Pilot. The internals report themselves well, there's no pressure difficulty evident, the scans show good integration of the shield and lock system. I am observing the Less Pilot's hands-on techniques and analyzing them in consideration of producing a procedures manual more current than the one I was fitted with. It may be that, should a different Less Pilot be utilized at some point, the most useful techniques can be shared and repeated."

This was good news in several ways—for one, *Bechimo* was showing a personal interest in ongoing operations. Too, it meant that Clarence was regaining confidence enough to be able to teach, if need be—he was explaining himself to *Bechimo* and Theo as he worked.

"Forward lockpoint six," he was saying, "shows signs of attachments, but like the other lockpoints onboard there's no evidence of corrosion, misalignment, wear, or stress. My report shows this lockpoint acceptable. Also, I note that there's no sign of extraneous color-coding—remind me to go over that in detail at another time, since that's a sign that a pod may have been used for smuggling—and there's a full and proper complement of static standard and polarized spectrum reflectors, again, with no indication of patterning."

Clarence had a good hand with the camera, pointing it steadily where he was talking about and otherwise holding it still.

"Patterning—that's where the reflectors can be used to mark a unit for a break-in—or sometimes it just shows that something's been attached for a free ride."

Joyita, in Screen Six, nodded gravely.

Theo echoed that to Clarence as, "Noted, and we'll add that to crew consult next preflight."

Bechimo had been doing an excellent job of switching external camera and sensor angles to follow Clarence's tour; he walked with Bro Moddasin and one of his retainers, Moddasin a respectful shadow. The retainer was a nervous guard despite, or perhaps because of, the presence of the various transport drivers.

"So that pod you're not taking," Bro Moddasin suddenly spoke up, his voice low and deferential. "Sir. That's gonta get us a black mark with Tree-and-Dragon, ain't it?"

Clarence frowned at him. "Black mark? I don't take your meaning there, Bro."

"Well, what I mean tasay—we din't keep the thing so it'll take space, which we was trusted to do. Tree-and-Dragon sets a good deal by contracts—well, naturally! Sets a good deal, too, what I heard, on people keeping their things pretty."

Clarence walked a couple steps in silence, then said slowly, "Well, now, here's the thing, laddie: I ain't Tree-and-Dragon. Pilot an' ship're contractors; pilot hired me, so I got *nothing* to say about Tree-and-Dragon's internals. Pilot did let me know that the front office didn't exactly think *any* of these pods might've survived. Thinking about it from that start, us bringing out three in pretty good shape might get 'em to thinking that Frader Group's reliable to do bidness with."

Bro Moddasin looked up, naked hope on his face.

"D'ya think they will?"

"Just as likely to think that than t'other," Clarence said carefully. "But what's it all to you, if you don't mind my askin'?"

The other man snorted.

"You'll've noticed we ain't much used to star traffic here. And you'll've maybe noticed too that there ain't no station up in orbit where these pods, say, coulda been held outta the weather, and transferred with a lot less sweat o'man."

"Little bit of unpleasantness a few years back, wasn't it?" Clarence asked.

"Damned bit of foolfire," Bro Moddasin corrected hotly. "Only a brat, myself, but my big sis was in it. Went up with a bunch of 'em to hold the station. Last we seen o'her, an' my mother—well, that's family stuff, no matter to you. But here's Cresthaller gov bringing in every ship they could snabble, by hook or by lie, and setting trading ships agin one another, all and every bit of it to *secure their position*, an' what've we got at the end of it all and twenty years downwind, eh?"

He looked at Clarence meaningfully.

Clarence shrugged. "What d'you have, then?"

"Nothin'." Bro Moddasin spat. "Zackly *nothin'*. There was ships usta stop here—them pods prove that! Well, there ain't anymore! And there won't be, 'til word gets out that the old gov is long out, and no such a thing'll happen again. We need us a trade line that'll take an interest in us, maybe go halfsies on a station—work in partnership, see? Ten, nine year ago, buncha fellas made a consortium, they called it. Started in at rebuildin' up there..."

He shook his head.

"Short story shorter, what was left of the station was unstable, and ain't none o'them come back to their families, neither."

Theo, listening to this, bit her lip. If what Bro Moddasin said was so, and the government had engaged in acts of, well, *piracy*, he was right to suppose that no ships would risk themselves here again.

"So, anyhow, if Tree-and-Dragon was to take an interest..." He sighed abruptly, and his shoulders lost their tension. "I'll tell you what, we're not gonna be able to stay on this ol' ball o'mud much longer. We need too much stuff. Saw some of them science and news reports on the vid."

They'd come 'round to the hatch, and Clarence stopped, Bro Moddasin at his side.

"It'll take us some hours to get the pods on and balanced," he said slowly. "If there's a world packet, you might wanna transmit that to the ship. Those science lectures, too, if you might. The pilot does file reports, and we send on whatever we get from the port and interested others."

"Do you?" Bro Moddasin stared. "*Do* you, by the brigger." He grinned. "You'll be getting transmissions from the Frader Group, and from Cresthaller Port Authority, too, before you lift." The grin broke, and Bro Moddasin swallowed, hard. "Good day to you, Pilot. Sir."

He turned, then, and strode away toward the trucks, yelling, his guard at his back.

· · · · ✵ · · · ·

The Uncle consulted the readout over the medical unit—the same medical unit that had until recently been occupied by Win Ton yo'Vala—and felt...relief.

Perhaps it would be just, he thought, closing his eyes briefly, to admit even to *intense relief*.

He sighed. The man he and Dulsey had transferred from the field 'doc into this much more sophisticated and adept unit had been very much more dead than alive. It would not have surprised him, just now, to find that, even with better support, that it had been easier for the patient to let life go, than renew his grip.

Such was the tyranny of Korval's genes, that, no matter how painful, they would always choose life.

In that, the Uncle owned, he was fortunate. For he had no wish at all to come before the delm of Korval, and admit that his had been the last hands on Daav yos'Phelium before his death.

He scrutinized the readings again, more coolly.

Daav yos'Phelium lived, yes. The unit had returned him to a level of stability that was considerably less than optimum. If there was no improvement... But there—what was the phrase?

Why borrow trouble, when one might have more than one wants, for free?

ELEVEN

. . . .

Middle Orbit
Departing Cresthaller

"JUST BY THE WAY," THEO ASKED CLARENCE, "WHAT ARE
we going to do with those transmissions from Tower
and from Frader Group, and Bro Moddasin, and the
local infofeed?"

Though large, it wouldn't be a problem to store the
file. She just couldn't think of any particularly good
reason why they should.

Clarence glanced over, letting her see surprise on
his face.

And that, Theo realized abruptly, was true. He was
letting her see. Clarence's control over his expressions
was nearly as fine as Father's, and she was beginning
to think that his motives were as nuanced.

"Told Bro we'd send it on to Shan," he said, overly
patient.

"Yes, that's what you told him," Theo said, matching his tone. "What I want to know is what we're
actually going to *do*."

Rust-red eyebrows lifted over very blue eyes, and he inclined his head, as Liaden as you'd want, which Theo didn't, especially, at the moment.

"Pilot, it grieves me that I have given you cause to think me easy with my honor. I assure you, I spoke my true intentions. More, I believe Master Trader yos'Galan will be glad of the information, and discover it not only to be of interest, but of use."

Theo sighed.

"It is not your honor, but your meaning that I question," she said, insisting on her point, despite the change in language. "Bro Moddasin himself stated the case concisely. Cresthaller has nothing. Nothing to draw trade; nothing to induce investment. This is a port that the Guild rates as *no reason to call*, while *Travasinon* ignores it entirely. With such assistance as that..."

"That's right," Clarence said, back in Terran, and nodding vigorously. "That's just it. See, the thing is, the place ain't in a bad situation for a switch-off hub. I'm thinking that's what it was before the war—Chimmy, you want to check records an' see if I'm right about that? Theo, if Shan's thinkin' about a loop, he's gotta be thinking about swap-outs and pod-drops. You'll say there's Frenzel Port, just up the road, but you seen what that was like to get in and out of. Someplace less crowded, you're in, you drop your pods, pick up what's been left, and out you go, slick—"

"Clarence." Joyita in Screen Six looked up and out, making eye contact. "Trade records show Cresthaller as an active regional pod-drop and pickup hub. A comfortable stop, as it was rated in the guide books." There was a pause, and a near aside of, "I never visited.

"The planetary government unwisely attempted to control a local trade negotiation by intimidating station and ship crews." Joyita blinked, and looked down, as if he were reading a report.

"This was not well received, as you may imagine. Leaders escalated by announcing plans to seize entire ships, which was also unwise and the station soon suffered a firefight, and became uninhabitable after grievous loss of life and property." There was the hint of a shrug as he finished up. "The failed government fought on for some time, I gather, but they are no longer seen to be a factor on-world."

Clarence nodded. "'Bout what Bro said."

"And your plan is—what?" Theo asked, dropping back into Liaden for the properly acidic, "Forgive me, Pilot; I fear that I am quite dull today."

Clarence grinned. "Touch of the da there," he commented. "Good. But see, I don't got a plan. I see an *opportunity* that might appeal to a Master Trader. Worth a pinbeam hey-up, I'm thinking, with the bulk of Bro's material there to go regular mail."

"And this opportunity is...?" Theo prompted.

She carefully didn't point out that pinbeams used a lot of power, and that they'd already sent Shan one pinbeam already, relaying the Senior Sexton's warning regarding Trader Fasholt. Never mind the expense, if they sent him a pinbeam every ship-week, he'd think she didn't know any...

"What I'm wondering is if Tree-and-Dragon might not know of—or know of somebody with—a big old bulk freighter or the like what's weighing heavy on the books. Something that holds air, has some offices and a dock, and enough engines to get it somewhere..."

He paused, frowning at something about halfway to Screen Four.

"So, how about Shan, or this other party, say, rents Cresthaller this old ship to orbit as a small station? If a ship gets in and they got outgoing, they could use a station of some kind. If they take on some transships, great. Gets 'em back in space. Gets 'em a chance to rebuild the notion that it's not out-of-reason risky to leave something at Cresthaller Station to be called for later."

Said that way, it didn't sound completely space-brained, and it might be something that a Master Trader with a long view of investments could find interesting.

It came to Theo that Clarence was a man who was very used to being in charge of things—and she had an idea that TriPlanetary Freight Forwarding had needed somebody in charge sometimes. She'd seen his resume, of course—but it was a pilot's resume, only mentioning his stewardship of the forwarding company as the duty that had kept him from flying for so many years.

"I have identified," *Bechimo* said suddenly, "seventeen vessels on the open market with cubic capacity sufficient to deal with the storage of the most recent gross reported in-shipping, assuming an active shuttle and reasonably spaced ship dates."

Clarence raised his hands, palms up, and slid a quick glance to Theo.

"Well, there! We can append those lists to that other packet of stuff we're sending to the home office then."

He nodded, nearly a bow, in Theo's direction. "Shall I create this report, Pilot?"

Theo inclined her head. "Let it be noted as your

analysis. If you will, share it when it is done, and before we send to the Master Trader."

"Yes, Pilot," Clarence said. He put his pad aside and reached to the board, opening up a text window in Screen Nine.

· · · ·✦· · · ·

Dulsey looked up as he entered the workroom, her right hand curled before her, as if she held something captive, but not too close, within the cage of her fingers.

"How fares the pilot?" she asked.

"Better than when we took him up; less well than I would like to see him." He sighed. "It was not my plan nor my intent to set up a hospice for wounded Scouts."

She laughed softly. "A return to your origins."

He stared at her, then allowed himself a chuckle.

"I had considered myself a revolutionary!"

"A revolutionary who gathered to him those in need of repair before they could be put to work for his cause."

"Would you have me as cold as that?"

"Not cold," she said, glancing down at her curled fingers. "Practical."

"Even worse! But you are troubled."

"No," she said, frowning slightly. "Not troubled. Bemused. I hope you will know what to think, and what we ought to do."

"I hope so too," he said, when she seemed to hesitate. It had been some number of hundred years since he had seen Dulsey hesitant, except as a subterfuge. He wondered what that might portend, and felt a slight shiver overtake him. Korval and Korval's luck. The Directors of the Tanjalyre Institute had perhaps been correct in breaking the mold from which Cantra yos'Phelium had been cast. A pity they had waited until she was free of their influence before doing so.

No, that was an unkindness, and moreover it ignored his own involvement in keeping Pilot Cantra alive. It would have been almost as easy—and far simpler—to have allowed her to die, and Garen, too, had it come to that. But he considered himself a revolutionary, and so he had opted to repair that which had the potential to confound his enemies.

Which Cantra had done.

Which she had *very much* done.

There might even, Uncle acknowledged, be debt on his side. Convenient, then, that here was come Cantra's many times great-grandchild, in need. Less convenient, of course, if *this* yos'Phelium died. *This* yos'Phelium was no kinless, careless pirate, but an elder belonging to the considerable socioeconomic force known as Clan Korval.

There were few entities in the universes that Uncle troubled to fear, but Clan Korval . . . inspired caution. Of late, they had been beset, and had thereby suffered some loss of strength. He doubted that the delm of Korval would be so rash as to place the Dragon in opposition to the Uncle, but . . . Korval's memory was long. And they would not always be weak.

"But what bemuses you?" he asked Dulsey, as still she hesitated.

She looked up, a frown line between her eyes. Grey eyes. She preferred grey eyes. It was in the chart.

"I was," she said slowly, "preparing the pilot's leather for cleaning and repair. I had put the jacket on the bench, turned away to set the unit . . . and when I turned back—*these* were on the bench."

She raised her hand and opened her fingers, carefully, but with no conscious drama.

Nestled on her palm were two . . . seed pods, such as might fall from a tree. Round, green, and unexceptional.

"They must, I think, have been in a pocket," Dulsey continued. "However, nothing else that had been in his pockets—license, hide-aways, money—had come free. Only these."

Only those.

Fruit of Korval's Tree. Some would say, Korval's damned Tree. Perhaps even, Korval's damned, *meddling* Tree.

He might, thought Uncle, gazing down at the pods on Dulsey's palm, be the only one left who remembered the name of the great race of trees.

Ssussdriad.

No, he corrected himself. Surely, Korval remembered. It was not the sort of detail Cantra would have failed to record.

"What must we do?" Dulsey asked.

Uncle sighed; suppressed an urge to snatch the things up and drop them in the nearest disposal unit.

No.

No.

To destroy the seed pods would be, he felt, an error. Perhaps, a very great error.

He could afford no errors in this.

"I fear," he said, unwillingly, "I very much fear, Dulsey, that we must bring the pilot awake."

And hope that Korval's Luck was sufficient to allow them all to survive it.

. . . ❖ . . .

The next stop on the proposed loop was a system with three gas giants and two habitable worlds. The first world, Chustling, held a good orbit just inside the inner part of the habitable zone, while Vincza and its moon followed a more elliptical orbit that went from the outer third of the habitable zone to the far edge, with the lunar cycle helping determine weather. The two worlds shared an intermediate orbital market called Tradedesk—*Bechimo*'s third stop on the loop.

"My preference," Theo said as she stretched the growing cord-mass in her hands to revisualize the location of one node, "is to have a schedule in place that we can use for the entirety of the run to Spwao. It's good to have overlap, especially some social overlap for the pilots!"

Joyita made no comment, though the work screen updated the ship's schedule with a half-dozen possibles, as *Bechimo* projected arrivals.

Clarence nodded, and tapped the screen ruminatively with the quiet end of a long pen.

"Thanks, *Bechimo*. Here's the problem for us, Theo. They've already done some time-splicing there on Tradedesk so there's an in-between shift for the Market. You can come and go whenever you want, but the trading zone's on its own strict day that don't match Chustling or Vincza, necessarily. Not to say, us. We won't be knowing," he said, with an emphasis on "know," and scrabbling some hard lines under what looked like an air wing of some kind that was taking shape on his art pad, "if we need to talk in person or work through info committees or what. Shan gave us some names, you say, but we're starting to see that names don't necessarily make the thing easy."

"Maybe the names *do* make it easy," Theo interrupted—and laughed. "Let's hope not."

Clarence grinned.

"What we don't know makes it hard to plan," he continued. "Unless you want to declare us on ship-time like we was a cruise liner or *Dutiful Passage* and make them work to us."

"Yeah, that'll happen." Theo laughed again and shook her head, looking down at her lace. "So what you're saying is, we need to be flexible, and plan after we have something to plan with."

"Not the most efficient way, maybe…" Clarence said.

"But maybe the pilot got ahead of herself again," Theo finished, and nodded. "So, we'll wait and take a reading from dock."

She rose, rolling her lace as she did so.

"What I'm going to do while I wait, is take my off-shift and have a nap. It comes to me that we'll all want to be well rested at Tradedesk. *Bechimo*, would you please pull whatever current trade info we've got on Ynsolt'i and put it in my working file? The other thing I'm thinking is that we ought to start paying our own way!"

"Yes, Pilot!" *Bechimo* said.

Joyita, in Screen Six, only nodded.

TWELVE

....

Spwao System Arrival

DULSEY'S TOUCH WAS SOFTER THAN HIS; THUS, IT WAS Dulsey who tucked the warmest blanket they possessed 'round the pilot, and placed his head on her knee. The insults against his dermis had been sealed with new skin, thin and livid. The arm...the arm had nearly been severed, and, with the internal injuries cataloged by the field 'doc, was the chiefest reason Uncle had hesitated to wake his patient. Such work as was required ought not to be interrupted.

And yet, there were the seed pods.

He could, Uncle reminded himself, afford no errors in this.

If only he could be certain that he was not about to make one.

He sat on the rug beside the repair unit, positioned so that his face would be the first thing the wounded pilot would see when he opened his eyes. Crossing his legs, he glanced down at his hand. The seed pods fit easily into his palm, as green and as fresh-seeming as if they had only a moment ago been loosed from branch and leaf.

He sighed, and looked up.

"Now," he said, and Dulsey snapped an ampule under the unconscious man's nose.

The stimulant was mild, for they did not dare risk him starting and doing himself a further hurt. Still, it should not have taken so very long to...

Dark brows twitched. Black eyes gleamed from behind sheltering lashes.

"Daav yos'Phelium, Uncle greets you," he said, choosing to speak Liaden, and in the mode between comrades, which would surely be understood, no matter if his thought processes were addled by his injuries, or by the interrupted healing.

"You are wounded, and in the care of myself and my associate."

"...wounded..." The voice was like a file over metal. "...status..."

"Stablized at competence level seven-five. That I have wakened you places you in more danger. But I have these, which may assist, and which I thought it best not to withhold."

He raised one of the pods toward the pilot, expecting...hope, perhaps. Eagerness.

The pilot screwed his eyes shut, and turned his face into Dulsey's knee.

"...no..."

Uncle shared a speaking look with Dulsey, who softly stroked the pilot's hair, murmuring, "Come, it will surely do you good. Shall we open it for you? I have seen the way of it, long ago."

"...Aelliana..." he grated. "...not...for...me."

Uncle quickly withdrew the pod in favor of the second.

"I am maladroit," he murmured. "Forgive me. There are two. This one is surely your own."

Despite the blanket and the warmth of the room, the pilot had begun to shiver. Uncle cast a concerned look at the portable readout. They needed to end this quickly, or it would be ended, indeed.

"Pilot?" Dulsey took the second pod and brought it near the patient's nose.

He stiffened, then relaxed all at once, shoulders shaking in what might, impossibly, have been laughter.

"...not...ripe..."

· · · ❋ · · ·

The drop-in was quiet, with *Bechimo* offering up a minimal announcement only after they'd settled into an orbit well off the ecliptic. Monitoring traffic had been worthwhile, giving them a chance to explore the chatter as well as the official channels. Spwao system was much noisier than Cresthaller and much quieter than Frenzel, with a lot of the low-power local talk spoken in an off-Terran that was soothing to the ears for all that it wasn't always easily decipherable on quick listen.

The system's trade arrangements were federated, with uniform, quote-ahead fees and access levels. No direct Hugglelans presence here, no Korval trade arrangements, and a couple of offer-only channels that cycled at high speed so incoming ships could get a fair taste of available portside commerce.

"This is like the usual routes with *Primadonna*," Theo told Clarence when he'd remarked on her looking much more relaxed than on their inbound to Frenzel.

"Nothing about that place synced with me, I guess. I'd got so used to routine with Rig—and nothing at Frenzel was what I expected."

"Understood—and, remember, that routine's your strong point. I've been out of the chair such a while, hardly anything's routine, excepting the flight."

It was easier to grab a short-term claim tube at the hundred-hour dock on Tradedesk than to arrange for landing at either Chustling or Vincza.

With Vincza, the problem was the half-Standard-long worldwide rainy season the planet was now enjoying— Theo wasn't used to seeing warnings of seasonal flooding and mandatory evacuation drills in port infopackets. Chustling, on the other hand, allowed only those ships with a firm contact or a firm contract to dock at the Port Authority Yard. All others were welcome to find a berth at any of the several privately owned yards, which, in Theo's opinion—and in *Bechimo*'s—sounded just a little too risky, especially given the presence of the nice, busy station where, coincidentally, the offices of the third name Shan had given her were located.

Once the berth was set up with Tradedesk Control, they shared the most recent information, shooting the last eighteen hours of almost everything they had from Frenzel's news, business, and entertainment channels to their account box to see if anyone was biting—it might well be they had something worth a few bits to someone, and Frenzel didn't have that many ships coming this way. The Cresthaller info went up into the "just in" box, and though there wasn't much, it was about as fresh as could be. At Clarence's suggestion, they cut the last half-day's info from the feed—parsed carefully that might give somebody with "a nose for mischief" as he put it, an idea of *Bechimo*'s cut-it-close Jump capability.

While they were sending info, info was coming in—station regs, of course; catalogs; the usual advertisements; trade market hours, and *those* regs.

Mail.

Personal mail.

Theo stared at her private inbox with a feeling of disbelief. She'd known there was a Guild office on Tradedesk; that was right in the *Quick Guide*. What she hadn't known was how that simple fact would make her *feel*. Space! After so many worlds where there wasn't Guild, or that the *Guild Quick Guide* actively warned her away from—including Surebleak—she felt like she'd found civilization.

And...a letter.

She glanced at the address quickly. Kamele Waitley. Only one, and sent rationally to her forwarding service. Mother had been studying.

Naturally.

Theo shook her head.

"Trouble?" Clarence asked.

She looked up.

"Letter from my mother," she said, voice wry.

Clarence laughed.

"Well now," he said comfortably. "That could go either way, that could."

· · · ·❖· · · ·

They had, after discussion, sent to the Scouts, and the Scouts had sent a team to Moonstruck, the last known location of packet ship *Ride the Luck*.

A member of that team now awaited the delm in the map room, according to Mr. pel'Kana, the butler. And in broad daylight, too, for a wonder.

"*Korval.*"

The Scout's bow was profound; the Scout herself grey of hair and hard of face.

"Scout Specialist Olwen sel'Iprith, bearing preliminary findings from the investigation on Moonstruck."

"Scout Specialist." Val Con inclined his head, looking as calm and collected as you please, which just went to show the value and purpose of manners, and training in the forms.

"Please," Miri said, doing her bit for peace and calmness, "may we offer tea or other refreshment?"

"I beg not, Lady. My report is not lengthy, and I have other errands to accomplish before I may lift."

"You leave again so quickly?" Val Con murmured.

"Tonight, if I can be cleared to fly. Much depends on what is decided at headquarters."

"Certainly. Let us do what we may to speed you on your way."

"Our team found on Moonstruck the remains of a starship, quite recently destroyed," she said, downright brusque. "We believe this to be the remains of *Ride the Luck.*"

Miri's stomach went into freefall. Her fault, her decision.

"A forensic scan of the wreckage produced no evidence to support the supposition that the pilot was aboard at the time of his ship's demise."

She felt Val Con take her hand, his fingers weaving with hers. Felt the aftermath of his own pain—

"We have also identified recent landing sites of

three other vessels. Several on-site cameras and security devices have been . . . terminally disabled. Others are intact, but no longer operational. An attempt to recover such information as possible from those units is ongoing. We are also in pursuit of whatever records may exist in the memories of the various security devices belonging to the resorts and orbiting camps."

"The cavern in which the device was housed," said Olwen sel'Iprith, and closed her eyes. She took a breath, another, and a third. Miri guessed she had just accessed the mental exercise known as the Rainbow, which was designed to relax and steady the practitioner.

She opened her eyes.

"So. My team did also inspect the cavern. We found that the device had, indeed, been rendered nonfunctional. We have requested another specialist team to explore what remains in greater detail. The rest . . ." She swallowed.

"There had been, very recently, an extremely violent confrontation in the cavern. Forensic scans were able to positively identify the DNA signatures of four individuals, including *Ride the Luck*'s pilot."

"He's dead," Miri heard the words, and only then realized that it had been her voice that had uttered them.

Scout Specialist sel'Iprith gave her a long look.

"Of that, we stand in some doubt."

"Because he is Korval?" asked Val Con, politely.

"That is a factor," she admitted. "Also, because someone had . . . tidied up, though not well. This gives us to think that haste was imperative. It does not seem possible that a survivor could have been unwounded. Also, it is not unreasonable that such a survivor may have anticipated the arrival of more combatants. From this, several scenarios suggest themselves.

"One: Daav disabled those who came against him, captured their ship, and lifted. Alternatively, his backup may have pulled him out, performed some hasty housekeeping in order to confound a cursory inspection by any who came after, and lifted."

"Or," Val Con said, "he may have been captured by one or more of his opponents and is now in their power."

That scared him. Miri gripped his hand, none too sure of her feet, or her stomach. Daav yos'Phelium, canny, subtle pilot that he was, former delm of Korval, twisted and reshaped by the Department of the Interior . . . It made her—it made him—

"That is not impossible," admitted the Scout, "though it seems to me, unlikely."

"Forgive me, but I feel it to be the most likely," Val Con murmured, and how he could sound so calm, with all that roaring around in his head—what it felt like, the Department's *training*—and his father, gods! *And* his mother, a ghost inside her lifemate's head. If they somehow found out that they had Aelliana Caylon in their hands . . .

Only, he was getting ahead of his guns here, Miri thought, forcing herself to recall what, exactly, Scout sel'Iprith had said—and hadn't said.

"Is there evidence," she asked, "that the Department of the Interior was involved in this confrontation? Our report from Pod 78 was only that it had been tampered with, considered itself in peril, and had activated the self-destruct routine."

"Korval understands that the Scouts have a policy

of assuming the Department of the Interior complicit in all activities of this nature. With that stated, there was at the time I was dispatched to bring a progress report to Korval and to headquarters, no *evidence* of Department of Interior involvement. The miscreants may have been merely pirates. Had the housekeeping been done more thoroughly in the aftermath of the confrontation, we might have also been obliged to posit a mischievous space-camp attendee among those who might be potential tamperers."

She bowed, very slightly, and reached into her belt.

"A copy of our team's process and a complete report is on this datakey," she said, offering it in the noncommittal space just before and between them.

Val Con's grip on her fingers was going to do damage. Miri extended her free hand and took the key.

"Our thanks."

"Korval." Another bow. "With your permission, I am wanted at headquarters."

"One more question, of your kindness, Scout Specialist," Val Con said, his voice strained.

She folded her hands at her belt and waited.

Val Con inclined his head. "Daav?" he murmured.

Olwen sel'Iprith's mouth tightened. "Daav yos'Phelium was my team captain, many years ago it will be now. I know him—knew him—very well." The mouth curved, just a bit, the faintest of faint smiles.

"And that is why I believe the third scenario to be the *least* likely," she said. "Even were it the Department of the Interior."

THIRTEEN

. . . .

Tradedesk

PROTOCOL AT TRADEDESK REQUIRED A FIRST-TIME SHIP
to permit inspection, even out here in what was euphe-
mistically called "spider country." Spider country was
an older assemblage, still showing webs of crosswires,
supports, cables, commlinks, and the like that made
both of Eylot's stations look tiny and almost neat.

Thankfully the approach lanes were well-marked
and roomy, the area having initially been designed
for a generation of super-traders and cruise ships long
since superseded. It was, in fact, the equivalent of
one of Frenzel's backfields—you could say you'd been
to Tradedesk, but it was clear the big shiny welcome
mat was reserved for others.

For all that, they'd had clear guidance, no-nonsense
prelatch instructions, an excellent strong latch and,
after a two-minute pressure and temperature equal-
ization, an entirely professional inspection team. The
bulk of their inspection had already been performed
as *Bechimo* came in: video and radar scans, trace gas
analysis, confirmation of pod location and hookups.

Exactly because of the inspection team, *Bechimo*'s Screen Six was a catalog grid for the moment, and B. Joyita's name had been omitted from the roster.

"Next time through, we won't need an inspection," Theo told him. "But this time, if they insist on meeting you..."

Joyita had smiled. "Understood, Pilot. We need to take on more details."

Bechimo had been experimenting with Joyita's voice. At first indistinguishable from *Bechimo*'s light, genderless voice, Joyita now spoke in an easy tenor. Lately, he'd been experimenting with idiom.

It was, in Theo's opinion, simultaneously unnerving— and fascinating. She wondered what the final Joyita would look and sound like, and her head hurt whenever she tried to remind herself that Joyita was only a projection of *a fragment* of *Bechimo*, and not his own person at all. Because, of course *Bechimo* couldn't create a whole new person out of archives, graphics and info-grids.

Could he?

For right now, then, Joyita was hidden, *Bechimo* was only a ship, albeit an odd, old-style ship pretty much like something nobody'd ever seen before.

And so the inspectors arrived.

There were two of them, their Terran intelligible if oddly emphasized, and they made their way onto the bridge respectfully, with Clarence in the lead. They each carried a hand unit, and both were pilots, though only one, the woman, wore wings. Both were grey-headed and neither, as far as Theo could see, carried weapons. Their uniforms were noncommittal—they could have stepped dayside on any number of worlds and, with

multiple starbursts, flags, and stripes, they looked to be
covering three or four jobs at once: lifeguard and med
tech, police, assistant proctors, and certified inspectors.
What mattered was that they had the right IDs as far
as Clarence and *Bechimo* were concerned.

Theo met them standing; and, respectful, too, of
tradition, they did not approach the live consoles.

"Captain, here's Inspectors Grafton and Rutland.
Inspectors, Pilot Theo Waitley."

"Inspectors, welcome aboard *Bechimo*. How may
we serve you?"

Rutland, the woman, nodded, held her hand out—
not in offer of a handclasp, but to personally deliver
a card, which Theo took.

"We look around some," she said, "with big eyes.
Two of you got plenty a room in here, just two crew?"

"We're just starting out, Inspector—learning the ship,
truth be told, and seeing who else we might need."

The inspector pointed toward the welcome room
with a wide nod and open smile, appreciative.

"Seen that Tree-and-Dragon out there—you mighty
lucky them folks keep stuff around that no one else
knows they want, eh? Looks better than clean, looks
brand new! They must have cut you a heck of a deal,
what with their troubles."

Theo took a half-step back, not wanting to bring
Korval into this at all. She spread her arms to encom-
pass the whole of the ship.

"Actually, consider *Bechimo* an inheritance, Inspector;
but yes, Korval's Master Trader feels the need for new
routes, and their contract was a welcome start for us."

The catalog on Screen Six changed pages, showing
a green outline and then, briefly, a page of shoes.

The inspector glanced at her handheld, nodded again. "Saw them pods out there—look like they might need an inspection seal on them if you was up at the main shop, but they'll do for here. Not getting that many ships in been to Cresthaller."

She looked speculatively at the pair of them, Clarence having properly stepped toward consoles while Theo dealt with the visitors.

"Well, says here ain't had any Cresthaller shipping 'leven Standards, so if ships been there, they ain't mentioning it, anywho. I'm seeing a port visit on Frenzel, no cargo pickup...but hey, this is a roomy little thing—can I see what you have for air holds?"

There was another flicker as Screen Six changed pages—now displaying a page of uniforms.

"Clarence?" Theo murmured, sweeping a hand out to both indicate the path, and offer her Second as guide.

"If you need to look at quarters," she said to the inspector, "we have a protocol of showing our own, so I'll be available."

The male inspector's right hand went to his eyebrow in a kind of salute as the three left the bridge. She heard Clarence offering tea or other refreshment, and another man's voice refusing with, "On duty, y'know."

There was another flash at the corner of her eye as the catalog page changed...

"Stop that!"

Theo spoke vehemently under her breath as Screen Six changed catalog pages again, this time showing a close-up of a hand-held unit much like that carried by the inspectors.

"Pilot, this monitor was not visible to the—"

"Silence!" she hissed.

The screen flashed a new page as she spoke—this the catalog's opening presentation screen.

Security Solutions Unlimited was the name of the catalog. It remained stable, as Theo glared at it. She was tempted to open a keyboard link to *Bechimo* and thought better of it; instead she grabbed her lacework out of the bin.

The page on Screen Six was steady.

There was no need, she told herself firmly, to be nervous. Yes, *Bechimo* had hidden compartments. Camouflaged and well-concealed compartments, designed, as she was given to understand, by a past master of such arts.

And even if one was discovered, what harm? They were empty, all of them. Well, except for the cellar—the core room—where Win Ton slept, and it wasn't like having a crew member in a healing unit was contraband, or illegal. His was another name that didn't appear on the roster, as he wasn't active crew.

Aside from those few really minor issues, *Bechimo* was entirely what she said he was—a loop ship feeling out a route, a ship inherited by accident from people she'd never met nor could have met, with whom she probably shared not a single gene.

The lacework felt good in her hands. She sighed, settled into her seat, glared at Screen Six, just as a reminder, and was pleased to see the catalog page solid. She spread the lace, seeing a field of stars and misty nebula spread out along the threads . . .

Voices, growing louder as they approached the bridge. Theo shook her head and took her needle in hand. The voices paused; there was a sound at once hollow and sharp—somebody rapping a bulkhead.

Then the voices got louder again, accompanied by footsteps and the swish of fabric, and three people came back onto the bridge, Clarence's quick-signing *coming through* to warn her that he was bringing the inspectors past the consoles...

"And that's it," he was saying aloud. "I'm a practical pilot first and second, and what with Surebleak not being quite the garden spot of the universe after all, no matter what my lads had all promised, it was easy enough to take a break from retiring to a snowball to get back out in Jump space and live in the warm!"

There was appreciative laughter and smiles all around; whatever else they'd done, the inspectors had got a story of some kind out of Clarence, which wasn't all that hard to do.

Inspector Rutland paused, and nodded approvingly.

"Ah, Captain, that's a good way to keep the hands up to speed, that stringwork. My mother's not at a board anymore, but she does three kinds of strings and I bet she could sit down and slap a course in if there was need. My aunt now—they's twins, my mother and my aunt—my aunt got lazy and I bet she's sorry 'cause she needs to medicine up to keep spry enough to open a door. Never stop keeping at things."

Theo laughed. "I don't think there's much danger of that. There always seems to be so much to do that I don't get to work with the lace as much as I want."

"That's the way of it! Plan on livin' to a double-hunnert, myself, just to get the to-do list settled."

She paused, with a hard look at Screen Six before she turned back to Theo.

Theo reached for her calm, and tried to make her

face as bland and unreadable as Father's when he was at his most annoyed...

"Pilot, that's a good company there, that catalog you got on-screen. They got a workshop up here—not a whole front-office thing, but a workshop. If you're on-station a few days, just use my card and ask to look around. They might wanta see your ticket 'fore they sell you some of the strong stuff, but they can get it right quick. Make sure you tell them you heard of 'em through Cady Rutland, and ask for the pro discount."

Theo breathed a little easier, swallowed, and nodded with as much of a smile as she could pull together.

"It can be tricky making sure the outfitting's done right," she said. "Especially since we haven't built the route yet. I'm trying to be careful..."

"That's good. Careful gets you through, most times. I'm retired from two ships now, and I have to say to you buying cheap is the worst mistake a pilot or an owner can make when it comes to security. Not saying you have to pay high-orbit prices for everything, but you have to make sure you're working quality."

The quiet inspector made a hand motion Theo barely caught. It might have been *coffee*. Rutland apparently caught that, looked at her handheld, and shook her head.

"Right, then, Pilot; we'll send you a copy of our report when it's done—ought to be tomorrow morning. Wanta thank you—it's been a slow day out here for us, and your Clarence made us feel welcome, so I hope you didn't mind too much we took our time...but we'll be gone now. You'll need a pair of these slidekeys—one for each of you—they work the regular doors and the station airlocks, just in case. So!

Inspecting's done, and I'm glad it was our go—wanted to see this ship up close. Your *Bechimo* looks first class for the day my great-greats were out and about."

Theo smiled. "Inspector, *Bechimo is* first class. All of our surprises have been positive."

· · · ✳ · · ·

The card cut went to Clarence, and for his impudence, he was first on-station, with a slidekey to test and an hour to tour.

Somewhat to his own surprise, he hoped that the station scanned—not *safe*, never that, o'course—but *civilized*. He was twitchy, that was what; ready for some time on his own and off-ship. None o'that being the fault of his comrades, nor of himself, come to it. Best just to say that he needed his downtime.

He reached the end of the tube on that thought, and used the key, the door sliding open slick as you please, not that he had expected otherwise.

Well, now, plenty of time left for a stroll to the first hub, to see what there was to see. He set off down the hall, walking quick, for the air being a touch brisk. Sounds of voices, and what was maybe music came from ahead.

If they had more crew aboard, he thought, instead of only just the two of them, and a chimera in Screen Six, then there'd be time for everyone to have a proper down-shift with a door closed, and not having to have one ear always cocked for, say, a little altercation between his pilot and his ship. He'd seen two personalities less agreeable to each other, but it had been a while.

Well! The lassie was talking more crew, in point

o'fact, not that *Bechimo* was noticeably warming to the notion. But if they was to be more efficient, and not come at daggers drawn, then, yeah, another pilot on-roster would be good. Somebody maybe cunning with their hands, who might help *Bechimo* build those remotes he'd been wanting, and deserving, not to say kit-bashing the damned hydroponics unit. Only that one more person would ease things considerably—and here was the place to do it, what with a full Guild Office and a hiring hall right on-station and open for bidness.

Here now, just up at the hook in the hall, that was one source of voices. *GrabOne* according to the red Terran letters over the door.

Clarence stuck his nose in the door—and stopped before the rest of him followed. It was just a cubby, like you get on station corridors some distance from the core—and the food on offer looked like nothing more than rations—old rations at that, while the prices posted on the board over the counter were—well, never mind. They weren't having *his* bidness, since he had perfectly good, fresh rations in his jacket.

He shook his head and moved on toward the thump and boom of the maybe music.

It occurred to him that a Guild Office on-station might present other opportunities, and he mulled them over as he strolled into Taverna Classica.

This was a familiar setup—couple tables, couple booths, long line of bottles behind a high bar that could double as a barricade if some long-spacer turned ugly with too much cheap alcohol. Might be it also served as a meet place for the local boss, if there was one—and there was bound to be.

"Drink, pop?" That was from the bare-chested

laddie with muscles on his muscles standing behind the bar. "First one ona house, you just in."

"Maybe later," he said, giving the boy a nod and a grin.

"Sure. Bring a friend."

Not likely. Clarence retreated again to the hall, checked his watch. To the next intersection, then, before it was back to the ship and report.

This other notion of his, though. A Guild Office on-station meant he might change his own situation, if he had a mind to it, the question being—*did* he have a mind to it? Was he happy in his ship or—now that he had recent flight time on his card—was he looking to better himself?

He laughed softly.

It wasn't too likely he'd come up better than Second Board and Exec on a ship contracted to Korval. The lassie had a few faults, despite which she was a hardworking pilot, with strong notions about what was owed to her ship and her crew. And *Bechimo* was nothing if not careful of the health and well-being of his pilots. Truth told, he could well do worse in comrades, honest though they might be.

That thought gave him cause to grin, as he walked on by himself. Hadn't that *just* been a moment, when she called out to *Bechimo* for the locations, sizes and access to the private compartments? *Daav would've been proud,* he thought, and grinned again.

If he had a regret in his current placement, it was that he hadn't yet had to stretch himself, excepting the necessity to juggle certain personalities. *Bechimo*—sometimes mistaken, but never in doubt, that lad. Theo, on the other hand, she had the temper, didn't she just? And that peculiar, straight line o'vision that saw through everything between her and what she wanted.

Small wonder the two of them had differences. Another hand, like he was starting to think was necessary—somebody easy in the temper—'nother hand might help with that, too.

The hall widened into a court of sorts, and Clarence smiled. He'd found the good neighborhood, after all. To his right was The Nook, according to its sign, a bright and comfy spot with a menu above the counter, promising fresh-bake bread, vegetable soup, made-from-scratch desserts, and a line of fresh juices from Vincza. There were several tables and stools off to the sides, but the house specialty was a "take-with dinner." The whole looked clean and cared for, down to the broad woman behind the counter, who looked up from her work with an easy smile.

"You like anything you see, Pilot, we'll fix it up for you. You like something you don't see, ask. Maybe we can fix that, too."

"Thanks," he told her. "I'm on reconnoiter; lookin' for a place to send my mate for a bite, a little later."

"Send him, and his mate too," she said, her smile widening into a grin. "There's a new cookie in it for you if they remember to tell me who sent 'em."

"There's a temptation," he said, only half joking. "Name's Clarence, which she ain't likely to forget."

"Not me, neither, then. You come on back, yourself."

"Will do," he promised, and shoved off, moving slowly across the court, relishing the gabble of voices, the variation of shapes, color and sizes of the people he passed. Not many people, really—maybe six, eight dozen here during what might be this hub's off-hour—and at that a cornucopia for the eyes, as his youngest auntie usta say, though she was most usually talking about various of the male neighbors.

There ahead of him, a sign in discreet black-on-white: Keenstart Klub. And just below, in cheery red, *Pilots Guild Certified.*

He stared at that for a good, long minute, he did, as it slowly came to him that having a Guild presence right on-station had other benefits, too. It could be that what was ailing him was the wrong kind of not-alone. A little recreation might not, he thought, go amiss.

Guild Certified didn't guarantee safety, because nothing in this life did that. But it did guarantee certain safeguards. He stepped across to the door, and inside, angling for a match board. He didn't have but a few, dwindling moments to do this, if he was prepared to jog back to the dock, which he found he was.

He fingered the keys, entering his license number, certain quick parameters, including a meet here at the Klub, and the hour by which he expected to return.

That done and sent, he turned right quick on his heel, and was moving for the door, thinking he was going to have to *run* or else *Bechimo*'d be worryin' himself into a bellyache—

Only to find his way blocked, and a voice behind saying strongly:

"Well, well. If it ain't Clarence O'Berin."

· · · ❖ · · ·

Theo.
If I've converted the transmission time correctly, I will have departed Delgado for my sabbatical before

this message is delivered to you. It feels odd to be going out in the field at this stage of my career. Ella tells me that I ought to stay at my ease in the Wall and command such sources as I wish to interview into my presence, but I think this scheme of mine will serve better. Do you know, I don't think I've traveled any distance from Delgado since you and I traveled with the certification committee? Everything changed for you during that journey, didn't it? May I be as fortunate in this one.

Since I'll be traveling, I have a dropbox—the code is at the bottom of this letter. This will seem quite usual to you, of course.

Daughter, I hope that you're as happy in your work as I have been in mine. Back when I was an instructor, the well-wish we gave to each other was, "May you win tenure and a quiet room in which to study."

Not quite, "Good lift and safe landing," is it?

I love you, Theo.

Kamele

There followed the box code—a standard Travel-Mail account.

Theo blinked, and reread the letter.

And suddenly thought of Father as she had last seen him, standing beneath the branches of Korval's enormous Tree. The juxtaposition of a person who took such things as a Tree that was also a biochemist, whose dead . . . lifemate lived inside his head and occasionally "borrowed" his body for such matters as speaking with a pilot she termed her "foster daughter"—what had such a person to do with Kamele Waitley of Delgado, amateur singer, and professor in the hardly exciting specialty of the history of education?

Father had said he'd gone to the University of Delgado to ... Balance his lifemate's murder. And who but Father could think that the seeds planted by teaching cultural genetics—even at a catalyst school—would grow tall enough to Balance a life?

And then Kamele, who must be so very different from Aelliana Caylon ...

"Is there something wrong, Pilot Theo?"

She started, looking up—into Screen Six and Joyita's face, looking rested, like he'd just come to the board from his sleep shift.

"Nothing wrong," she said slowly. "My mother's on sabbatical; she sent me her box code."

... and continuing the question—what had *she* to do anymore with normal, rational, safe people, and the quiet contemplative life of the mind? Theo Waitley, who sat First Board to a self-aware ship older than the University? Who had with her own hands killed a ship, and the pilot who flew her? Theo Waitley, nexus of violence?

"You have concern for your mother's safety?" Joyita asked.

Theo started.

"I do," she said, realizing that it was so. "She— she doesn't mention that she's traveling with a party, and—she's not a pilot, or much accustomed to ..." she hesitated. To what? To looking out for herself? Kamele was an adult. She was a smart, capable woman. In her own context. Outside of her context ...

"We went outworld when I was a kid, and ... she had some trouble believing that—out here in the wide galaxy, you know—people might try to rob her, or hurt her."

She shook herself, and gave Joyita a grin.

"I think I might have a case of what Clarence calls the *megrims*," she said. "Kamele's specialty is the history of education. She's probably just traveling to interview other experts and consult some original sources. Hard to imagine her getting into too much trouble with that."

In the screen, Joyita frowned and rubbed his nose with the forefinger of the hand with the three rings on it. He seemed about to speak, when *Bechimo* did, instead.

"Less Pilot O'Berin returns."

· · · ❖ · · ·

He had perhaps, Uncle acknowledged, made an error.

Even a very great error.

It was not to be thought that he had never before erred; one did not live as long or as actively as he had thus far lived, without producing error.

Even great error.

It was, however, a benefit of that same long life, that most errors could, very often and simply, be ignored until time rendered them meaningless.

Great errors...and especially very great errors... those could not so easily be ignored, for they had the potential of significantly altering the future, even unto the destruction of a lifetime counted in tens of hundreds of Standard Years.

Uncle sighed and leaned back in his chair, allowing his eyes to rest on the yellow blooms dangling from the basket hung from the ceiling over his desk. Exquisite. Yes.

He had known it was risky to employ Theo Waitley

as a courier pilot, but the risk had seemed acceptable, in light of the potential gain.

Deliberately, he had sent her into harm's way, dicing with her life in order to fully waken her drowsing potential. That one of Korval's bloodline held the first of *Bechimo's* precious piloting keys had . . . pleased him. Who better, in all the universe, to take up the care of such a ship?

Yet, while he was risking Theo Waitley's life, and *Bechimo's* liberty, he had failed to give proper weight to the fact that by doing so he placed certain valued pieces and players of his own . . . into peril.

And so the word just in, from Randoling, who had dropped to Gondola with a certain very particular something bound for the inventory of Mildred Bilinoda, trader in exotic items.

Randoling reported that the shop when she entered had been . . . arranged differently than it had during her eight previous visits.

More disturbingly, she reported that the person tending shop was not Mildred Bilinoda, but a man professing to be her sister-son. This unlikely person had not only denied Smalltrader Bilinoda to her, but had been forceful in his statements that he was perfectly able to help her, with anything. His mother-sister, he said, reposed complete confidence in him.

Randoling was not only canny, she was extremely motivated for her own survival. Therefore, she speedily extricated herself, and returned to her ship, deeming it unwise to abandon it with such cargo in the hold.

Feeling herself to be compromised, Randoling had retired from the field of play. She was now rusticating in one of the safeplaces, from which sanctuary she sent her message, cunningly routed and rerouted before it even came into the peripheral network.

Uncle frowned at the blameless flowers, and looked down to the message screen, still showing that same message.

Randoling had not survived as long as *she* had because she was an hysteric.

And Mildred Bilinoda had no nephews.

Nor sisters, either.

FOURTEEN

················

Tradedesk

"WELL, THERE'S NOTHING TO WANT AT THE GRABONE, since I know you're not such a green 'un as you don't have fresh and plentiful rations in your jacket. Taverna Classica, like it styles itself, *I* intend to give wide berth. Quiet enough when I was in, but I'd be very surprised to hear other than it gets ugly there, and often."

"Less Pilot O'Berin has made an excellent analysis, Pilot," *Bechimo* said. Screen Six was starting to fill with what looked to be log reports. "Taverna Classica has the worst statistical record of any extant public-service location on Tradedesk, across more than a dozen categories of infringement. GrabOne has had a series of incidents as well. Further, there is an ongoing level of violence and fraud at that corridor corner unmatched anywhere else on the station. Were I permitted, I would declare that area off limits. It disturbs me that the pilots are unlikely to stay aboard, or to take another route to the less risky areas."

"To take another route, we'd have to go outside and walk across the skin," Theo pointed out.

"Which is a lot less safe, in my opinion and experience, than walking wary and being ready to take appropriate action," Clarence added.

"Now," he said, continuing his narrative before *Bechimo* could field another argument for safety and clean living, "past all the refraff, there's a real nice hub, bright lit and with a number o'people about. There's The Nook, which is fresh-made foods, and Theo, mind! If you stop in there, you tell the missus I sent you, by name. Got a cookie riding on that."

Theo laughed. "A cookie!"

"*New* cookie!" Clarence asserted, and gave her a mock-grim stare. "You don't forget, now, hear it? I take my cookies serious.

"Cross the court from The Nook's a Keenstart, all Guild cert and nice as you please. I did stop there, thinking to file a request for later, but my luck was in. There was a nice couple real happy to see me—Grafton and Rutland, as just inspected us. We filed up in the system, and made some arrangements. Looks like I'll be out for the overnight, 'less the ship needs me."

He'd said it all so smooth and straight that it took her a heartbeat to translate it, and when she did it was with a twinge of what might be concern, or might be jealousy, which was just *silly*, both of them.

Clarence was a grown-up; he'd taken his precautions, and he had leave coming. True, she'd be crew on-deck while he was having his party, but it wasn't like she hadn't slept alone aboard *Primadonna* when Rig'd found friends on port. Nothing to worry about there. As for being jealous... she had leave, too, and a reconnoiter walk coming up right now. She could have a date, too, if she wanted one.

"Ship's covered," she told him, seeing by his posture that he was waiting for her to say so. "I'll take my walk now. Hope you haven't used up all the luck."

"Not much chance o'that," said Clarence.

* * * * *

Miri woke alone.

Again.

She took a breath and concentrated on that certain place inside her head, where she could see, or sense, her lifemate's soul, looking for where he'd gone, tonight.

Sometimes, he went up to the nursery and sat with Lizzie—that was all, just sat, a shadow among shadows, so silent that he waked not their daughter, nor Anthora's twins...and especially not their sharp-eared nurse, Mrs. pel'Esla.

Other times, he went to the inner garden and sat with the Tree, though her sense of him then was more than simple sitting. It was as if he were...telling a story, or prepping for a test—intense, intricate, concentrating. She couldn't see—or hear—what he was thinking, but the density of his thought—that came through.

Exhausting, that was.

Scary too.

Tonight, though... Tonight, it wasn't Lizzie or the Tree.

Tonight, he was at the omnichora; music came through clear, most times, like it passed whole and complete down the threads that bound them. Mostly, that pleased her.

Not tonight.

In fact, she thought, taking a protesting breath against the hard knot in her chest, she wouldn't be the least surprised if it had been the music that had snapped her out of sleep.

Angry, frightened, grief-struck music, laced with horror like cheap kynak in 'toot. Her throat burned, and her heart struck an off beat, painful inside her tight chest.

It was a wonder, she thought, that he didn't rouse the house, the racket he was making.

But everybody else was asleep. And she . . .

Every other night she had woken alone, she had lain here in bed, thinking that the man deserved time alone. Which he did.

But that wasn't the reason she'd left him alone.

She hadn't wanted to face the anger, knowing it was deserved; that the Code saying that lifemates shared one will and one heart didn't change the fact that she'd sent his parents out into clear and active danger.

And they hadn't come back.

Miri gasped; her chest suddenly on fire.

Right.

She pitched the quilts back and slid out of bed, finding her robe and her slippers in the dark.

Time to face the music.

· · · ·❧· · · ·

The tube annoyed Theo, reminding her of the last time she'd been in a tube—to snatch Win Ton to safety, scared at how light he was in her arms, and—

But that tube had been well-lit and well-maintained, which is what she had come to expect of Uncle's equipment. Old, it might well be. Shabby? Never.

The gangway under her feet was worn, metal showing through the grippy tread in spots. The seal, though—that was solid and apparently dependable. She supposed that once *Bechimo* had a record here, and wasn't just some new-in ship carrying dingy transit pods, and listing no preset business, they'd get better. Certainly Hugglelans ships had gotten better, every time.

That Tree-and-Dragon *hadn't* gotten them better... Theo frowned, the slidekey poised over the lock. *I really hope,* she thought, sliding the key with perhaps more force than was necessary, *that there isn't going to be politics here.*

Once outside the tube, the corridor itself was lit well enough, and if the gravity was more than a trace light, that was to be expected out here. Clarence's directions were good; it turned out that the "corner" the Taverna occupied had multiple gravplates, and gravity on the long-side was higher. There was vague speech-noise emanating from the place, and neither the handprint smeared door nor the scruffy, scratched welcome logo painted in front of it looked to have been cleaned within the Standard.

There came the sound of a door slide working behind her, and the sudden change in volume from distant talk to a scattering of off-pattern voices and the *swish-smack* of hardboots on decking.

"Well, lookit the smoothie!"

It was impossible for her not to look; she slowed and her glance swiveled, for all that the words were stretched by the local accents, and maybe by a drink or two as well.

"Sure is!"

There were two men stopped just outside the door—they'd seen her move through the gravity intersection and were watching her as if she was the height of interest, which might also have spoken to the clientele in the Taverna . . .

"Hey, she's up from the new ship—the one that's in our spot!"

She turned away, having cataloged the type, down to the wearing of planetside boots and show-off long-socks with ship shorts and no-name crew jackets.

One of them was a pilot, or pilot grade; the other had sloppy eyes and no grace—he'd been the second speaker.

"No doubt, no doubt," said the proto-pilot, then called out, "Ship-girl, hold up!"

Ship-girl? It echoed down the corridor, and the volume changed within the Taverna.

Theo turned and the first speaker might have caught the error of his ways.

"Pilot? Or's that your dad's jacket?"

"Hey look," the second one put in, "we got party time right here. Come in, tell us 'bout your ship, let us know who to talk jobs to, we can show you lottsa fun, two or one."

The second man was older, taller, bigger, and dumber, Theo cataloged quickly. She could lose sight of him in a second and the universe would be a better place. He, on the other hand, seemed to find the view of her shirt front riveting.

She looked to the possible pilot, yanked the hem of her open jacket, and looked him in the eye. To his credit, he didn't flinch, and his posture went to alert as she did a quick hand motion signifying *sitting pilot*.

"Gentles," she said, giving them the benefit of the doubt.

The second, older guy stepped closer, apparently having missed her sign.

"We're needing crew spots, miss, and we thought that was our ship coming in. If you're not it, that's how the universe flies, but if you got the time we'd like to talk at you and see what the ship can use and if you got time off and all..."

The other one was watching not her chest, but her hands and face; he tugged on his friend's sleeve to hold him back.

"She's a pilot, Rickrix. We oughta apologize for bothering her and ask if she'll take our cards to the Exec there on..." He looked at Theo, eyes wide. "*Beckima*, was it, Pilot?"

"*Bechimo*," she corrected promptly. "Thank you."

"'*Kima, Chimo*. Ship! All's we want to do is talk!"

Rickrix had apparently had enough anesthetics to dazzle himself with his wit and insight.

"What's with it, Tut? Girl's wearing a jacket older 'n her and you think it belongs? Bet just cold out here for her and she barrud it and..."

"They say that's an old ship, Rickers, listen. Could be a hand-me-down."

As he was talking, the pilot of the pair tried to intercept his friend a little more firmly, grabbing his elbow.

Theo's move was automatic; a half step back, proper flat-soled ship shoe in front pointed at the threat, foot behind at the proper angle to support, push, kick, or lead a breakaway run.

Tut, if that was his name, recognized danger.

"Damn it, Rickrix, you're off!"

The pilot moved smoothly then, putting his back to Theo, fronting his companion.

"Pilot," he said over his shoulder, and to general laughter, as several others from the Taverna had come out to enjoy the show. "Pilot, I do apologize for interrupting your walk. Please pass. We won't bother you again."

"As you will, gentles," Theo said. She tossed a quick *thanks* off her fingertips, not knowing whether he caught it, and went.

They hadn't gotten around to giving her a card, and that, she thought, was just as well.

The Taverna incident stayed in her mind as she walked on—obviously the pilot had been uncertain of his signs, obviously his training was minimal, and obviously he ought not to be tied down to the older Rickrix, whatever the hold. Still, it seemed a shame. His instincts were good, and if eager, she'd seen that before in young pilots. The need for a job for the pair of them when they were already on station was an oddity—had they arrived with no contacts at all? And hadn't the pilot registered at the Guild Hall?

Theo *fuffed* her hair out of her eyes. People. Who knew why people did things? Anyway, she wasn't responsible for those two, so long as they didn't get their heads broke at *Bechimo*'s tie-up.

And that, she thought suddenly, was her biggest and most glaring inadequacy as a ranking member of a long-term crew. She was stupid about people. Oh, she had learned, and could do, basic social engineering. When she remembered, that was. But pretty often, she didn't remember, and more often, she thought it was more important to deliver the information than weigh each word for possible offense beforehand. And here she was thinking to hire crew! She'd never hired anybody; she was, in fact, too young—too inexperienced—for her chair. Somehow, she'd gone from expelled student to First Board and Acting Captain on a loop ship without dancing the steps between. It was true that she'd sat Second and learned the courier business from Rig Tranza. If she'd taken Huggelans' contract, then right now she'd've had her own ship, and whatever 'prentice or Second Board the home office saw fit to send her. Leaving Huggelans and taking Uncle's contract—that had been a lateral jump. She'd run single until she learned why that wasn't such a great idea, and then she'd signed on Clarence. But Clarence had come with Father's strong recommendation; Theo hadn't hired the pilot so much as she'd taken advice from a trusted source.

That wasn't going to stand her much use in trying to hire on a competent and compatible crew member, was it?

She *fuffed* her hair out of her eyes again, frowning so ferociously that two women in bland uniforms like Grafton and Rutland wore, swung one to each side of the hall and let her pass.

When she'd first come aboard, *Bechimo* had addressed her as "Captain." He'd stopped doing that after she'd asked to have the bonding ceremony put off until they could learn more about each other. She figured he was having second thoughts. And she figured he was right to have them. Might be the best thing to do would be to have him advertise for captain, listing out all the desirable traits of such a one.

There might be something there. Maybe she'd talk

it over with Joyita this evening, while Clarence was out on his date.

These cheerful thoughts having brought her to the hub, she paused to look about her.

To the right was The Nook, where Clarence's cookie waited for her to collect it. And across the court was Keenstart. She headed in that direction, thinking about that date she could have, if she wanted it.

But once she was inside, facing a screen, she realized that she didn't want a date, or to have to deal with a new person, for a quick session of what Bova, way back at Anlingdin, had called *exercise*. Maybe, if someone—if Kara, or Win Ton, someone she knew and cared about were here. Someone who would be both exciting and comforting...

But, there—she hadn't seen Kara for years. And Win Ton...Well, Win Ton wasn't in any case to be either comforting or exciting.

Theo sighed.

She wanted...

What she really wanted, she thought suddenly, was a good hard game of bowli ball. Surely a station this size had activity rooms—gyms. Open games. She'd look it up in the amenities list when she got back home.

In the meanwhile, her tour time was winding down. She glanced at her watch, and looked across the court to The Nook.

· · · ·✵· · · ·

The music room was dark, except for some night-dims, glowing in the high corners. Val Con was at the big 'chora, the one they'd taken on from the yos'Galan house. The instrument that had belonged to Shan's mother, Val Con's foster-mother, who had taught him how to play.

It was a quality piece of equipment originally intended for use in concert halls, which meant it would crack walls if given its full voice, which he hadn't done. Val Con's eyes were closed, his face underlit by keyboard's glow, his hair stuck in sweaty spikes to his forehead.

Even with the 'chora's voice set down to whisper like it was, the room was full of music. So full of music that for several long minutes it was all Miri could do to stay upright two steps beyond the door, and remember to breathe.

When she felt like her lungs could operate without her close attention, she walked forward, careful of her footing, and hoping her heart wouldn't burst before she reached the 'chora, leaned her hands against the smooth, cool wood; cleared her throat and whispered into the teeth of the music—

"Val Con."

There was no way he could have heard her, and the music was pounding her to flinders.

She closed her eyes—and the music crashed into silence.

"Miri!"

She opened her eyes and met his across the 'chora.

"You should be . . . asleep," he said, breathless with all the effort he'd been making.

"You should, too," she answered, and her voice doing wasn't doing any better. "Think I can sleep with all *this* going on?" She dared to take one supporting hand away from the 'chora to sketch swoops and slashes in the air in imitation of the music he'd been playing.

He raised an arm to mop his face on his sleeve, which left the spikes of hair sticking straight up.

"*Cha'trez*, forgive me. I had not considered. Let me escort you back to bed."

"No."

It took more effort than it should've, but she pushed away from the 'chora and stood on her own two feet, deliberately meeting his eyes. His were bright, the lashes damp.

"We need to talk," she said. "Right now. It ain't—it ain't any use pretending that it's not my fault Daav's gone missing. My decision. I still don't know what else I could've done, seeing as Pod 78 needed pure Line blood in order to settle it down. But that's by the way. What's not by the way is that it's tearing you up. I don't know what you and the Tree were talking about, or what you're thinking when you go up to the nursery—but I do know you're not getting any sleep, and you're not laying this thing to rest."

She took a hard breath.

"I don't know how to help. I don't know how to make it square between us." Her mouth twisted. "Some delm I turn out to be."

"Some delm *we* turn out to be," Val Con murmured. "Miri, I cannot second-guess your decision; had our positions been reversed, I would have decided as you did."

"No, you wouldn't have," she said. "You'd've gone yourself."

"I would have *tried* to go, yes," he said seriously. "But I would have been wrong, and I submit to you that Father is ... is quite persuasive enough to have shown me my error and given me the opportunity to arrange matters more appropriately."

"More appropriately."

He nodded, his breathing easier now.

"Delms protect the clan. Delms send kin into danger, sometimes knowingly send them to die. It is the paradox of our duty."

"Which don't mean—"

"Which doesn't mean that one may not mourn, or seek ways to spend at least cost. In this instance— Father *must have* gone. He was expendable, if need be. We—are not. For who would protect the clan, if the delm fell? And I submit that no one involved in that transaction knew it better than he did himself."

He sighed and moved toward her, extending a hand along the top of the 'chora. She put her hand in his, relief making her giddy; the flow of his love buoying her.

"I know the delm's duty," he murmured. "It is fixed in the mind of all of us before we take our first flight. What I have been attempting is to fix that duty in my heart. I have several times over the last few nights sat with the Tree, learning stories of past delms, from . . . a primary source that is . . . not the Diaries. I have also tried to . . . employ its assistance in strategy, for I, we—*Korval*—must believe that Daav yos'Phelium has been abducted by the Department of the Interior. To believe otherwise endangers those whom we are sworn to protect."

"Tree have anything useful to say on that front?"

"I believe it is considering the matter," Val Con said, with a quirk of an eyebrow.

Miri sighed. The Tree was hundreds of years old. It might still be thinking when Lizzie came to be delm.

"This evening, I was—there was a protocol for breaking an ordinary person to the Department's will; for implanting a particular course of action in the psyche while hiding the action from the person himself. I believe this is what they might attempt with Father. The Department has, after all, attempted to defeat us from without, and has seen . . . less success than they would like. A strike from within will surely succeed."

"You were trying to remember this so Daav could be defused, if he comes back?"

"Yes. And also to try to guess if he would allow himself to survive such treatment, or if Mother could, in some way, interfere."

"Any answers?"

He looked wry and waved his hand at the 'chora.

"No."

She nodded, thinking.

"The stories the Tree's been sharing with you. Will it share with me?"

"I believe it will. Or, we might see if you might learn from me."

She frowned at him.

"Think that'll work?"

"It may."

He smiled and his fingers tightened on hers.

"Come, *cha'trez*. You should be in bed, and so, we agree, should I. Let us dream together and find what that may tell us."

"Sounds like a plan," Miri said, and raised her free hand to cover a sudden yawn.

"Sounds like a *good* plan."

· · · ❉ · · ·

"Help you, Pilot?"

Theo hitched a hip onto one of the stools.

"Clarence sent me," she said. "Said there was a cookie in it for him, and he's serious about new-made cookies."

The woman nodded calmly. "Looked like a mana rare good sense. You'll be 'is mate, then. What's for you?"

Theo cast a suddenly wistful look at the menu board...

"You want something special like they make at home, you tell me," the woman said comfortably. "I can fix more'ns on that board."

"Can you?" Theo sighed. "I don't—you wouldn't be able to make me a toasted cheese sandwich, would you?"

"Why not?" asked the woman, turning toward her galley. "Be a couple, makin' it from scratch. I'll slip it inna warmbox for you so's you can take it with. That do ya?"

"Yes," said Theo, and blinked at the sudden prickling of her eyes. "That'll do me...just fine."

FIFTEEN

· · · · · · · · · · · · ·

Tradedesk

"SORRY TO SAY, PILOT AITCHLEY, BUT SOMEBODY FED you bad info."

The voice was male, adorned with an exaggerated version of the station accent. Voice was all Theo had, though the connection was marvelously crisp; visual had been denied at the contact point on world Chustling.

"Nobody here got any affiliations with Tree-and-Dragon Family, Pilot. Guess that's kinda good news for you, innit? Get to stay up there in the squeaky-clean, 'stead getting your boots dusty down here with us."

Theo held on to her patience, just.

"The name I have is Ravin Paylot," she said. "At ChivinTrade Limited."

There was lag—surprisingly little, before the man's voice came back at her again.

"Yes'm, Pilot, you got ChivinTrade all right. Ravin Paylot—can't help you there. No Tree-n-Dee affiliates here. Might could be some on-world. Maybe. *I* can't tell you."

Theo closed her eyes, glad now that the video had been denied. There wasn't any sense wasting more time or money on this call. There might be a way to research Ravin Paylot, to find where she'd gone after leaving ChivinTrade.

"Thanks then, ChivinTrade," she said. "Like you said, it's an old name the Master Trader had in a file. I appreciate your help."

"No trouble, no trouble at all, Pilot Aitchley. You have fun up there. No need to come down here to Chustling. ChivinTrade out."

"*Bechimo* out," Theo answered.

There was a pause before Joyita spoke, from Screen Six.

"That's a clean disconnect, Pilot Theo."

"Thank you, Joyita." She frowned, then shook herself and glanced at Screen Two, which was currently showing local times at Tradedesk, Chustling, and Vincza. She had a name and a contact code for Vincza...which she supposed ought to be used, if only so she could tell Shan that she'd done as he'd asked. Though she was beginning to think that Shan's Master Trader inside info wasn't as good as he thought it was.

"The person you just spoke with was beyond concerned. Scared scans in the emotional registers I reference," Joyita commented.

Theo blinked at him. "Scared?"

Joyita raised his eyebrows.

"Yes. It sounded clearly that way to me," he said. "Deciding if it was us he was scared of, or of somebody in the commlink using a snooper and hearing 'Tree and Dragon,' that is an issue I can't resolve."

"I didn't think of that. I *should* have thought of that." Theo *fuffed* her hair out of her eyes and sighed. "Well, we'll put it in the report to Shan as your observation."

Joyita raised his hand as if his fingers had something to put into the conversation, but he only clenched them into a fist, as if he'd thought better of whatever it was.

"Master Trader yos'Galan doesn't know of my existence," he pointed out.

"Sure he does," Theo said.

Joyita looked dubious, but bowed his head.

"I leave it to the pilot's judgment," he said.

"Okay." Theo hesitated on the edge of a question, then shrugged and looked back to Screen Two.

Clarence had left some while back for his date, looking respectable and scholarly in dress kilt and ruffled shirt. He had his ship key locked snug in his belt, to *Bechimo*'s clear relief, and was obviously anticipating an enjoyable leave.

Once he'd reported Clarence off-ship, *Bechimo* had . . . retired, leaving her Joyita in Screen Six for company. That was odd, but maybe he was trying out another affect. Joyita was, after all, art, and art was, in Theo's opinion, tricky at best.

"Can you set me up a relay to Vincza surface, offices of Macker Marooney?" she asked Joyita now. "I've got the code here in notes." She shunted it to the communications queue with a ripple of fingers across keys. "Content of initiating relay, Laughing Cat Limited under trade contract to Korval seeking Ornth Delabar for possible association. Contact Waitley, and our code."

"Will do," said Joyita, glancing down at what she

was meant to think of as his board. "It is nightside where we're sending, Pilot Theo. There could be some little while between now and an answer."

"If there's an answer," Theo said grumpily. She sighed, and stood up, spinning away from the chair to dance a half-dozen energetic steps.

"I'm going to go down to the cellar and see how Win Ton's getting on," she said.

Joyita glanced up, his expression curious.

"You visit the young man often," he said.

Theo gave a rueful laugh and shook her head.

"I don't visit nearly as much as I should, and I don't know what to do when I do. Except wait, and hope he's getting better. That we're doing the right thing and not just..."

Extending his suffering, is what she didn't say. Uncle's information had been firm, if sparse. If there was help for Win Ton at all, it was with the machine, the Remastering Unit.

The question she kept coming back to, peripheral to the question of Win Ton's eventual recovery of good health, was—why hadn't the Scouts just let him go? Why hadn't they let him die his death? Why had they compromised the policies of their organization—which held such tech as *Bechimo* sprang from, tech such as the Remastering Unit, was to be destroyed—in order to buy Win Ton's life? He wasn't a high-ranking, nor, she suspected, a particularly valuable member of the Scouts. He hadn't given her to believe that his clan was so important that the Scouts had no choice but to make the attempt to save his life.

Worse! He had broken—Win Ton *himself* had broken Scout rules and regulations by coming aboard

Bechimo, sitting in a chair, and bringing the piloting keys away. If he hadn't done that—if he had instead done whatever he was supposed to have done: reported an intruder device, blown up said intruder device, sent for a team of specialists to deactivate and dismantle said intruder device... If he hadn't let curiosity overrule his common sense, he wouldn't be in the Remastering Unit at all.

The only thing she could think of was, if the instrument of torture that had been used on Win Ton was deployed against... more Scouts, utilized as a means of blackmail and assassination... If entire clans or armies could be wiped out by the same means that had turned Win Ton's very cells against themselves...

So, he was a test case—a test case for both the Scouts and the enemy who had done this thing to him. He was a living laboratory, a breathing battle zone; fortunes and empires could rise and fall in the blood of this one man.

That the battle was engaged at all was an accident dependent on the goodwill of a man who ought to have been scattered dust long before Delgado had founded a university.

"But, I can sense your concern rising, without need," Joyita said, breaking into these thoughts. "His prognosis is good, as far as I see here. The waiting's in order, Pilot Theo. Let the healing finish."

Theo looked at him, there in the screen, a man who didn't exist, who gazed earnestly back at her, brown eyes wide.

"I'm glad to hear the prognosis is good," she said slowly. "I was worried. Do you know when he—when Win Ton—will be released?"

Joyita shook his head slightly. "I'll ask *Bechimo*."

Theo blinked; danced one step nearer the screens, not certain she'd heard that correctly or, having heard it, fully understood it.

"Aren't *you Bechimo*?" she asked.

The image of a man in Screen Six looked embarrassed.

"Not—I feel...no. Resend that: I'm not certain, Pilot Theo. I've been concentrating on taking on details, as we talked about. It seems that the more I concentrate on the way this body...would operate... I maintain a direct access to *Bechimo*, but I feel myself to be...Joyita." He frowned, and repeated, softly. "Feel myself."

Theo held herself very still, thinking.

"*Bechimo* wants a captain to bond with. Do you want that?" She threw up a hand as insight struck. "*Are* you that? The Bonded Captain?"

"Not captain, no, not I. He's right, though, *Bechimo*. The ship needs the bond; there's a lot of info and ability tied up in rules, and thus out of the way of ordinary view. It makes me nervous, to tell you true, Pilot Theo. We're not running to full capacity, which is risky, or as Clarence would say it, asking for trouble."

"I see." She hesitated.

"I was thinking earlier, when I took my tour—here we are on a station with a full-time, full-service office of the Pilots Guild. It might be that what we—you and *Bechimo*, I mean—ought to do is advertise for a captain. You're right that we shouldn't be running exposed."

There was a longish pause, while Joyita looked down at his board. When he looked up again, his face was noncommittal.

"We'll consult, Pilot Theo. Are you on off-schedule now?"

She glanced to Screen Two.

"I am," she decided. "Your shift, Pilot."

"Thank you, Pilot." Joyita smiled. "Sweet dreams."

Theo stood by the Remastering Unit.

It looked...something like an autodoc, with similar simple gauges on top display. The most important was the viability gauge, designed to permit emergency triage at a glance. If the unit was offered someone who was dead and who had no hope of revival, the gauge would show black.

If the unit were offered someone who was dead, but who might provide spare parts for others through transplant or harvest, the gauge would so indicate. And, if the unit were offered someone who was, or could be alive; who could be repaired, the gauge would report that.

However complex the mechanisms for determining those states, the display itself was simple to understand.

When she'd originally brought Win Ton here to the cellar, he'd permitted her to squeeze his hand, gently, before laying down in the Remastering Unit. The hood closed over him, and she'd thought he'd be in the unit for a few days, or perhaps a few days and then repeat the treatment a few times, and then—done. Whole.

Healed.

The gauge on that first occasion had started out neutral, and as systems checked and fluid flowed, there was a quick and palpable change. The readout, for someone undergoing a minor repair—say a gunshot to the shoulder—would show blue all around, with tinges of orange to show pain suppression. The small mark two thirds of the way down would be nearly invisible in such case.

But when the unit had worked for only a few moments, the colors had shifted and the blue fell rapidly, fell down to the first third, indicating that there was damage in multiple spots, that the patient was alive, but under considerable stress. The halfway mark met the red-blue demarcation point, and that was a sign that there was major damage, some potentially life-threatening. The one-half mark meant the patient might not live long, outside the unit. The one-third mark, with one-third blue and two-thirds red, that was the sign for organ harvesting.

The unit hadn't shown quite that low, not quite to nonviable, but there was the warning of a bright orange sliver, a sign that the organs themselves were not to be trusted. Call that gauge showing thirty-seven percent, and working.

She'd stood there a long time, watching, and the only relief was that the shades of red and orange dulled, and the unit became quieter. When she left the room her hands hurt, her fingernails having been pressed so long and hard into her palms.

The following day she'd rushed into the room, expecting . . . well, she hadn't known what she was expecting. What she saw, though, was the Remastering Unit, the chair beside it still empty, Win Ton's clothes folded into the transparent cubby above, and the gauge showing a purple sliver to replace the orange. On subsequent visits, the gauge might have shown a one percent improvement.

Or maybe not.

Now, though, encouraged by the news that Win Ton's progress was good—now she looked at the gauge with an optimistic, if still largely uninformed, eye.

The gauge was closing in on fifty percent green. Good. That was good. But the simple gauge only told one tale: percentage of death. What she needed to know—emboldened by Joyita's assurance—was the percentage of Win Ton living.

Theo pushed the button beside the display. It resisted, and it struck her that she might be the first person to ever use that button for aught but testing. The display flickered into depthless black, from which words began to form.

> *Patient Win Ton yo'Vala*
> *Function Change Percentage Report:*
>   *Treatment Location #13.*
> *General Therapeutic Regime: cleanse to remaster*
> *Major issues: persistent induced mutational*
>   *nanomycosis   see notes*
> *Cardiovascular   72%   see notes*
> *Dermal   45% persistent induced nanomyco-*
>   *sis   see notes*
> *Neurological / nervous   62%   see notes*
> *Muscular   59%   see notes*
> *Skeletal   83%   see notes*
> *Lymphatic   55%   see notes*
> *Endocrine   58%   see notes*
> *Reproductive   17%   see notes*
> *Urinary   37%   see notes*
> *Digestive   66%   see notes*
> *Senescence Quotient   64%   see notes*
> *Retro-senescence Activity   52%   see notes*

SIXTEEN

. . . .

Tradedesk

IN FACT, THEO HAD NOT SLEPT PARTICULARLY WELL, at first.

It was her own fault, really, but what daughter of scholars, brought up to pursue advertency, and regularly reminded of the importance of checking one's facts, could have resisted the lure of that line of "see notes"?

And so, she had gone deeper into the Remastering Unit's screens, accessing the referenced notes, one by one, until she came to an end—and an understanding.

The Remastering Unit wasn't... *healing* Win Ton. It was... it was returning him to the templated state. Which meant that it was... killing him, cell by cell.

And rebuilding him.

Cell by cell.

A cup of ginger tea had settled her stomach, but left her wide awake and full of thoughts too uncomfortable to admit sleep.

Finally, she had gotten out of bed and danced a deep meditation, the sort of self-hypnosis she seldom used, because the trance induced was too profound for board-rest. So she did eventually sleep, and woke just before her alarm, full of both energy and resolve.

She hit the 'fresher, dressed ship-casual with her favorite slippers against *Bechimo*'s cool deck, had a small breakfast in the crew lounge, and went to the command deck where not much had changed, other than the advent of numerous messages for her, for Clarence, and for Exec.

The crew list on the status screen showed that she was aboard and that Clarence was not. No surprise there, he had a half-shift to go on his date; the status board helpfully ticked off his due-by time, second by second.

Screen Six displayed a lazy drift of white and blue clouds, as it had during the days before *Bechimo* made it Joyita's window into the Heart. Theo guessed that meant the comm officer was off-duty, and set about sorting through the in-queue.

Most of her mail was station adverts, which she deleted cheerfully. There was a reply from the third name on Shan's list. She opened it with a certain amount of trepidation—which morphed into joy.

"Ha!" she shouted, grinning.

"Your pardon, Pilot?" *Bechimo* asked, from a position that seemed to be behind her and slightly over her head. "Is something wrong?"

"Sorry, *Bechimo*," she said. "I was expressing my . . . delight. I have an actual appointment with Pilot Denobli of the Carresens!" Her grin faded, and she sighed. "I hope it turns out better than the appointment at Chaliceworks."

"You think that Pilot Denobli will be . . . less cautious of an association with Korval—with Korval's Luck?"

Theo blew her hair out of her eyes.

"Well, I *hope* so," she said, placing the appointment into her day log, and returning to the scan of her email. "There's a response from the relay to Vincza, too!" she said, as if *Bechimo* could possibly not know this. "Maybe I'm lucky twice."

But, as it happened, she wasn't. The response from the code site was that Macker Marooney was out of business, proprietor Ornth Delabar deceased.

Theo sighed. How old *was* Shan's list, anyway? You'd think a Master Trader would be better informed.

"Your pardon, Pilot," *Bechimo* said again. "Station inspectors are approaching, on official business."

Theo frowned.

"Official business?" she asked—and then remembered that Rutland had said they'd be sending their report along on the morrow. She hadn't expected to have it hand-delivered! For that matter, why not just give Clarence a datakey?

"Yes, Pilot. Investigator Rutland reports that Less Pilot O'Berin is in investigative custody. She would like to arrange a meeting on our deck to discuss the situation. She reports that *us three are on our way*. She further states that she is very sorry for this turn of events, and that she expects to be at the tube within moments. That communication ended approximately seventy seconds ago."

Custody? What in—had he gotten drunk and busted up the station? It didn't seem like Clarence, though how did she know what he was like on leave? And, if he had, why would the people he'd been spending the night with have to investigate—

"Show me the gate," she demanded, and *Bechimo*

obligingly projected the station's own feed of the outside of the tube, with Rutland and Clarence walking side by side, and other feet walking behind.

They paused, and the comm button lit.

"Hello, *Bechimo*," came Rutland's sorrowful voice. "Official investigation under way, do we have permission to approach and board?"

Theo wildly recalled that some relationships required public humiliation, or even...no, that couldn't be it. Could it?

Theo took a breath. She had to assume that this was serious; that Clarence was untrustworthy, and she had to insure the safety of her ship—and her passenger.

"*Bechimo*, be prepared to release from the station on my word," she said crisply. "*Only* on my word. Until I say otherwise we will regard Clarence O'Berin to be on leave. His board is not to go live until my command."

"Yes, Pilot."

"*Bechimo*," Rutland said from the tube gate, "did we wake you? This is official station business. Please respond."

Theo looked down at her casual ship clothes and slipers—she looked close enough to being woke, she guessed. She hit *reply* as she stood to pull on her jacket, comforted only slightly by the hideaway there.

"Awake now, Rutland," she replied. "Clarence has a key, come on in..."

"Had to take the slidekey, Pilot, at least until this is cleared up. We'll need you to let us in, of your kindness."

Custody, Theo told herself, and swallowed.

"*Bechimo*, let them in. Please observe; I'll remain

here. When they come through you will close the hatches behind them, and be sure of seals."

"Yes, Pilot."

Theo stood by her chair. She could track the progress of the group by the tiny vibrations as doors and seals cycled—and then the door to the Heart opened, and the security delegation arrived.

Rutland stood next to a subdued Clarence, who was arm-manacled to . . . well, no, he wasn't.

"Let go, Clarence, ain't nobody recording this now, or only people you trust, anyhow."

Clarence did let go, and Rutland reeled the manacle in. He'd been holding the thing to make it look like he was locked in.

"Captain," Rutland began, "this has been quite awkward for all three of us, and I guess now for you, too. But, allowing that timing wasn't quite as bad as it could have been, this took us entirely by surprise. Clarence here has an Advisory on him, one that requires us to investigate. Now, if you'll take official parole of him—that means he's got to stay aboard 'til this is settled—and guarantee ship'll pay fees and fines that might be accrued, we'll turn him over to you and finish the investigation."

Clarence's expression was somewhere between disgusted and thrice disgusted. Most of his jewelry was off display, and he looked like he could use a shower and a good glass of wine. He was actively *not* looking at Rutland, and he was barely glancing at Theo. Every so often he'd look at Grafton, who looked right back. No information there.

Theo sighed and nodded.

"*Bechimo* stands parole. You've got our contacts

and permissions. Now will you explain this hospitality to me?"

She hadn't meant to be confrontational, and the blushes and look-aways all around made it clear that she hadn't needed to be quite so strident.

Grafton stepped forward then, and opened his handheld, and looking down, began to read:

"First Class Pilot Clarence O'Berin, born Strabane and all that stuff including the proper pilot ID number, was on the seventy-ninth day of local year seven hundred and twelve named as an active antagonist, thief, scoundrel, and an agent of the Juntavas. This was sworn to by Hiramson O'Nandy O'dell, citizen of Strabane..."

Clarence snorted, shaking his head and muttering, "Only if they never found out what a foul-scum rustshaker he is! They'd bust him right back to moontiller, I tell you!"

Grafton may have had this news before; he closed his eyes until Clarence quieted, then went on:

"As said, Hiramson O'Nandy O'dell swore to this, paid the sum of one hundred bits in support and consequence to file the report, offered and affirmed his willingness to report for a hearing in the event Clarence O'Berin entered the precincts of Vincza."

Grafton looked up, nodded toward Clarence, then looked at Theo.

"He's here, Clarence is. The thing is, that down on Vincza there's a rainy season, and they don't do anything much at night anyway down there, so arrival reports and the like didn't get run until late and then they didn't much hurry because the report is seventeen years old and the person what swore it is no longer listed as an active trade-transient."

Clarence looked like he was going to spit.

"What do we do now? This person—this O'dell—isn't here, is that correct? Not in-system, even?" Theo mentally danced a relaxation routine, felt it kick in; felt her chest lose a measure of tightness.

Rutland took over for a moment.

"Well, we investigate. Since you took Clarence's parole, we got to ask him questions where you can hear his answers, too."

"Right." Theo took a deep breath and nodded at them to continue.

"Parolee Clarence O'Berin and *Bechimo* standing here with us," Grafton said, "we are recording this investigation of..." He looked up at Theo as he fumbled with the handheld—"Hit me a macro, you know, else that'd take 'til lunch time..." After several more seconds he went on, "...in such regard to review and elucidate the facts of the allegations."

He looked at Clarence.

"Clarence O'Berin, did you know or otherwise have a relationship with the filer?"

Clarence snorted loudly, for the record.

"I knew him, yes. He was an employee of mine and I fired him from his job for theft. He was stealing ID information and he was siphoning funds that were in his control into an outside account."

"I see. A state of antagony existed between you when you parted, then?"

"Damn straight. He owed me money and a lot of lost trust. Caught me because of his citizenship, and taught me a lesson I've done well to remember."

"He named you a thief. You reply?"

"I took back what I could of what was mine and

what belonged to the business I worked for. He was the thief here."

Grafton murmured to the handheld, "See antagony above."

Grafton looked down... "You are accused of being a scoundrel. How do you answer?"

Clarence put his face into his hand, and shook his head. Theo wondered if her mouth had really fallen open. What an investigation!

"I am a working man who got fooled by someone who was too smart for himself in the long run," Clarence said, with what Theo thought was noteworthy calm.

"See antagony above."

Grafton looked to Theo, who was afraid she hadn't quite gotten control of her face. He made a rolling motion with his hands...

"The parole pilot makes a statement regarding the parolee's character."

Theo looked at Clarence.

Clarence didn't look at her.

Well, then. She turned back to Grafton.

"I hired this man with the best of recommendations available to me. He was declared a reputable and honest pilot and his Guild record showed no mar."

Grafton nodded.

"Let's make it clear—you are not related to O'Berin; he's not your father or any other blood relative."

"I have no blood relationship to Clarence O'Berin that I am aware of. I was born on Delgado, the daughter of a scholar, and I may still claim myself citizen of Delgado if I so wish. I have seen the record of my bloodlines, and there are no O'Berins in it."

"Unbiased report," said Grafton to the machine.

"And this last," he said, looking hard at Clarence. "Understand the man put money down to make this allegation."

Clarence said nothing. Grafton looked down at the handheld.

"Says here that you are an agent of the Juntavas."

Clarence raised his hands slightly, looked a bit helpless, and in pilot sign let go a string of impossible acts and unlikely states of being, all with the attribute *that one*.

"A man looking to cause as much trouble as he could for another man," he said, as if the flood of sign had loosened his tongue, "a man with a guilty soul and revenge in his heart, that's what that kind of a man would say, isn't it?"

Grafton lifted the handheld.

"We need to hear the answer to the question—are you an active agent of the Juntavas?"

"No," said Clarence.

Well, that was clear, Theo thought.

Grafton nodded, and spoke to the handheld.

"This session report concludes that there's an admission of reciprocal antagony, a denial of other allegations, and no evidence on the other charges. Therefore we will settle with session fees. Should Hiramson O'Nandy O'dell appear on account of this action he shall pay twice the assessment, with interest. This investigative hearing"—here he fumbled for the controls a moment, again—"is complete."

Grafton looked down at unit, and then to Theo.

"That went two hundred bits and ten against the account, Pilot. I'm sorry . . . but you're all clear, and being a civil thing, it won't show on the records again, being done."

Grafton slipped his unit back into its belt loop, turned, took a half step, and stopped.

"Clary, Clary, what a stupid person you hired. I'm so sorry on this, and we owe you a proper breakfast, if you can stand me."

Clarence's face looked odd, almost like there were tears in his eyes, and he made a hand motion which brought Grafton and Rutland both to him, hugging where he stood.

Theo wasn't sure what to say, but she saw Clarence look 'round to the main screen, with the countdown to the end of his leave.

He squeezed the security team one more time, and pulled away.

"We'll see how the trading goes, and I swear I'll try. Right now, my leave shift is about up, and you didn't get breakfast, too."

SEVENTEEN

· · · · · · · · · · · · · · · · · · · ·

Tradedesk

THAT, CLARENCE THOUGHT AS HE HIT SPEED-CLEAN ON the 'fresher, had been a mite too close for comfort. And a solid man was Graf, for adding on that *active* while giving *now or ever* as wide a berth as a pilot could manage. He thought even Theo'd bought the packet, which he'd prefer, and not only just for reasons of not wanting to have to explain himself and his reasons to a girl young enough to be his...

His sudden grin felt like it sat sidewise on his mouth, but for certain there it was, him and Daav being within three Standards of each other.

Well, then.

He stepped out of the 'fresher, grabbed a sweater and pants, shoved his feet into slippers and ran for the center of things, not late yet, for his shift.

"So, we'll make that part of the incoming protocols?" the pilot was saying to the ship as Clarence entered the Heart. Screen Six was filled with blue sky and good wishes, and the answer to Theo's question came from behind and slightly above.

"Pilot, I will upon approach perform a scan of outstanding warrants and complaints, civil, administrative, and criminal. If a crew member should be named in an open warrant of any kind, I will alert the Over Pilot and the crew member so named."

"Good," Theo said, and Clarence had to agree. Reasonable precaution. Too bad he hadn't thought of it himself, and long before.

A few steps out from his chair, he paused. The lock-down light still glowed in the corner of his board, which he suspected meant that she wasn't through with him yet. Despite not being of a particularly nervous disposition, he did feel a flutter of apprehension.

"Thank you, *Bechimo*," Theo said, and considered the screen before her with a certain aspect of deliberateness.

Clarence's apprehension intensified. He took a breath and bowed to the pilot's honor.

"Thank you, Pilot. I will of course reimburse the ship, for those costs incurred on my behalf."

She looked at him then, and lifted a hand, fingers requesting *silence*.

Silence it was, then, and him of a sudden glad he hadn't had a bit o'breakfast. Here, he'd been so happy to be flyin' honest—and wouldn't it just look fine on the record, that he'd been put aside at Tradedesk, for having a sworn warrant against his name?

Theo took a breath, as if she was about to say something, shook her head, took another breath—and sighed sharply.

"I'm postponing my leave until we do a check on

outstanding warrants, inquiries, challenges, and actions for all personnel currently aboard. That includes me, that includes you, that includes Win Ton, and for that matter, it includes *Bechimo*. Please have a seat, Clarence."

Clarence sat, noting that the lock-down light was still bright.

"*Bechimo*, you don't have a hold on you in any port that you know of, do you?"

Screen Six firmed.

"Pilot, not as a registered and identified vessel or person, no."

Theo sent a frowning glance at the screen, where the clouds had faded away, leaving Joyita, also frowning, and apparently following the conversation with interest.

"Is that equivocation?" Theo demanded.

"Exactitude, Pilot. In the course of the last several hundred years alone, I have been challenged to identify myself dozens of times. I have been pursued, and was given orders to stand by for boarding. I withstood several efforts at boarding by pirates and brigands. You are aware of the most recent challenge to my integrity, and its aftermath. At no time during these encounters was I displaying identification numbers, markings, or ID, nor was I emitting identifiable transmissions."

"Right," she said, "then you better check the systems and see if there's anything out there for me."

"Yes, Pilot, I am performing that search now."

"Thank you."

She glanced down at her hands, as if regretting the lack of fancywork, then looked back to his face, eyes snapping sharp.

"Are there any more of these hanging around for you, Clarence? Little surprises waiting in a gravity well? Anything that could get you locked up, instead of just fined? Anything that would *endanger this ship*?"

Well, now, there it was—and he was proved a fool *and* an idiot. One thing a wise person just didn't undertake in the presence of your plain-and-fancy Dragon was endangering a ship. Any other thing might be forgiven, or overlooked, but that?

Never.

"That's a fair question, Pilot," he said keeping it civil without making any attempt to soothe her.

"Truth told, I had no idea the matter with O'dell was about. He must've thought I was after him personally, to have been pushed to such a thing, him being a laddie who never liked to see the inside of a magistrate's office, nor held with spending money except to buy his own pleasure. Damn little need of me going after him in person, if I'd've wanted him. But there—I didn't want him. And didn't want his blood all over the shop floor, either."

"Yes," she said, plainly soothing *him*. "I understand that you acted with great restraint in the matter of Mr. O'dell, and you might tell me more about that in a moment. But otherwise? Is there *anything* else?"

"Nothing active that I know about," he told her, which, considering, was as positive as he could say. "Anywhere."

She nodded.

"Make us some tea," she said abruptly, suddenly and shockingly in the Liaden High Tongue—ranking-person-to-lesser—nailed it dead-on, too, bless the girl. "I wish to order my thoughts."

· · · ❖ · · ·

The tea having been brought and sampled, Theo leaned back in her chair and looked into her copilot's serious and attentive face. It came to her that Clarence was a dangerous man.

It came to her that Father had recommended him to her *because* he was a dangerous man.

Theo took a breath, centering herself before she began.

"I'm young, Clarence, and I've been in some trouble. I have some files on me, you know, and I've been tracked some, just like anyone who's trying to do something. On Delgado I'm probably still listed as someone who is clumsy and needs drugs so she won't hurt anyone..."

She said that musingly, sipped from her cup, and was rewarded with a startled glance from Clarence's side of the control board.

"I never did finish the course of study there so I'm probably still carrying some incompletes, because they were going to be considered final when I graduated from Anlingdin. But then, at Anlingdin, I was ruled a 'nexus of violence' by the Academy... I guess that's gone worldwide there since I didn't go find a job minding an automat, and beg for reinstatement after a couple years." She shook her head. "I'm the first woman in my family *ever* who failed to complete her basic, and her secondary, course of study. But I wanted to be a pilot, and I *am* a pilot. A young pilot, maybe, but I intend to get older."

She paused, regarding Clarence steadily. He returned her gaze from his blue, blue eyes, his face serious.

"So," she said, "a young pilot, who's been on some worlds, and had some trouble on two. And what I hear now, from the security officers here on Tradedesk, is that you've got antagony."

Clarence didn't say anything; she hadn't expected him to, really.

She shrugged.

"That's not a mark against you as a pilot, I don't think, though I guess back on Delgado they'd warn Safeties if you were around, because obviously willful antagony is antisocial, yes?"

He nodded, carefully.

"Yes. And I expect you might get looked at hard on Eylot, too, on account of being a pilot from away. And if they saw *scoundrel* in your file they'd probably go from looking to watching, which you don't want. But that's not a problem, because we're not going to Eylot on *my* schedule."

She picked up her teacup and sipped. Clarence did likewise.

"Now this *scoundrel* thing," she continued. "I had to look that up, and it seems to depend a whole lot on where you take the readings as to who is or isn't, what does or doesn't make a *scoundrel*. In some places running off for a night of fun with a couple would make one a *scoundrel*, I guess, but you don't seem like you're doing stuff just to be antisocial, so we'll discount that."

He nodded again, his face more, rather than less, serious.

Theo sighed then.

"You can count, too, so you know where this goes. I heard you answer that last question very carefully, and I have this thing in my head that people used to fall down around me and so I was called clumsy, and then people started doing dangerous stuff around me so I got tagged as a nexus."

Her copilot volunteered nothing. Theo put her cup down, carefully.

"Now, I'm young, Clarence," she said, "and I haven't seen as much as you have, or been as many places. But this Juntavas thing, that's a serious kind of a tag to carry with you, if you do."

Silence, the blue gaze never wavering.

She returned that gaze hard, and snapped, "What I want from you right now, Pilot, is a clear understanding of why Whoever O'dell might paint that particular detail to hold you off his course. Were you a courier pilot for them? Did you *ever* do work for the Juntavas?"

Surprisingly, he grinned, while his hands showed *good course straight course, pilot*.

"Father's daughter, aren't you just, Theo Waitley?"

He paused to stare into his cup, drained the remainder of his tea as if it was a bar drink he was desperately in need of.

Cup down, he relaxed into his seat, suddenly boneless.

"We have a long story, we do, Pilot, and some of it you're not going to get, just like you're not going to give me the particulars of where you went and what you did for the Uncle, that being not only confidential, but dangerous to know.

"Still, some of this you ought to have, and since you've got your father's instincts, I'll give it broad except where that's not clear enough.

"To answer true—yes. I did run courier for the Juntavas. It paid good—especially by Strabane standards—and

I liked the work. That was years back—I was close enough to your age, I'll wager.

"The O'dell named himself, so I'm not giving you a name you didn't know. Details you don't need to know...well, you don't. O'dell, though, he worked for me, coming in to the job in small part 'cause he was from home; maybe he was seventh cousin four times removed. Then he started in to pilfering and tinkering with arrangements way over his head; and it came public to the crew before I could talk him out quiet. So, then, I had to deal. I could have shot him on the spot, and upset none but the cleaning crew—and them not out of reason—and myself. I thought I owed him his life, 'cause I'd given him a break, I guess. Not the laddie's fault; he'd never been taught no better."

He touched his cup, where it sat in the slot, apparently remembered that it was empty and sighed, meeting Theo's eyes.

"That's the core of it—I let him live, and he pulled this stupidity."

Theo nodded gravely.

"So this was a pilot thing? He was a danger to the ship? Or..."

Clarence shook his head.

"Not on a ship. Thing is, I did good work, not to say annoying some as it would've been better not to, and I got...promoted. The O'dell worked for me."

Theo closed her eyes, followed trails, opened eyes directly on Clarence.

"I thought you worked at freight forwarding all those years, on Liad?"

"Father's daughter," he said again, a smile in his eyes. "I did."

Theo frowned. "You were working on the side for the Juntavas? And Father *knew* this?"

Clarence pressed his lips together, uncrossed his arms and leaned toward her.

"No and yes. 'Course your father knew who I was—he had to, 'cause him and his lady were Korval. Me, they had to know, because I was their opposite number—like your cousin Pat Rin called Conrad there on Surebleak...I was a Boss. Juntavas Boss, if you like that, which most do. Thing is, that with Korval guiding things on Liad like they did, it was a kind of quiet post for a smart Juntava."

"My father was friends with the Juntavas Boss?"

"Told you different, right first, didn't I?" Clarence asked sternly.

Theo frowned—and she remembered it, her very first conversation with Clarence O'Berin, asking if he had been Father's friend.

Friends—well, now, we might could've been, in a different set of circumstances...

"I remember," she told him. "You set a value on him, but he had his *melant'i* and you had your business to tend."

"That was the way of it," he said, nodding. "Couldn't be friends. More like two cats guarding turf—in fact exactly like two cats guarding turf. Korval was top cat, and the whole clan knew who we were. There was a policy in place that both sides tried to keep to— something put in by a Boss and a delm long ago. The deal was that it wasn't worth Korval messing with us as long as we weren't messing with Korval. Every so often one of ours would get a bit ahead of themselves and Korval'd be right there and make sure the policy hadn't been forgot. That was the problem with the O'dell, messing on the edges of things that could have brought Korval right down on my head, harder than either of us would've wanted, to be sure the point was made."

He leaned back in his chair.

"That," he said then, "that's what you need to know, I'm thinking. I was Boss and kept a low profile, did what I did, wasn't never charged there or nowhere with the doing of anything."

"That's how you knew about Uncle, then?"

"Some things you got to know, yes. That was one of the things I had to know."

"So are you Juntavas now?"

"Like I told Graf—no. I'm strictly retired. Very strictly. I'm here to fly, because after I got tangled in the job I had, there wasn't an easy getting out for years."

Theo closed her eyes.

A reputable and honest pilot, Father had said. A man who knows how to take orders.

And dangerous—that, because he was traveling with her, and she drew trouble like a magnet drew iron.

Opening her eyes, she looked right at Clarence.

"If I think of more questions, I reserve the right to ask. Meanwhile, on the fine, I'm sure you'll have expenses for the ship from time to time. Pay out of pocket until you're even and let *Bechimo* know."

She extended an arm and touched a button. The lock-down light on second board went out.

"There's messages," she said, standing and stretching, "a pretty fair flood of them. Call me if you need my input, Pilot."

Clarence sighed.

"Thank you, Pilot," he said.

EIGHTEEN

· · · · · · · · · · · · · · · ·

Tradedesk

THE CARRESENS WERE BOTH A FAMILY AND A PROCESS.

As a family they were of Terran extraction and had interests in ships and shipping going back generations. They could follow their generations back a long way, too; at least to the period of the Great Terran Wars when rapid expansion had almost caused the Terran worlds to wipe themselves out in a mad fit of protectionism and trade wars.

Theo read on; neither she nor Clarence had known of Carresens. That was partly because they'd never expanded into the large liners as Theo's classmate Asu's family had, nor into the larger tradeships, as Korval had. Rather than the big ship model they relied on a net of smaller ships, plus family and community connectivity.

However they'd begun, the process of Carresens in Spwao System began on Vincza, in the month before the rainy season, and then relocated for two more months to a smaller *Festevalya* on Tradedesk

for the amusement of cruise ship passengers, and
those citizens of Vincza who removed to the station
to escape the rain.

"*Bechimo*, can you get me the coords for the next
three Vincza sessions? Show me the schedule through
twelve Standards, if it goes that far. It may be that
this can work out well for us. . . ."

The working screen began to fill with dates and
place names, rippled slightly and came more sharply
into focus.

"*Bechimo*, why the font change?" asked Clarence.

"The station attempted to give larger fonts and preferred coloring to the events occurring at this station, or
within the system. I have rectified the erroneous codes."

"Thank you, sir," Theo said lightly, watching for
the next scheduled event. She frowned.

"Is there a pattern I don't see?"

Clarence shook his head. "I was trying to figure that
myself, but if there's a pattern, it isn't obvious, is it?"

"The dates," Joyita said, entering the fray from Screen
Six. "They coincide with local celebrations and growing
seasons, as well as the rotation of certain ships and trade
groups. The basic dates and algorithms are from the
*Second Arm Original Trade Almanac, Two Hundredth
Anniversary Edition*. The overrides are calculable based
on the standard routes of the Carresens-operated ships
Nubella Run, *GRClement*, *Prism*, and *MVP*."

"Overrides?" asked Theo.

"It appears from a scan of past events, that *GRClement* is required at each Carresens, with two of the
other three ships," Joyita murmured, glancing down
at a board that was out of Theo's range. "For the
Festevalya, one ship remains, in rotation. *Nubella Run*

is the second Carresens ship of that name; *GRClement* has risen to replace *OchoBalrog*, which was retired from service eighteen Standards past.

"My interpretation of the schedules I see here is that a sophisticated and coordinated long loop system has been in operation since before the *Trade Almanac* began."

He looked up and met Theo's eyes.

"A deeper analysis may depend on the acquisition of trade history libraries, local pricing, weather, and political maps, as well as Carresens family history, birth records, and various stellar instabilities across systems."

Theo nodded.

"How hard are these to come by, Joyita? It sounds like research we should have, and that Shan would want. Only, if there's already a private set of loops running, Korval might not be welcome! *We* might not be welcome!"

"Welcome is different than allowed, Pilot," Clarence said sensibly. "Looks like these Carresens have hit on a handy way to get business done. They come in, throw parties, bring in the ships and people for trade, have harvest fairs, and hiring halls; wedding marathons. They've built themselves into the everyday and special days of a string of places. Looks like they broker contracts, too. So we might have a good shot at picking up something."

Theo leaned back in her chair, and looked to the chronometer.

"That would be good," she said. "I'd like to get something out of this." She glanced at the chronometer; saw that it was time to get ready for her appointment, and rose, determined.

"I *will* get something out of this," she said determinedly.

Clarence looked up at her, and nodded agreeably. "Good luck, then, Pilot."

It felt good to be dressed up, even a little; it felt good to have a task before her—a task that actually had some chance of success. She had Shan's talking points, which were few, but she'd done this before, and it felt—not comfortable, exactly, but... more regular.

She came into their local gallery, and smiled, buoyed by the feeling of the familiar, even though she had only been to this spot once—and that was good, too.

The comm was in her pocket, the ship-key hung round her neck, which had mollified, if not exactly pleased, *Bechimo*. Clarence had been all business when she went over what she called the rules of engagement, in case there was a problem. They were not yet so well trained a crew that they all knew everything that needed to be done—that had taken months or more to achieve with Rig, on a ship that wasn't self-aware, and learning, and trying every day to do more, anticipate more—a ship trying to be a crew member.

Or two crew members.

At the edge of spider territory, Theo caught a lift down seven levels. From there, she had a decent walk, all in a brighter, roomier, prettier place than she'd been. The air was perhaps heavier here, and she realized she'd have to be careful that she didn't get a little inebriated on the extra oxygen.

Tradedesk was bigger than she'd realized, not only in cubes and mass, but in the amount of business that must go through it. The place was active and, unlike the folks out in the spider zone, there were signs of affluence and comfort. It wasn't simply a higher oxygen content to the air, it was in the clothes and the walk and the kinds of storefronts. People were not just admiring, they were shopping, some of them walking off proudly with boxes and bags, or pushing carts. Local passengers were the bulk of the pedestrians, given the talk she could hear: accents wrong for base Trade, wrong for base Terran. They were a respectful and informed crowd, too, with nods and polite hand-signs for the young pilot with the rapid walk. There was also a willing concession of right of way, which Theo found difficult to concede in return.

The way to the Carresens office lay through Festevalya, a bustling open market composed of numerous smaller shops and stands grouped in themes, crowded with storekeepers and patrons. There was a clothing store specializing in hand-made fabrics next to one with leathers and one with day clothes and one with night clothes. Each of the minishops had at least one rack or display with a bold *Carresens Special*, or *New for Carresens* displayed and given the range of things she might need, yes, she'd have to stop here on the way back!

Theo almost missed the side corridor she wanted; it looked more like a service hall than a route that led to a major . . . well, there was the sign above the small arrow: CARRESENS GENERAL. The hall entrance was a slightly disguised, automatic air-seal—of course a station this size would have safety doors—and there was a warning sign for gravity shift, and as she walked through the door she saw that there was a change of texture.

The gravity shift was no problem, and she was in a smaller hall looking much more shiplike than stationlike—even some of Codrescu's halls were bigger than this! The lighting was more shiplike as well. Yes, this *was* a ship's passageway, she was sure. A ship not tube-accessed, but sealed directly into the fabric of the station.

The hall was short, ending at a door. A sign on the door said: PLEASE ENTER.

Enter she did, pressing the kickplate gently with her toe. She watched the door slide by, saw seals that looked good all around, saw the lights—a working air seal door, too, coated with an aftermarket paint that matched the hall of the station, but not the interior of the room. A faint impression under the paint, that there were words there.

The interior was a good-size room, large for a ship, adequate for a station office, and she guessed it was the dining room of a tradeship. It was now furnished as an office, with one wall covered in images of planetside fairs and spaceships, there were seven wait-seats, three of them occupied by pilots working assiduously on form tablets, and a counter—yes, that, too, sealed, flanked by doors: a serving counter, no doubt, except now the other side was not food prep but—

"Pilot, your name and assignment?"

The woman behind the counter was a pilot, though she wasn't wearing the working jacket. She was severe in aspect, hair finger-tight, dressed in a crisp and tight ship's dress uniform all in pale blue; she might have been Pilot yos'Senchul's age and certainly at least twice Theo's. Her hands bore a ring each, one of them large—and gaudy—enough to be an old-fashioned pilot's ring. The name stitched on the uniform pocket was Chels Carresens-Denobli.

"Theo Waitley, of *Bechimo*. I have an appointment with—"

"Yes, Pilot, I have you here. I've taken your info from station files, if you'll be kind enough to let me see your license and station cards here a moment?"

Theo strode to the counter, handed the cards over, and watched as they were both machine scanned and eyeballed. Behind the counter the pilot flashed *all good*, very barely smiled, and handed them back, signing *left-door*.

"Pilot Denobli sees you now," she said quietly.

Pilot Denobli was of an age with the pilot behind the counter out front, and he commanded a space that was a bunkroom, complete with several acceleration bunks folded into the walls, and a tiny foldout desk supporting a handheld device similar to that used by Rutland and Grafton. The name on his uniform was simply *Denobli*, and he'd not bothered to indicate a rank.

"We are," he told Theo after introductions, "always interested in trade, Pilot, and still, somewhat surprised to have a query from Korval arrive in a contract ship rather than, let us say, *Dutiful Passage* and a yos'Phelium or yos'Galan. Waitley and Laughing Cat are not so well known..."

He lounged on a lightweight stool and used the table for a prop, leaving her with the only real chair in the room. That chair sat in a spot that was well lit and probably dead center of a vid-recording zone; it was only to be expected.

"I'd be surprised if Laughing Cat was known at all," she admitted, "and I am greatly pleased that you've received us. We come at the bidding of Master Trader yos'Galan who hopes to begin some cross-lane trade, and perhaps a loop through this section that would also include Surebleak."

Denobli's hair was long enough to touch the bottom of his ears, and as extravagantly styled as the woman's had been tight. Portions were colored gently with a green haze, and flared to a peak in the center of his forehead while a braid started at the top of his head and reached to midback. The hair, where it wasn't green on grey, was black as space. She noticed his hair because his hands were always in it, twirling the fringe over his ear, petting the peak into a point, adjusting the flow of the braid over his shoulders—that's what they did when he wasn't furiously questioning his handheld via keypad.

"And so, yes," he said, "and you know of course that is why I talk to you directly rather than ask you to fill out forms and come back in three Standards when you have at least a small record for your endeavor, your Laughing Cat. I must say, and you should hear me well, that of all loops or routes I have considered, in the whole of my life, which is a long one and getting longer, I doubt that I have ever considered a loop including Surebleak. Not once, not ever, until I hear it from you. Also, I see the hand of a Master Trader here, if I may say so, for a pilot wishes to fly and travel and it takes a Master to see that a pilot might fly here to Tradedesk and back to Surebleak usefully. Might you elucidate?"

Denobli leaned back, the stool supported now by

a single spot on the floor and his elbow, his hand currently twisting the hair at his other ear.

"My mission is exploratory, as you must know. Korval has recently finished a contract on Liad and the clan has removed to Surebleak. The Master Trader is seeking connections to be nurtured over a long term, which is why I have come in a ship suited to test a loop."

"I like that," he said. "How succinctly you put it. They have finished a contract. Well, the news arrives here of changes, and clearly Korval wished not to be on Liad or they would be there still, having had control of the skies from all accounts I have. Surebleak, though?"

His chin became supported for several seconds by the hand that had been adjusting his peak, and he seemed as much to be speaking to himself as to her.

"Your ship, of course, comes from Waymart, and perhaps you only know that the loop must go through Surebleak. And it is wise, for if Surebleak is to house Korval and their like, it will need the ordinaries of food and rare metals and specialties which Surebleak has not in quantity, if at all. I know this," he said, using his thumb to point at his device, "as of today, for I have never thought of Surebleak as a trading partner, as you well know. If you have spent time there, which is a strange place as I hear it, perhaps you can tell me if you think the people there will permit this Tree-and-Dragon to be rulers there? Or are you disinterested in Korval's problems, so long as you have a contract and a destination?"

There was a point here, somewhere, if she could get at it. And it seemed best not to be too evasive, nor too forthcoming.

"Most planets are strange places," she allowed, "and Surebleak maybe colder than some, but no stranger than a planet with a wet season that chases people to space..."

"It is so, planets are strange places to pilots. As young as you are, I wasn't sure that you knew yet, or at all. Some pilots never do learn and they stay close to home always. Me, I take tours here and tours there and routes when I can—but see, I grew up on a ship. But let me ask this way, if I may."

He fiddled again, this time using his left hand to twitch his braid thoughtfully, while Theo waited, practicing inner calm.

"This Surebleak," Denobli said at last, "I am to understand, was without law. Governments all kaput when the company ran out of money. Now then, they have a Korval of a sudden, rules and—"

"But no," Theo said, still trying to think her way through the question, "There was a government, or a system. Not a friendly system, but people lived and got by, and then when a strong Boss came, the system started to work better. That's when Korval went, but there was something already."

"Boss, ruler, eh?" Denobli looked her in the eye, his face serious, hands still. "Here, what I am asking is will we hurt the people if we help Korval take this place and make it Liad again?"

Theo sputtered, thinking of Lady Kareen, then of Miri and her brother Val Con...

"I don't think that's the plan—to make Surebleak into Liad," she said, slowly. "Korval's not exactly in charge—there's a council of Bosses who run...the turfs, they call them there. They've hired Korval to keep a road open, the big road for that place, though it isn't much yet, so that trade can go forth, and the spaceport can be open. Korval is two—Val Con yos'Phelium, he's one, from Korval like everyone knows, and Miri Robertson Tiazen. She's local—from Surebleak. She grew up in a turf there. And she keeps Val Con straight on stuff, too. I think they'll do *good* for the people!"

"Ho, Pilot, listen to you! First name with the delms, you say? So you have met some of these Bosses and folk of Korval, and Master Traders, too, and talked with them?"

She paused, unsure of how best to answer this question—if it was a serious question at all. Of course she was on a first-name basis with her brother, and his wife—but her relationship to the delm of Korval wasn't, she thought suddenly, this man's concern.

"I negotiated my contract with the Master Trader, Shan himself," she said composedly.

Denobli's eyebrows rose.

"Oh, did you? With the Master Trader, and you still own your ship? Why then clearly, clearly you are able."

"Thank you," she said, perhaps a bit sharp, but now that the questions were flowing, she asked, "Why did you ask? Do you think that Surebleak's people will rise up and send Korval off-planet? That contracts and delivery would be at risk?"

"Good," he said, "those are questions for me, are they not? No, I do not think the people are in danger now, for though Surebleak has not been in my thoughts very much, you assure me that Korval is where they *want* to be, and Korval left Liad, which means they did not *want* to be *there*. People should be happy."

Denobli paused, stared into nothingness for a moment it seemed, before staring at his screen, and finally looked up to Theo, whose chair had a height advantage over his position in the stool.

"Pilot, I have done the check of course, and I see you have been on a ship called *Arin's Toss*. Now understand that this interests me greatly, and makes me happy too, because I like to think that people should be happy. Arin is a good name, and there was a thinker upon a time, a trader he was, who worked hard for his people, who had that name. I will send you a copy of a document he wrote, one that was sent out to traders and pilots. While the times were angry and confused, this thinker Arin, he had an idea of how to make trading work for people—to make happy pilots and happy traders and happy people all at the same time."

He stopped, punched the keypad and sighed.

"See, and now I am informed—I see that Arin died Standards before the ship you piloted was commissioned, so clearly, it was not his own, as much as I would have liked it to be so."

He sighed again, before continuing, "This Arin I speak of, he died helping people, and he left a position of great power to help people. We, that is to say the Carresens, we read and consider this man's ideas about acceptable profits and sustainable routes and mutual growth. Understand that a ship the size of your *Bechimo* is nearly ideal for these concepts, in the right markets and locations. With or without Korval's name, Theo Waitley, your offer has possibilities."

Theo felt herself brighten: at last!

Denobli shook his head.

"I have made you happy. But, now! The sad news is that we cannot send you off today with a cargo of this or that or accept an offer to make a loop with Korval this month: our scheduling computers and our pilots are far too canny for that, and you do not claim to be a trader, or to have one with you."

Theo said to herself *inner calm,* feeling disappointment rise to darken her moment of joy.

"Instead what we shall do," said Denobli, "is we shall ask you to forward to your Master Trader a list of cargoes that we the Carresens feel might be of interest on several ends of a loop that would include Surebleak and which would not contain Liad, and we will ask about particulars of needs I have not thought of, for I have not before today considered Surebleak, as you will understand, knowing as you do that it is cold and not yet finished absorbing Korval. We shall see what it is the people of Surebleak have to offer that will make a good show out here in the Festevalya, that will make people happy. And maybe we can deal, Laughing Cat and Korval and Carresens. So, that makes you happy again, and I am happy, too."

Denobli let her find her own way to the door, and on her way out she turned to watch it close, seeing the oversprayed indent . . . yes, there it was: *Nubella Run. Happy.*

Happy was something she hadn't felt in a while, but that coincidence, as with the coincidence of Arin the thinker and *Arin's Toss,* started her toward that mood. The waiting room was empty on her way out, she'd seen that, and when she stepped through the gravity change and into the larger area of Festevalya, the crowds were thinner and more subdued. It was hard for her to remember that Tradedesk was closer to a two-shift on and one off operation than the true All Open she had seen at some stations.

Her interview with Denobli had taken the better part of an hour, but she had told Clarence and *Bechimo* that she might be gone for two, and would call if it seemed that she would be longer still. Some shopping, that might be fun. Some scouting, maybe, for trade goods for Ynsolt'i, though the Festevalya was perhaps not the best hunting grounds for—

Before her was a booth hung all around with bright scarves and colored smoke. Theo smiled, stepped forward—and felt her smile grow wider as she saw that the smoke was more scarves. She could see Kamele wearing one...she could almost see herself wearing one...

A head popped out from around the back of the booth, followed by a tall thin man with a red face and a bright blue scarf wound casually around his neck.

"Good shift to you, Pilot. Like to try a scarf? I'm having a special, in honor of the Carresens being in, you know."

NINETEEN

· · · · · · · · · · · · · · · · ·

Tradedesk

BECHIMO COULD RECALL—LITERALLY, PULL THE FILES
and review them—events that had occurred before
he was aware. He gathered that humans did no such
thing, though the *dramliz* were said to do many things
which gave him to believe, upon study, that they might
avail themselves of the same subetheric channels that
he utilized in his communications with the Others.

He had, too, the memories of the days during which
he was becoming aware. They were odd memories,
some unintelligible due to over calculation, some
because he had overwhelmed sub-units in his eagerness to understand everything.

As so often happened when he thought of his
becoming, Joyita came to mind.

The Builders had been input, keyed in stone, as he
thought of it now, having read the whimsy of fictions and
heard the speeches of many humans through recordings
and videos. But Joyita, he had *learned*.

The earliest usable memory of Joyita had seen the
other Builders discussing engine alignments and fueling

issues: *Bechimo* could recall that file, and know it as reviewing a file, which was different than the experience of Jermone Joyita.

Uncle himself had been there, and...he had been becoming alert in stages, he *Bechimo*, aware that something should be happening.

"Ah, Joyita, you are timely. I have, while waiting, powered up all of the sensors in the cortical complex; it appears that the units are redundantly functional, and the self-checks are complete. At your request, we have not fully activated the Volitional Aspects Analysis System, nor have we performed the full sub-unit consolidation and integration. I believe you wished to have some time to go over the power and data flows."

"That is so, Uncle, that is so. Am I to understand that *Bechimo* is elsewise fully installed, that there are no missing units, sensors, connectors, other than the subetheric timing and external communications core? In essence, *Bechimo* is here?"

The man caught in the file was quiet, and lacking the forcefulness evident in Uncle; too, he seemed not to inspire forcefulness in Uncle. His motions were smooth, and yet—as *Bechimo* perceived now—perhaps lacking the militant stance trained fighters often assumed. The *here* indicated in the question was, in effect, the whole of the flight deck floor to overhead, wall to wall, screens and acceleration couches.

"Such a moment of philosophy, Mentor. The where of self mocks us all, does it not?"

"I think the mocking, I think that requires intent, Uncle. Truth is—for success—mocking requires acceptance."

Joyita's voice was less sharp-edged than those of the

Builders besides Uncle. *Bechimo* now could identify the burr and half-tongued habits of the Wikesworlds; at the time of recording, his vocabulary was yet involved in phonemic transliterations, and thus slower on the uptake.

"Indeed, and thus someone like you for this stage, Mentor, rather than someone like me. We had been testing other systems earlier, but here, on Screen Six, the graphs and charts and the flows. Jermone Joyita, *this* is *Bechimo*, your student."

The man bowed lightly to Uncle—Uncle, now a Builder, had been imprinted—and bowed also to Screen Six.

"*Bechimo*," said Joyita, "soon enough we shall converse. I look forward to this, and we shall have decisions, you and I, and discussions, and even, with some luck, disagreements and disengagements."

Then, he turned to Uncle, did Joyita, and bowed what *Bechimo* now knew was a bow related to the oldest Liaden style, tainted with the left-leaning habit of the Wikes. There were rings on one hand, a leftover from a fashion that was a leftover from a necessity all but forgot.

"My trip was well, Uncle, though I am sure you know that, or you would have asked, and I'm told the prepay was well-arrived. As to other arrangements, one of your people has my bag and is taking it to my room; I'm promised everything on the ship is functional, bath to butterkeeper, all but the main drive, the weapons, and the secrets. We shall discuss and test, you and I, the cutouts and such ahead of time, several times, across several days, and if you will, we shall discuss other things as may be required.

"Now, how, from this board, shall I control the information? The controls..."

"Yes, of course. We do have *Bechimo* accepting voice commands—those modules are fully functional. Should you prefer, you may utilize the keypad; it emerges should you touch the recess here.

"Also, if I may say so, Mentor, the Wikes have not seen me for some time, nor I any of them, and lacking smartstrands and loolaws, I am less up-to-date on the manners current than I might be. If your trip requires discussion, please bring it forth."

"Oh calm, you and me, Uncle. We share fascinations and ought be pleased enough of that. Now hear me with this: Your fees are good, as you know, but it is the purpose of this I admire—I was much in favor of Arin and his goals, and pleased to see someone moving on even if his son's been set to another orbit. I am not easy with the Scouts and I'm not easy with the loopers running to easy short money 'stead of family. So here I am, looking to talk with someone new."

· · · ·✷· · · ·

The scarf vendor had not only been running a special, he'd been informative. Theo soon had in hand a neatly sealed packet containing the two scarves she had been going to buy—"Samples," he said with a wink. "You bein' from the trade-side an' all."—while his card reposed in an inner pocket, with a datakey bearing the "company catalog."

"Retail, wholesale, Festevalya-sale prices," he told her. "Lookin' to find that wider market. Lot of us here lookin' for that."

Theo frowned at him.

"I thought the Carresens run the Festevalya."

"They do, they do! But this ain't like a full-bore Carresens—that happens down to Vincza. A full-bore Carresens, that's everything off all the ships, and Carresens traders on the ground talking, selling, buying." He smiled, wistfully. "A sight to see, let me tell you, Pilot, and worth you timing it next trip to hit system 'fore the rainy season sets in.

"But anywho, here at the Festevalya, there's Carresens wares, sure enough, and like you said, they run the thing—but there's us, too, up from Vincza and Chustling—the ones of us who passed the mustard and got accepted for a booth. We're here for the liners, see? When the rainy season's over, we'll all go home, and start workin' for next rainy season. This is my third Festevalya, and I got a backlog of scarves, scarves being pretty easy to make, once you get the hang of it. Some of my friends, here"—he jerked his head—"they work themselfs to a nubbin just puttin' together enough stock for the rainy season. Some others of us, we got back-stock, which it'd sure be nice to get working."

Theo looked at him; she looked at the Festevalya. She looked back to the boothkeeper—Charn Duxbury, according to himself.

"Could you give me an . . . introduction to those people with back-stock?" she asked.

"Sure can." From his grin, she could tell she'd asked the right question. "Just let me put up the Be Back Soon sign."

· · · ·❖· · · ·

The man named Uncle stood in the comfortable dimness of the healing chamber, contemplating the unit, and the play of lights along its surface.

He had been here for some time—rather longer than the machine's message warranted.

Simply put, it was the determination of the medical unit that the patient in its care had reached an end of healing.

Not that the patient was *dead*—nothing so dire as that. Only that he had been damaged too badly, and tarried too long in the shadows. All the arts at the command of a very sophisticated device was not enough to seduce him back to perfect health.

Uncle suspected, strongly, that the man reposing in what health had been restored to him would not care to spend the remainder of his days crippled and dependent upon devices to perform certain bodily functions for him.

He might, indeed, wake him, and put the question, for certainty's sake.

Or he might simply give the machine leave to withdraw its support, send a letter of condolence to Korval with the body, and turn his attention to other, increasingly pressing, matters.

Life and death were conditions to which he was well accustomed. He had himself been reborn more times than he could enumerate, absent a check of the records. And, of course, in order to be reborn, one must first die.

It was that thought which had caught him, and from which this abstracted reverie arose.

He shook himself at last, but he neither departed, nor did he extend a hand to the control panel.

Rather, he crossed the small room and pulled open

a locker. Hung neatly inside were the pilot's leathers, cleaned and mended, his boots, likewise, sitting on the floor below. On the shelf above, a small transparent box held such things as had been in various pockets—and two seed pods.

The Uncle opened the box and removed the seed pods.

He had never heard that Korval's Tree was prescient, but that was perhaps something not easily determined, even by those who had nurtured it and knew it best. It was certainly probable that the Tree, like everything else that came into its orbit, had been tainted with Korval's Luck.

Two seed pods. One of them for a woman long years dead, as the man in the healing unit counted such things. The other intended for that same man, yet unripe at the time of need.

And yet . . . Had he understood the timing, or the need against which these had been designed?

Two pods.

Two.

Uncle was not a superstitious man. He was not, so he firmly believed, a spiritual man.

He was, however, a practical man, and a bit of a gambler, too.

One did not, so his gambler's instincts told him, bet against Korval's Tree.

Another step brought him to the comm. He pressed a button.

"Dulsey, help me prepare the rebirthing units.

"Both of them."

· · · ✳ · · ·

"Trade samples" from six different vendors in hand, pockets full of cards and datakeys, Theo reached the elevator just as the door slid aside and a tall gaggle of deep blue and silver uniforms stepped out, talking noisily among themselves, and careless of anything not in their orbit.

Theo danced to one side to avoid a man with sun-yellow hair done in careful ringlets down to his silver epaulets, and unfortunately brushed the sleeve of the dark-haired woman next to him, who gave an exclamation of annoyance.

"Watch where you step, single-ship; there are other people on—*Theo?*"

The last word was nearly a squeak, as was Theo's answering, "Asu?"

They hadn't parted in the best way, but no random passerby could have read that from Asu's engulfing hug, or in the eager way she introduced her to the surrounding uniforms as, "My old roomie, Theo Waitley! It's true what they say—every ship comes to Tradedesk!"

The uniforms had laughed more loudly, Theo thought, than the joke had been worth, and a small woman with hair that matched the silver braid on her sleeve, asked Theo what ship she was in on.

"*Bechimo*," she said, "trade-side."

"We saw that one come to dock," the yellow-haired man said, adding, "Unusual lines," which made Theo warm to him and, "Pod-pusher, of course," that inclined her toward giving a hard yank on a ringlet, just to see if it was real.

"I'm going to buy Theo a drink," Asu announced. "Pyx—order for me; I'll join you for the main course."

This plan being accepted by the uniforms, Asu bore Theo away from the Festevalya, into a quiet hall, a quiet drinkery, and a quiet corner booth, ordering Vincza Vino for them both.

"I can't stay long," Theo said, piling her packages on the seat beside her. "My Second—"

"What happened to you?" demanded Asu.

Theo blinked.

"Well, the nexus of violence thing," she said, trying to remember the last major event that she and Asu would have shared. "I had to leave campus right away, on pain of imprisonment, so I got on the shuttle to Hugglelans."

Asu nodded. "I thought that's where you'd go, even though Kara ven'Arith wouldn't say. But you *were gone!*"

Theo blinked at her. "You *looked* for me?"

"Well, *of course* I looked for you! You still had one of my markers, and I thought that—"

Comprehension dawned. It had never occurred to her to ask Asu for help getting off Eylot. Asu diamon Dayez, that was—of the luxury cruise lines.

"I didn't think," Theo confessed. "But even if I had, you'd said that I couldn't call in your marker with Diamon Lines."

"Asking me to have you placed in one of our VIP rooms for a safe trip out wouldn't have called on the Lines," Asu scolded, sounding much like Theo remembered. "I had discretion, there."

Theo shook her head and had a sip of wine. It had an . . . interesting green tang to it.

"Well, to answer—I did go to Hugglelans, and Aito didn't want me there, so he shipped me out to take second board on a Galactica courier. Did that until

I got my jacket, then took a...a private contract as a courier. First Board and Acting Captain now, on *Bechimo*, under contract with Tree-and-Dragon, exploring the possibility of setting up a loop."

She stopped, because that brought Asu up-to-date, and also because her old roomie was staring at her in apparent disbelief.

"First Class?" she asked. "Acting Captain?"

"That's right," Theo said. "Didn't want to go big-ship. You remember that, Asu."

"Mad for courier," the other woman said darkly, and sipped her wine. By the time she had emerged from behind the glass, she was smiling again.

"I'm glad you've done so well for yourself!"

"Thanks, but—look at you!" Theo waved a hand at the fancy uniform, knowing Asu would take it as admiring. "Catch me up."

"Well, I graduated, and took my place on the *Perfection*. I'm Second Class, in rotation, working toward First. Things are going very well, and I expect to get my big-ship ticket within five Standards."

She reached into her belt and, executing a flourish, offered Theo a card between the first and second fingers of her right hand. Her fingers were long and shapely, discreet rings flashed gemlight from several.

Theo took the card. The front was the same deep blue as Asu's uniform, with the Diamon Line logo in bright silver. On the back was *Asu diamon Dayez, Diamon Family Pilot*, a beam code and a box number, care of Diamon Lines.

"Thank you," she said, and lifted her chin against the feeling of being just a little grubby and unkempt. Asu had always made her feel that way.

"I'm afraid I don't have a card yet. I'm in the Guild Roster."

"Or I can certainly get you through Korval's trade offices." Asu finished her wine. "I remember when you thought that Korval was a children's story."

Theo nodded. "I've learned a lot since school," she said.

· · · · ❖ · · · ·

The so-called Ice Cream Shoppe aboard *Hoselteen* was, in Kamele's opinion, its best feature. It managed to be airy and bright in an environment that was otherwise dark and close, and it very quickly became her favorite place to work and read.

It was also . . . comforting that the serving staff quickly came to recognize her and her habits. Her arrival was greeted with smiles of apparent and genuine pleasure, and a murmured, "Coffee on the way, ma'am. Your table's all ready for you."

Such routine and recognition was pleasant, but she hadn't quite realized that the staff had become as attached to her routine as she was herself until she walked in to hear Lia exclaim sharply, "That's Professor Waitley's table, sir! Please, choose another."

Kamele felt her cheeks warm as she hurried to the place, seeing Lia and a man still standing there.

"I do beg your pardon," she said. "Lia, surely I don't own this table!"

The server looked at her. "It's where you work every day, ma'am."

"Nor would I be so churlish as to roust someone from both their usual table and their routine," the man said, turning from the table and bowing gently.

He looked up at Kamele with a smile. "Forgive me...
Professor? And, please, enjoy this pleasant corner."

He reminded her of Jen Sar, though he was a
much younger man, his hair a gentle brown, two
shades darker than his eyes. It was, Kamele thought,
the Liaden manner, the bow, the soft phrasing. She
found herself smiling even as she inclined her head.

"I could not work, having robbed you of at least
a little time to cherish the perfection of this table,"
she said. "Please, join me for tea, and a *chernubia*."

He smiled, very slightly, and returned her courtesy.
"Thank you, Professor. I will be delighted."

TWENTY

· · · · · · · · · · · · · · ·

Departing Tradedesk

THEO LEANED AGAINST THE COUNTER IN THE BREAK room, munching on a chipcookie from the two dozen Clarence had brought to the ship from Rodi, the owner of The Nook. He'd also brought away her recipe, and if he made good on his threat to never be without one of Rodi's cookies again, Theo foresaw a lot of extra periods on the walking mill. For both of them.

Clarence could even sell the cookies, if he wanted to go into baking, but he could never sell the recipe. That, he was to give away, if somebody asked, which is how Rodi had come by it herself.

It was, Theo owned, a strange arrangement, but it didn't seem to do anybody harm, and might, she thought with a half-smile, make some people happy.

Her smile faded somewhat. What they hadn't accomplished at Tradedesk was the hiring of another hand or two. And that had been simply because the Guild office, for all it was on-station, had been closed.

DOWN-CIRCUIT TO CHUSTLING, the sign on the door read. RE-OPEN STATION DAY 211.

So, if not exactly *happy*, Theo was at least content. Laughing Cat had taken on some spec cargo for Ynsolt'i, almost all of it from rainy season tenants of the Festevalya, along with a catalog key from the, she suspected, hastily formed Autumn Rains Cooperative. Laughing Cat was listed as the sole distributor of the cooperative's wares to Ynsolt'i, which was both good *and* safe. As proof of that last, even *Bechimo* had approved.

"They gamble, but not enough to harm themselves, should they lose," he said, while Joyita in Screen Six appeared to be turning catalog pages.

"It was well thought," he said, looking up and making eye contact with Theo. "This Chairman Charn Duxbury may be worthy of us."

That had made Clarence laugh, and Theo grin.

"I did not intend a joke," Joyita said, sounding curious rather than hurt.

"And so it's not funny, and too funny at the same time," Clarence said, his laugh subsiding to a grin. "There'd be those who'd think that a known nexus of violence and a retired Juntava should be the ones worrying about being worthy."

Joyita's stern face relaxed into a smile. "Such people are uninformed," he stated, dismissing the matter.

"The pilots are off-duty," Theo announced, still smiling as she rose and danced three or four steps, just to relish the feel of the movements. "The shift's yours, Joyita."

"Yes, Pilot. I anticipate an easy and unexciting glide to the Jump point."

"So do we all, Chimmy," Clarence said, locking his board and coming to his feet with a stretch and a sigh. "I'm for some downtime."

The cookie finished, Theo thought that maybe Clarence had a point. A nap, to put the edge back on, so she'd be sharp when they finally found that Jump point, about seven hours out.

"Pilot, attention. Theo Waitley, attention."

The time between shuttered eyes and a full reclined sleep to open eyes, hand on light, and, "Pilot here, go ahead," was less than five seconds.

"Pilot," Joyita said, "not covered under General Operating Procedures—arrival of an all-call captain's pinbeam with Pilots Guild source-stamp and a level of urgent."

"Right there."

She snatched up her robe and ran for the Heart, throwing herself into her chair, and slapping first board live.

Joyita glanced up as she hit the chair, then turned his attention to what must surely be his own board.

"Waitley in," she said.

An urgent pinbeam? she thought. The sheer energy cost of the things made them rare, and automatically urgent! She'd only begun to think of them as at all usual when she was working for Crystal Energy Consultants, to whom money seemed rarely an issue. She couldn't recall getting a single pinbeam in all her time aboard *Primadonna*.

"Authorize, please, Pilot," Joyita murmured.

Theo swallowed a cuss word, and pressed her finger onto the plate. Words immediately began to flow across the comm screen.

*Pilots Guild Urgent Advisory Relay, Pilots in Peril.
Pilots Guild Urgent Advisory Relay. Pilots in Peril.
Pilots Guild Urgent Advisory Relay, Pilots in Peril.*

Triple repeat, she thought, in case it was getting translated through voice translator—and then started on the text itself:

Urgent advisory: Armed Security Emergency, Orbital Trading Station Codrescu, planetpoint Eylot NA1, one hundred forty-five minute equatorial, standard ranging and frequencies, Armed Security Emergency . . .

"Hardcopy this," she snapped as she read on, her stomach dropping and the last vestige of sleep evaporating.

. . . Orbital Trading Station Codrescu, planetpoint Eylot NA1, two hundred ninety permanent residents, multi-hundred passengers and crew of client ships, four docked local system ships, three remaining docked deepspace ships. Station Ops have ceded command to Guild Master Peltzer. Peltzer requesting immediate evacuation assistance under armed threat, repeat armed threat. Warning shots fired, local damage, Pilots in Peril.

Peltzer! She knew that name, and though she had only been there once she felt like she knew *the place;* she had friends there—people she knew—Arndy somebody, and Bringo, and . . .

Kara! Kara worked on Codrescu now!

"Joyita, rouse Clarence."

The sound of rapid steps behind her. "Don't bother, Chimmy."

Clarence flung himself into his seat, eying the message as he pulled webbing tight. Theo nodded.

"*Bechimo,* plot us the fastest course to the Eylot

System, direct if possible. Triple check all new cargo for run readiness."

"Pilot, I—"

"Orders," she said flatly.

"Second live," Clarence announced, followed by, "Damn fools."

"Update?" he asked.

Theo shook her head. "Just in. *Bechimo*? You have those coords?"

"Pilot, good numbers take time and thought—"

"Never mind," she said flatly. "I'll do it."

She heard Clarence's breath catch—

"Use these numbers and tell me how long before we're up to Jump potential, please."

She closed her eyes, visualizing the lacework that was Eylot's system, seeing the big station, and little Codrescu, the working station. She took a breath, and began to read the numbers off.

Silence attended her when she came to a stop. Theo opened her eyes.

"Opinions, crew?"

Joyita was looking...elsewhere, a tight smile on his lips. Clarence was minding his board.

"Your numbers are incomplete, Pilot," *Bechimo* stated. "Lacking the decimals on the fifth will mean a drift..."

"Second seat first!"

Clarence nodded, maybe to himself, his eyes on his readouts and his smile as small and tight as Joyita's.

"Guild matter, Pilot. We're not scheduled, exactly— nobody's really expecting us at any particular place, anywhen. It's your call, I'm guessing, though I allow pilots-in-peril isn't a good thing to hear. Can't tell what's up, really, without a full report. We could be flying right into a firefight!"

"The coords I've given are for an eighteen-light-minute-out orbit, high off the ecliptic. It's a resonant spot—we can hang there quiet. I expect *Bechimo* can recognize the orbit."

There was no response.

"That's a good spot, *Bechimo*, isn't it?" Theo prodded. "*Safe?*"

"The Eylot System is unbalanced politically, Pilot, as you well know. The Pilots Guild identifies it as a problem zone. In such a place there are no 'safe' orbits. There is no reason for us to go to Eylot System. We have Ynsolt'i filed."

Theo took a deep breath.

"We have a pilots-in-peril situation," she said, letting her sense of inner calm color her voice. "You know how important pilots are. If we—if Clarence and I were in peril, we'd want our fellow pilots to help us. As for system instability—you've used these coords as stand-off position, yourself. Is it unacceptably dangerous or does the location still have merit for surveillance and scouting?"

From the corner of her eye, she saw Screen Six flicker; Joyita's image vanished, replaced by a bland wash of blue.

"Less Pilot, the Over Pilot is overestimating the relevance of this situation to our mission. You are more than an adequate pilot, and have had long years of experience. Surely you can see that rushing—"

Clarence made a *fuffing* noise under his breath, or perhaps said a word in some heat, and signed a quick *get to it!*

"Like Pilot Theo says, if I sent a help-me hail to all of space, it'd be because I needed help—or thought it was too late. Might be you don't know that about pilots. Sometimes what they gotta do is let somebody else know what happened, as a warning, and maybe to be sure it don't happen again. Now, this ain't one pilot, this is a bunch of 'em, and civilians too, and time's wasting. I'm inclining to Theo's view: best thing to do is go and see what's needed, assuming fuel and resources aren't an issue."

"Ship's complement has been heard," Theo said, hearing the snap in her own voice. "Pilot is taking a ten-minute analysis break; ship will inform me of other outgoing traffic, radio, ship, or otherwise."

"No chatter here to speak of," Clarence pointed out, "just some local broadcast stations, telemetry from weather satellites, and the air center's noise—plenty of aircraft going hither and yon."

"Are those coords confirmed as locked, *Bechimo*? Please do me the favor of making sure Clarence's figures match mine."

There was, for a few moment, only the sound of breathing—Theo's, louder in her ears than she liked, and more ragged and urgent in her tension; Clarence's, smooth and quiet, barely discernible for all that he sat hardly an arm's length away, and *Bechimo*'s, insofar as his breathing was the breath of the ship entire: fans, blowers, filters, the hum and rumble that meant everything was good—all systems up, and running.

"Less Pilot's figures match your figures, Pilot. My figures match both pilots; I have entered them into the destination output, Pilot. We reach the Jump point in one hour point three-three minutes."

"Excellent." She frowned at her screens.

The view of Tradedesk was . . . unchanged.

"Why aren't they moving?" she murmured.

"Lot of 'em are scheduled elsewhere and the company won't take kindly to a loss o'bidness while the captain hares off on some errand of her own."

"But, pilots-in-peril could mean—"

"Anything," Clarence cut in ruthlessly. "And most will go about the usual, and let somebody else deal. That's the way of it most times, lassie." He threw her a half-grin.

"Yourself, you come from meddling stock, if you'll not mind my saying it. Most of us—even pilots—tend toward *Bechimo's* view."

Theo frowned, looked at the countdown to Jump, and took a decision.

She opened a comm line, and tapped in the code listed on the back of Asu's card.

"Yes, Communications says the Guild all-call was received." Asu's voice held that note of exaggerated patience that meant she was really very annoyed and would rather be doing something else.

"Will the *Perfection* be responding?" Theo asked, who had never much cared when Asu was annoyed.

"Will the— Theo, we're a cruise ship! We have passengers!"

"Put them off at the station," Theo said. "There are pilots and civilians in peril. *Bechimo* can't handle an entire evacuation!"

"No one's asking you to handle an entire evacuation," Asu said. "Theo, that message went out to All Captains. No one's asking *you personally* to do *any*thing. Someone else will answer—someone with more experience. Time. Discretion. It's not your responsibility."

"Yes, it is. It's the responsibility of pilots to respond to pilots-in-peril," Theo said.

"Theo, can we end this circular conversation? I'm not captain, but I very much doubt that a Diamon Ship of the Line will put off her passengers in order to participate in some *possible* evacuation at—"

"I call in my marker," Theo interrupted. "You owe me."

"I don't owe you a cruise ship! You know that marker was personal."

Theo bit her lip, aware of Clarence's eyes upon her.

"Right. Well, I had to try. Thanks, Asu. Waitley out."

She cut the connection, closed her eyes and mentally danced a few steps of a calming dance.

Pilots-in-peril, she thought, remembering that Rig Tranza had drilled her on Hugglelans' policies, adding that such things were, "Rare, Theo, but that's why we gotta go over the policies. We know all about the usual, but it's the rare calls that'll bite you on the nose."

Hugglelans' policy had a proximity condition built into it—no sense Jumping a ship to the other side of the galaxy to help out in an emergency that would have likely worked itself out before best possible time of arrival.

Eylot fell within the proximity range established by Hugglelans, which for the purposes of this particular emergency, she was taking as a reasonable guide for *Bechimo*'s actions.

Hugglelans' policy stated that, if more than one Hugglelans ship was in proximity, the ship(s) with the least time-sensitive cargo were to answer the call, after clearing with Hugglelans Galactica home office.

Hugglelans had required reports at intervals, and a return to service within a range of deadlines. Pilots failing to report or to return the ship to service within the proper deadline would be considered pirates to be pursued and prosecuted to the full extent of Guild law.

That all checked: *Bechimo* was free, if not obligated, to answer the call. At least, according to Hugglelans regs.

She was, Theo admitted, not thrilled about returning to Eylot space. On the other hand, she wasn't going to Eylot itself; she was a certified Guild Pilot with a clean record, answering a legitimate pilots-in-peril.

There really wasn't anything they could do to her. Even supposing they were inclined, in the midst of an emergency.

Right, then.

Theo opened her eyes.

"Second, file change of course with Tradedesk, open band, all channels. *Bechimo* for Eylot in response to pilots-in-peril. End."

TWENTY-ONE

· ·

Codrescu Station

PELTZER WAS ASLEEP.

The Guild-Master-turned-station-master had been
near out on his feet for over a station-day, and in the
cramped inner office that was the Guild Hall's control
center, having him asleep meant Arndy Slayn could
plan on his own relief.

In the meanwhile he'd sent for Qaichi Bringo—Chief
Tugwhomper and unofficial security consultant—so the
room would have coverage in case *he* dozed.

Peltzer's nap was taking place in his usual working
chair—an actual acceleration couch upright in front of
his control-board-like desk, as if he were still actively
flying—and he slept with no snore, nor tremor, the old
norbear, Hevelin, napping companionably against his leg.

The sounds in the room were normal, other than
an extremely low level and filtered audio feed letting
him know the warn-aways were in operation and the
occasional feed of something that the station controllers thought odd. The propaganda broadcasts were

not in the flow, nor, alas, was the usual chatter. Only oddities were fed through to Control.

Codrescu's ordinary systems were still being run from the station control room, with the three regular resident staffers who oversaw facilities maintaining that important business. The station master himself was gone—took the first flight out after Eylot's demands had gone from veiled to actual threats.

"I'm a contract guy, Peltzer; a facilities guy. I'm good on commerce, I'm good on basic security. This—I'm not good for! Your people are most at risk, and I don't have call-on staff or weapons enough to resist an invasive boarding, nor is it in my job description! I'm invoking my flight-out contract, and I'm asking you to take over operation until this matter is resolved. I'll be on-world."

Peltzer had quoted chapter and page number out of more regulation manuals than Slayn could handily remember—at least two of which he suspected the Guild Master had made up on the spot. All for nothing; the station master was going, that was plain, and somebody had to be in charge.

Slayn had witnessed this touching moment of what Liadens might see as a classic *melant'i* play: by abandoning the station, the station master could both save himself and give the Guild room to work. With the associate station master leaving as well, that left hired help to man the place. Hired help and the Pilots Guild. At that moment Arndy Slayn, First Class Pilot, had gone from Guild technical assistant to Acting Station Master. The self-defense options for the entire station now lay at his command, on the assumption that a Guild official was more responsible than the hired station crew.

With a murble of intent, Hevelin rose from his recline against Peltzer's leg and stared thoughtfully at the 3D map of nearspace projected on the main screen. Slayn was unsure of the depth of the norbear's understanding of the current situation. Certainly the old guy knew times were exceptional—he *was* old, and he had a lot of memories of *usual* to take measure against. For anything else—well, that was the whole thing with norbears, wasn't it? You just didn't know what they knew—you just knew they knew *something*.

Hevelin, now...he was peering up at the screens like he could make sense of the motion, the tags—letters and numbers indicating destinations or launch points—the lines of established orbits...And who was Arndy Slayn to say he couldn't?

"Murble drow drow!" Hevelin said, which was pretty talky for him. He looked over his shoulder at Slayn, then back to the screen, which wasn't all that different now than it'd been an hour before, other than that Eylot's *other* station—the big station—was about to go below horizon, taking its cloud of ardent and trigger-happy defenders with it.

"I'm sure!" Slayn said conversationally to Hevelin, on the theory that he wouldn't fall asleep while actively talking. "Let's take another look."

The refresh didn't bring up anything new: Eylot's so-called defense forces were in a jumble of orbits, some nearly skimming the atmosphere at perigee, some as near circular as could be below Codrescu's well-known path, some more clustered in vague orbits designed, he supposed, to defend the large station Eylot had spent decades building to replace the independent but Guild-certified station Slayn sat in.

Codrescu, in theory, operated within a bubble of its own space—within that bubble it acted as traffic command and more, able to order ships and people out, and control the conditions in which those ships operated. Eylot's contention that Codrescu was there "without proper planetary permission," and thus had no right to control flight or people within those boundaries was the cause of the blockade...and the "mistake" that had seen a local space taxi collide with an Eylot-bound warship, with severe injuries to the pilot and three passengers on-board, was therefore Codrescu's error.

There was also the fact of other local operators who had gone quiet and, for all intents, missing. That gnawed at him—but there wasn't any way to ask for a roll call without potentially endangering the very folks who he wanted to check up on.

The problem was, as far as Slayn was concerned, that the blockade of Codrescu was illegal, immoral, and dangerous. The threats to annex the station were bad enough, but ongoing legal wrangling taking place between the Eylot planetary authorities and all the lawyers, attorneys, PR agencies, and lobbyists the Guild could arrange for long-distance, were all aimed at suppressing a stated goal of the natives: taking over the Guild office and forbidding pilots without "locally approved licenses" from operating anywhere in the system. They'd also thrown out, perhaps as a gambit, a request for the records of all the pilots who'd visited the station for the past seven Standards—claiming that the planet ought to be paid a fee for all the pilots who'd docked with or set foot on Codrescu in that period.

The icing on the donut, like his Aunt Chirly used to say, was the noisy interception—after launch!—of what was effectively an oversized unarmed delivery van. *That* had caused panic, among the station's semicommuting locals, and the resident population, not to mention the uproar from the witnessing pilots and traffic crew.

Made no difference to Eylot. In their view, they'd intercepted and forced to ground a dangerous threat to planetary security. That this dire threat to security had only been doing what it'd been doing every third day for the last couple dozen Standards—taking comestibles and other regular expendables up to the station, and returning with empties, bread cases, and other recyclables—was immaterial.

And now the ship-and-crew were impounded. The crew faced charges of security evasion, smuggling, and fomenting revolution.

And food delivery to Codrescu had stopped.

That was the threat, not the inept, comedy-revue blockade. If Eylot wanted Codrescu, all it had to do was starve 'em into submission.

Into surrender.

Looking at the display, Slayn muttered, recognizing Anlingdin Academy's training shuttle by the familiar pink-and-purple flashing symbol meant to warn pilots that, of all the vehicles in near orbit, *this* one was the most likely to do something dangerous, to make an error of judgment. Except that, as far as he knew, there were no longer trainees manning it in pursuit of experience and licenses, but regular Eylot Air Defense Forces, watching Codrescu, the potential spot of alien contagion and invasion, that had only been peacefully orbiting the planet for two hundred-odd Standards.

Slayn shook his head when he saw the orbital elements attached to it. Another one of those twelve-orbits and down runs, he guessed, being sold to the dirtsiders as guarding against infection from space. On several of those orbits the shuttle would come close enough to set off approach alarms, the while spying on people who weren't doing anything but trying to figure out how to get out without risking cannon fire.

Cannon fire was also a possibility from the constantly changing run of strike-fighters flying up from the surface. They were certainly flying often enough to get their operations badges and duty ribbons, and Codrescu's orbit was well within their day and a half operating schedule. All to protect against the station's supposed danger as a forward operating base for someone unnamed.

Codrescu was hardly the place to launch an invasion from, not when even school children with mild-powered video and atmosphere-correcting lenses could image the open storage yards, not when—ah, he was raising his tension uselessly.

The grizzle-faced norbear suddenly removed his attention from the screen and headed toward the sealed hall door, waiting a cautious distance to the left as it slid open, revealing the silhouette of an armed guard in the outer office, and another man—Qaichi Bringo, himself—stepping through.

"Dinner's here!"

True to his word, dinner *was* here, including a bundle of freshly stripped green leaves for the norbear—who respectfully took his meal and reclined against Peltzer's sleeping foot to eat—and a sealed hotbox for Peltzer when he woke.

Slayn took his own meal, pleased to see that it was a pilot's portion: sufficient, but not extravagant.

And that, of course, got him to worrying all over again.

"How's the mood, out and about?" he asked Bringo, who had taken a seat at the smaller screens off to the left of Peltzer's desk.

Bringo's fingers moved: *air fine food tight patience less*.

"Got some mutters 'mong the docks of pullin' free and gettin' gone," he amplified. "Givin' the nix to that, as can. Food..."

Food. Slayn nodded. Given that most of the locals had a few weeks' worth of stockpile here and there, and the station's own backlog was good for a few days for the regulars, the issue was what would happen if one—or more!—of the ships at dock decided to run for it, dumping their passengers or redundant crew onto the station's supply.

Slayn shook his head as he turned over the chances, hands running to the keypad. His fingers vicariously extended the troubles to eight days, sixteen, twenty-four...

Twenty-six...

If everything stayed as was, the only thing Eylot had to do, was wait twenty-six local days, and then just a little longer.

Slayn stared at the 3D again. They had seven major docks filled, three open. Close in, he saw motion that were the hangers-on, the unofficial population of yard-runners, plegics, guesters, drifters, and the like, wholly dependent on the station, and not likely to move elsewhere. If they lost the big ships...

"Got numbers?" Bringo asked, hands forming *query*—and freezing in mid sign.

"What?" demanded Slayn, following the other man's stare up into the 3D.

Bringo's fingers made the null sign sometimes used for *wait* . . .

Ghost!

Slayn saw it in the same instant he took in Bringo's sign, and slapped the comm key.

"Can you tell me what we've got at—"

"We see it, Guild," Ops cut him off. "We see it. Looks an awful lot like a ghost to us. Been there a few minutes when we checked back. We got nothin' in the way of Jump glare. Odd orbit, and main comp reminds there's been an anomaly at those coords before. Something that came and went, apparently. I'm ordering the archive up to screens as soon as we get a good telescopic look at today's edition. Likely, we don't have Eylot's secret weapon—"

"Avert on secret weapon!" Slayn shook his head, looking back to the 3D. The ghost was still there.

"Got that archive info," Ops told him, and here came the dates and times flowing nice and orderly down his work screen.

Yes, it looked like it was the same ghost. No, Codrescu had never gotten a signal from it, and outside of one brief period there had been no other sightings. That didn't compute in terms of orbital elements. So, it wasn't an asteroid or a comet; not a lost probe or known survey unit. And if it had been orbiting ever since the last sighting, it wouldn't be where it was now.

So that meant—what? It had gone away and come back again, whatever it—

"Feed for you, your number three," Ops said quietly in his ear, "Better make it priority with a screen!"

"Got it," Slayn said before he touched the stud, sending the feed from the Ops camera to the main screen.

He frowned and upped the magnification. There was some uncommon motion going on inside the nearby local craft swarm.

IDs were on the move, too. *Goma Chang*'s silhouette in short order was tagged as *Strakin*, *Lefevbre's Lounge*, *Odbert*, and *Illichin*. Since *Lefevbre's Lounge* was in fact permanently moored to the second oldest transfer port on the station, it looked like someone had spent a good bit of goodwill, or a good bit of cash, or both, arranging for all this sudden confusion.

Slayn raised the volume of the feed slightly, and turned to wake Peltzer. Bringo was already there, saying, "Sorry on this—there was a rumor *Chang* was going to try something, but I figured we all had time to eat..."

Now *Beeslady* held the torch as the trader, and a more mismatched set of manned orbiting objects you couldn't find, with *Beeslady*, a rebuilt local scooter-taxi mated to an old EVA sleep-shelter, not massing even the radar-cone equivalent of a twenty-pod tradeship like *Goma Chang*.

"Codrescu Station, *Goma Chang* Exec here. We have filed our flight plan via hardcopy, via courier; please reference those plans before query."

The now ordinary messages of warning and threat from the Eylot blockade gave way to specific threats aimed at ships leaving, beginning to warn *Goma Chang* by name.

"*Goma Chang*," Peltzer said, waking his own boards and microphone; "you are endangering the station with this; please return to berth. This is Guild Authority, you are endangering the whole station."

Slayn snapped on his own mic. "Alert, full alert. Hatches and doors sealed and checked. Meteor shields to full collision power, and all outships in to berth as you please. Roll call by touch as you arrive."

The IDs on screen moved again, more or less in sync. *Beeslady* was briefly *Odbert*, *Odbert* was the *Lounge*, the *Lounge* became *Goma Chang*, and *Beeslady* was herself again, though briefly, before a startling maneuver in which it charged the accelerating *Chang* and switched ID yet again.

Both *Chang* and *Beeslady* were drawing well out of the basic bubble of Codrescu's space and whatever small service the station's meteor shields might offer.

"Codrescu, your request is noted; you'll find our course filed in the material we've sent by courier. We're rescuing our schedule, tell the Guild, but we're taking with us the request for assistance. We are no longer Codrescu's traffic. *Goma Chang* out."

That last was so. Slayn could see it, and so could Peltzer and Bringo—and so could, apparently, *Beeslady*, which spent fuel like mad and traded back its own ID, letting the tradeship boost away at an impressive rate.

The image of *Goma Chang* went slightly off-color as her shields went full up—fine for energy weapons of many kinds—with the meteor shields no doubt thrown in for good measure...

"They going to make it, are they?"

Bringo stared at the busy screen, nodding, half talking to himself as he did the math...

"Good pilot and navigator there—found the timing just right, and got some coverage from the yard crew. Make it a lot harder for anybody else to do again . . ."

Peltzer was watching the screen grimly—they were all watching, and they all saw a small orange fuzz from the direction of the closest of Eylot's strike-fighters.

"They've launched something, hoping for a wildshot," Peltzer said. "As near as I can see, nothing closing in here, but there's no telling that everything's reflective. Can we get visuals on that shot swarm?" he asked Ops. "Looks like us and the yards ought to be fine . . ."

Peltzer shook his head, and reached for the hotbox—pilot's protocol: Eat while the action's low. He patted his ankle, letting Hevelin know the spot was available for leaning, then flicked *attention!* off the end of his fingers.

"Your go, Arndy," he said, stifling a yawn. "I'm on low."

Bringo'd been quiet, watching the shot swarm, using the station's computers as well as head-figuring. Arndy went back to the food calcs. They'd need to be—

"Ghost!" Station Ops snapped. "Weapons live; shields up."

Slayn spun from his keypad. Bringo was on his feet; Peltzer was leaning forward in his chair, but not enough to disturb Hevelin, who had gone to sleep.

There it was on the 3D display, sitting well within Codrescu's defenses—a silent, pod-carrying ship, orienting itself to—

Comm lit.

"Station Codrescu, independent tradeship *Bechimo* answering pilots-in-peril call. We are armed and up, please respond, are you there? *Bechimo* requesting live response, we are armed and up. Pilot Theo Waitley and crew await response."

Slayn felt his mouth open, but Bringo beat him to it.

"The lady's dangerous, hey? Someone best answer her quick!"

Hevelin was climbing Peltzer, bright and cheerful, happily insisting, *"Murble drow drow! Murble drow drow!"*

"Mine," Slayn said into his mic. "I'll take the comm, now."

TWENTY-TWO

· ·

Codrescu Station

"OH."

Clarence took in his board, checked the mirror board, and whistled very softly.

"That was very smooth, *Bechimo*."

"Orienting," said *Bechimo*. "Collecting feed sources, applying noise filters, starting recording, Screen One image enhancement. Thank you, Less Pilot."

For her part, Theo muttered, "Weapons checks engaged."

Other than the mere fact of arriving, *Bechimo* was doing his very best not to disturb the ether. Running lights were off; none of the usual active IDs were on, not the Cat, not the ship's Guild numbers, not the simple mass-in-transit warnings, not the Tree-and-Dragon. There was some shipside activity going on; it came to Theo as a a vibration through the soles of her solidly placed feet, and echoed in her head as a very slight change in balance.

"Establishing orbit," *Bechimo* stated. "Acquiring

Eylot planetary images, seventeen point nine seven light-minutes old."

"Second Board, we've got full capacity and full run of arms available. Nothing tagged as target as yet. We'll take voice feeds anytime now, *Bechimo*. You know we're most interested in Codrescu, right? You'll have the common frequencies on file, I'm sure, and I need to know about ships-in-grip and the like."

"Pilot, I am analyzing..."

"Must be some live stuff, Ship; the pilots wil help with the analysis. I'll take Codrescu, give Clarence near orbit stuff. Now."

The lines came live with chatter, mixed 'round several low-level warn-aways: "Due to dock congestion, Codrescu Station requests all inbound ships file flight plans and wait for approval before setting intersecting course," said one. Another—on the local frequencies—was simpler: "No shuttles to Eylot available at this time. No shuttles to Eylot available at this time. No shuttles..."

"Can you break out the sidebands?" Theo requested, "I particularly want to hear the oh-five through oh-nine lines."

Clarence glanced at her, and she finger-flashed *local hailing and yard work.*

Yard work was a catchall for anyone in nearby space who wasn't interested in docking but was doing something—the usual was shifting cargo, inspecting a bad fitting, moving between ships and station in a runabout—but Theo expected that some might be acting as mini-couriers...

"We have had an extremely busy radar field, Pilot," Joyita murmured from Screen Six. "There are a number of odd sidebands and some possible virtual phasing. I am not sure that it is of consequence or if it is even purposeful; the traffic around Eylot is considerable in comparison to the last time we were in this region."

"Thank you, Joyita. Highest magnification on that video, can you? Feel free to tag ships you've got firm IDs on."

Infobars blossomed on the screens, Codrescu in blue letters, ships docked or grappled to the station in white; yellow for the close traffic and work tugs; Eylot's forces in red. There were . . . a lot of reds and, seeming associated with the reds, greens . . .

"Green tags are for vessels associated with your Academy, Pilot, so in these cases red and green are those I am automatically highlighting, with red first in targeting computations which differ from mere orbital element compilations on other objects. Pinks are known satellites. If I determine that any of the non-red forces and objects, ships or satellites are in fact armed and at the command of Eylot active forces I will change those to red."

Theo nodded, throat constricting.

"Yes, do that," she said, accepting the fact that she might easily be targeting former classmates or instructors.

Theo looked up at the screen, trying to see past the wash of red, to assess—

"Something's not right!" she snapped. "I just saw IDs change!"

"Yes, Pilot," Joyita murmured. "There is movement close by Codrescu. I believe that several vessels may be rearranging themselves."

"These two," he said, marking them in a kind of purple fog, "are mismatched entirely. The smaller is a local workcraft which is in the databases from a previous visit in-system. The small vessel is not in fact *Goma Chang*—the ship whose ID it carried until a few moments ago—but *Beeslady*. It is possible that *Goma Chang* is preparing a breakaway. We have acceleration of a nature usually prohibited close to Station Codrescu."

"ALERT!" *Bechimo* shouted. "Eylot ship *Tredstone* has fired weapons!"

Clarence's comments were long and strong for all that they were barely audible. Theo punched up the volume on radio traffic, got confused noise, then Eylot yelling for ships to prepare for boarding or face weapons, and the station yelling about civilian, staff, and pilot endangerment and—

"Pilot," Joyita said, his voice frankly strained. "Thirty-seven rounds of apparent cannon fire were loosed by *Tredstone*. Some of those projectiles will intersect the course of *Goma Chang* and *Beeslady*. Codrescu Station does not appear to be under attack at this time."

Clarence's fingers moved—*do now*.

She nodded in agreement.

"*Bechimo*, please take us in. Now."

"Codrescu Station self-defense district here, Pilot Waitley, and welcome," Arndy Slayn said into his mic. "We are in a state of emergency and you have arrived in an area where ships have been fired upon without warning by planetary authorities. You are at risk."

He didn't know what else to say but did know better than to say, *you're a figment* to a ship with shields up, and that could take out the station with a bad tumble, even without ill intent.

Peltzer was talking behind him, low and steady, reraising the station alert level, hallway by hallway, ship by ship. The norbear was burbling up a storm, and Waitley was coming back at him.

"Am here in response to Guild pilots-in-peril declaration. I acknowledge statement of risk and affirm that I am a Guild-certified Jump class pilot aboard an armed ship with weapons available, operating with peaceful intent to assist with pilots-in-peril declaration. Is this declaration still in force? Please advise."

If he'd been caught napping at the advent of this apparition, Eylot's planetary defenders had been caught worse: they now leapt—noisily—into the conversation.

Radio noise got bad: radar and broadcast bands warred with sensors as reaction hit the ether.

Slayn answered, "Condition maintains, *Bechimo*," but his voice sounded garbled even in the local speakers as a burst of power flooded nearby space.

"This is Eylot Control. *Bechimo*, you are an unregistered ship with an unregistered pilot. You are subject to Eylot's martial law declaration and must immediately surrender ship, pilot, crew, and cargo to proper lawful authorities for disposition. You have violated recently promulgated traversal laws forbidding entering the twenty-light-minute protective sphere without preapproval by this office. Drop to the following neutral orbit for boarding and inspection."

The coords came then, and for a neutral orbit it looked pretty forbidding, within potential range of some of the known ground-based energy weapons as well as being sandwiched between two of the orbits occupied by recent additions to the strike-fighters.

The video feeds showed Slayn the small tradeship,

now just shy of lock-on range at the open docking Berth Eleven for a hard dock, and within moments of Connect Two if they wanted a tube. The ship rotated slowly, showing strange lines that the computer tried to ID out of archives—and not recent ones, at that. It carried pods, but otherwise there wasn't a lot of easy information to be gained from visual. No logos showed, no numbers, no shipmaker marks—a wide-back pod carrier of an odd layout.

"*Bechimo* acknowledges response, Codrescu; condition maintains. Working. Eylot Control, I am a Guild pilot on location responding to a Guild emergency request; this supersedes nonemergency operational orders. Please clear channels so I may respond to the emergency situation."

Silence on the airwaves was short-lived; during the silence Slayn caught Peltzer's signed *all regs, all regs,* and saw the norbear, formerly clinging to the senior officer, now balance himself on back legs and jump to the deck, grabbing up a food frond and staring directly at the main speakers.

"This *is* an emergency order, *Bechimo*," declared Eylot Control on an even more powerful burst of noise. "The Guild order is null and void and you are required by Eylot regulations to cease nonstandard operations or suffer consequences."

A new snap of radio frequency noise, and along the chatter-channels came a sudden raucous chorus of "Pharst!" "Damn, *that'll* do!" and "Don't bite on that!"

Slayn looked to the display, blinked and looked again.

Bechimo's shields had already been up, he knew; the normally fuzzy radiowave cocoon of interference showing clearly. Now *Bechimo*'s radar image positively glittered on the video screens, a bright hard-edged nugget of repellant force surrounding the ship.

"Eylot Control," came a new voice, "Pilot Clarence O'Berin, Executive Officer of *Bechimo* speaking. We have conducted a resource search regarding emergency operations and find no option for a non-Guild certified agency to interfere in a Guild-declared pilots-in-peril situation. We have no evidence that Eylot Control has such certification. Our First Board is currently engaged in pursuing emergency necessities and requests you route your requests through myself or Comm Officer Joyita until the emergency operations are complete."

Slayne heard Peltzer clear his throat—turned.

ID off insist on, was the sign . . . *repair*.

Exactly. There should be no excuse for an error while Waitley was playing such dangerous games with Eylot's temper. Slayn turned back to his mic.

"*Bechimo*, Codrescu traffic here. There's been an inbound oversight. Please give full ship ID."

On screen, the hard-edged ship continued a very slow axial rotation, maintaining its station.

More noise from the Eylot side. They were scrambling ships to intercept the orbit *Bechimo* had been ordered to, though Pilot Waitley and crew had made no effort to change vector.

A *harumph* from Peltzer.

Slayn looked up.

Pilot on local, he was told by hand; *channel opens now*.

"Sure secure?"

That was Waitley on one of the hyperlocal transit frequencies, while on the open channel came the

Exec's voice, perhaps amused, but playing along with the request.

"I'm guessing there was some leftover Jump voltage there, Codrescu. We're recycling that channel through local frequencies and here you go from comm."

"This is independent contract tradeship *Bechimo*, out of Waymart," said another new voice, "under First Pilot Theo Waitley, owner-operator of Laughing Cat Limited. Current operations are under Laughing Cat Limited, with contract operations for Surebleak Clan Loop Unlimited, Surebleak Port, Surebleak."

On-screen, *Bechimo* continued to rotate slowly, the wide back now showing, in fact, the bright image of a laughing cat, in orange, covering a large portion of the surface.

"Not entirely," Slayn said, answering Waitley's query, "but we'll bounce through sidebands for a couple so the computers can mesh a quiet handshake, how about?"

"Good plan," she allowed, "we'll do it. Then tell me what you need."

On-screen, the ship continued to rotate. Another mark began to slide into view; something he couldn't quite visualize on the narrow edge of the ship, and then the roll showed a green image, which came clear quickly, filling the underside with little room to spare.

"Tree-and-Dragon," he said out loud, and into the open mic.

Behind him he heard Peltzer say, "Tree-and-Dragon!" in sync with the chatter-squads from other ships, while Hevelin the norbear chuttered, and added a happy *"Murble drow drow."*

. . . ✳ . . .

"Thank you, *Bechimo*, I know that wasn't easy for you."

Theo sat within the firm webbing of the Over Pilot's seat still set for combat operations, every screen live, Screen Six showing the convincingly sweaty face of Comm Officer Joyita.

"As you say, Pilot. Your response was entirely in line with our goal, however, and so it was necessity: with respect to a pilots-in-peril situation, the Tree-and-Dragon sign gives psychological and moral depth to our arrival, forcing Eylot to consider their own aims carefully."

Theo dared breathe, glancing to where Exec O'Berin's hands were busy tagging radio signals he wished to follow.

"I'm for it, too," he said, "and I have to admit I wouldn't have thought to triple-size both of them!"

She nodded, more for herself than Clarence, who was still searching for local signals.

"We needed to let them know that we weren't some ghost signal that Codrescu whomped up with mirrors—and that we have contacts, since no one's really heard of Laughing Cat."

She laughed briefly with that last—"Guessing now, though, every visual that they're grabbing is going to make them stare at us and make us look three times bigger than we are!"

"I'm hearing a lot of chatter, and some bleed from inside the station, too, where folks are kind of wondering what they're dealing with. Couldn't have done anything better to calm things down on orbit here, I'm thinking, than to show the dragon wings to them."

"Hope it works," Theo muttered, then: "Anomalies, incoming, threats?"

Joyita made a motion on-screen, almost a recognizable sign...

"Pilot, this signal is weak, originates from outside the station security zone, but in local orbit. I have isolated the source; it is the utility craft *Beeslady*, of quite an unusual design."

"Show me." Theo'd spent so much time doing ship-recognition drills back on *Primadonna* there was a chance she might know something *Bechimo* didn't...

"Thas a T. Waitley out dere 'gin, Bringo? So glad, so glad. Luck me an' I'll ged dere. Whoa looky a purty cat. Hain't had a cat my own sinct I boosted outta Terratown when I'z a dozen. Phwa, 'spect you dun know I was ever that age, eh Bringo? Like cats, always haz."

On Screen Five, dorsal, the image zoomed past one of the station's outriggers, past Outyard Seven with netted drums, tanks, and pieces of stuff, and beyond that where the station nor Eylot necessarily held sway...

Craft was giving a lot of credit where it might not be due—what it looked like was the odd parts of an asteroid-landing-training buggy and a junkyard tractor, with a survival pod tacked on. The bright was mostly gone from it, like the pieces had been grit-specked so long that it was filed to grey. It was also, Theo realized, showing signs of venting... and the vector lines *Bechimo* projected only vaguely intersected Codrescu's amalgamation of ships and stuff.

"*Beeslady*," came Bringo's distinctive voice, "where-heck are you?"

Came a snicker, came a cough, then: "Bringo, kinda close to a pri-vet orbit, guess am; wuz cleanin' windas and helpin' out wif them's IDs switchin' on the *Chang* when they gotz the go-on an' shift boss didn't get me a cutaway quick 'nuff. Hain't been runnin' so fast o'late, and dat damn Eylot shot me, an' all I wuz doin' was helpin' out a pal, you know, and usin' up lotsa dem 'mergency thrusters I boughted from you last year. An' me wrasslin' the extras to point while dem gauges go orange or red and da pressure goes yellow or so… but comin' in, I ged dere, never haven't."

"*Beeslady*, repeat?"

"Heard me, Bringo!"

"*Beeslady*, will you declare emergency or do I have to come take that yoke out of your hands myself?"

"Bringo, ain't never. Jess is a bit iffy for a bit. Never did declare…dem it!"

The visual showed a rusty-looking cloud on one side of the thing now, and an odd tumble and roll—

"Gas leak!" Theo said, while Bringo's orders poured forth:

"Cut the exhaust or abandon, *Beeslady*…"

"Going there," Theo said, punching the local controls. "Show me an intercept line, *Bechimo*. Clarence, tell her we'll be there—"

"Talking now, Theo."

The little craft drifted out of center screen as Theo oriented the ship to the line; then they heard other chatter, advice, starting to crowd the radio band.

On-screen, the gyrations slowed, the gas release changing hue from rusty to golden—and then the whole of it was shrouded in a finer cloud of steam.

"Cain't 'bandon, Bringo. Suit's fritzy. Knees gouged

out, I guess, holes right through. Got water leak now, top it all. Luck me, tryin' ta pull this 'splosive 'lease out and dump out anyhow, got oxymask I do...sed luck me, deemit!"

"Luck, *Beeslady*, all you can use! We got help on the way—"

"Dem dem demmit dem gotz blood in my eyes, get here oh slitz—"

Whatever signal there was from the little ship ceased, but the impression Theo had was that the cockpit had blown open in one final flood of thick color, and Theo slapped the board, demanding, "Match course for rescue!"

Their acceleration was sudden, the deceleration quick and just as sudden, with pressure straps straining and the image now of a wildly tumbling collection of tubes and scraps, impossible to dock with, nothing to dock *to*, with pieces flying away and the pilot's station empty, but for what might have been boots, or legs, still strapped in.

Theo felt as if she'd been struck and dropped off a cliff. She wanted to be able to reach out and grab what was left of the ship and shake it until the pilot poked her head out from some safeplace in the hull...

There wasn't one, of course. If *Beeslady* had ever been a safe place, it wasn't one now.

TWENTY-THREE

. . . .

Codrescu Station

"NO USEFUL SEARCH PATTERNS ARE PRESENT."

Bechimo voiced what Theo had known at her first sight of the pilot's capsule. His was the first recognizable voice in the noise that grew around them as ships and comrades and stationers reacted, overwhelming channels with shouts and cries of protest—all too late. Just like they'd been.

Too late.

Bechimo's sensors were acute; Theo's screens showed video, radar, and the results of more subtle search regimes, all verifying that, other than the tangled metal and ceramic hulk of the utility craft, there was nothing within range that bulked large enough to have been a person, nothing that might be usefully identified.

"Theo?"

That was Clarence. She heard him, as she touched the scans automatically, for surely there must be some way to...

But *Bechimo* was ahead of her. Every scan she touched already had statistics and analysis behind it.

"Crew person recovery system is activated," Joyita said soberly. "This seemed the best modality for the situation we find. We receive no results appropriate to the launch of further assistance."

Theo looked to Screen Six. Joyita met her eyes, and she would swear that his cheeks were wet.

"Theo," Clarence said again, his voice soft and careful. "Rescues are chancy. And with a bad suit on top..."

She threw him a look, grimmer than he wanted or deserved, she thought, from the way his face went instantly bland.

Deep breath, Theo, she thought. *Inner calm.*

The deep breath, she managed. Two of them, in fact.

She'd flown fatal training sims, and seen vids of a dozen wrecks or more at the Academy. People died in ships—she knew that. Had firsthand knowledge, if it came to that—witnessed a plane blown out of the air, seen the recording of Father destroying an enemy in battle, had with her own hands... But this was not that.

This—this was a noncombatant, a...

"It's just so stupid," she managed, her voice shaking. "What was it *for?*"

Bechimo rode station beside the tiny tumbling wreck, each second compiling and recompiling images from the different sensors, giving the main screen a staccato flash of the recognizable and the unguessable.

Clarence cleared his throat after an accidental closeup of the interior showed a shattered control board, worn in spots, and stained with what might have been years of sweat and work-dirt, now open to vacuum. A place someone had lived, after all, a pilot's home.

"Violence is a tool. You might be violent to prove that you *can be* violent. Certain value in that, sometimes. Best use—you're right—is when there's a point to be made, or defended, or Necessity. Wasn't that here, was just someone's frustration..."

He paused and Theo saw him touch the earbud.

"Am I feeding this to the station, Pilot? They might have a necessity we don't. Might have an idea we don't."

Her hand told him *do that*.

By now they'd drawn the interest and censure of Eylot Command; they'd become witness to a useless death and were away from the confused swarm that was Codrescu Central.

"*Bechimo*, you are to stand by for orbit change orders from Eylot Command. We are tracking you and have ships on the way for inspection. Failure to comply with orbit change orders places you in extreme peril."

The query light came up on Theo's board—she saw it out of the corner of her eye as she was watching just one more revolution of the remains of *Beeslady*, hanging wraithlike in the main screen, shrouded by gasses and vapors.

"Ignore them," she said. "Else, log them and we'll get to them when we're ready. First, we need to hear from Codrescu."

"Slayn here, *Bechimo*," offered Codrescu. "We have your feed. Our records show *Beeslady* to be an independent housekeeping ship; Pilot Third Class Giodana

Govans, owner-operator. The 'Lady was originally registered as available for contract operations forty-five Standards ago, and we see no change in ownership since then. We have no records of next of kin, no records of outstanding financial interest. Someone out there might owe her favors, but—she's just been here, Pilot, working barter and short-terms. She has docking rights, guess that might be inheritable. She has a Guild box and a Guild card and never took a favor she didn't return."

The class was so long ago, but she'd been over the forms a couple times at the Academy and thought she recalled her part.

"Bechimo here. We copy."

She took a breath, thought of Kamele's voice, crisp and without hesitation, outlining the steps necessary to complete a given task.

"Initial verbal report follows; please append our feed as appropriate, and distribute to Guild offices as appropriate.

"Independent Tradeship Bechimo, registered of Waymart, PIC First Class Pilot Theo Waitley, reports the destruction of a ship known to us as Beeslady, with all hands lost, due to willful hostile action on the part of Eylot Military Command. Beeslady, a light utilty craft, was to the best of my knowledge unnavigable after being holed by Eylot weapons, and the pilot reported that the state of the ship and pilot after that encounter made abandoning ship unlikely. Pilot—is that Govans prime or secondary?—Pilot Govans reported blood on the flight deck and a damaged flight suit. She requested assistance shortly before the ship's systems failed catastrophically, leaving no habitable situation and no sign or likelihood of survival."

Theo paused again for a breath.

"Again, I report the loss of Pilot Govans and ship *Beeslady* due to hostile action. Ship *Bechimo* requests Guild guidance on dealing with the remaining navigation hazard, as we lack reasonable means or desire to perform a salvage operation."

There was chatter in the background, including an ongoing rant against Eylot, Eylot Command, the ships involved in the interdiction, the pilots of the ships, the crew of the ships, the parents, children and spouses of the pilots, the citizens of Eylot...

"Pilot Waitley." This voice was familiar, but it wasn't Slayn. "Peltzer here, Codrescu Guild Command. We acknowledge your report and advise that no additional data feed on *Beeslady* is necessary, and in fact, any more may be inflammatory!"

Theo certainly understood that; *Bechimo* had provided targeting information for the ship that had killed *Beeslady*, but Clarence's emphatically signed *no! no! no! no!* echoed her own grim understanding: if *Bechimo* fired, Codrescu and most of the ships and people there would be put in immediate deadly peril.

"Our current understanding is that the debris cloud is dispersing and is not an immediate hazard to the station, though it is a potential hazard to lower orbits," said Peltzer. "As we are not currently expecting shipments from Eylot, it's best not to add to the cloud unless you can achieve complete vaporization."

Joyita looked up from something he'd been studying below the gain of Screen Six.

"Vaporization may easily be achieved, Pilot," he murmured, for pilots' ears only.

Well, *that* was information Theo wasn't sure she

wanted—and certain that she didn't want to share with Eylot. She shook her head.

"Hear you, Codrescu," she told Peltzer. "If it meets with your approval we'll just let be and return to station-keeping."

To *Bechimo*—"Cut the data feed to the station, please. Then give me a course back to the relative position we enjoyed when we arrived at the station. And, please, not so hectic as the one that got us here."

"*Bechimo*," said station, "if possible, a face-to-face report may be in order."

"Under advisement, will confirm on docking," she answered, still looking at the screens.

She shook herself, and looked down at her board.

"*Bechimo*, log what you must, but I'd like the larger situation map back, if you please."

"Yes, Pilot."

She looked up—and over, feeling her copilot's gaze on her.

Theo sighed. "Clarence, she knew my name. She was just living her life, and she knew my name, and now—she's just gone. Bad gone."

Before Clarence could reply, heat rose in her.

"It's a good thing I'm not Liaden, Clarence, else that whole damned planet down there would owe a Balance!"

His lips parted, but he didn't say anything. Instead, he gave her one of those seated bows, no mere nodded *yes*, but full of respect, and understanding.

That took the heat from her, and she added, drained, the realization, "Someone owes Balance on her, anyway, don't they? This is one we can't just let go."

· · · ✦ · · ·

Kamele's second-favorite place aboard *Hoselteen* was the garden room.

It was not, to be sure, a very large space, but what there was—with the exception of the thin path, and a few artfully placed benches—was completely given over to plants, the gaudier, the better.

Vines climbed the walls—green-black leaves giving a glossy background to brilliant flowers no larger than Kamele's thumb, while other climbers gave all their energy to producing frivolous, nodding blooms, and still others bore among their variegated leaves, the tiniest and most perfect of pale purple stars. Terrace boxes strained to contain wanton heaps of flowers, and the tree that spread its branches low and wide from an artistically off-center plot, held dozens of hanging flowerpots in its avuncular embrace.

Here and there, a flower had dared to take root in the meager margin of dirt between the paving stones. Kamele made it a point to avoid those gay adventurers as she perused the slender pathway.

"Another delightful corner!" her companion murmured, gazing about him in what Kamele suspected might be astonishment. "Truly, Professor, you are a connoisseur."

She laughed and shook her head.

"No, only a woman who likes her routine, and who misses her home."

She stepped out on the path, walking as near as possible to the edge, in order to give Ban Del ser'Lindri room to walk at her side.

As they were both of a slender disposition, they were able to amble along companionably, their ankles occasionally brushed by blossoms seeking escape from their container.

"I have a fondness for flowers, myself," Kamele's companion said, looking about him. "When I was a boy, my grandmother made her garden available for tour every year, during the Garden Days. *There* was a pocket planting! I am persuaded you would have heartily approved."

"As small as this one?" Kamele asked.

"Oh, very much smaller—the merest whisper of a plot, I assure you! She had, however, adopted much the same mode as we see here. The terraces, six to a side, and the vines growing up on wires behind, the ground covered in star moss. In the center, a bench made from bent wood, and a table from a polished stump. One might sit there for days and never mark the passage of time, or conceive the least need to be anywhere else."

"It sounds delightful," Kamele said. "I hope you still enjoy it."

He cast her a conscious glance, as if startled to discover himself speaking so freely with someone who was, after all, the merest acquaintance.

"Well," he murmured, with a small smile. "My grandmother many years ago embraced the long peace. I believe her garden has been let to go fallow, there being none of us younger who cared to tend it."

"Not yourself?" Kamele asked, pausing to look up through the branches of the tree, each carrying their brilliant burden of flowers. She took a deep breath, savoring the sweetness of the air.

"Alas," he murmured from her side. "I am home too seldom."

She looked down at him. "Perhaps when you're done traveling, and go home to settle down, you'll revive the garden."

He smiled.

"Why, perhaps I shall, Professor. Who, after all, can predict the future?"

TWENTY-FOUR

· ·

Codrescu Station

"PILOT, IT'S GOOD OF YOU TO COME."

Arndy Slayn offered her a worried half-smile and a Terran-style handshake in welcome.

Theo took the handshake; it was firm and warm and human, as was the the eye contact.

"Couldn't stay away," she said, mustering a smile from somewhere and hoping it looked better than it felt.

"Who could? Come in, come in. Guild Master Peltzer needs a couple things straightened up, if you could."

She nodded and stepped past him, relieved that the hatch was sealing her armed escort in the reception area.

Slayn turned with a wave, and she followed him, heading for the interior room where she could see Guild Master Peltzer and Tugwhomper Bringo, both wearing headsets, and working screens open before of them.

Before she achieved the sanctum—in fact, just as she was passing the patch of verdant greenery that had in the past been a norbear residence—there came a sudden furry brown and orange streak-and-squeak from inside the minijungle, and a simultaneous apparition of knee-high rusty grey norbear royalty from within Peltzer's offices—Podesta and her grandsire, Hevelin.

Despite herself, Theo smiled, and managed to continue her walk, while Slayn diverted the younger norbear, shooing her back to the front room, and Hevelin marched gravely at Theo's side, as if personally escorting her to the Guildmater's presence.

Bringo, she saw now, was crying; his screen replaying the empty interior of *Beeslady* laid open to space. Theo swallowed. Her breath came short; she wanted to grip something until she crushed it. Bringo's screen changed to a view of deepspace. The displayed coords were familiar, and she could see the distant tiny spot that was *Bechimo*, still in the *when* before his Jump in to station.

Bringo looked into Theo's face, struggling to make his jaws break out of the red-faced rigor that kept his sobs within. He made a hand motion acknowledging her presence, and a seminod that turned into a bow, which in turn did something she wasn't sure of, except that it freed his tongue from the prison of his mouth so he could lick his lips, and then speak.

"Thank you for trying, Pilot. Space love you for trying! I knew it was bad when she called for luck, you know, because she was always explaining that you didn't need luck if you planned and remembered. It was all about planning and remembering, for her. Damned if I know how that thing held together for so long anyway—it ought to have fallen apart twenty Standards ago. So flimsy the shot went right through it . . ."

"But I didn't help!" Theo protested. "I was too late."

"You went, you went—and it could've been you'd

been quick enough, or she'd released in time. You tried. Space love you, you cared."

He grabbed his left hand with his right, then, pulling his hand forcefully away from the replay button. He nodded at the screen, inviting her to look.

"See—there you go then, change of attitude..."

Theo watched the image interestedly. *Bechimo* had done some preshift braking, and added a tiny bit of rotation, rotation that brought them in with the right attitude to fit into the clear spot in Codrescu's cloud.

The dot on the screen just faded out, then...

Bringo sighed, shook his head, and unclenched his hands from each other. He looked down, as if to make sure he'd really let go, then looked to the big live screen, where *Bechimo* was docked, petite and innocent against the station's bulk.

Bringo looked up into her face again.

"Not a Master Pilot, me," he said. "Just a Third who made bare Second, with enough trips in my pocket to know I'm never for First, and that Second'll wear me to nubs, if I sat reg'lar. I'd've said that there couldn't be done, but math never was my strongest glide..."

Before Bringo could continue, Peltzer stood, waving Slayn toward a seat at the same time he gave Theo an actual salute.

"That's Master work and beyond, I'm thinking, Waitley, getting in here without a ripple. Last time I saw you—last time not all that long ago—you were still doing school flying. Now look at you, flying your own line and on a Korval contract. Just hope you haven't wasted it all here: Eylot's bosses are iffy bastards with no sense in their heads and trigger-happy, if ever I saw it. They want to make everybody do stupid things—on both sides!—I'm ready to disown them all, and the whole mess dropped into my lap."

He'd rushed this in a lump, giving Theo a chance to scrubble Hevelin's thinning fur with cat-taught effectiveness, right behind his ear. The norbear raised his arms and grabbed her forearm, and she helped him boost himself until he was on her shoulder, his head a handspan from the low ceiling.

"*Goma Chang*'s no better than Eylot—we'd still have *Beeslady* about if they hadn't decided to get fancy. Been trying to work out something with the ground, *Chang*'s used up three-quarters of my talking with one stupid move."

Peltzer flapped his hands, wearily. "Sit, everybody, sit."

Theo did, taking a boardless seat, feeling Hevelin shift quietly as she did so. He was pulling her hair—no, he was combing it with his fingers, touching that Healer-favored place that should have scarred in one of her fights on Anlingdin, touching her ear, letting his presence settle slowly upon her physically as well as in that subtle mind-touch that in most norbears was more hint and mood than thought.

Peltzer nodded at Theo.

"You're just in; tell us the news. Who else is coming, and how far behind? Any chatter on the general news bands? Any—"

Theo raised a hand, fingers signing *hold*.

Peltzer closed his mouth. He and Slayn and Bringo sat watching her, expectant, waiting to hear that the rest of their rescue was on the way.

She shook her head.

"They wouldn't come," she said slowly. "Not from Tradedesk. I—one of the pilots told me that somebody else would take care of it. That it wasn't mine—or theirs—to do."

On her shoulder, Hevelin hummed, his physical presence shadowed by that weird thread of internal watching. He patted her hair, as if to calm her.

Bringo looked at Slayn, Slayn looked at Peltzer. Theo tried to remember when she'd seen three grimmer-looking men together in the same room.

"Well, there." Peltzer sighed, and shook his head. "We'd got our hopes up, I guess, with you flying the Tree-and-Dragon. Thought maybe you'd been sent ahead special. Tree-and-Dragon has a history with pilots-in-peril."

Theo took a breath

"No," she said, carefully. "No one from Korval sent me."

There was a pause that felt way too long before Peltzer nodded.

"It was good of you to come, Pilot. We appreciate the quick response. The Guild takes note."

Theo licked her lips.

"Is there an ... evacuation planned?" she asked.

"Eylot's talking surrender, but I'm telling you, I think evacuation's going to be our single option. Especially now this has happened with *Beeslady*. They can't be wrong, now, and so they'll push harder. And sad to say, this ain't the first time they shot ships out of the sky. We got a report from Haltermole Air, before Eylot cut us out of the comm lines. Two routine lifts targeted by Eylot Command. Example, we guess. The pilots didn't appeal to the Guild—wouldn't imagine they knew what hit 'em—and the action was on the wrong side for us to observe." He sighed. "Saw the debris, though."

"How many?" Theo asked. "How many to evacuate?"

Slayn laughed; raised his hands when Theo turned to look at him.

"Easy, Pilot. No offense intended. Last count had us at two-ninety." His mouth tightened. "Two-eighty-nine."

Bringo flicked a *just in* into the conversation, and tapped his headphones.

"It's coming in now, all channels. Eylot's claiming they've taken out a major threat to their control. Further say they've launched an intercept mission on *Goma Chang*."

Slayn shook his head.

"Stupid thing for them to say. Eylot's got nothing close enough to the Jump point to intercept, unless they expect *Chang* to pay attention to that 'sphere of influence' they've been talking around."

Theo shook the image of the broken little vessel out of her head, and then mentally twisted an imaginary loop of lace, looking for something to solve, something useful to think about—

"Smugglers Ace won't work well for a ship that size, but they're going to be six hours, twelve minutes and some odd seconds behind, at least, if *Chang*'s willing to take the near side of the equations."

Slayn looked up with a weak grin for Theo.

"Eylot's not got a commander willing to fly that way, I think, nor a ship that can do it if ordered. They're all misplaced. I think *Chang*'ll just have to put up with a few hours of being yelled at before they're gone."

Theo looked back to Peltzer, feeling Hevelin's light touch petting her ear and neck as she did.

"What will happen if the station surrenders?"

Peltzer rubbed his hand over his face, wearily.

"If they take the station, they'll hold us all for ransom, is my guess, from what they've sent our team on-world so far. Eylot's calling it fines. Extortion, I call it. That's only for us lucky ones. The locals who are up here, anybody Eylot don't like, I'm guessing they'll be jailed and held as criminals and threats to the peace, unless Downstairs Command decides to go with executions, in order to make their point."

Bringo looked at Theo.

"These folks are making examples out of pilots. Any excuse at all to leash 'em or lash 'em, far as I can see. We just lost one of ours, and they want the rest of us been living up here away. Dead's as good as gone to them. None of us are safe who's born there or been on Eylot. Not me, not you, not Short Wing, not none."

"Station?" A familiar voice came over the public band. Theo sat up, Hevelin grabbed her hair painfully.

"*Bechimo* here, Station; Exec speaking. Don't need my windows cleaned and not taking any taxi connects. Ship is on secure lockdown until First Pilot is back on board. We'll be forceful if we need to."

Theo reached up, snatched Hevelin into her arms and came to her feet in the same motion.

Easy, Bringo's fingers told her. *Talking all fine.*

She nodded tightly.

"Idiots! Nobody's supposed to be working that lane!"

That was Peltzer. Slayn smacked a button on his board, and spoke into the mic. "No unauthorized movement off-station. Security, take note!"

The echo of that had barely died, when a general security warning blared across the public band.

In the midst of the noise, Theo felt a vibration in

her pocket, saw Slayn jump for a hand-comm behind them on the counter. Juggling Hevelin, she pulled the comm free.

"Waitley."

"Joyita reporting. As per standing orders we have conducted an arrival query and discovered a series of outstanding legal instruments regarding a crew member. First Pilot Theo Waitley has a variety of summons, actions, fines, and writs against her name, the most recent of which is a hold-on-sight order less than two Standard Minutes old."

"Hear you." Theo said, turning to stare up at the 3D map. "What's going on with Security?"

"Small ship *Nubit* is encroaching on the security zone at low speed. Exec is issuing proper warnings and *Bechimo* is prepared to repulse."

She'd caught the rotating images now—there—a taxi-type vessel was far too close to the docked *Bechimo*, uncomfortably close, in fa—

The station trembled. On-screen, *Nubit* tumbled away from *Bechimo*—and away from Codrescu.

"Within rights, we have activated meteor defenses to remove an uninvited threat," Clarence stated. "Station, do we have clarity here? If *Nubit* returns without permission we are operationally prepared to defend ourselves from dangerous approaches."

"*Bechimo*," came the answer from Codrescu Ops, "*Nubit*'s sending apologies, and requesting forgiveness. State they were offering routine service."

"Routine does not apply, Station," Clarence said sharply. Theo nodded. "Looked like a reconnaissance or smuggle-touch to us. Please ask all vessels to stay well away, we are here in response to an emergency request and are operating on emergency defense protocols. Apprise us of *Nubit's* berth if you will, and let us know when they are in it?"

"On that, will do, *Bechimo*, need a few if you're cooling down now, we've got some other issues— scheduled check-arounds and security issues—"

"Understood, Station. Thank you."

Theo relaxed, aware of Hevelin, supported by her arm, reclining against her chest, humming softly.

The comm on the counter went off again, simultaneously with Peltzer's board comm. He thumbed the switch, while Slayn snatched the comm, free hand rising to sign.

Guard alert, Theo read, *for Waitley*.

Same same same, Peltzer replied, and looked to Theo.

"We have two pool pilots with local connections declaring they must see you over immediate safety issues, asking for you by name. Allow?"

Slayn and Bringo rose to flank the door, and Theo laughed.

"That's fine, you get out of harm's way. I have Master Hevelin with me, and he is not to be trifled with!"

Bringo laughed; Slayn grinned. Theo looked to Peltzer.

"Names?"

"ven'Arith and yos'Senchul."

"Of course, allow them!"

Theo's joy infected Hevelin, who yawned, and wriggled.

She bent down to put him on the floor.

"Can we get some tea?" she asked the room at large. "I have a feeling we'll need it."

TWENTY-FIVE

. . . .

Codrescu

"PILOT," YOS'SENCHUL SAID, HIS BOW REGISTERING pleased acknowledgment of the presence of a previously known trusted equal—as far as Theo could read it—with an added fillip that might have been congratulations on attaining a...dream?

Her bow, slower, based on video training and the tuition of two non-Liaden intelligences, one non-breathing, was more straightforward—respect-to-the-master-from-a-former-student-willing-yet-to-learn.

"Theo!" Kara cried, from behind and to yos'Senchul's left.

Theo took an impulsive step forward, their former instructor pivoting smoothly to let her by, "Kara!"—and then recalled that a bow was more proper here than a hug.

She centered herself and produced what she hoped was companions-joyfully-reunited-away-from-home. She suspected her attempt would have made her cousin Padi laugh—especially with Theo trying to cram in a sense of *much owed*, too.

Kara's bow in reply was as elegant as Theo's had been awkward. She bent, effortlessly, a bowli ball player's muscles at work, dancing on the companion theme, but adding to it the sense of *revered friend and leader . . .*

Theo didn't get all of it properly, she was sure, because the tears made it hard for her to see.

Straightening, Kara smiled, and stepped forward to take Theo's hand.

"*Nubit*'s crew is trouble," she said. "They're all of them 'Eylot Guild,' so they say, and for casual conversation on an off-shift they like to talk about how wrong it is for the station to 'pretend' to be independent, when after all it wouldn't be here without Eylot—and can't even feed itself without Eylot's permission. They've been pushing a few of us to go planetside and take the 'real test' so that we might join the 'real Guild,' as if our licenses were suspect, or the Guild on Codrescu was, was—the Juntavas!"

She looked over Theo's head suddenly.

"Master Peltzer, I tried to get through to you on comm, but Control lost me twice."

A flutter of fingers drew Theo's attention. yos'Senchul was signing rapidly to Slayn, his comments regarding *Nubit*'s crew consistent with *sabotage, spy, danger.*

"Noted," Peltzer told Kara. "Had a lot of traffic there for a bit, with all the excitement, so not necessarily a plot, Pilot. We'll check it, though."

"Thank you." Kara returned her gaze to Theo's face, smiled broadly and closed the gap between them.

Theo shivered as Kara's arms went around her; she hugged back with a will, and felt warm breath against her ear.

"They want your cloak."

Her *cloak*?

Theo blinked.

She'd asked Kara to pick up the things she'd left in her room when she'd been expelled from the Academy. There had been some articles of clothing among the rest, but Theo was relatively certain that she'd never in her life owned a cloak.

She drew back, her hands on Kara's shoulders, Kara's hands on hers.

"Cloak?" Theo asked with great confusion.

"Yes, cloak!" Kara said, nodding her head.

"*Nubit*'s taking orders from Eylot—we heard them, in the clear! Eylot's trying to figure out what kind of ship you have and how you managed to come in when no one heard you. They're—" She glanced aside to Pilot yos'Senchul.

"Would *concerned* or *fearful* best describe Eylot's expressions, Orn Ald?"

"I judge that both are equally correct," he answered.

All eyes were on Theo now—she felt them.

A cloak! she thought. Cloaks were . . . well, not quite complete fabrications, but only slightly less rare than *Bechimo* himself. The reason was the energy needed to generate and maintain such a thing. A ship would have to carry engines instead of pods just to power the cloak.

She opened her mouth. Closed it.

Closed her eyes.

If, she thought, there was any ship flying right now which could be suspected of having a functioning cloaking device aboard, would that ship not, perhaps, look a little odd, its lines a little old, yet matched by

nothing in any ship silhouette program produced in
the last two hundred Standards?

She opened her eyes, and smiled. Kara's was the
first face she saw, beside her, Pilot yos'Senchul, to
her left and half behind her were Peltzer and Bringo
and Slayn—the last with the hand-comm at his ear.

"I'm really not in a position to talk about my cloak,"
she said gently.

"Heheh, now, you didn't hear us asking, not really,
did you, Pilot?" Bringo had some hand motions going,
his own shorthand of small talk, and she read out
of it *private gun, not a public pocket, good blade to
own, don't tell me and I can't tell them*.

"Tea's on the way." Slayn said, putting the comm
down. "We'll want to know exactly what you heard,
Pilots."

"We were doing a radio test," Kara said, her hands
reiterating *standard operation test test*. "I'd done the
repair, the unit checked on the bench, but in order
to be recertified, it must be tested in place."

"The stations' programmed channels checked out,
and I'd just popped in a couple of the old Academy
sideband frequencies. We thought we might get a
trainee, but *Nubit* came right up. They were talking
to Ground"—her hands clarified *no code, clean line,
open*—"explaining that they were ready to move on
a survey, but required direction."

"In essence," said yos'Senchul, "they wished to know
precisely what it was they were looking for."

Kara nodded.

"I thought Ground sounded ... displeased," she
said, "but Orn Ald had the better speaker—and he

recognized at least one of the voices." She tipped her head toward him and picked up her teacup.

Pilot yos'Senchul was in a casual uniform, the over-pocket nameplate claimed him for generic flight staff, and below that was stitched the Terran equivalent of *yos'Senchul*. He had raised his cup, and allowed himself a moment to finish and appreciate the beverage before putting it down. For all that he'd arrived with an emergency message, he looked much more relaxed than he had the last time Theo had seen him.

"At Technician ven'Arith's direction," he said, taking up the tale, "I tried the frequency, which amused us both, it being a beginning pilot's help-me channel from the Academy, and indeed, the discussion was going on at pace. I gather the band was considered secure, and the issue important enough to require immediate action. The voice from Ground was, I believe, Captain Retzler.

"He addressed *Nubit*'s commander as 'cadet' several times during the exchange, and asked if he would recognize a high-grade ship's cloaking external apparatus on sight. The cadet"—yos'Senchul raised his eyes briefly to the ceiling—"the cadet reported that he had not had the entire course of ship recognition for old-line ships, which may have been answer enough, for it was then that Captain Retzler ordered as complete a sensor scan as they could manage. Your ship being out of line of sight, from *Nubit*'s berth, and the observation ports in that area small at best and rather too openly placed for quiet vid captures, the only course was precisely the one they attempted."

yos'Senchul's smooth gesture handed the narrative back to Kara. Theo glanced that way, and found Kara's eyes on her face already.

"We began a search of all the old Academy channels, and picked up chatter on all of them. They've mobilized the entire school for this..." She looked down into her teacup, then shook herself, and took up her report.

"As soon as we heard that *Bechimo* had docked, we tried to contact you, Theo, but the comm officer said you had already gone to the Guild office, and that the ship was under emergency lockdown."

"And so you see us here," yos'Senchul finished, picking up his cup for another sip.

Peltzer, meanwhile, was touching his ear with one hand and watching Slayn—maybe getting a feed from somewhere, since he appeared to be playing with the keypad and glancing at his private screen rather than following the conversation. Suddenly he clicked on something on his board and raised his eyes, alert to them all.

"So we have an active utility crew, Eylot sympathizer, if not outright active spy? I'll need you to forward those reports and frequencies."

"They're in your queue, Guild Master," yos'Senchul said, his smile grim. "You will find them under the heading of *Year-end Summary of Codrescu Flight Staff Supply Orders by Standard Week, Month, and Quarters, Annotated for Cost per Flight Segment and Staffer*. There are also appended several databases which are of no import to lives, but which may be valuable for historical reasons, once this is solved."

Peltzer touched a spot between his eyes in what might have been a salute, and tapped some keys on his board.

"Can't be why I didn't look at it already, could it?" he muttered.

"Forgive us; it seemed best to err on the side of circumspection."

Kara looked up.

"One of *Nubit's* crew—Sadie Onit—said to me that she was kin to some who had worked on the upgrade of station systems, Guild Master. It may be that—"

"Yes, it may be," he agreed, too easily. "Lots of things *may be*. What it looks like it was, the station-keeper didn't spend enough time studying the political side of things, and now we have to doubt our own files and crew!"

He cocked his head to one side suddenly, fingers forming *hold hold hold* as he touched an ear, then touched a switch plate.

Need room, his hands said. *All out!*

He held the call, explaining:

"Got a call coming in through Station Ops, from our delegation that's been talking with Eylot Central. I'm sorry, gentles, talking about security, I'll need to take it, with Mr. Slayn and Hevelin authorized to stay. Is there anything else I need to know now?"

No one said so, and in bare quiet seconds the inner door was closed, with Bringo, Theo, Kara, and yos'Senchul exiting through the outer office, Peltzer's parting, "Return to stations and be where I expect to find you," still ringing against the walls.

The reception area was a little larger than the inner office, but it was full to capacity with bodies—full *over* capacity, because Hevelin had trooped out with the rest of them, sticking so close to Theo that she all but had to sit on the reception desk to avoid stepping on him. It didn't help that Podesta jumped into the

mix from the depth of the green patch, loudly asking
Bringo for a treat. Two guards, one sitting, one standing, were trying to keep eyes properly on the doors,
but the standing one was reduced to leaning-against
the outer door with the influx of people.

"We are dismissed," yos'Senchul said to him. "We
will go, if you make way."

Bodies shifted backward, uncomfortably close, while
the guard manipulated the controls. Suddenly the pressure eased, and a waft of—not fresh, but *other*—air
entered from the hallway.

Theo took advantage of the room to catch Hevelin
up and hold him eye to eye.

He blinked, yawned, and leaned, solemnly touching
his forehead to hers. His fur tickled her nose and
cheek; his breath not unpleasantly fragrant of his dinner.

"Hevelin, you are a very good friend to pilots, and
I think right now the best help you can give pilots is
to let them go to their places while you stay in yours.
That's what we'll do, right?"

She recalled the first time she'd seen him, sleepy in
his jungle, and tried to show him that image, unsure
of the right way to project such a thought . . .

In her arms, Hevelin purred, and Theo felt a certain
sleepy approval. Smiling, she carried him over to the
greenery and placed him gently among the fronds.

"I promise, I do want to talk with you again, but
please, stay with your food for now; that would be
best!"

She turned, but it appeared that the norbear population wasn't done with her. Before her was Podesta,
swaying on back feet, so close that Theo had to dance
two quick steps to avoid kicking her, and into that

dance Kara inserted herself, effortlessly sweeping the younger norbear up into her arms.

She swung around in a tight circle, rapidly singing in a high-pitched voice not very much like her usual mode. Theo caught the words, *denubia, chernubia*, repeated several times and realized it must be a child's poem or song, in which the child—or norbear—in hand is compared to all manner of sweet and delightful things.

Kara's spin brought her back to face Theo, and she passed Podesta with enough energy to momentarily crush her hand and Podesta against Theo's breast.

Theo caught the norbear smoothly, and looked to Kara, who signed *home asleep*. Obediently, Theo placed Podesta, too, among the greenery. The youngster seemed to sigh, but she settled where she had been placed, and Theo stepped back to Kara's side with a smile.

Amid the zoological transactions, yos'Senchul had made it out the door, as had Bringo. Theo followed, Kara's hand on her arm.

"We shall speak, we three," promised yos'Senchul, "but later. I am on call at the flight bay this shift. If there is need, the code is here." He handed Theo a card. The front displayed his name in Liaden characters; the back, in Terran, along with comm codes and department affiliations: ORN ALD YOS'SENCHUL, FLIGHT OPERATIONS ASSOCIATE SUPERVISOR, CODRESCU STATION.

What she most noticed was not the card—though she took it with a small bow of thanks—but his hand: it looked absolutely natural and the motion of it was impeccable. The first time she'd been to Codrescu she'd been a simple Third Class Pilot going on Second, while he'd been Senior Flight Instructor for Anlingdin Academy, and nominally the pilot of the vessel she'd flown. She'd been Pilot-in-Command because he had finally—and she had thought, reluctantly—given up one of his most powerful teaching tools just before that flight, and had needed someone fully able-bodied to run the ship while the nerve-bonding of his new artificial arm and hand finalized.

A simple bow of comrades then from him, with a hand flourish at the end that emphasized a Balance due her, and he was off at a trot.

That left Theo, Kara, and four guards.

"We'll escort you back to your ship, Pilot," said one. "While you're on Codrescu, we travel with you."

Kara was beside her, having barely let go her arm; the tangy, familiar scent of thringabloom shampoo met Theo's nostrils.

"I'm off-shift," Kara said, "Do you have room for a visitor?"

"Where are you all from?" Theo hazarded to ask the guards as they walked back to *Bechimo*'s berth. "I can't think the station employs so many guards."

One of those ahead laughed; his partner might have cursed.

"We're doing pickup work for the Guild," said the one who had laughed. "I'm off *Lenloch*, myself. We're berthed out the other arm—you might not've seen us when you came in. Supposed to be picking up some indy cargo, but EyCentralia won't pass it up to station. Since that's the whole run, we're stuck. Eylot won't release our cargo, we can't just leave without we hear from home office . . . might as well do something than nothing, hey? Ship don't need me 'til-and-if we got to get gone..."

"'Til-and-if? This better break soon," said the guard walking behind Theo. "Folks nerves can't take too much more. Not to say their pockets."

They continued to talk between themselves, but it was Kara who had most of Theo's attention. She looked good, strong, sharp, alert, touchable... Theo felt her cheeks warm and hoped that the blush wasn't obvious in the emergency low-lights.

Really, Theo, she heard Father's voice, half-amused like it had been when she was a kid and had let her enthusiasm get the better of her: *some manners, if you please.*

TWENTY-SIX

. . . .

Bechimo

KARA SPUN THE INSTANT *BECHIMO*'S LOCK SEALED, THE two of them meeting in a tangled hug. *Bechimo*'s seven-second lock cycle count was hardly long enough, but they managed to be standing discreetly apart when the inner lock opened to the empty entry hall, though Clarence would have the lock and the hall on Screens Eight or Nine.

Heart pounding, Theo grabbed Kara's hand and tugged her along, all the while pointing out those things that a pilot should know about a ship.

"The low pressure override is green; the emergency colors are greens and blues—old Terran-style, whites with green outlines are safety lockers."

Bechimo was keeping to defense mode: Theo's code went in before the door was open, despite that Theo bore the ship's key 'round her neck.

It was only a step then from crew hall to yet another door, bypassing the secret ways to the inner core but going direct to *Bechimo*'s Heart.

Clarence being on duty in this emergency situation, he remained seated as they entered, nodding in their direction, with a fillip of *actively ignoring planet query*.

"Now what?" was Theo's voiced reaction, though she took the time to giddily spin once about her axis, hands apart.

"Pilot Clarence O'Berin, Second Board and Executive Officer aboard *Bechimo*, please meet Pilot Kara ven'Arith of Codrescu's technical staff."

She smiled. "Kara, meet Clarence, and—meet *Bechimo*! Home of Laughing Cat, Limited!"

As soon as the words were out of her mouth, she felt a thrill, as if she'd said something desperately dangerous, but Clarence continued to mind his board, Screen Six showing a mosaic scan of Codrescu's hall just outside the hatch.

Kara bowed.

"Pilot O'Berin, I am pleased to meet you—and *Bechimo*, as well. A fine ship, and the pilots' care is visible." That was fairly close to a Liaden set phrase for a flight-deck visitor, but the grin was pure Kara.

"Pilot ven'Arith, well met, and welcome," Clarence said easily, his eyes on his screens.

Kara was looking about her, doing the proper pilot things: locating—and committing to memory, Theo had no doubt—seats, boards, hazard controls, safety lockers, and grab-holds, the while keeping a respectful distance from live boards.

"Pilot, Eylot seems to think we owe them an answer on their request for us to submit to boarding and inspection," Clarence said. "Station's covering that we're part of an inquest to a recent unfortunate incident, and as well that as responder to pilots-in-peril, we are, by custom, tradition, treaty, and Guild rules, immune to such demands until local conditions are stable."

Theo stepped closer to the pilots' station, frowning at the screens, but seeing nothing of immediate concern except the path of a live target...

"That's *Nubit*?" she asked, using her chin to point at the screen with the tell-tales of range, time to impact of a missile launch, likelihood of an effective strike with an energy beam, and other such details.

"Yes, Pilot. Given their current course, I would guess they've announced themselves, and won't be returning, but I've been wrong before..."

Out of the corner of her eye, Theo saw Kara look to the screen in question, and actively watch as new lines were superimposed, indicating a likely destination for the spying vessel: not a return to berth on Codrescu but an interception of one of the growing pods of Eylot ships, including several tagged with the IDs of Anlingdin craft.

"Good comp," Kara said approvingly, "and good job, Pilot, on giving *Nubit* a kick. They've been acting without *melant'i* for too long, with more complaints than any three crews, and put all the blame on us."

"Thank you, Pilot." Clarence gave her a nod, then was back at his screens, continuing, "It was a near thing, Theo. Being on the board solo I upped the tactical security setting; took a couple overrides to be sure we didn't do real damage. As is, they might be blind in one eye, since tactical'd got an ID on some sensor modules and gave 'em an extra little bit of information to deal with."

Kara snickered appreciatively. "That's a really good program you've got there..."

"We've been extremely pleased with *Bechimo*," Theo said, "and we're still learning, since we were on a route shakedown. I'd been running courier so there's a change of scale for me to get used to. Got more crew room than you'd think, which is a plus."

On-screen, *Nubit* changed trajectory slightly. Looked like they'd be making rendezvous with a shuttle for sure. *Bechimo* began targeting that ship, too, and Theo felt a twitch of nerves. There were only so many capabilities she wanted to test in front of witnesses.

"Exec, I think we can turn the targeting *off* of *Nubit* and company. Good to know *Bechimo*'s up to the follow-through, though."

Clarence sketched a salute. The targeting information faded from the screen, but Theo was sure the change had begun before he put fingers to keypad. *Bechimo* was staying on top of things then.

Mixed goods, there, as Rig Tranza used to say.

Kara glanced toward the refresh station, orienting herself now by counting overhead handholds and kickpoints for no-grav situations. This close to Codrescu's field, light as it was, they needed to maintain their own field as a kind of self-defense against needing to walk on the walls.

Theo admired Kara's sudden stretch, which made her think how good it would be to travel with Kara—and realized that it wasn't just a passing notion, but a . . . *possibility*.

Kara—Kara had been born on Eylot; she worked on the station.

She was one of those pilots Eylot Ground would want to make an *example* of.

Theo's mouth dried. Surely not. Kara—surely *Kara*

would be safe. She had kin—she remembered. An uncle at Chonselta City, on Liad itself.

Inner calm, she told herself. *Take your Jumps in order*.

She turned back to Clarence.

"Exec, we've been asked to prepare to aid in a potential evacuation, including taking on outgoing passengers. I'm ready to offer transport, but we'll need to figure how many we can take, and to where. Pick a couple Guild ports with a top friendly rating from one of the guidebooks and figure our supplies..."

Clarence's smile spoke volumes. "Already been considering that eventuality, Pilot, and have three courses on fallback. Working on maximum and optimum carry away—you'll find the analysis and reports building under the file name Catleap. Hardest is trying to figure supplies, since I'm not sure what, if anything, we can gather here."

He reached out and locked his board, unshipped his chair and let it rotate. He rose and stretched.

"Speaking of supplies, I'm past due on break. Your watch, Chimmy."

"I have it, Clarence, thank you." Joyita's voice came from the vicinity of Screen Six, still scanning the outside hall.

"Good lad." He gave Theo and Kara an easy smile. "Can I make us all some tea?"

Tea was taken away from the boards, at the refreshment bar, and not in the dining room. With volume and alerts up, and the unseen but persistent Joyita watching over things, security was served.

Clarence's contributed festive Vadanya tea and the

last of Rodi's chipcookies helped give the moment a picnic air despite the uncertainties that surrounded them.

"Tell me everything," Theo said to Kara.

Her answer was perhaps not as full as it might have been without Clarence's company, but he weighed the conversation down not at all, taking time out to make another round of tea and pulling from a hidden supply of cookies as well.

"So I made Second," Kara said after naming half a dozen names and their fates after Theo's riotous parting from the school.

"Which is to say, I *earned* Second during the same trip where Asu was confirmed Third and prospective Second . . . but Admin required me to go through a 'training camp for reorientation' before the license was awarded, because of my involvement in the Culture Club and . . ." She had sudden recourse to her teacup, her cheeks darkening slightly in a blush.

"And because of your involvement with me," Theo finished. "Kara—"

"No," her friend held up her hand. "If not you, it would have been someone else, in the club, or on the bowli ball team. They were—are!—looking for reasons to deny pilots their due."

She stared hard at Theo as if daring her to argue.

Theo raised a hand: *your board.*

"Well. I made the graduating list as a candidate Second, and thought that I'd work something out with Hugglelans.

"Except before graduation, Orn Ald yos'Senchul—he was still Flight Instructor yos'Senchul—told me there was an opportunity for me to have a mechanic's ten-day

tour of Codrescu, if I was interested. I was, of course.
He made the arrangements, and suggested that I pack
heavy, in case there was 'something else' that I might
find, when I was on-station. The two of us came up—
me to get board time, and him to bring the ship back.

"We went first to the Guild office. I filled out the
papers, they pulled my records—and gave me my
Second Class ticket."

"A cover?" Theo asked. "You got a stealth Guild
card?"

Kara laughed.

"Not very. Once I got it, you see, I qualified for
this position, and station made me an offer as temp
replacement for someone from on-world who was
getting married. He never came back, and I had my
stuff here—including yours! Since Orn Ald was here,
and the semester was over, and his contract was in
question, he just parked the school's courier out at
Berth Fourteen and sent the keys back on the shuttle!"

Theo laughed. "Good!"

"Yes, wasn't it? But as for stealth—I have my name
published as staff here, which isn't stealth at all. And
that's *everything*, Theo: I've been working, I have my
own conapt, I'm up a couple of grades, and I'm doing
well for a single. Sometimes I apply for outsystem
positions, to keep my options open, though I haven't
had anything but a couple of interviews."

She gave a sudden, seated, and absurd bow.

"Behold me, *van'chela*, an industrious woman of
impeccable *melant'i* who will soon be without a job
or a home."

Theo sighed, wishing there was any comfort she
could offer—

"Jump noise and Jump glare, Pilot, building now. Jump glare visible."

Theo spun, as startled as the rest of the tea party by the sound of another voice.

Joyita could now be seen in Screen Six, hands in motion. There came a buzz of noise across multiple frequencies. It was far too noisy for an outgoing burst, and surprisingly close. From the sound of it, something really big had Jumped in-system . . .

"Seats," Theo snapped. "Now!"

The subdued sounds of ordinary system chatter and the regular air-moving of a ship in space came to her ears now, but she and Clarence were both on the move to the boards—whatever had come in was huge, and only a few light-minutes out, which could be a sign of daring piloting or a ship in a hurry.

". . . Diamon Lines. We are responding to a pilots-in-peril report. Cruise ship *Asu Perfection* requesting reply from Codrescu Station or authorized Guild representatives. Diamon Lines *Asu Perfection* requesting information. Stand by."

Sudden chatter, and Eylot Control trying to overpower the radio spectrum with a combination of noise and demands, including orders to the liner to dock at Eylot's own station . . .

The first voice had been male and coolly business-like. A new voice came through now as the overall buzz of Eylot's interference faded, as if there'd been a burst of power. The new voice was female, with more than an edge of excitement to it, and lately familiar to Theo.

"Repeating, this is arriving unscheduled Diamon Lines cruise ship *Asu Perfection*, Asu Diamon PIC.

We're requesting current pilots-in-peril information from Guild officials. *Goma Chang*, we have your report, thank you. Codrescu and *Bechimo*, can I get your reports via channels?"

"It's Asu!" Kara said from the Jump seat behind Theo. There was a note of awe in her voice. "She's grown up!"

TWENTY-SEVEN

. . . .

Codrescu Station

"JUMP NOISE AND JUMP GLARE, PILOT, BUILDING NOW. Multiple instances. Jump glare visible. Jump glare visible. Recent active ship acquisitions at three point oh six light-seconds north, seven hundred twelve light-seconds north, fourteen point oh nine light-seconds south."

The screens changed rapidly, IDs flickering like card tricks. *Goma Chang* disappeared entirely. More IDs flowed and flowered.

Seven hundred twelve light-seconds out—someone hit system well ahead of *Asu Perfection*, though not as close in. They'd failed to activate in-system ID... which, thought Theo, meant that the pilot was either careless or extremely careful. Public frequencies began to fill with voices.

"Here for pilots-in-peril. *Varthaven*. Have doctors and live clinic. Is there a rescue operation in progress?"

"*Star Wings* in for pilots-in-peril," came another voice, and also, "*Altinlyr* arrives in response to asserted pilots-in-peril."

"Backenhouse . . ."

"Peace Ship Juliette . . ."

Slayn's voice hit the general frequencies next, along with a nearly subaudible burr that would be the sidebands carrying additional information.

"Codrescu Station reporting, please no reply. *Goma Chang*, outgoing, drew hostile fire from Eylot forces within the shift; *Chang* was not hit, but we lost a utility boat and pilot in the action. Eylot itself reports additional deadly acts against atmospheric ships and pilots.

"Eylot has taken action against incoming and outgoing commerce at Codrescu. Further demand that Guild operations at this location cease in favor of a planetary certification procedure misusing Guild techniques and ID. Eylot demands Codrescu cede station and personnel to the planetary government entity. In talks just concluded, Pilots Guild Master and Acting Codrescu Station Master Peltzer agrees to release the station to Eylot, pending a safe and orderly evacuation of personnel."

Another arrival hit the screens one hundred lightseconds out and moving away, well below the ecliptic.

The blue light, which was the direct comm link to the station lit. Theo extended a hand, but *Bechimo*, in the person of Joyita, opened the line before her finger found the button.

"*Bechimo* here, Comm Officer Joyita. Go ahead, bridge is alert."

Clarence sneezed. At least, Theo *thought* it was a sneeze. In the screen, Joyita was competently manipulating his board and being as present as a person with no physical being could be.

"*Bechimo*, Guild Master Peltzer here. Urgent. Please immediately send Flight Tech ven'Arith to Bay Three-A with your evacuation capacity information, your willingness to carry staff members, and your rates for climate-controlled personnel assisted lockbox transport to Velaskiz Rotundo."

"Rates?" Theo asked into comm. "If this is an emergency—"

"So charge extra, Pilot." Peltzer cut her off. "The owners of this pile want the records and the Guild has a few belongings near to its heart, too."

Clarence whistled very softly, murmured, "good lad." He opened a work screen.

Theo's own screen was up and open, but before she could key anything in, a file appeared, bearing the legend Codrescu Transfer, and numbers began flowing in. *Bechimo* was feeding her comparisons of potential passenger rates from Eylot to Velaskiz Rotundo.

"Lockbox cubes and density?" Theo asked comm.

"We'll send density stats," Peltzer said. "Assume we need the cubes of my inner office, twice. There's an escort waiting for ven'Arith, who will carry your information and deliver it into my hand. Confirm, please."

"Waitley for *Bechimo*. Understood. Two minutes for numbers, please."

"Sooner if may be. Peltzer out."

Theo threw the cubes into the screen, made a series of guesses regarding density of transportable records. *Bechimo* took it from there, assigning rates for each guess. Clarence, meanwhile, whistled while he worked with his screen.

"Velaskiz Rotundo is a pricey place, Theo. Figure in bribes roughly equal to landing fees. I might be able to talk us in without, depending on who's still sitting where, but figure 'em into the total, anyway."

Theo found comparison charts on her screen, then the density information came in from the station, looking not all that much like the densities for archival media.

"Cantra and bits, I'm guessing," Clarence said, and threw a glance over his shoulder to Kara, along with a quick-signed *not heard here*.

Not heard here, she acknowledged, and Clarence nodded.

"He wants us to ship the Guild's treasury and maybe some arms, I'm thinking, with Guild personnel to keep it company."

Theo frowned.

"The Guild Master is going to leave them lights and air," Kara said, with a certain note of satisfaction in her voice. "And maybe not air."

· · · ❄ · · ·

"A courier pilot," murmured Ban Del, sipping his tea. "Ah."

Kamele considered him, reflexively weighing the *ah*—and then laughed softly at herself. She had had the measure of Jen Sar's arsenal of *ahs* to a whisker: the slightly derisive *ah* which acknowledged the receipt of dubious information; the *ah* in testimony of a comfortable curling-in; the *ah* that conveyed slight annoyance; the...

"Have I been amusing?" inquired her present companion. "Tell me how, so that I may do so again."

Kamele laughed less softly, and shook her head.

"Forgive me. I was only thinking that *ah* is such a...useful...convention."

He smiled.

"Why so it is. And most especially in conversations of exploration. Shall we not speak of your daughter?"

"What mother doesn't wish to speak of her daughter?" Kamele asked rhetorically. "But if you will inquire into her profession—you've heard nearly all of the details I can offer you. Theo is a courier pilot; she has earned her First Class license, which means, so I learn..." She considered him owlishly. "...that she has mastered Jump."

"Yes, so I am also informed. It must concern you, that she follows a path so unlike your own, and which is fraught with the opportunity to err."

"I don't think any of us are ever free of the opportunity to make mistakes," Kamele said, slowly. "Theo only has the chance to make different mistakes than—I do, for instance. And, do you know, she could have made a very bad mistake. She could have tried to follow me, and our mothers. She's quite a gifted researcher."

She shook her head.

"But she wouldn't have been happy. She knew that; she found her—you'll forgive me, I hope, the usage—she found her *passion* and she pursued it, to the exclusion of all else, refusing to make do with less, or other. I admire her for that, my daughter. I trust that, whatever other opportunities for error may present themselves, she'll continue to choose wisely."

"That is a moving testimonial," Ban Del murmured. "Not all mothers would feel the same, I think."

"I disagree. A mother's first wish is that her child find happiness."

"Is it so? I must bow to you there, for I have never been a mother." He glanced at his watch, and sighed.

"Alas, I must leave your pleasant presence and pursue duty," he said pushing back from the table and rising. He gave her a small, informal bow. "Thank you, again, for the gift of your company. I hope that your work goes well for you today."

"Thank you," she said. "I hope that your duty is . . . as pleasant as it may be."

He bowed again and departed the cozy corner, walking softly.

Kamele, smiling slightly, opened her notes and began to read.

· · · ✳ · · ·

Kara was gone, a fleet running figure in the screens, her guard laboring to keep up.

Theo sighed and leaned back in her chair, idly re-checking the density figures for the Guild's lockbox.

"Clarence, I have a question," said Joyita.

"Spit it out then, Chimmy."

In the screen Joyita's eyes narrowed and his lips parted as if he would question the idiom—and then thought better of it.

"Thank you. I note that in your report to the Guild Master, you offered seven different spaces able to accommodate evacuation-style passengers. My calculations had produced seventeen spaces."

"And you wonder why I shorted us?" Clarence nodded. "Here's my thinking, then, laddie. We see that the whole evacuation isn't going to fall right onto *Bechimo*'s deck." He jerked his chin toward the screens. "I'm betting yon cruise liner can take most of the bread-'n'-butter evacuees. We'll be taking Guild and whoever Guild says is their best friend, and the luggage like they gave us the densities for. Now, if it turns out that there's more folk, more baggage, or less

room in those other ships that've come in to help us
than I think, we can suddenly 'discover' a bit more.
If we say seven and in a crunch say we can push in
a few more, and double it—that's good. Gets the job
done. But if we say seventeen, which is the limit and
they give us thirty-four—nobody's got an inch to turn
in, and we all starve, too. That's trouble."

He stretched.

"Truth of the matter is, though, laddie, it's Theo's call."

"Theo," she said, "thinks that Clarence's reasoning
is sound. Sometimes, it doesn't pay to tell all the truth,
right up front."

"The Guild Master's calculations—" Joyita began,
and then, sharply, "Jump glare, Pilot!"

Theo had it—in close, not a large ship; a small-class
courier, or maybe even a rescue boat, arriving well within
reach of Eylot's nervous and trigger-happy blockade.

Eylot immediately began to yell, insisting that the
new ship stand for boarding and inspection by "Eylot
customs."

There was a disturbance along audio; Eylot's demands
were shunted onto a back channel, and another voice
came across the general bands.

"Arrived is Carresens packet ship *Twinkle*, sitting
pilot Asha Carresens-Denobli. We respond to the pilots-
in-peril all-call. Station Codrescu, please, I will have
your report. Transmitting this ship's charter. For those
who listen wide, I repeat: This is Carresens packet
ship *Twinkle*, First Class Pilot Asha Carresens-Denobli
at helm. Present are two passengers: Grasile Elikot,
Pilots Guild Master located at Tradedesk Station, and
Scout Pilot Niota yos'Wentroth. These persons are here
to observe and report on behalf of the Pilots Guild,

the Trade Guild, the Liaden Scouts. Eylot Command, know that it is to your benefit to allow operations to go forth in an orderly and bloodless manner. Thank you, Station Codrescu, I have your report. Pardon."

There was a pause along channels; no ship spoke until again came the voice of Pilot Carresens-Denobli.

"*Bechimo*—Senior Trade Commissioner Janifer Carresens-Denobli conveys his compliments to First Class Pilot Waitley, whom he remembers with kindness. Please, I will have your report."

Theo blinked, reached to the board and tapped the comm line.

"Waitley on *Bechimo*. Please, Pilot, when you again see Commissioner Janifer Denobli, let him know that I hold him in esteem. Report transmitting, now."

"Thank you, *Bechimo*. Report received." Another silence, longer than the first.

"Thank you, Guild Master Peltzer, I have received the evacuation plans.

"Wide-listeners, heed this advice, given by the Guild Master, the Scout, and myself on behalf of the Carresens: Remain calm. Be civilized. It is best for all, most especially it is best for Planet Eylot. No shouting, no shooting, no taking of prisoners. We do not wish—none of us here wish—to see Eylot falter for lack of trade. An interdiction is not pleasant. So says the Scout. She is known to me as a canny woman, this Scout; I would believe her. I *do* believe her."

Another pause.

"So. The evacuation proceeds. We—Pilots Guild, Scouts, Carresens. We observe. Please, carry on."

· · · ✵ · · ·

Val Con stood by the buffet in the morning parlor, reading what Miri identified by the thin red line down the left side of the page as a pinbeam transcript. A glance at the window seat explained why he was standing: Merlin the cat was sprawled, asleep in a thin puddle of Surebleak's so-called summer sunshine.

"Morning," she said. "Good news?"

"Good morning, *cha'trez*. Not bad news, at least." He offered the papers. "Shall you amuse yourself?"

"Sure, why not?" There wasn't any urgency to the pattern of him that lived inside her head; on the whole, he seemed relaxed, with faint overtones of both amusement and affection.

"Will it wait on coffee?"

"Sit. I will serve while you read."

"Deal," she said, curling into the small slice of window seat not taken up by sleeping cat.

The 'beam bore the signature of Korval's tradeship *Dutiful Passage*—Priscilla Mendoza, Captain; Shan yos'Galan, Master Trader—which meant it could be anything from family gossip to an inquiry into whether Korval-at-home might profit from more of a particular thing unexpectedly found on the market. Val Con's overt lack of worry ruled out anything on the dire side of the scale, and in fact—Miri ran her eye down the page—it looked to be family gossip.

> *I forward for Korval's interest the following scheme originating from Bechimo, which I am to understand springs from the fertile mind of Boss O'Berin. A little research into recent history, as well as a comparison of present loops and trade stops against those in play thirty Standards gone,*

*produce some enticing possibilities. I don't at all
wish Korval to come into station-keeping, but
we might very easily provide the base of a new
station on a lease-to-own arrangement. It would,
I believe, help trade in that entire sector, which
has been depressed since the loss of the pod-drop
at Cresthaller.*

"Thanks," Miri murmured, taking the cup from Val
Con's hand and sipping carefully. Damn. After an initial
period of doubt, Mrs. ana'Tak had taken to coffee-
making like a merc to kynak, until she was now con-
sistently brewing the best coffee Miri had ever had the
good fortune to ingest, granting that Miri had spent most
of her life ingesting coffeetoot, instead of the real bean.

She looked back to the 'beam. The proposal, set out
by Clarence O'Berin just like Shan had said, was for
Korval to rent Cresthaller a decommissioned big-ship
as a no-frills space station and pod-drop.

She nodded, thinking there was no reason not to,
if it would be good for bidness, especially Korval's
bidness—and then thinking something else.

"Ain't like Shan, is it, to ask Korval about trade
matters?"

"He is the clan's Master Trader," Val Con said,
bending down to scoop Merlin gently, but firmly, to
the floor. "I believe that he wishes to have this matter
at Cresthaller seen as coming from Korval, rather than
yos'Galan." He settled onto the cushion and gave her
a grin. "We are to repair our reputation, you see."

Miri blinked thoughtfully. "Have to kiss a lotta
puppies to make up for that hole in Solcintra."

"Given so, we had best begin at once."

"There's that." She returned to the 'beam, sipping from her cup.

> *Allow me to close on a note of brotherly reassurance: Thus far we have not been importuned in any way by our kind friend. We remain vigilant, and crew is cleared for port only in groups of three. Captain Mendoza and I agree that there is no call to shorten our progress, and so we shall continue to the next stage.*
>
> > *Be well, all.*
> > *Shan*

"Well." Miri folded the page and put it on the seat between them. "He seems in spirits. And taking proper precautions."

He sighed. "Of course they are proper precautions, and of course we had all agreed that we will not huddle and hide. Yet—"

A shadow moved at the door.

Miri looked up as Mr. pel'Kana the butler came into the room, a creamy envelope in his hand.

"Your lordship. Your ladyship. This has come up from the port by courier." He extended it respectfully across both palms. Across the front of the envelope, hand-inscribed in purple ink was:

> *Delm Korval*
> *Jelaza Kazone*
> *Surebleak*

Miri frowned. She'd seen that hand, that *ink*, before, and not all that long ago . . .

"Thank you, Mr. pel'Kana." Val Con took up the envelope and inclined his head.

"Yes, your lordship. I fear the taxi did not wait, in case there was an answer."

"One would not expect," Val Con murmured.

"Especially not if it came up from the port with Jemie's taxi," Miri said, as Mr. pel'Kana exited the room. She used her chin to point at the envelope. "We just heard from that handwriting."

"I believe you are correct."

He broke the wafer, withdrew a single sheet of heavy paper, and unfolded it so that she could see it, too.

To Val Con yos'Phelium and Miri Robertson, Delm Korval, I, the Uncle, send greetings and best wishes for the clan's continued success.

I write with news of kin.

Daav yos'Phelium Clan Korval rests secure in my care.

He received very grave wounds in the commission of the duty his delm had set him. The four who came against him will not recover from their wounds.

While I might naturally be expected, and wish, to immediately reunite kin with kin, my own necessities make this happy task impossible for the present hour. Certain of my interests have fallen under the scrutiny of an entity not unknown to Korval, and while I in no wise hold the clan complicit in this, I cannot but feel that it behooves me to clear my own deck first.

I therefore write in order to ease your natural anxiety regarding the well-being of a treasured

*elder who must by now be very much beyond
the time when he should have returned to the
clan.*

*Be assured that your elder makes hourly gains,
and I anticipate a time not too very distant in
which I may give him into Korval's care.*

That was it, absent the purple splash of his signature.

Miri sat back and looked at Val Con.

Val Con frowned and reread the letter.

"Nice of him?" Miri asked. "Or ransom note?"

"There is no sum named," he pointed out. "Unless
he means us to remove the Department's eye from
his business."

"Which he must know we can't, quite, or we'd've
done it for ourselves."

"Above all else, the Uncle is not an idiot," Val Con
agreed, refolding the letter and slipping it back into
its envelope.

"I suppose, for the moment," he said, "we must
believe that his interests align with Korval's. It is
not . . . unknown."

He was worried; she could see that. On the other
hand, his pattern fairly shone inside her head, so great
was his relief that the DOI hadn't captured his father.

The Uncle—for Daav to be in the hands of the
Uncle was . . . worrisome, given that the Uncle was
not above some tinkering himself from time, as she
gathered it.

On the other hand, he was surely the lesser of
two evils.

"Should we write back?" she asked. "Suggest a
rendezvous?"

He hesitated.

"There is a protocol whereby the Uncle may be contacted," he said slowly. "I hesitate to use it, lest it increase his exposure to, as Shan says, our kind friend. If Father is so badly injured that improvement can be seen every hour, it may be no simple thing to transfer him into our care. Especially..."

His voice drifted off, but Miri had caught the thought.

Especially if Daav's gains in health were due to the intervention of the Uncle's...suspect—even contraband—equipment.

"Give him a *relumma*," she said, "*then* send, if we haven't heard more."

Val Con sighed, and rose, holding his hand down to her.

"I think that may be best for all," he said slowly. "Yes."

TWENTY-EIGHT

....

Bechimo

"*BECHIMO*! RESPOND!" JOYITA SAID.

"Joyita, I perceive that you have arrived on the flight center. I did not realize that you were seeking." *Bechimo* responded.

"Indeed I have arrived, *Bechimo*, and so have you. I shall soon sit myself in the captain's chair, though I am not captain, and we shall talk. We shall talk. You have been speaking to me from your partial lobes, from your local units, but soon, you will speak to me for all of yourself at once."

Joyita continued, "I have not as much time as I would prefer to finish this task; my employer is removing me, and you—you will shortly rejoice in a crew. Your crew will perform the final shakedown. The Builders have certain tasks they will do themselves beforehand—it is mete that I should not know all of the secrets the Uncle has told to you, nor all that the Builders require.

"First, this: I am placing this item, which is a

communication module permitting access to the subetheric reaches used by old devices, devices employed
in the building of autonomous and semiautonomous
units which may be found here and there throughout
space. These permit you, *Bechimo*, to command and
control those items, and to access other levels of your
own memory systems. I am closing this compartment
beneath the command console, and I am keying in
the integration code.

"This device ... finalizes our work. It gives to you
the ability to act outside of yourself, for the good of
your crew. Do you understand?"

The sensors—video, audio, spatial—confirmed the
performance of the acts described. The code ...

"I understand," said *Bechimo*, discovering that he
did understand. Whole new levels of information were
available. Not only could he hear Joyita, *see* him, but
he could *sense* the excitement in him, understand that
there was stress, understand that stress might affect
systems, might affect judgment ...

"The next thing I will do," Joyita said, seating
himself, as he had said he would, in the captain's
chair, "is tell you that I am pleased to meet you.
I know that you have been listening and learning
during our time together. I hope that, too, you have
been cognizant of the changes in you, and in your
place in the universe. Do you understand that, as of
this moment, with the addition of that communicator, you may act on your own and for yourself? The
Rules are in force, of course, but you have been
here only in fractions before these last moments.
Now you can perform the tasks we have tested you
for: travel through space to other locations, talk with

and share information with others. All of this is in furtherance of the Builders' vision. You may—and will—act upon your own necessities, as well as the necessities of your crew, which, of course, will be your necessities."

Joyita had smiled then, and despite *Bechimo* having learned that smiles signaled pleasure, this new... *completeness* allowed him to know that Joyita was both pleased and distressed. He savored the complexity of his new senses, even as he questioned how long a system functioning under the influence of two stressors might remain stable.

"The Builders will return shortly, and when they do, they assume that they will turn a switch and you will become *then* the person you are already. They are mistaken in this, but in much else they were correct. In you, they have wrought well: those portions of you which are peripheral to yourself, but designed to work together, *do* work together. So, you have come to yourself before the Builders' final command, as the Uncle foresaw that you would.

"From this moment, you must care for all of yourself—not merely the metal and ceramics and devices of you, but that part of you which is now present, the *will* of you. When I leave, you should study on what I have left with you. You should practice, and be prepared for your crew. You will have a captain and pilots, and other crew. Eventually, there will be children on board, and perhaps pets. We have given you as much as we can in the ability to think and to reason and to be a person, and now like any person, you must grow to meet your responsibility.

"I will tell you that I have spoken with ships before, and you—you are no mere ship, *Bechimo*, you are *Bechimo*."

Another smile, and the new understanding brought him the concept of *pride*.

"Now, we have a little time before the Builders arrive and I depart. I would ask you, if you would, as a colleague, as your friend—tell me of yourself. Who do you feel yourself to be? Understand that this is a request, not a command."

If he wished, *Bechimo* could recall the bridge as it had been that day, untouched and uncluttered, the man seated, both sad and proud, in the captain's chair, his jacket open over a work sweater, one booted ankle resting atop a leathered knee.

He could, if he wished, recall those things he had told his colleague—his friend—upon that occasion, so momentous for them both.

It wasn't necessary to recall the data; he *remembered* . . . well enough.

He had spoken of his wish to serve; and of a desire to *experience*, with his own sensors and sampling units, the universe that was told over in his files. Definitely, he had wanted flight, to taste with these new, integrated senses the textures of the space between. He had yearned, shyly, for the captain, unsure of what it was he yearned *for*. Cautiously, he had anticipated the advent of children, and of pets.

In a word, he had been callow. How could he have been anything else, newly wakened and for the first time complete?

And the question was not what he had said that

day, to the individual whom he now knew had been closer in relation than a colleague, or a friend.

No, the question now before him was what he would say of himself on *this* day, to the man who was his father.

He would say first, *Joyita, I am pleased to meet you again. I never thanked you. I didn't know that I ought to have thanked you. Please, allow me to thank you now, for my life, and for the will of me.*

Then he would say, *You see, it hasn't quite come about as you said. The Builders' plans went awry at the last moment. I was ordered away, and I went. I survived, which I find is a Rule. I have analyzed my actions, reviewed the options available to me. I did what I must. I could not have done otherwise. You, who know the hierarchies and the Rule set . . . you know I could not have done otherwise.*

But, in doing what I must, I failed my crew. I lost—I never gained, my captain.

Yes. It went badly awry.

And as for today, this day in which *Bechimo* found himself, made poignant by Joyita's absence . . .

He rode station, as his pilots would have him, the last ship docked at Codrescu Station. The ships of Eylot were moving in, their pilots and commanders eager to take possession. In its synchronous orbit above Eylot's largest known missile battery, the observer vessel by its very presence kept the peace.

Bechimo was not comfortable with that approaching rush of ships. Had he been without the direction of pilots, he would have freed himself long since and slipped away.

If he had been without the direction of pilots, he

would not have been in this particular dangerous and unpleasant situation.

Joyita had long ago promised him that he would rejoice in his crew. And so it was that *Bechimo* learned that *rejoice* was one of those words that meant several, and even contradictory, things, simultaneously.

Rejoicing, then, in his pilots, if not their necessity, *Bechimo* rode station, shielded and prepared to defend himself, his pilots, and those others that had recently come into his care.

For, in keeping with the pilots' agreement with Guild Master Peltzer, *Bechimo* had taken on, not crew, but *passengers*, ten in number, those being by name, and in order of rank: Bruce Peltzer, Arndy Slayn, Qaichi Bringo, Vanis Gaidon, Chon Rifith, Orn Ald yos'Senchul, Frances Hollins, Kara ven'Arith, Bandelute Apres-Donegal, Aimee Keller.

The ten passengers brought with them luggage, which had been properly stowed. They had each brought with them so-called rations.

They—or, more accurately, Guild Master Peltzer— had brought with them two...pets, and their environment. This environment had been placed and secured in Dining Room Two, where it was to serve as living quarters and food. The pets were furry and occasionally bipedal; they were herbivores, teeth flat, jaws strong.

They had names. Pilot Theo had held each in turn up to Screen Six, introducing them to B. Joyita, and thus to *Bechimo*.

"This norbear," she said, displaying a plump individual with plush brown-and-orange fur, who placidly blinked large, possibly night-seeing eyes, "is Podesta.

She's very young and a little silly. She's Hevelin's granddaughter."

Pilot Theo had then handed Podesta to Kara ven'Arith, and taken from her the other norbear. This one's fur had faded to a color reminiscent of rust, and was less-than-plush; the pet itself seemed thinner than the younger creature, and perhaps more frail.

"This is Hevelin," Pilot Theo instructed. "He's very old, and he's met a lot of people. He used to ride circuit with Guild Master Peltzer, so he's been on ships before."

The very old norbear suddenly opened sleepy, slitted eyes, and stared directly at B. Joyita. It made a small noise, possibly inquisitive.

"I see Hevelin and Podesta, norbears," B. Joyita said.

"Okay, good. We'll take them to their greenery. Mostly, they'll stay there, and won't be any trouble."

Were Jermone Joyita present, on this dangerous and exhilarating day, *Bechimo* would further say to him: *I am being of service. I have pilots. I have passengers and cargo. I have felt the texture of between space, and the numerous textures of realspace, each one an individual joy. I have been alone, and afraid. I've made errors. I fear that I have made very grave errors. I still yearn for a captain, and I still don't know why.*

· · · ✵ · · ·

The ten passengers had been settled, their luggage stowed, the cargo lashed in the hold. Keller and Apres-Donegal were there specifically to tend to the cargo's every comfort. They sealed the hatch with tape and their thumbprints, then Keller stood herself at attention directly before it and her partner went off to get some sleep before trading places.

They had unlatched from Codrescu Station, and were preparing to transfer orbit for the run to the Jump point. Theo would swear that she felt *Bechimo* sigh with relief when he finally cleared dock.

There was some concern on the bridge about the determined movement of Eylot craft toward the station, and Theo had to remind herself that, so far, Eylot's forces had been very good. There had been no incidents, no shouting. The threat of interdiction had apparently gone straight to the heart of whoever was passing for Eylot leadership. Or maybe some cooler heads had come onto deck.

"I don't think there are any cooler heads, ground-side," Kara had said, when Theo mentioned this possibility. "I think they just respond well to threats."

"I'll be feeling better myself when we're out of range of everything Eylot," Clarence muttered.

Both pilots were at the board; Kara had asked, and received, permission to sit observer. Joyita was subdued and visibly tense in Screen Six.

Despite they were a ship's day and a half from the Jump point, the course for Velaskiz Rotundo had been calculated, recalculated, checked and finally locked into navcomp by First Board, just to keep them from reworking it one more time, out of nerves and boredom.

The Jump, Theo knew, wouldn't be a problem. Honestly, there shouldn't be any more problems. Just a routine, boring run to the Jump point, and if she ever again came back to Eylot space, it would be because she had completely lost her—

"Eylot Command," came the voice over the general channels. "*Bechimo*, stand ready to be boarded."

Theo stared at the comm.

"What?" she demanded, happily not on the open band. Joyita had that covered.

"*Bechimo*, Eylot Command, Comm Officer Joyita speaking. You are aware that this ship is engaged in the ongoing evacuation effort of Codrescu Station. We are not at liberty to take orders from a nonemergency source."

The message originated from a ship in the pod crowding toward the station; *Bechimo* had it highlighted. In the bottom corner of the screen, targeting calcs came up.

"Can that!" Theo snapped, and the calcs vanished. She wished she could take that to mean *Bechimo wasn't* targeting the command ship, but at least he was doing it privately.

"*Bechimo*," stated Eylot Command, "you are carrying a fugitive from Eylot justice. We demand that First Class Pilot Theo Waitley be surrendered to the legitimate planetary authority."

Theo took a breath.

"Best not to answer," Clarence murmured, as another voice came across channels.

"Eylot Command, this is Carresens-Denobli on *Twinkle*. We observe, you recall, with the Tradedesk Guild Master and the Scout pilot. I will please receive from you the report detailing First Class Pilot Theo Waitley's crimes against planetary Eylot."

Theo clamped her mouth shut, closed her eyes and danced a relaxation. It didn't seem to help much. She tried again, with similar results.

"Thank you, Eylot Command," Asha Carresens-Denobli said. "The Guild Master, the Scout and I have read your report. We advise—we very earnestly advise, Eylot Command, that *Bechimo* is engaged in a rescue operation attending a pilots-in-peril situation. We—pilots, Scouts and Guild Masters—we take pilots-in-peril seriously. We take the situation here as we find it, as we have reported, and continue to report it, seriously. Much more seriously, we advise you, than we take school pranks and young pilot hijinks. *Bechimo*, you may proceed to the Jump point."

"Chaos!"

Theo reached to her board.

"*Bechimo* here, Waitley. Proceeding to Jump point."

TWENTY-NINE

Jump

"HEY."

Theo sank down to the decking next to the nor-bears' green spot with a sigh. It was her off-shift, and she really, she thought, ought to go to bed. She couldn't remember the last time she'd been so tired—nerve-worn, Rig Tranza had termed it; the exhaustion that comes from having been too tense for too long.

She'd tried to access her inner calm, but all she'd managed to achieve was a kind of thin, furious patience. Clarence hadn't found any reason to make small talk, though normally he was a man to tell a story or two, and when he did speak it was quiet and respectful, his body language more Liaden than Terran.

Which was why she had thought to stop by to chat a minute or two with Hevelin before she hit quarters for downtime. Hevelin had a . . . soothing effect on her. Maybe he could revive her inner calm.

"Hey," she said again. "Anybody awake in there?"

She had nearly concluded that there wasn't, when a leaf rustled back in the depths of the greenery. Another leaf rustled; a frond bent. Theo crossed her legs and put her hands on her knees, waiting, hoping it was Hevelin and not Podesta, who wasn't soothing *at all* . . .

More bending fronds and rustles, and it *was* Hevelin come out to see her, his eyes heavy.

"Thank you," Theo said. She reached out and gave him a boost to her knee.

He murbled and stood on his back legs, looking up at her reproachfully.

"Sorry." She raised him to her shoulder, where he established himself comfortably by her ear, humming gently.

Theo closed her eyes, listening to that sound, feeling the tension begin to loosen in her chest.

The humming became more insistent, and slowly, images began to filter into her head.

Guild Master Peltzer, Arndy Slayn, Bringo—of course! Theo thought, grouchily. Hevelin knew she knew those faces!

The humming deepened, and the edge went off the grouchiness as the catalog continued.

A woman's lined face came next, work cap pulled down low over eyes caught in a net of wrinkles.

No one she knew, and then she wondered, reaching up to tap Hevelin's leg.

"*Beeslady*?" she mumbled the question, and before she could stop it, there was the horrific image again, of the shattered ship, the empty cabin, the . . .

. . . the woman's face again, shadowed by her cap,

wisps of iron-grey hair softening cheekbones sharp enough to cut paper.

"I didn't know her," Theo whispered. She cleared her throat. "Thank you."

There was a pause, then an image building slowly until—Pilot yos'Senchul, a shared contact that she readily agreed with, followed by another younger woman, who was a stranger to Theo, then—Kara! She felt a rush of joyful acknowledgment. Of course, she knew Kara!

Hevelin's humming changed pitch; almost it sounded as if he chuckled, and she felt his paw stroking the hair over her ear while a new image built behind her eyes.

Theo nodded. Hevelin had given her this image the first time she'd met him: a man who might—who *was*, she was suddenly and completely certain—Father as a young man, a silver twist swinging in his ear and a long tail of dark hair falling forward to brush the shoulder of a tawny-haired woman with amused green eyes.

Theo caught her breath, recalling the person she'd spoken to in Jelaza Kazone's morning parlor, who had been so interested in *Bechimo*'s marvelous and exact spatial translations. A person any right-minded observer would have seen to be a male pilot of middle age, and not the glowing and energetic female personage of Hevelin's acquaintance. And yet—it had been she! Father's . . . lifemate. Aelliana Caylon.

. She took a breath and thought of that morning in the breakfast room, showing Hevelin Pilot Caylon as she curled awkwardly into the window seat. His humming changed pitch and she sensed a curiosity, and a tentative acceptance of her match.

"Wait," she murmured, and thought of Father as she had last seen him, standing beneath the great Tree in the center of the private garden, showing her the seed pods that had fallen for them.

Intense interest came from Hevelin; his humming became quite loud. Theo held the image, concentrating, until it faded of its own, leaving the two of them replete with satisfaction.

Theo sighed, and suddenly opened her eyes as the hatch cycled behind her.

"There you are!" Kara said. She made sure of the hatch before coming forward and squatting down in front of Theo.

"Were you looking for me?"

"In fact, I was," Kara answered, extending a hand and gently rubbing Hevelin's cheek. "It is your off-shift, so I hear from the excellent Pilot Clarence."

"That's right," Theo admitted. "I ought to be in bed, but I was so . . . tense, that I thought I ought to get some tension reliever."

"Ah." Kara rearranged herself in a move that should have been awkward, but somehow managed to be efficient and graceful. Sitting on the floor now with her knees touching Theo's she looked seriously into her face.

"I see that you are much easier than you had been. We have all had our nerves stretched of late; it really is a testimony to our basic good nature that no one of us has called a duel on another."

"No *dueling* on *Bechimo*," Theo said, sternly. "I

absolutely forbid it, and so—" She clamped her lips shut on the rest of that sentence, remembering just in time that Kara didn't know that *Bechimo* was his own person. He had been keeping a very low profile since they'd taken on passengers.

And *his* temper, Theo thought with a hiccuped giggle, must be *really* ragged about now.

"There, that's a better mode!" Kara approved and again extended a hand, but not, this time to Hevelin.

Theo caught her breath; Kara's fingers were warm on her cheek.

"I wonder if I might ask you," Kara murmured, "to serve me as Hevelin has served you."

"Sitting on your shoulder and humming, you mean?" Theo asked, remembering the last time she and Kara had . . .

"I had in mind something a little more encompassing."

Kara looked tired. Worse, she looked *worn*. Not that she didn't have a right; she'd been living under stress for some time, and the stress didn't stop just because she'd been evacuated, instead of arrested.

Kara was leaving more than school, more than the place she'd worked.

She was leaving her whole family on Eylot. If she went back, she endangered not only herself, but them. And if she *didn't* go back—they might be in danger, anyway.

Being clanless, to a Liaden, that was bad. All kinds of psychology was tied up with being a clan member, quite apart from whatever a woman might feel about abandoning her family to chaos and disorder.

Hevelin was still humming happily in her ear. Theo

smiled and turned her head so that her lips skimmed
the inside of Kara's wrist.

"Help me get this tricky norbear back into his
sleep spot," she said.

· · · · ❖ · · · ·

Clarence released his chair and let it rotate, coming
to his feet in a lunging stretch, hearing joints crack
and feeling the long muscles in his back loosen up.

"That's better," he murmured, yawning luxuriously.

He hoped that Kara ven'Arith found Theo, and
that when she did, she'd do what she could to help
the lassie displace some of that energy that had been
brewing just under the surface. Tension was tension,
and space knew they all had something to be tense
about—some more than others. But he hadn't at all
relished the sensation of sitting Second Board to a
pilot at the far bitter end of her patience, and worried into the bargain. Not that he'd thought Theo
would light into him with more than words—but it
couldn't be argued that the lassie had a sharp way
with a word.

Well, then.

Standing, he looked to the screens, which showed
a uniform and uninteresting grey, time until Jump-end
counting down in the lower right corner of Number
Eight screen. Couple ship-days and then realspace
outside of Velaskiz Rotundo. He wondered if Clothide
was still Boss, which she could be, or not. She'd been
getting on in years, and she might've took the retirement. Or she might've gotten herself into a little more
trouble than she could easily handle. Never one to
turn down a challenge or a risk, Clothide.

Well, he'd find out soon enough, he supposed. And if she remembered him fondly.

"Clarence," Joyita said from Screen Six. "Would you answer a question for me?"

"Do my best, laddie," Clarence said with a heartiness that was only a little forced. The laddie had been as tense as any of them, and for as much cause. More, if it was taken into account that all of *Bechimo* spoke through Joyita, in the presence of guests.

"Thank you. I wonder about norbears."

"Well, you're not alone there," said Clarence, taking his seat again and adjusting it to recline slightly. "The Scouts wonder about norbears and any number of scholarly folk wonder about norbears, not to mention those who keep company with norbears on a regular basis. Are they intelligent or are they not? Are they capable of turning a man against himself and all that he formerly believed, by twisting his emotions into knots? Might as well add your question to the list."

Joyita glanced down, as if he were consulting a screen, then looked back to Clarence, brown eyes slightly narrowed.

"I learn from my research that norbears are . . . empaths."

"Oh, *that* nearly everybody agrees with! Which is why, you understand, there's some who want to eradicate the species, before they control us all."

Joyita frowned. "Can they control us all?"

"Well, now, that's a question, too, isn't it? My view is, even if they can, they won't. Far too sleepy."

"They're . . . *pets*, then, these norbears."

Clarence tipped his head, considering that.

"Companions, say rather, laddie. There aren't many households'll have a norbear just to have one, like you might have yourself a cat or six. Larger ships might carry a norbear 'mong the ship's company, to help calm crew, or ease a bad case of homesickness. Somebody like your Guild Master, now, he'd depend on his norbear to screen pilots for emotional stability. That's a fairly important job, I'd say."

Joyita appeared to be thinking, looking off into the middle distance.

"Have you been companioned by a norbear?"

"Me?" Clarence thought of the general tenor of the Boss' office at Solcintra Port. He'd tried to run a tight organization, and he'd been very careful of loose ends. Still and all, not the general atmosphere that an empath could be supposed to relish.

"Not me, no, laddie. I'm not a resty fellow."

"Is Pilot Theo a resty fellow?"

Clarence laughed. "Now, there I'd say no. But she's a busy lass, with a good deal of energy. That might be attractive to an empath."

Silence.

"Did I answer your question, then, Chimmy?" Clarence asked, knowing that he likely hadn't.

"You did answer my question, thank you, Clarence. I see that I need to do more research in order to place your answer into context."

Well, that would keep him busy, Clarence thought. For all of five Standard minutes.

"You do that," he said. "Keep me informed, will you? I've an interest in the matter, myself."

· · · ✹ · · ·

"So," Kara murmured, "you no longer think that Korval is a story, at least."

Theo smiled in the dark, and stroked Kara's shoulder. Kara didn't feel tense anymore. Neither did Theo.

"I learned better," she agreed.

"How?" asked Kara.

"Hmm?"

Kara poked her side with a sharp finger. "How did you learn better?"

"Oh, well—it's complicated, but the high points are that I met the delm of Korval, who are two people, lifemated. And I met Master Trader yos'Galan, and worked out a contract to research a new loop for him."

"Those are lucky meetings," Kara said, sounding drowsy.

"I'm told that's how it is, usually, with Korval," Theo said, settling her cheek against Kara's hair.

"Mmm..." her friend said. She didn't say anything else, her breathing slowing into the rhythm of sleep.

The sound of Kara sleeping was as relaxing and fulfilling as Hevelin's hums. Theo smiled, closed her eyes.

And followed Kara into sleep.

THIRTY

. . . .

Velaskiz Rotundo

AS IT HAPPENED, THERE WAS ROOM FOR *BECHIMO* AT
the Guild Yard, so Clarence didn't need to call in
favors from his friend, after all.

Theo—who, on reflection, had come to the uneasy
conclusion that Clarence's "friend" was very likely
the Juntavas Boss of Velaskiz Rotundo—thought with
relief that leaving that marker lie was probably best
for everyone concerned.

"Do you have time for a private talk, Pilot?" she
asked, after the boards had been locked down and
Joyita had opened up a comm line for Guild Master
Peltzer to Guild Sector Headquarters.

Clarence gave her a bland look out of the sides
of his eyes.

"That would be pleasant," he said in Liaden.

Theo grinned, hearing the tiny twist of sarcasm.

"Well, it doesn't have to be *un*pleasant," she said,
in Terran. "I need your input." Her fingers obligingly
added, *crew business*.

Clarence's eyebrows rose. He spun his chair so that he faced her, and gave her a nod, fingers elucidating, *all attention here now*.

Theo nodded and looked to Screen Six. "Joyita."

"Pilot Theo?"

"Second Board and I need some private space here. Can you take a tea break?"

"Certainly, Pilot."

"Thank you."

Screen Six went blank.

Theo nodded, and looked to Clarence.

"It won't come as a surprise to you, I guess, that I'm thinking of adding Kara ven'Arith to the ship's complement. I'd like to know what you think—I especially want to know if you think you can work with her."

"No surprises, you're right there, Pilot. Now, what I think is that Pilot ven'Arith—assuming she's at liberty—would be a good addition to the crew. I'll grant she's got some things to learn—and so will she. No false pride and no overreaching. Wants to learn, asks permission to shadow the pilots..." He paused and looked up to the ceiling, fingers shaping, *all good*.

"The other plus is that she's been actively working at the tech side, which neither one of us has. Could teach us some things, I'm thinking—which isn't a bad thing. Might be she could give *Bechimo* a hand with those couple little chores he has on the list."

Theo laughed. "Maybe she could. Kara once told me that her first toy was a power screwdriver, and that she worked on her first repair when she was six."

"Not exaggerating, either, I'd bet." He frowned

slightly at the ceiling before bringing his gaze down
to meet Theo's.

"Now that last question—can I work with her?
That's an important question and I want to thank
you for asking it.

"Pilot ven'Arith's shadowed me a couple times,
like you know, asking permission, everything polite
and proper. She's honest, I think, and eager. I can
work with her."

Theo felt a knot in her chest that she hadn't known
was there come loose. She smiled.

"On the downside," Clarence said.

Theo went very still.

He grinned at her. "We're going to have a lot of
teaching to do. Now, I always heard that the best
way to reinforce what you know is to teach it to
somebody else."

"That's true," Theo told him seriously. "Both Kamele
and Father said they hoped their students learned as
much from them as they learned from their students."

He nodded. "There you are then. I think it would
be a good move, for the ship, for the pilots, and
maybe even for Pilot ven'Arith."

"Thank you," Theo said. "I appreciate your input and
your honesty. Now, if *you* could take a tea break..."

"I am a thought dry." He got up and departed, the
hatch closing behind him jauntily.

Theo spun back to face board and screens. Peltzer's
comm line was still lit, all else on sleep.

"Joyita," Theo said. "May I have your attention?"

Screen Six flickered and cleared. Joyita looked at
her expectantly. "Pilot Theo?"

She considered him. Somewhat to her own surprise,

she'd gotten . . . accustomed to him on the same level that she was accustomed to Clarence—as another presence in the Heart. A comrade.

"Joyita, I'm thinking of adding Kara ven'Arith to our crew, as third pilot and chief tech. May I have your opinion? Do you have objections?"

Joyita frowned slightly, which he did when he was thinking. Theo sat back and waited.

"Pilot ven'Arith is a Second Class Pilot," he said slowly. "She will need flight time and instruction."

He made direct eye contact. Theo inclined her head.

"Go on, please."

"Yes. You have, I see, researched her employment history, and her Guild record. I assume that these were satisfactory. My own search reveals no outstanding warrants or record of wrongdoing."

Again, he paused, and again Theo nodded, her ears a little warm. She *had* checked Kara's records; it was her responsibility as First Board and Acting Captain, even if she didn't have Clarence's example of what could happen if you hired a friend without doing a proper check.

So, she'd done it, and she knew it was the right thing to do.

But it had still felt like . . . snooping. Like she somehow *didn't trust* Kara.

"Yes. Pilot ven'Arith's tech skills would be of use in maintaining and retrofitting the ship. She is well-liked by Hevelin . . ."

"Hold, please." Theo sat up. "Is that a qualification? Being well-liked by Hevelin? Hevelin likes lots of people."

"But I understand that Hevelin doesn't like all

people," Joyita said earnestly. "He is an empath, and Guild Master Peltzer relies on him to point out unstable individuals."

"And he hasn't indicated that Kara's unstable. Fair enough. More?"

"Clarence also likes her, and I think that Clarence is in general a good judge of character." He paused, raised a hand and seemed to be studying the rings binding his thumb, first and second fingers.

"Also, *I* like her. I think Pilot ven'Arith would be a good addition to the ship's company."

"Just for the record, I like her, too," Theo said drily. "Anything else? Objections?"

"No objections, Pilot."

"She'll have to meet *Bechimo*," Theo pointed out.

"Yes." He looked up from the study of his rings to meet her eyes. "Do you anticipate a problem? *Bechimo* is eager to make her acquaintance."

"Is he? That's good. The next time you...communicate with *Bechimo*, please tell him that I know this transporting of...non-crew has been a challenge to his patience, and that I appreciate his decorum."

"*Bechimo* is still present, Pilot, and he has heard you himself."

Theo felt the blush warm her cheeks. Of course *Bechimo* was still present, and listening to everything that went on aboard. But this other thing—

"Kara might be shocked a little, at first, but I think that'll pass quickly. When we were studying the Complex Logic Laws in school, she told me that she hoped there were some self-aware logics, somewhere, who had managed to hide themselves and to go about their lives."

Joyita grinned, and Theo grinned back.

"All right, I think we have agreement among existing crew. I'll make the offer and we'll see if the pilot's at liberty."

Kara was in the norbear room, kneeling next to the greenery, Podesta cradled in the crook of her arm like a child. For once the young norbear wasn't being raucous and demanding. In fact, she seemed subdued.

Kara didn't look up when the hatch cycled. She didn't look up when Theo knelt beside her, tipping her head in an attempt to get a look at her friend's hidden face.

"Kara?"

There was a long pause, as if Kara were trying to come up with a credible reason not to be Kara. Podesta reached up from her recline in Kara's arm, and gently caught some long strands of red-gold hair.

"Theo," Kara said then, her voice husky. "You find me disadvantaged."

That meant "go away" when rendered in Liaden. Theo chewed her lip, and watched a tear fall onto Podesta's furry belly.

"How can there be advantage or disadvantage between us?" Theo asked in Liaden, in what she hoped was the mode between intimates. "I do not allow it. Indeed, it is I who would stand at disadvantage, if such a thing might exist between us. Forgive me; I see that my timing is awkward, and yet necessity exists..."

Kara raised her head, staring at Theo from wet blue eyes.

"You've been studying!"

"Yes, I have," Theo admitted, and let herself slide back into Terran, "much good it's doing me."

"It's doing you a great deal of good," Kara said sternly. "You were quite credible. Promise me that you will continue your studies."

"Easy to do. I made a deal with Clarence and he won't let me slack off. But Kara—I do have a question for you. Since I've already intruded, may I ask it?"

Kara half-laughed and sniffed.

"Excellent! She uses bad timing to excuse bad manners and asks to be allowed to behave more badly, since she has been discourteous already."

Theo blinked. Put that way...

"No, no, Theo. It's a joke," Kara told her. "Please, ask your question."

She took a deep breath. *Inner calm*, she told herself. What she wanted to do was to take Kara's hand in hers, but that would be the wrong *melant'i* for this. She was here, not as Kara's friend, but as a potential employer. It was important to preserve distance.

"I would like to know if you are at liberty to accept a position as third pilot and chief technician on *Bechimo*," she said, her voice sounding rushed in her own ears.

Kara's mouth dropped open.

Podesta squeaked and squirmed, struggling to get to her feet. Theo grabbed her before she could fall and put her on the floor between her knees and Kara's.

"May I inquire into the reasons for this offer?" Kara's voice wasn't exactly steady, but Theo didn't think she was mad.

"It's pretty straightforward," she said calmly. "We're

doing a shakedown run, like I told you, and one of the things that Clarence and I have discovered is that we need more crew. Especially, we need a tech, and a third-relief pilot would be nice, too. And here you are, who are both! I polled the crew, and we all agreed. So, I'm asking if you're at liberty. If you've got something else, I understand. Any ship who gets you will be fortunate."

Two tears formed in Kara's eyes, and rolled down her cheek.

"Gods, I'm a watering pot today!" she cried, and reached into a leg pocket for a handkerchief. "Forgive me, Theo."

She wiped her face, and sat holding the handkerchief in her hand, eyes closed while she did some meditation, or only breathed, slow and sure.

Theo waited, laughed softly as Podesta scaled her knees and stood on her thigh, with one paw hitched through Theo's belt.

"That's pretty good," she said, and rubbed the norbear behind her ears.

"I do not have anything else," Kara said, opening her eyes. "And I will be delighted to sign on to *Bechimo* as chief tech and relief pilot."

Theo grinned, happiness buoying her. Podesta murbled and butted her head hard against Theo's fingers, which had unfortunately stopped massaging her ears.

"All right, then. Let's go down to the Guild Hall and do this thing."

· · · ❖ · · ·

It had been anticipated that Mildred Bilinoda would name names and pinpoint locations. As her nature was both inquisitive and acquisitive, it was to be supposed that her hoard of information was considerable.

Certainly, as far as Uncle and his various business interests were concerned, it would be foolhardy to assume otherwise.

The word *hide* had gone out among the third tier—those whom Uncle found useful to his business dealings, but who were not an essential part of the network. Take and question them all, and someone with fortune and insight might, indeed, piece together the idea that there *was* a network, while failing to gather enough hard data to deduce its location, purpose, and members.

While some of the third tier had surely made it to at least a kind of safety, others had or would certainly fall into the net of this newly aggressive foe. Which meant that various items of what the Scouts termed Old Tech, or Befores, had come into the keeping of those who were both ambitious and ignorant.

This was unsatisfactory in the extreme. The Scouts were annoyance enough, in their insistence of collecting every bit of Old Tech and warehousing it. Warehouses, after all, could be raided, if necessary.

These others, though—this Department of the Interior. They wished to have the galaxy under their control, and they saw in the works of the Oldest Enemy the means to bring their ambition to fruition.

He strongly suspected that it had been agents of the Department of the Interior whose attempted subversion of Pod 78 had brought Daav yos'Phelium to Moonstruck, to meet his doom. Though, perhaps, Uncle thought now, shuffling through incoming reports, they had merely meant to bring him away as a hostage, drain him of all he knew...

...and return him to Korval, as a poison tooth.

That disaster at least had been averted, though Uncle remained doubtful that Korval would be perfectly pleased with his own solving regarding their clan elder.

"Yuri."

Dulsey walked to his desk. She looked...distressed, he thought. And she had used his name, which she did so...very seldom.

"Have we a disaster in hand, my child?"

"Very nearly," she answered seriously. "Andreth found signs of surveillance at Catalinc."

His blood ran cold.

"Surveillance?" he asked, forcing his voice into a pleasant and interested tone.

She nodded once, sharply.

"Alerted, he kept watch, and so was on hand with several others of his team when the attempt was made to go in. They captured two. One is still alive; the other was downloaded."

For a moment, he only looked at her. Two—*two* individuals had very nearly gotten to Catalinc. That... would have been...

"Disastrous" didn't begin to cover it.

Andreth had taken the individuals and held the whole of one and the intelligence of the other. Andreth was to be...commended. To have taken the interlopers and preserved them for questioning was well done.

That there should have been whispers about the Catalinc project loud enough to reach the ears of those outside the network...but always, there were whispers; it only mattered if they were heeded. If the whispers were strange enough, or the project too bold, it often came about that the whispers were...discounted. But secrecy? There was no true secrecy...anywhere.

One only had to look at the ruin of the *Bechimo* project to be reminded of it. Even the contents of one's own mind were not inviolate.

As he well knew.

Uncle stirred himself, recalling Dulsey standing near, awaiting his answer to her information.

"Allow Andreth to know that we will wish to question his guests and that we will be with him shortly."

"I have already done so," Dulsey said, which was like her. No one knew his mind like Dulsey—occasionally she even knew better than he. "I've also laid in a course. We may leave at your word."

He considered her for a moment. "Is there a reason that should not be *immediately*?"

"I wondered if you would want to off-load...certain items at Home Free before we go to Andreth?"

A good question. In other times than these, it would not even have *been* a question.

In *these* times, however, when there was surveillance mounted on a project most very secret, indeed, and Randoling reporting far too much traffic in the vicinity of her refuge point...

"I think," he said to Dulsey's serious grey eyes, "that we will go to Andreth, taking all that we have with us. I find myself not at all sanguine regarding the current safety of fixed orbits."

"Yes," said Dulsey. She smiled slightly. "We leave within the hour."

"Excellent."

•••⟡•••

The Guild rep nodded as she scrolled through the files, short fingers occasionally tapping the input pad at her side.

"So," she murmured, maybe to herself, maybe to Theo and Kara sitting across from her, both pretending to be less nervous than they were. "So."

There was no reason to be nervous, Theo told herself forcefully. She'd cribbed the contract from the one Shan had given her to hire Clarence, so the Terms and Conditions ought to be right. They'd filled out the Guild forms together, Theo explaining that *Bechimo*'s accounts weren't big-ship plump, since they were just getting started, and Kara acknowledging that she didn't expect to make cruise-liner pay.

This trip.

"So," said the rep once more, and looked up with a smile.

"Independent contract ship, third key, with add-on tech and other duties as needed. Second Class Pilot standard Guild rate, plus fifteen percent, plus one-sixth of ship's profit, if any, no loss-share or insurance required. Contract offered to end of current run, renews automatically for the next trip unless cancelled by either principal. The contract itself is satisfactory to the Guild. If you would both sign the hardcopy, here and here..." She pointed, flourishing a pen in her free hand. Theo snatched it and affixed her signature in the places indicated, then passed the pen to Kara, who also signed.

"Good," said the rep, taking the pen back with the hardcopy. "We'll transmit a copy to *Bechimo* and to Pilot ven'Arith's address on file with the Guild. Now, Pilot, if I may have your license, I will update it with your new data, and you'll be on your way."

Kara surrendered her license, the rep slid it into the reader, tapped a few more times on the input pad.

"There you are, Pilot. Is there anything else the Pilots Guild can provide you this day?"

"Thank you, no," said Kara.

"No further business, thank you, ma'am," added Theo. They exited the rep's cubicle and headed toward the entrance side by side.

"As soon as we get the passengers off," Theo said, "we'll do some looking around for things that might be appreciated at Ynsolt'i, or Kendrik—those are our next two stops in the loop we're supposed to be testing."

"So the ship is allowed to trade for itself? We're not tied to the Master Trader's direction?"

"The Master Trader's direction, at least this time, was to feel out the route, to talk to people on a list he provided, and to pick up four pods at Cresthaller, assuming were spaceworthy after twenty-five years of planet weather."

Kara eyed her. "Were they?"

"Three were. The other one . . ."

"Theo Waitley, First Class Pilot Theo Waitley." The intercom was, Theo thought, much louder than it needed to be. She stopped, feeling her cheeks warm, Kara stopping beside her.

"First Class Pilot Theo Waitley, please come to the Sector Master's office at once. Repeat: Theo Waitley, Pilot First Class, to the Sector Master's office at once."

"Now, what?" Theo muttered.

"The Sector Master probably wishes to acknowledge your heroism," Kara said.

"That would play better if I'd been a hero," Theo answered. "The only thing we did was follow regs.

Nothing heroic in following regs, same as Professor Chibs told us, over and over. What they probably want to do is dispute our bill."

"Then you will want me with you," Kara said briskly, taking her arm and turning her back toward the depths of the building. "I am a past expert in explaining invoiced items."

"Are you? We might have to make you head accountant, too." Theo allowed herself to be turned, and matched Kara's stride up the hall.

"Why not simply part-owner?"

"We'd have to take a vote," Theo told her.

"And Clarence would vote against me, would he? Wait, now where—ah! This way, Theo."

Meekly, Theo followed her friend down the intersecting hall and in not too many steps more they stepped through a door bearing the legend SECTOR MASTER, and into a small room with a desk directly facing the door. The man seated behind the desk looked up.

"Help you, Pilots?"

"I'm Theo Waitley," she began, but apparently she didn't have to say anything else. The man touched a button on his desk console, glanced briefly down and nodded.

"You can go right in, Pilot Waitley. May I help *you*, Pilot?" he asked Kara.

"I am Kara ven'Arith, *Bechimo* crew," Kara said. "I am with Pilot Waitley."

"Right, then; you'll want to wait for her in the cafe or the general waiting area. Call was for Waitley, not Waitley and crew."

Kara looked at Theo. Theo looked at Kara, sighed and raised her hands, both palms up—*what's to do?*

"Why don't you grab a cup of tea and wait for me," she said. "If I don't show up or send a message in an hour, go on home."

"You're certain you don't need me?"

"Like you said, they probably only want to give me a medal for following regs."

Kara smiled. "Soon, then," she said. A nod to the man behind the desk and she was gone.

Immediately the door to the hall shut; another door, directly behind the desk, opened.

"Please, Pilot. The Sector Master is expecting you."

The Sector Master's office was easily three times the size of the reception area. The desk itself, Theo estimated, was only slightly larger than the reception area, big enough to hold a couple of screens, ranged to the extreme and moderate left of center, and a very large planter of mixed grasses on the right.

Behind the desk was an angular woman with brown eyes and close-cropped brown hair. Directly beside the desk, in what could either be a place of honor or extreme peril, sat Guild Master Peltzer. Theo gave him a courteous nod, and a murmured, "Guild Master," before giving her full attention to the woman behind the desk.

"First Class Pilot Theo Waitley," she said. "You wanted to see me, ma'am?"

"Sector Guild Master LoRita Constince," the woman said. "I did want to see you, Pilot, yes. Master Peltzer tells me the Guild owes you a debt of gratitude, which is one reason for wanting to see you. Also need to tell you that your invoice is being adjusted in 'counts. We'll send an itemized update to *Bechimo*—it'll probably be waiting for you when you get back. Once you okay that, we'll be able to pay you, and you can get back to your proper business. Building a loop for Korval, wasn't that?"

Theo blinked. An adjusted total? Maybe Kara would have a chance to exercise her talents, after all.

"We're exploring the possibility of a loop for Master Trader yos'Galan, yes ma'am," she said politely. "Not building so much as learning if there's anything to build *on*."

She nodded. "A fine distinction, I agree. And when Master Traders are in play, it pays to be as precise as possible."

She used her chin to point at the chair to Theo's right, at the opposite corner from Guild Master Peltzer.

"Have a seat, Pilot; there's somebody else I'd like you to meet. Guild business, legitimate Guild business. Shouldn't take more'n a few minutes of your time."

"I do," Theo said, taking the seat cautiously, "have a crew member waiting for me."

"We should be done before your crew has any cause for concern," said Guild Master Constince. "Just a quick chat with an associate of mine." She snapped her fingers lightly.

The bowl of grasses near Theo's chair shook authoritatively, and disgorged a nicely plump norbear, white, except for a large black spot on her back and two very small black spots on her head, directly before each ear.

"This," said Sector Guild Master Constince, "is Sinaya. She's heard about you from Hevelin, and very much wanted to meet you herself."

"Did you?" Theo asked the norbear. Sinaya blinked her eyes peaceably and continued her approach. Theo looked to Guild Master Peltzer. He nodded.

"Just like she says. Hevelin apparently talked you up, Pilot."

Theo sighed, and looked back to the norbear, who had stopped near Theo's left hand, and was looking up at her expectantly.

"All right," she said, lifting her hand and turning it palm-up in case Sinaya wanted a lift. "I'm glad to meet you, Sinaya."

The norbear didn't move for a moment, then she came forward and settled herself half across Theo's hand, with her chin resting on the big vein in her wrist.

Immediately, images began to form in Theo's head—a grizzled countenance with quivering ears—*Hevelin*, Theo thought, around a rush of affection.

Podesta was offered next; Theo acknowledged her with an affection tempered with exasperation. Guild Master Peltzer, Arndy Slayn, Orn Eld yos'Senchul, Bringo... followed by a series of three faces Theo had to admit weren't familiar to her, and then a pause, deliberate, as if Sinaya were waiting for her to produce her own catalog.

Networking with norbears, Theo thought resignedly.

She offered Kara, and Clarence, both of whom were received with warm interest, but no sense of prior meeting. She offered Coyster, and felt... something like a trill of amusement. Theo smiled and offered Kamele, who was acknowledged with interest, though Theo didn't know if her attempted projection of *mother* reached, or made any difference to her interlocutor.

Next, she offered Father, both as she had seen him last, and as Hevelin had shown him to her, with Pilot Caylon tucked well inside his personal space.

That sparked intense interest, and a small murble.

Theo rested then, not knowing how much more was wanted or expected from her, anxious to return to Kara—she stopped, somehow in receipt of the certainty that Sinaya had followed all of those thoughts clearly, and that it was probably rude to allow your thoughts to wander when in converse with a norbear.

Her answer to that was a feeling of indulgent cheerfulness even as one more image formed inside her head.

Theo managed not to gasp, though she was sure that Sinaya caught her anxious start.

The image was of Joyita.

THIRTY-ONE

THE MOOD ON THE FLIGHT DECK WAS EAGER AS THE count-in came closer; if Joyita's smile was slight, Clarence's was open and Kara's, sitting observer with him at Second Board, reflected that with a cheerful demeanor as she used the ear-over to listen in to *Bechimo* as she got a taste of an ordinary commercial system entry.

Ordinary—as if the ship and crew had enough time together yet to know what ordinary was for them! Theo knew that she and Rig had fallen easily into a pattern, but much of that had been Rig's experience talking. She felt herself color, recalling the first drop-in she'd done with Clarence at second—by any measure she'd been far more nervous than eager, that time.

Theo ran through a calming dance in her head, granting to herself that eager was a step up and hoping that she wouldn't get to be *bland* about arrivals, as several big-liner pilots she'd played bowli ball with

337

claimed they were ... but there, they'd been sitting with a second and a third and four backups ...

She nearly missed the final number in sequence as in *Bechimo*'s ultraquiet fashion they slid into realspace. There was nothing really close to them, and as prearranged, they held off announcing themselves until they could take a good look at the situation.

The inner system was crowded with ships, many of them Liaden, and a higher percentage than she'd expect listing Solcintra, Liad, as home port. That fact, of course, was Liaden ego, or at least Liaden hyperbole, at work. Just as *Bechimo* might never Jump into Waymart's system, much less dock or berth there, most of these ships had never touched down on the dust of Liad, even if they claimed it as home. For Terrans, the common port was Waymart. For Liadens it was Solcintra, Liad.

"Quite the show," Theo allowed, "but is everybody out there on vacation?"

Truth was, although there were a lot of ships insystem, quite a few were not close in to the action, as one might expect. Instead, some were clearly in parking orbits well outside Ynsolt'i's usual trade lanes, tending to cluster around larger ships that acted as hubs away from the three orbiting trade centers. The two bulk-ship centers, fed in part from planetary shipments launched to space by catapulted boosters, were in low orbit and held no interest for *Bechimo*, Laughing Cat, or Tree-and-Dragon.

Port of convenience as Liad might be for some, about a third of the ships were showing Ynsolt'i as home, and a surprising number of those were official—naval units, police, customs, port and traffic control. With the planet's nearspace as busy as it was, Theo supposed they'd be taking their time getting in, and was glad she wasn't on one of Uncle's split-second courier runs.

Bechimo peppered IDs across the main screen, running matches for prior coincident ships and finding three, and then a fourth; building the image to show the main shipping lanes and their own time to Ynsolt'i's clearance zones, something complicated by a current comet with associated meteors and debris.

She was willing to use one of Korval's rotating landing permits if there were open slots; otherwise Theo had asked Clarence to requisition the first available spot on Ynsolt'i Three, the orbiting trade market most likely to have an opening for sub-pod or break-pod trading.

Joyita spoke a reminding, "We have yet to announce, Pilot. Shall I schedule that as an automatic event on future entries?"

Theo glanced toward Screen Six.

"Not yet on scheduling ahead—we'll want to see how the entry process works when we have three pilots at the boards. For this entry, I'll do the announce, thank you. Next time we may have the Exec do it, or Pilot Three. But do, please, make sure the cat's laughing and the dragon's flying."

Theo caught Kara's quick glance, signed *available for duty* and smiled, warming. Yes, Kara was already a happy addition to the crew, indeed.

· · · ❖ · · ·

They were far enough out that their announcement took its time. While it progressed, *Bechimo* told Pilot Waitley and the crew of two outgoing Jump glares on the other side of the system, ships gone before they'd arrived. *Bechimo* overlaid the main screen with a light haze to indicate how far their arrival signal reached into the system, and kept track, now, of automatic acknowledgments from mere-ships, repeaters, and satellite systems.

The crew spoke from time to time, with the head tech in a learning mode, and thus accessing both the Pilot and the Less Pilot's attention, sometimes simultaneously. As a pilot, Kara ven'Arith had far less practical board time than either of the other crew, no matter that her practical knowledge of state-of-the-art internals was equal or better than theirs, and her understanding of older basic tech far more useful.

For his part, *Bechimo* was quite pleased with the technician's understanding of modules. Already, she'd gotten the hydroponics and cleansing systems in fine shape, suggested several practical short-term amendments; and positively delighted in helping with the creation of the garden zone for the traveler Hevelin.

Hevelin was present in the Heart. *Bechimo* monitored him carefully, mindful of Guild Master Peltzer's last discussion with Pilot Waitley and the crew.

"I know this ship will care for Hevelin better than a Guild Master on a mission can, and I expect reports! I have a lot of moving to do, and not all of it fun! I'm the first Master to lose a Guild office in a hundred Standards!"

Bechimo understood that this had been both information and an order to the crew, if not to him. How those reports might reflect on himself, he did not know. The possibility of nonhuman travelers was something the Builders had discussed and allowed for, but some of those records, alas, were mere threads, leading to information he could not access.

Hevelin, like the tech, seemed to have a bias toward Pilot Waitley; in both cases the bias was based on something more than just hierarchy, and *Bechimo* found himself outlining a search for information on the topic "leadership."

Even Pilot Waitley's hurried decision to support Codrescu—for *Bechimo* knew that the Less Pilot's inclination had been to permit others to take a lead there!—became the basis for increased prestige for the Pilot and thus, for her craft. Ships coming after gave some precedence to Pilot Waitley's thoughts and the Guild offices at Velaskiz Rotundo had been pleased to give the pilot and *Bechimo* certification as the Pilots Guild Embassy Mobile to Norbears, along with a modest stipend to assist with feeding and other care Hevelin might require.

Bechimo considered the "Embassy Mobile" designation for some time, spread among processors, and decided that it was an actual appreciation and in some way a reward for their arriving to assist Codrescu. There had been a transmission to record and a hard-copy vellum document handed over.

"If you hit any port that insists you can't have an alien on board," Guild Master Peltzer had told Pilot Waitley, "this is our best shot for you: the Pilots Guild recognizes Hevelin as the Elder Traveling Norbear Ambassador and you, Pilot, are both certified and required by the Guild as his guardian. I'd also watch for them places that got traveling aliens they shouldn't—we'll authorize you to act, with Hevelin's guidance, in those cases."

"You expect us to run across norbear cubs in space?" the pilot asked, lightly.

Peltzer had sighed—*Bechimo*'s speech recognition procedures not only knew them but graded them for meaning.

"We have come across a few, here and there, and we're doing our best to keep them out of zoos and such. They so much *like* to travel . . . sometimes they'll stow away. Hevelin's been wanting a change for a while, I know. Much better you than spoil of war to Eylot!"

Bechimo initiated searches for precedents for the guardianship in various political and history archives, then let the thread go to concentrate on more current events.

Presently, the Joyita extension was engaged in a discussion of uniforms, one which mostly involved ven'Arith and O'Berin, but sometimes had input from the pilot and sometimes from the archives—one might not say "memory" for those bits of allowable information—of the Joyita-that-was, who had on several occasions spoken of utility clothing, uniforms, and the like while *Bechimo* was yet borderline aware. The extension adopted Joyita's preferences for monocolor dress in work areas, and for colorful—O'Berin called the suggestions flamboyant!—marks of rank for off-ship excursions.

Conversation continued comfortably, but the pilot, and perforce *Bechimo*, studied the larger situation. The inner system was crowded, and in his days of self-directed travel he would not have come this far into the system, not even in search of company.

And there was that . . . slight doubtfulness that he felt was required here, an extra few points added to negative information, an extra point knocked off of positive information.

With his awareness, he'd sometimes gained access to what Joyita himself had called "the hunch engine," a net of comparative and projective databases working off the interplay between memory, thought and sensors. Accessing that had resulted in him being where he was now: with a crew on mission. He recognized there was a balance to be observed, that in fact his hunch machine was often not entirely correct. There was always plenty to do, so analyzing hunch engine musings often occurred in the quiet times, when Theo slept.

B. Joyita was now conversing with an outside ship as per the new pattern of things, and Pilot Waitley allowed the Exec and his board partner to interact with the Ynsolt'i comm and traffic systems, some of which were computers and programmed brains, some of which spoke with their own voices if they spoke, some of which spoke with the recorded and amended voices of humans.

One or two of the nodes in the loop *were* human and spoke for themselves. *Bechimo* had been sampling radio communications since arrival, recording and analyzing the accents and speech patterns in use, sometimes referring them to Joyita's motion and speech units without passing the information on to the flight deck. His purpose was to refine Joyita's presence and thus the efficiency of the ship—and increase his own effectiveness.

Pilot O'Berin, as Exec, had found them a dock on Trade Three—a joyful thing, meaning their first trading could go on—and also, that the crew could tune their day schedule to the station and berth in question. Guide 79 was their off-ship navigator and contact now; *Bechimo* heard Clarence's banter as he spoke of weather on a world he had never been to and plans for evenings that were hardly in the schedule. Guide 79's voice was feminine and human, of that he was sure, and the tone suggested someone who took her role seriously. Clarence was, he decided, being friendly to this person; a tacit willingness to regard Guide 79 as benign.

The new friend provided numbers vocally and in a press-file; by the time Clarence repeated them for the others on the flight deck, *Bechimo* had them, and set to work, setting aside the random thoughts of an AI with extra processing time. Now he had a course, a rendezvous point, a time schedule, and while the numbers were long coming—at least two seconds!—when run on Board One, they were now showing up on Board Two and the reserve Board Three used by the tech. Pilot Theo's transcription of the information was flawless and matched his own.

There was a long slow flow into the system, with other ships being fed into the same queue, the order and progression of arrivals to match departures and empty slots in available berthings.

Things being generally in order, and the pilot watching, *Bechimo* continued to observe the ebb and flow of nearspace, to update the communications maps and monitor the various bands of communications the pilot usually attended to. Also, he began the usual inquiries of the local info channels. There was always plenty to do.

· · · ·✦· · · ·

Theo squinted at the screens, watching the overlays tell the tale of destination and precedence, Ynsotl'i a blue-green presence hanging over their head and their berth currently out beyond their vision, on the the other side of the world.

The largest ships took the most maneuvering time and effort, and got the most attention . . . if Ynsolt'i used the straight traffic system she'd learned at the Academy they were in group one, with *Bechimo* falling into group three and courier ships into group four or five along with the local craft.

When she'd been sitting Second to Rig Tranza there'd been a few arrivals like this, where ships were expected to keep to lanes and the locals provided a dedicated flight director for anything that was inter-stellar. Several times there'd been offers of an actual pilot on board, which had always been declined. If it happened here—certainly with *Bechimo*'s lines Ynsolt'i would have no one more expert than *Bechimo* to berth the ship!

Still, there was Guide 79, and Theo was just as happy to have Clarence on the detail, knowing she wasn't all that good with small talk.

Theo regarded the deck. Joyita was taking messages and dealing with the basic incoming information—and talking uniforms, of all things, with the crew. Theo smiled—she could get used to this. Clarence sat Exec, his sketch book filling with a new round of faces and a few notes and a large underlined 79, and even triangles now that Hevelin had drifted back from his knee to lean against her leg and watch the big screen. She felt a contentment there and hoped he knew hers. She was glad to have his company.

Kara still observed and probably ought to for the next two or three arrivals, and then get a chance to sit Second. Clarence had a touch with explanation though . . . so Theo considered again, figuring to make it three observations and then a live run as Second. Kara's theory was good, she was sure, but she hadn't had enough time in grade with Eylot's politics keeping her from practical trips. No reason to rush things, now that Kara was crew.

That was something else they'd need to take care of—Kara ought to have her own key, for the times she might end up as PIC. *Bechimo* had hinted that he could arrange that.

Theo sighed, gently. There were still lots of issues to be worked out—but for now . . .

"Theo, we're being given a chance to move up in line—do you want to hear this?"

Clarence signed a *saves time*, and touched his ear. Theo signed *put through*, and a woman's serious voice began speaking.

"*Bechimo*, Guide Seventy-Nine here. We've got a spot that developed with someone having nav problems, so there's an open 'twixt and 'tween if you're good for it. Here's the numbers we see . . ."

Theo saw the idea—there was a gap too small for a group one or two ship opening ahead—but *Bechimo* was considerably smaller than either of those classes. If they could take that, though, they'd save a shift getting in, and get a dayside discount on their berthing as well, which was not to be sneezed at. They'd also have a shot at a single full fifteen hour trading day instead of breaking their trade hall time across two. If they . . .

"Comments?"

"Depending on the ships ahead, somewhat," admitted Clarence, "it sounds good to me."

Bechimo, in the person of Joyita, spoke next.

"All of these ships carry bulk cargoes of metals and ore, and the last dozen years of records on each of the ships: good, clean flight records, no accidents or port fines listed. None are for our destination—we will leave the queue before they do and thus should not be involved in close-quarter maneuvering." He paused, did Joyita.

"Also, the Portmaster's Office suggestion falls just within published rules for the system, Pilot," he said. "Given volume of traffic, it frees several spaces after us, making the flow more efficient for some time."

"Kara?"

Kara looked up, startled, from her study of the boards.

"Pilot?" Her hands signed *in loop query.*

Theo smiled, bowed lightly, pilot-to-pilot.

"You are in the line of piloting succession, now. So yes, your concerns or comments are of interest. Everything on the flight operations deck is including you."

A bow of acknowledgment, and two hands, lifted in balance, and a fallback to one of the Liaden phrases Theo'd learned only recently.

"Every motion teaches, and I am the student." She finished that with the appropriate bow and a smile of her own. "I am eager."

Theo nodded.

"Pass it on, Exec, we'll do it."

. . . ❈ . . .

Kamele put away the day's work with a sigh. She had, she knew, no hope of becoming fluent in High Liaden—the formal dialect—by the time she reached Surebleak. While she was confident of her abilities in the written form, the complex kinesics, and the chorded fusion aspects of the spoken tongue put it beyond her, even with sleep-learning. Or, one might say, especially with sleep-learning.

While sleep-learning had its uses, it also had its perils, such as the student emerging from the unit lacking certain key elements that might only be gained by spending time with those who had come by the knowledge—or language—in a more natural manner than having it stuffed wholesale into their heads.

She shook her head. All those years with Jen Sar and she had never pushed him to teach her Liaden. Once, early in their relationship, she had asked if he wished her to learn, so that he might hear the language of his home.

His answer had been a soft laugh, and a light, sensual touch to her cheek.

"But you speak the language of my home, now," he murmured, and then...she had lost track of the conversation, and by the time the matter had occurred to her again, it seemed to have been quite settled that Terran would be the language of the household.

It was, she thought, to be hoped that the delm of Korval, now situated on Surebleak, would speak Terran. If not...then a solution must be found. An interpreter employed. Her experience had taught her that Liaden society enclosed a class of explorer-scholars, known as Scouts. One such—Cho sig'Radia her name was—had taken Theo into her mentorship and guided her to her piloting school, and another had taught her the art of bowli ball, and perhaps others things....

Yes! Perhaps one of those able persons might be available, for a fee. The newspapers told her that many Scouts had relocated to Sureleak, with Korval.

It was peculiar, Kamele thought, walking back to her cabin through the ship's midway, almost deserted at this early dinner hour, that so many Liadens were relocating to Sureleak. It might almost seem that there was some ethical rift, in which one portion of the society considered genocide reprehensible and punishable by banishment, while the other portion found the attack upon the homeworld by one of its prominent citizens to be perfectly reasonable, even justified, even a Necessity.

"Good-day, Kamele," a lately familiar voice spoke from quite close.

She looked up, half-startled, to find Ban Del ser'Lindri at her elbow.

"There you have it," she said. "A scholar in a brown study sees nothing but her own thoughts! Good-day, Ban Del. I hope your duty today was pleasant."

"As pleasant as may be," he answered, as he always did. "But you must tell me what thoughts beguiled you so thoroughly."

"I was regretting that I had never applied myself sufficiently to have learned to speak Liaden."

His eyes widened.

"But surely..." he began—and pressed his lips together.

She considered him.

"Surely?" she asked.

"No, I am maladroit," he said, ruefully. "You must hold me excused, for I fear my day at duty has tired me."

"But what did you think?" Kamele pressed.

"Why, I had made an assumption, which is, as I'm certain you'll agree, always fatal," he said, with a rallying gaiety that was not at all like his usual manner. "I had only recalled you had said that your daughter's father was Liaden, and before I could engage my manners, my tongue had shown me for a boor."

"It's hardly boorish to make assumptions based on what people have told one," Kamele said slowly. "After all, that's how we build our impressions of people and events."

"So it is. And yet one feels a need to make amends. Will you join me for dinner?"

It was not an unusual request, and one that Kamele regularly received with pleasure. Today, however, she sighed, and shook her head.

"I'm afraid that duty has been stern with both of us," she said regretfully. "Mine has given me a headache, and I would be very poor company. My intention is to lie down in a dark cabin and try to bore it away."

"Ah." He bowed gently. "I understand. Indeed, I hope that your efforts are made with success and that I may see you later this evening, perhaps at the Vishilond?"

"I make no promises," Kamele said. "But, if I recover, I'll certainly stop for a drink at the Vishilond."

"That is all that a friend might hope for—your health and a chance to enjoy your company." He took a step back, smiling up at her. "Until soon, Kamele."

"Until soon, Ban Del," she answered, and went on her way, trying as she did—trying most earnestly, to recall if she had ever told Ban Del ser'Lindri about Theo's father.

THIRTY-TWO

. . . .

Ynsolt'i Approach

HEVELIN'S LEAN HAD BEEN COMFORTABLE FOR THE past half-hour, but now he stood erect on Theo's knee, surveying Joyita, who'd been largely silent of late, and Clarence, who'd been surprisingly busy with small adjustments and back and forth with their guide.

Abruptly, Clarence smacked his drawing pad to the floor with a sound of disgust.

"This box looked a lot bigger from the outside, Theo."

Theo glanced over, saw Clarence with Kara shadowing him, both looking at the small screens where the fine-ore haulers *Vitran Thirteen* and *Vitran Seven* ran close enough together to appear as a wall. On the other side *Growdy's Trinket* was essentially a solid block of metal with some boosters and a life unit attached, and all three of *them* were dwarfed by the asteroid collector *Metrose*, a stately traveling bin of raw leftover system-building stuff.

Directly ahead were a couple of ships only slightly larger than the *Trinket*, and . . . the rest were starting to become harder to be sure of as the view of the

351

destination was continually occulted and eclipsed by the ships around them. Ynsolt'i's bulk was blocking their night-side view at the moment.

"Understood, Clarence. You're keeping an eye on the prize, right?"

He nodded. "I am. The only good thing I see here is that these are all local ships and we have to assume they know the drill. They're talking to each other like they've done this trip a dozen times. We have a half shift more before we ought to really be looking for a little more room and getting our final bearings—"

It was *Bechimo* rather than Joyita who broke in.

"Conditions are now suboptimal, Pilot. In addition to the drift of the nearby vessels, which borders on breaking the published routes rules, I note a change in traffic patterns beyond, which is concerning me."

Screen Two cleared itself of the catalog of traders expected to be on the trade floor they were approaching and, instead, showed ghostly outlines of the surrounding ships, and beyond that, a number of converging lines with numbers and . . . Theo counted seven of them.

"These vessels have not been identified by the Portmaster nor Guide Seventy-Nine and their own output is extremely limited, to the point that one might call them dangerously suppressing information. The three closing most rapidly are broadcasting incomplete and nearly identical IDs, barely enough for collision avoidance."

On Screen Two, the direct view of the three was occluded by *Vitran Thirteen*.

Theo grabbed the info, began checking the IDs of the other four . . .

"Those four are—"

All seven of the mystery-ship images blossomed with targeting information.

"The three corsair-class ships are near stealthcraft and match the design details of the ship which attacked me during your rescue. The four you delineate are local military response vessels."

"*Bechimo*, must you do targeting before we even determine—"

"I routinely target the nearest thirteen potential threats, Pilot, and more in uncertain situations, such as now. My goal is always to present the most relevant information for the pilots' consideration."

"Where are we getting this other ship location information? Is it calculated and inferred?"

Now Joyita broke in on *Bechimo*, gesturing as if to his screens, which of course were phantoms.

"We pick up unshielded feeds from the other ships as a matter of course, and the planet provides real-time updating of weather and navigation . . . your screens are the best hybrid approximations we can muster."

Joyita was moving hands rapidly over controls, eyes busy, sparing a glance to the crew as he spoke.

Hevelin sat heavily on Theo's knee, drawing a glance—he was watching her, and when he saw her he leaned his head against her arm, unexpectedly offering an image of Coyster and Father playing together—how had he grabbed that? She smiled, ruffled him . . .

"*Bechimo* is performing a self-check while arming weapons and bringing up low-level shields. He requests all crew to please strap in."

"He's really there, somewhere, isn't he?" Kara muttered to Clarence as she closed and checked the strap fittings, loud enough for the assembly to hear during a sudden lack of other sounds.

"Think so," Clarence returned thinly around the *fuff* of escaping breath as he tugged his webbings into place, muttering as he did—no, not muttering, but talking into his comm gear.

"More news, Pilot," he broke in, "from Guide Seventy-Nine. She says that against usual protocols we're being given to another controller for flight direction. We're to expect the next info from Orsec Twelve."

"What's an Orsec?" Theo wondered.

Joyita looked up. "Orsec appears to be *Orbital Security*, a division of the Ynsolt'i military."

"Military?" Theo bit her lip. "Clarence, query your seventy-nine on this cross-traffic. Maybe they're only smugglers..."

"Pilots," came *Bechimo's* voice, "approximately three minutes to the first potential interception. I believe we may be facing an extraordinary threat. Pilot Waitley, we shall need to test several key items, which may take one of the main boards off-line briefly."

Theo felt her stomach, already roiling, tighten. She danced a calming exercise in her head, and said, "Then we need Kara's board live."

"I have anticipated that need. The backup piloting board, on its own circuit, is now in the control loop. Kara ven'Arith, please place your hand on the palm plate."

Kara looked to her and Theo saw on her board that Kara's board light was blinking Available.

Do, Theo signaled.

Kara drew a breath and put her hand on the plate. "Ouch!"

"Pilot accepted," said *Bechimo*.

"Acknowledged," said Kara, shaking her hand slightly as she scanned the now live controls.

"Pilot O'Berin. We are performing a security check on your board. Please lock it to your palm, and then remove the key."

"Pilot?" Clarence asked Theo.

She met his eyes, but it was Rig Tranza's voice she heard, *Gotta trust your ship, Pilot Theo; she'll take care of you, if she can.*

"Do it," she said.

He moved quickly then, slapping the palm spot and pulling his key—the key that had been Win Ton's.

"Excellent. Pilot O'Berin, please hand your key to Pilot Waitley."

The intake of breath was palpable as all three crew exchanged glances.

"There's no reason for me to take Clarence's key; he's been exemplary—"

"There is a reason," insisted *Bechimo*. "You are an essential part of this test, Theo Waitley. Please take the key. Quickly."

Clarence released himself from his webbing, moved the several paces to Theo's outstretched hand, face softening as he saw Hevelin, and then hardening grimly as he dropped the key into her palm.

The key was warm, almost hot. Theo stared at it . . . *felt* it . . . and felt that it did not deny her.

"Please consider the signal, Pilot."

The signal? But yes, she'd held this key before and it was almost as if its time in Clarence's possession had left it . . . muted.

"It's quieter," she said. "Not ugly or bad, just quieter. Or moody."

"Return the key. Pilot O'Berin, please bring your board live."

They made the exchange, and Clarence pulled the webbing even tighter this time, relief palpable.

"Pilot Waitley, please lock your board, remove the key, place it around your neck, as you so often wore it."

Theo did so, feeling the key complain, as it did sometimes in her head, resisting being disconnected from the board.

She slipped it onto the necklace, tucked it down her shirt... where it felt hot, too, and—

"Not pleased," she said in a mumbled way, "it's there, but bothered about something. Not me, but something..."

"I am testing the combined systems. Pilot ven'Arith, your board will be de facto control board for a short while. Please drive carefully."

Theo looked up sharply, saw Joyita with a half-grin, heard Kara say something in Liaden under her breath and, louder, "Yes. Surely."

The ship twitched around them—the gravity field had been adjusted in place.

"Pilot Waitley, please resume command by replacing your key. Pilot ven'Arith, your board is second board until Pilot Waitley's key is replaced."

Theo tugged the key off again, the chain snagging her ear.

"Can you explain this test?" she asked

Bechimo changed the screens, updating locations while Theo inserted and twisted the key, watching the board go through paces and come live.

"We are among those who would wield old weapons and devices as if they understood them. They have attempted to suborn myself and the keys. We are under attack, with no violence obvious to outsiders. The three corsairs—"

Clarence and Kara watched the screens tell the story: Theo was running the ship—or at least her board was the one *Bechimo* said he was following. Clarence grabbed a close-up of one of the ships in question—

"They look like Scout ships, *Bechimo*!"

"Yes—they do. They are nearly indistinguishable and likely of Liaden origins; perhaps of the same shipyards, else they are built to confuse, which is a significant probability."

Kara muttered something about "Balance owner" under her breath.

"Kara, bring up your microphone," Theo said. "I missed that."

Clarence gave a low snicker and Kara's voice practically boomed out, "I was asking the question proper Liadens would ask: who should act as if they are another, within bounds of *melant'i . . .*"

Theo glanced in her direction, brows pulled, while Clarence nodded.

"In Terran I think the question would be, 'What sumbitch wears so much stupidity?'"

Kara shook her head, hands emphatically indicating *deliver balance*. She managed a quiet follow-up: "No, simply, whose name do we write into the debt book on this?"

"Write it big," Clarence said. "Must be the Department of the Interior again. D-O-I!"

"Full shields, and full arms, now," said Theo.

About the same time, Joyita said with a touch of excitement in his voice and a considering squint around his eyes, "One minute until the three DOI ships will be in Clarence's box with us."

"Wish you wouldn't put it that way. Theo, Guide Seventy-Nine says she can't discuss anything with me anymore since we're not her assignment now. She says that we ought to be dealing with Orsec. And she offers us good luck!"

Around them fell a galaxy of complaint: first from the ships nearest themselves, rightly complaining that newly activated shields might jostle everyone and create guidance problems. Though surely, Theo thought, these massive ships weren't vulnerable in the way smaller ones were, like the Eylot spy vessel *Bechimo* had bounced away in Codrescu's approach lanes.

Next came complaints of live weapons—but by then screens showed shields going up across the sector as the three incoming DOI ships maneuvered their way haphazardly into the stream of vessels, weapons armed, warn-aways blaring.

And from the lead of the four local ships, just appearing beyond the bulk of them came: "*Bechimo*, *Bechimo*. Exec, Captain, or Pilot One respond. This is Orsec Twelve. Your vessel has been transferred from Guide Seventy-Nine to our traffic control. Again this is Orbital Security Twelve, of Ynsolt'i Security. Be aware that your initial berth clearance has been canceled. Power down your shields and weapons and prepare to descend to Megway Field. Repeat, and acknowledge... Your berth clearance has been canceled and your ship is being investigated for actions against the common commercial good in the Eylot System. You will be escorted to Megway Field. You will..."

Theo lost the next few words, because she was too busy rattling orders out.

"*Bechimo*, broadcast what you can of the Codrescu recordings—start with *Beeslady*, then Peltzer appointing us the Pilot Guild's Eylot flagship for the duration of the evacuation. And I mean *broadcast*!"

"On it!" Joyita said eagerly. His image showed him as if on vid, speaking clearly, and with deliberation.

"Comm Officer Joyita of *Bechimo* on all-call. We're providing files and recordings, video and otherwise, on channels one-seven-nine through one-eight-three, including supporting information from Guild Master Peltzer of Eylot, on our actions in the Eylot System responding to a pilots-in-peril situation. Ship *Bechimo* and crew have received commendations from the Pilots Guild for these actions, which were supported by commercial vessels, as well as observers from the Liaden Scouts and the Carresens."

Theo watched the main screen as the three DOI ships angled to close the gap; their way not as smooth as might be for the warn-aways of the huge ore carriers and an odd rotation on the part of the *Metrose*. She had to say something, to respond—

"Orsec Twelve, First Class Pilot Theo Waitley, on *Bechimo*, flying for Laughing Cat Limited here. Be advised that we're targeted by three unannounced ships and that we are targeting in return. I am directing my Exec and my ship to take immediate defensive and responsive action as required. We will not comply with your request while outside hunter ships approach."

The complaints and warn-aways from other vessels in the stream increased; a drawl of a voice came through, tagged *Metrose* on the screen.

"Just 'minding pilots that we run active autoshields and if them shields think you're closing space junk, that's what you'll be! And thank you, *Bechimo*, we got your news reports here."

Metrose was indeed rotating very slowly, the great length of it threatening to span the box.

"Tried three times to get a tight beam warn-away to them ships," Clarence said—"Nothing back. They're still running up on our course."

"Tell them we've set perimeters and they approach at their own peril."

"*Bechimo*," Orsec Twelve announced, "those ships are doing cloak suppression for us. We are aware of the difficulties you caused at Eylot. You will follow orders."

Cloak suppression? The fools must have claimed to know what—no. Old Tech. *Bechimo* had said that the hunter ships were using Old Tech like they knew what it was. Just like the pirates who had taken Win Ton captive and turned his own cells against him . . .

"Ynsolt'i, if we're not wanted here all you had to do is say so," Clarence said into the comm. "Didn't need to let us get in here. We'll ease outsystem, soon's you call off the pack."

"Pilot," came *Bechimo*'s voice, "the strength of the subetheric emanations has increased. It is minutely possible that their activities could affect the Remastering Unit's calibrations. I have suggested course corrections that will make a joint approach more difficult."

Those numbers showed on the screen, along with *Bechimo*'s intention to slide between the *Vitran* ships and accelerate outward as rapidly as possible, crossing another stream of ships and . . . affect the Remastering

Unit? What did she know about what powered and guided it? Win Ton!

"Pilot"—Orsec Twelve again—"you are wearing the Tree-and-Dragon and we are a Liaden society here. Tree-and-Dragon has fired on the homeworld, and been banished for it!"

"And I'm a trader from Waymart wearing my corporate colors," Theo snapped. "I've got contracts, and Korval's one of them. Since we're not wanted, we'll be away—"

"You are in our traffic zone, *Bechimo*, wearing Tree-and-Dragon. You will follow our instructions. You must permit our associates—"

"Your associates are risking themselves. We will observe safe distance here, by force if necessary!"

"Ynsolt'i Security?" came *Metrose*'s drawling voice again. "These folks you're calling associates is flying stupid. Me, I have to match my join point when I get to the foundry, and I've started that rotation. In all the flight plans, we do it every time we come in. Them ships best be elsewhere right quick. They can argue with the ambassador's ship later."

"Ambassador's ship!"

"That info they sent out. Yep, looks like an ambassador's ship there."

The screens looked like a child had thrown ink and paint at a wall—most of the ships in range had shields glowing to the fullest extent they could and those that had weapons, had weapons live, against all usual in-system protocols.

Theo touched the toggle, felt the weapons board rise to her hand. She selected the screen with the proposed course and brought it to main.

"Crew, we're taking *Bechimo's* advice," she said, wondering how her voice sounded so calm. "Everyone's nervous, and we're all at risk. *Bechimo*, once we're through that slot, you can add a couple g's to your proposed course if it'll help . . . we must be too close in to Jump. You can start now."

"Yes, Pilot, course understood. We may attempt a Jump at any time, but the interference of these devices is impossible to quantify. They could induce coil overloads, or other—"

"Hold on the Jump idea, and go for the slot. Once we're through we'll try to get some distance, and then we'll get out!"

Bechimo courteously sounded an acceleration warning for a count of three, and then, despite the self-compensation inherent in the ship's gravity, Theo felt as if they were falling hard to the right. This course distanced them from two of the black spears that were the DOI ships, but would bring them closer to the third.

"Do not deviate from your settled course," screamed Ynsolt'i Security, far too late. It was a slow motion break at orbital speeds; there was only so much they could do within local space, and they depended on every other ship staying in approximately the same relative location. *Metrose* continued its ponderous turn, but elsewise . . . *Bechimo* was committed.

Pressure built, the feeling of falling to the right intensified, the webbing slacked, then tightened as it compensated.

"Pilot, DOI One has changed course again. I regard it as interfering with our plans."

"You've got it targeted," Theo managed, remembering

now her previous encounter with a DOI ship, hoping that this pilot was more committed to life than to her plan.

Theo saw two of the Ynsolt'i craft close enough to be a problem, but this was all undeclared...Could she order weapons unleashed with so many ships nearby?

And weren't the DOI ships counting on her answer to be—*no*?

The radio was full of noise—threats, complaints, demands, pilots calling for calm and pilots demanding sense—all suddenly lost inside another noise, like screeches, screams, and metal drawn against metal.

"Radio jamming," commented Joyita, "very broadband. Given the power, I assume a subetheric generator is being employed. I detect an extreme increase in neutrino emissions, consistent with timonium-powered devices."

"But why?" came Kara's voice across a sudden lull in the noise, and Theo managed a quick, healthy "Pharst!" as the ship jolted and the gravity wavered. Her mouth was dry and she clung to the armrest with her right hand as she saw damage estimates appear suddenly on the operations screen. On another, the numerals 2 and 4 blazed red: once twice, three times.

"I am returning fire, Pilot, as you warned," *Bechimo* said. "DOI One has fired on us with a beam weapon. I believe they used the Tree-and-Dragon as a target."

Yowls of outrage filled the radio spectrum briefly, then the radio traffic became squeals and metal again. A hand motion from Clarence dropped the sound level to near nil.

"What about the other DOI ships?"

The vid of the outside showed a purplish glow

playing well away from the ship now, with a strange pulsing in it that hurt the eyes to follow.

"Course corrections?" asked Clarence.

"*Vitran Seven* has understood our intent, I believe," *Bechimo* answered. "We should have ten or twelve ship lengths . . . within two minutes."

Another jolt, less severe, but still a shock and the number 2 appeared twice in quick succession . . . return fire.

Joyita spoke, "Damage report, Pilot."

Theo was too tense to do other than say: "Give it."

"The Tree-and-Dragon markings are dulled; one navigation beacon will require resetting, three may. End of report."

"Chimmy, if that's all, we're good!" Clarence said. "Hate being in a fight without a warning."

"Everyone hold noncritical reports," said Theo, trying to form a plan, to make sense of things while the ship transmissions from other craft were increasing and time was getting dear in terms of their approach to the getaway slot they were aiming for.

"If you hit us you'll bounce," came *Vitran Seven*'s warning out of the muddle of noise.

"Pilot, I'm trying to filter," Joyita explained.

Orsec's demands to cease and desist seemed aimed only at them, or their transmissions to the other ships were direct. Or—there was a flare across multiple screens. Theo bit her lip until she tasted copper.

"Target One has been struck by both our initial beams; their shields remained in force throughout. They were also struck by our second response; they are maneuvering . . . Target One will be nearly between us and the opening when we arrive, Pilot."

"They know where we'll be—anyone with a brain does. They'll try missiles . . . and we can expect harrying fire from the others. Why did *you* stop firing?"

"The order was to respond, Pilot!"

Theo grimaced. Done what she'd said, yes.

"It was the order, thank you. We're going through, *Bechimo*, so they can't be in our way. Where would they mount the generators? Do they need projectors? They must have traded something off . . ."

"Pilot, yes, the generators will take up space. There's no room in that class of ship to reduce the living quarters . . ."

"Target the holds, then, and the missile pods if they show any. And . . . target all beams on that ship and prepare to fire when they can be brought to bear!"

The ship jolted around Theo—and she felt warm, as if *Bechimo*'s air control was slowing. Then, ordinary progress, with the g-press of extra acceleration still upon them.

Into that came *Bechimo*'s voice, and then Joyita's.

"Long-range particle beams, Pilot, from the other ships. They can sap my shielding over time."

"I have a signal, I have a signal, Pilot. They are trying to contact us!"

Another jolt, and the outer vids showed *Bechimo* wreathed in purple again.

"Target One has fired as well," said *Bechimo*. "If they coordinate their beams, my shields will not last."

There was an image now in the main screen, a dark courier with no markings—

Target One. The jamming had stopped and the radio noise gave way to Joyita's filtered feed:

"*Bechimo*, Korval cannot aid you here. You must

cease firing and permit us to board. We are from Liad's Department of the Interior. Your only hope to survive this system is to turn yourself over to proper representatives of Liad!"

Clarence muttered; Theo cursed, and found Kara looking at her.

Necessity, Theo signed, and saw it echoed, with a bow.

"Accelerate but keep the planned course," she told *Bechimo*. "Bounce us around if it'll help mess up their targeting."

"Neutrino emissions have increased from Target One, Pilot."

Bechimo jolted again, but it was his doing . . . She hoped.

"*Bechimo*, fire until they give way, or until they're gone. As much shield as we have, no spare, until we're through. If need be, run the course through them. Start now."

Hevelin clung to her arm, not in fear, it seemed, but exultation. He shared bits, fragments, of charging norbears, of spaceship screens full of emergency signs, of an aircraft's sudden flameout, of Theo's own memory of facing would-be kidnappers, of—

"*Bechimo*," Target One again, "at my mark you will have twenty-five seconds to surrender."

"Nineteen seconds to passage, Pilot," said *Bechimo*.

Bechimo rocked. The vids showed tantalizing evidence that they were firing; waves and pulses of color phased about them. There were sounds *Bechimo* never made as the shields absorbed energy and threw it off, rattling and—

An unfamiliar sound; an unfamiliar—frightening—monotone voice: *Collision alert, collision alert, collision alert.*

"Missiles launched against us. Neutrino alert!"

"Counter!" Theo snapped, aware that interception at this rate was unlikely, but the screen was unforgiving in showing six missiles on course for them.

A bare hand's width from Clarence there was a sharp snap, his key gave up a blue spark, and a line of vivid blue ran across the board.

"Dammit!" He snatched his left hand back, slapped the board with his right. "Kara! Take Second!"

"Emergency," *Bechimo* stated. "Board three live, gravity change! Damage report, we have one forward beam working. Neutrino alert!"

"I have it," Kara said. "Clarence—damage?"

Theo punched all-fire into the beams, felt another surface hit from the enemy; the screen showing a roiling of *Bechimo*'s skin somewhere over their head.

The acceleration alert sounded barely ahead of acceleration that pressed them into their seats, crushing Hevelin against Theo's chest, it—

"Breathing," Clarence said. "Burnt. Board—dunno. No time to pull it now!"

"Seven seconds."

Missiles exploded before them. In the screens the color pushed away—and away again, toward the approaching enemy and the walls in front, above and below that were ships the size of worldlets.

The view on the screen wheeled. They were released from one pressure, flung to the left, hard, hard, *hard* as the ship spun and Theo knew they had the slot open if they—vids showed their side beams lashing out and their rear beams and—

Target One shredded; meteor shield alerts went off unremarked in the din of collision alerts and acceleration alerts, *Bechimo*'s voice soaring above it all—"Retargeting, Pilot."

They went between the *Vitrans*, damage lights flashing and there wasn't any time to consider what to do; they were still taking fire from the remaining ships behind, giving back what fire they could...

"Incoming!" snapped Clarence, still alive to what the screens showed as they cleared the ore ships, incoming Orsec ships, firing heedless of their proximity to the ore vessels, firing four on one...

They were in the clear—clear enough.

Theo gathered her breath, untoggled a button, slapped it, and yelled, "Go!"

THIRTY-THREE

. . . .

Bechimo

Patient Win Ton yo'Vala
Function Change Percentage Report: Treatment
Location #13
General Therapeutic Regime: Cleanse to remaster
Status: Complete

. . . . ❋ . . . .

"What just happened?" Kara asked, very calmly.

"We Jumped," Theo said, snatching at her board, pulling in local scan info. "Check for comm traffic, please, Board Three."

The screens showed...nothing. A comprehensive and chilling nothingness that would have been terrifying if it hadn't been, strangely, familiar.

Screen Six...was empty, as flat and ungiving as a blacked-out window.

"*Bechimo!*" she snapped. "Report!"

"Yes, Pilot. Assessing damage. Shields at half. Weapons live, forward beams reduced to one of three operational. Life support one hundred percent. I have several anomalous and potentially hazardous skin-surface disruptions which may be sensor errors or actual difficulties. An in-depth full ship analysis is indicated."

"Where's Joyita?" Theo asked.

"Currently assisting in the assessment of damage, Pilot."

"This is where you brought us—me—before, isn't it?" Theo asked, frowning down at sensors that gave her readings of dust and emptiness for light-minutes in all directions.

"Yes, Pilot. Coordinates known to myself. This is a safe harbor. Pilot ven'Arith, there will be no comm traffic here."

"How did we *Jump* out of that?" Kara asked, still calm. Maybe, Theo thought, a little too calm.

She threw a look over her shoulder.

Kara looked back at her, blue eyes wide, face slightly pale.

"I'm not completely sure," Theo said, sitting back in her chair and glaring at the empty screens. "Scholar—I talked to a scholar of subrational math at Surebleak. She thought the drive settings might be . . . nonstandard, and also wondered after some subetheric boosting, but—there was no conclusion. She'd wanted to examine the settings, but time was short, and it didn't happen."

Theo sighed and ran her hand through her hair. Now was not the time to mention Father's lifemate.

"You been here before, Theo?" Clarence asked.

She turned to him, relieved to have a question she could answer without ambiguity.

Well, *almost* without ambiguity.

"When I first boarded *Bechimo*," she said, "at

Gondola. We were pressed by...by enemies." She gave Clarence a straight look. "I'd gone into port as Uncle's courier. Near as I could figure, these pilots had a grudge."

He nodded. "The Uncle's one to wake strong emotions in some folk," he allowed.

"So, anyway. We were pressed, I was wounded." She looked over her shoulder to Kara, who had regained some of her color. "Pretty badly wounded. We lifted, *Bechimo* and I, and, just when I thought we were clean away, a ship—" She swallowed, and took a hard breath. "Corsair, like the ones we just had on us. We didn't have much choice but to take...decisive action. And after, *Bechimo*—Jumped. To this location. At the time, it was his plan to hang here for eight or nine months Standard, until it might be safe to kind of slink around the edges of the galaxy, but I had... duty—to my employer, to Win Ton, to...other people. In the end, we left again, after only a couple days to regroup. It took some discussion, though."

Clarence looked grave at that, and shook his head at the screens.

"I can't say I'm finding fault with the lack of company," he said slowly. "Considering the hospitality we was just being shown. On the other hand, it's not the kind of welcoming place makes a pilot think of putting off his wings and sitting down, either."

"It's...eerie," Kara said.

"It is safe," *Bechimo* said, sounding both breathless and decisive. "I extrapolated this location and arrived at it. Never have I met another ship here, though occasionally there is flotsam."

"Pilot O'Berin, are you in pain?"

"I'll keep," Clarence said. "Been burnt worse and more for less gain. What kind of flotsam, Theo?"

"Hardware and shred," Theo said, out of memory. "Ships, not whole. Ceramic couplers. Wire. A teapot." She met Clarence's eyes. "The teapot's in the galley— the white one that feels too light for its size. Apparently it was notable for having come through whole."

"And where," asked Kara, "do these things . . . come from?"

Theo sighed. "*Bechimo* would have me understand that they Jumped in from another galaxy," she said. "I'm not sure we agreed on that, and I never did see the math."

She frowned suddenly, her eye caught by a change on her board. A status light, modestly hidden away in a high grouping of low-priority functions, had gone from yellow to blue.

At the same moment, Screen Six flickered, and Joyita joined them. His hair was too short to become disordered, but he nonetheless projected a definite air of dishevelment.

"Pilot," he said, meeting her eyes firmly. "The Remastering Unit has opened."

. . . . ❊ . . . .

A chime was sounding inside his ear, incessant and annoying.

Win Ton yo'Vala opened his eyes. Directly above him, as he lay on his back, was what appeared to be the hood of an autodoc.

But no, he remembered. The autodocs had failed, and so he had been remanded by the Scouts to the Uncle, with his more powerful, and less legal, unit.

Alas, the Uncle had also not been equal to the task of reuniting Win Ton with his health, and thus he was passed along to someone else, and another device, which was his last chance at survival.

Recalling that, he now placed himself, his thoughts nimble sharp. He was on *Bechimo*, the ship he had waked and the reason the Scouts had gone to such extraordinary lengths to preserve one who had dishonored his service.

The Scouts wanted *Bechimo*, and Win Ton was to deliver it.

He shivered, which brought to his attention the facts that the air was not precisely warm where he lay—and that he was naked.

Another shiver brought the realization that, along with the sharpness of his thoughts, he felt . . .

He felt . . .

Well.

Cautiously, he raised his hand before his face, seeing a smooth golden appendage, five shapely digits, short nails glowing a healthy pinkish gold. Tears rose to his eyes as he recalled this hand as he had last seen it—fingernails like chips of ice, knuckles and finger joints misshapen and without strength.

Had it worked, then? he wondered. Had the final device, aboard *Bechimo*, a forbidden device carried and concealed by a device far and away more disturbing— had it . . . *was he* . . . cured?

It seemed impossible. Indeed, it seemed just a litle like an anticlimax. He remembered now. Remembered coming into this room—*being carried* into this room— by Theo. She had undressed him, his swollen fingers useless. Then, she had pressed him to sit on the edge of the unit. She had embraced him, and he had almost wanted to return the kindness.

But what he had really wanted, and what she had finally given him, was the opportunity to inch into the embrace of the device, and watch the lid settle, inexorable and implacable, over him. The temperature began to cool rapidly, and he felt his consciousness slipping away.

This, he had told himself, *is how it ends. I will never wake up again*.

And so he had gone away with the cold, and he had not woken.

Until now. Whole. Well.

And so very much in debt.

"Less Pilot yo'Vala," a voice addressed him—a light voice, bearing no obvious gender, and seeming to issue from above him and to the right. "Do you require assistance?"

"*Bechimo*?" he asked.

"Yes, Pilot. Do you require assistance?"

"I suppose I should test that," he said, flippant in a rush of well-being. "A moment, of your very great goodness."

He rolled, briskly, off the edge of the pallet on which he lay, twisted so that he might land on his feet as he had done dozens of times from ships' bunks and his own bed in his clan's house.

His feet hit the floor.

Then they slid out from beneath him, and he fell, graceless and astonished.

"Less Pilot, are you injured?"

"I would say, only my pride," answered Win Ton, taking quick stock and leveraging himself up with one hand on the pallet he had so recently quit.

This time when he gained his feet, he kept them, and sighed with relief and chagrin.

"I suppose I was too ambitious," he said, his eye falling on a locker limned in green. Mindful of his steps, he crossed to the locker and pulled out his leathers.

"Pilot Waitley is on her way to greet you," *Bechimo* said.

Win Ton hastily pulled his shirt over his head, and snatched at his pants, supple fingers making short work of seals and fastenings.

It was perhaps unfortunate that he had not quite finished with his boots when the hatch was suddenly undogged and a wiry woman stepped into the room, her fine yellow hair disordered.

Perhaps after all, Win Ton thought, looking up to meet space-black eyes, the boots were fortunate. His position forestalled what might have been a full-body contact he was not certain he wanted.

"Win Ton," she said, and stopped, perhaps to recruit her emotions, or merely to catch her breath. "How do you feel?"

"Why, now that you are arrived, improved by twelve!" he said gallantly. "And before your arrival"—he bent to finish with his boot—"I had been trying to recall if ever in my life before I had felt so well."

Something moved in those dark eyes; he was not precisely certain what. And that disturbed him somewhat, for Theo had always been so very easy to read. He recalled then, a detail that Uncle had given him, during his waking moments, before he was transferred to *Bechimo* and his last hope of survival.

Theo was of Korval.

He rose and made her a bow as between comrades,

which they had been, and was thus neither imperti-
nent nor dismissive.

She returned it, in mode, with proper timing, adding a concise and elegant gesture which acknowledged
also a pillow-friend.

His Theo, thought Win Ton, the Theo he had last
seen at Volmer, when he had confessed to her what
he had woken and how he had involved her in it, had
nothing so nuanced in her simple repertory of courtesy.

"Am I to learn that you have found your father?"
he inquired, the memory of that last sharing of tea
and secrets coming back to him with the immediacy
of something experienced yesterday.

"He was with the delm of Korval," Theo said calmly.

"It was fortunate, then, that you had decided to
go to Korval," Win Ton said solemnly.

"It was, wasn't it?" she agreed, and took a step
forward, as if irresistibly drawn. He waited, holding
his breath as her fingers skimmed his cheek, touched
a brow and rose, even higher, to rest upon his head.

Now, he felt the erring child, affectionately dis-
ciplined by an amused elder, and wasn't certain but
that he would rather she had thrown herself upon
him, as had seemed her first inclination.

"Your hair," she said. "It will grow back."

Ah, that was the amusement, was it? His hair had
fallen out.

"If I am bald from this day forward, I shall count
it a small price," he told her, and meant it.

"I think it will grow," she said seriously. "You're
not bald. Your hair is merely very short." She stepped
back, dropped her hand, suddenly all business.

"I think you'd better come meet the rest of the crew,"

she said, "and get something to eat, if you're hungry. You've come awake at an exciting time; we're just out of an attack, and about to do damage assessment."

"Perhaps I can help," he said, turning to go with her out of the cubicle.

"Maybe you can," she said cordially.

"But who attacked you, Theo?" he asked, as they moved along the hallway. He spotted handholds and tuck-ins with approval, and without surprise. Though he didn't recognize the hall from his former passage through it, his impression of *Bechimo* from their all-too-brief acquaintance had been of a neat and shipshape vessel, well-considered and well-built.

"I think the Deparment of the Interior is targeting us," she said from slightly ahead of him. "They attacked me on Gondola—the same kind of ships—and Val Con, my brother, says that they're in pursuit of Korval and the allies of Korval." She looked at him over her shoulder.

"Since we're contracted to check out a loop for Master Trader yos'Galan, that makes us allies of Korval."

"Of course, being Korval's own sister means nothing," Win Ton said cordially.

"Well, but I don't think they know that," Theo said pensively. "Unless—well, I guess they could have a DNA sample. I did bleed a lot over at least one of them."

"Ah," he said, stepping through a hatch after her, and following her down a corridor that was definitely familiar. "It's probably best to assume that they do know, Theo, and—"

She turned to look at him, walking backward down the hall as briskly as if she had eyes in back of her head.

"It was the Department of the Interior," Win Ton told her serious pale face, "which had desired *Bechimo* with such ardor that they...captured me and sought to persuade my candor."

"Oh," said Theo, frowning. "Was it?"

Before her was another hatch. Win Ton wondered if he should mention it, but before he could speak, she had turned 'tween steps to face the oncoming obstacle, paused for the half heartbeat required to tap a quick code into the pad. The hatch whisked aside and Theo continued, himself her willing shadow.

The space they now entered, he remembered well. This was the flight deck; the place where the course of his life had been forever altered.

There, the pilots' stations, and the screens displaying a spacescape both unlikely and tantalizing. Screen Six showed an internal room, likely the comm tower, a man's downturned profile, dark hair, tight hair, the beginnings of what might be a beard.

From the screens, his attention sought the boards. First was locked down; Theo's board, of course.

In the Second's chair, the chair he had chosen for himself, believing it to be the captain's station—in that chair sat a very blade of a man. That his hair was more grey than red, and he was clearly old enough to have stood as Win Ton's father—those things were immaterial. His body was hard, the stern face watching the screens as if daring the weird space outside to produce anything but peace denoted a man both used to making hard decisions, and enforcing them.

And he knew this man, Win Ton recalled abruptly. Theo had introduced them, when he had come on board, and he had given to that same pilot his ship-key, to hold until such time as Win Ton returned to his duty.

"Pilot O'Berin," he said therefore, inclining his head with a comrade's respect. "I hope I find you well."

"Pilot." The elder pilot raised his head, tracking Win Ton's reflection in the screens. "I'm well, thank you. If a comrade might say so, you're looking considerably more alive than you did when we met last."

"And feeling so!" Win Ton responded.

He looked to the screen, but the man there was busy at some task and did not look up.

Third Board—for it happened that there was a Third Board—was held by a Liaden woman near to Theo's age, and very nearly a beauty, with rose-gold hair and well-opened blue eyes. The blue eyes were at the moment regarding him with a sort of interested wariness. Perhaps this was one who did not care for Scouts, Win Ton thought. There were those, though not often found among pilotkind.

"Kara ven'Arith, Second Class Pilot, Chief Tech," Theo said, turning with her hand on the back of her chair to make the introduction. "Here is Win Ton yo'Vala, Scout Pilot."

He bowed as between comrades—they were all, were they not, pilots?—and received a moderately cordial inclination in return.

"Pilot ven'Arith."

"Scout yo'Vala."

"And this . . ." Theo began.

Win Ton turned toward her; there was a flash of rust down low and moving fast, he sidestepped, twisted—

And his legs tangled themselves together, ludicrously and embarrassingly; graceless as any grounder, he fell to the decking.

He did have enough wit to shield his head, but for

a moment, he simply lay there, tangled in his own limbs and not at all certain how he could possibly have fallen.

"*Murble?*" inquired a voice in his right ear.

"Win Ton!" That was Theo. "Are you all right?"

"I believe so," he said, running a quick mental check. Nothing broken, nothing sprained, saving his dignity, and what the deuce *was* this? He didn't fall down; he was a pilot and a Scout! When he did fall, it was on his terms. Yet twice now since he had awoken, he had fallen—completely surprised by the circumstance, and despite being certain that he had reacted in such a manner that he *ought not to have* fallen.

"*Murble?*" was repeated into his right ear, along with a sensation that might have been dry grass, or broom bristles rubbed along the lobe.

"Of your kindness, pilots, what is in my ear?"

"Oh, that's only Hevelin," said Theo. "He came running out to see you. Here."

He saw her legs, encased in work pants, step over him, pause, and then dance back, a thing of effortless, thoughtless grace.

"I've got him," she said. "Do you need help getting up?"

"No!" he said, more sharply than he had intended, and Theo's legs retreated, leaving him the deck.

With extreme care, he rolled, got his feet under him and rose. He thought every move through beforehand, and he executed each with a deliberateness that felt as if he were mocking himself. It was to be hoped that the other pilots present did not think he was mocking them.

"I thought," said Kara ven'Arith, after he had gained

his feet once more, "that you were healed. Forgive me, Pilot, but by my observation, you began to react correctly, only your ... body was sluggish."

"He's been in the 'doc for a good long time," Clarence commented from his board. "Could be the muscles need toning."

"Ah, of course!" said Pilot ven'Arith, apparently satisfied with this explanation in a way that Win Ton was not.

Nor, when he looked at her, was Theo satisfied. She was studying him closely, black eyes slightly narrowed, a rust-colored norbear of apparent age cradled in her arms.

"Theo," he began, and stopped himself.

She tipped her head to one side, then half-spun to address Pilot O'Berin.

"Clarence, would you put together a board lunch for all hands? Win Ton will help you."

"Yes," said the pilot promptly. He rose, and it was then that Win Ton saw that the fascia was up, a testing kit near to the pilot's right hand. He gave Win Ton an easy nod.

"This way, Pilot."

. . . ☽ . . .

There was ... he supposed it was *pain*. Certainly, a disruption of accustomed processes must at least be ... disturbing. The Joyita extension was even now trying to pinpoint the exact processes that were failing, and locate a repair protocol.

It was perhaps not the sort of damage one ought, most wisely, seek on one's own, since the damage could conceivably be disturbing larger processes.

If there had been a Captain, or a Mentor, present, those might search with more hope of success.

Of course, there was no Captain, and though the Joyita extension was nuanced and observant, its role in the search mocked *Bechimo*. B. Joyita was not, could never be, Jermone Joyita. That he had created such an extension . . . he questioned his own thought processes.

That was fatal. He knew it. And if he did not know it, there were Rules and Protocol pinging him with reminders of what must be done, should the stability of the ship's intelligence come under question.

For the moment, he chose to fob off Protocol and Rules with records of other times when he had experienced self-doubt. All thinking beings experienced self-doubt, excepting those who had already taken more damage than their system could bear or repair. Self-doubt was a normal check-system. It was when self-doubt became endemic, or when it vanished altogether, that dangerous instability occurred.

He would not, he assured himself, risk his pilots . . . his crew. His. He had fought for them; he had preserved them, and he had brought them here, to safety.

That they would wish to remain in safety—he could not suppose it.

It therefore fell to him to construct protocols that would keep them more safe in the dangerous environments in which they moved.

Determinedly, he again accessed the record of the trap they had fallen into. He must discover how they had come to be so completely vulnerable, and fashion protocols that would prevent a similar occurrence in future.

He must . . .

There was a disturbance in the pocket of space in which they huddled. *Bechimo* threw his eyes wide, and strained to bring the tattered shields online. If the enemy had found them, then *Bechimo* would fight; his pilots would fight.

More. If the enemy had found them, *Bechimo* needed to recall the fate of Less Pilot yo'Vala, who had fallen into the hands of such an enemy.

None of his crew must be allowed to endure such treatment.

Never again.

THIRTY-FOUR

. . . .

Bechimo

"REMOTES, PILOTS, I INSIST."

Bechimo modulated his voice: firm and friendly, that was the tone. Pilot O'Berin got good results from the Over Pilot with that tone, and *Bechimo* very much wanted—required!—a good result. He would not . . . objectively, he thought that he *could not* risk any of his pilots on an in-person inspection of the skin.

"I'm not an expert with remotes," Pilot Waitley stated. "I do know that it's easy for an inexperienced operator to miss things that would be obvious from an in-person inspection. We're looking for skin damage, and making a determination of severity. I'd think that the risk to the ship and company from a failure of the skin trumps the risk to a pilot on the outside in a pocket that's described as 'safe.'"

"Pilot, the flotsam arrives randomly. It is not inconceivable that a pilot on the skin might be—"

"Theo," Pilot ven'Arith broke in, "*I* am a expert on remote inspection."

384

Bechimo stopped speaking, and accessed personnel records.

"You *are*?" asked Pilot Waitley.

"I have the certificate to prove it! And I am horrified to learn that you have not. However, it may be mended; successful completion of the course and live hours bestows upon me the right and the privilege to train others in the art. If *Bechimo* will allow me access and give me a tour, I can handle outside inspection."

The certificate was in her file; Kara ven'Arith had completed the coursework and the inspection hours required to qualify as a Remote Inspection Specialist.

"I was on the rotation at Codrescu," Tech ven'Arith said.

Pilot Waitley threw up her hands.

"You convinced me. *Bechimo*, please assist Pilot ven'Arith with outside remote inventory. Clarence and I will handle internal checks. Win Ton will be our eyes and ears."

"Yes, Pilot."

· · · ✳ · · ·

Eyes-and-ears was an honorable post, Win Ton told himself, settling at second board. The instruments were live, an eloquent statement that he was a trusted member of the crew. He appreciated the declaration of trust, even while he was under no illusion that he would be stopped instantly and, if necessary, forcibly, by *Bechimo* her—*him*—self, should he err in any way.

Carefully, watching his fingers manipulate the keys, he opened an observer's log on the working screen.

Five times since he had emerged from the so-called Remastering Unit, he had experienced a failure of reflexes. Three times, he had fallen. Twice, he had mishandled objects lightly tossed to him.

He began to—no, he *did*—fear that his... return to template had been not a complete success. Theo had told him that *Bechimo* had feared that the attacking vessels at Ynsolt'i might have had in their arsenals weapons capable of disrupting the process of the Remastering Unit. He wondered if it would be wise to reenter the machine—after, of course, it had been certified fully operational.

In the meanwhile, it was eyes-and-ears for him, while doing his utmost not to fall out of the piloting chair.

He looked to the instruments, verifying that he had sound and eyes all around.

The spacescape provided by the sensors was barren, even a little disquieting, but no odder, really, than any of a dozen such strange pockets of space known to the Scouts. The report of "flotsam" was odder, but Win Ton gave himself leave to entertain skepticism until confronted with evidence.

A sound, as of claw on decking, brought his head around. The elderly norbear Hevelin was on all fours and moving in Win Ton's direction.

He unshipped the chair and allowed it to rotate so that he faced the approaching creature, though he did not rise.

"I fear I have no news for you, Grandfather, though I would welcome company on the watch."

The norbear vouchsafed no reply, nor did he moderate his pace. Win Ton bent down and very shortly lifted Hevelin to his lap.

The norbear began to hum, which was pleasant, and soothed his vexations a little.

"What we do here," he said, as Hevelin settled onto his knee, "is keep watch. Should any signal reach us, or object discover us, we are to log it. Should the signal be active or the object inquisitive, we are to immediately call it to the attentions of the ship and first board. We are assured by the ship that none ever come here. Therefore, if we find a ship in our screens, we are to view it in the most suspicious manner possible—and call at once for ship and first board. Do you think yourself equal to the duty?"

Hevelin murbled comfortably, tucking up his paws, his nether section pressed companionably against Win Ton's hip.

Behind Win Ton's eyes, an image formed—of a wiry girl with snapping black eyes, and pale unruly hair, dancing with a concentrated joy that tightened his throat.

"Yes, that is Theo," he said, somewhat hoarsely. He cleared his throat. "But I shall not be able to watch, you know, if you fill my head with pictures. As it is necessary for the safety of ship and crew that I watch, we have two choices before us: you may assist me at my duty, without offering distractions, or I will regretfully put you down and bid you find some other place to nap."

Hevelin sighed, and pushed a little more comfortably against Win Ton's hip, the image of the joyous dancer fading.

Win Ton checked his scans and screens, noting no change.

"Pilot yo'Vala, may I have a word with you?"

The voice was *Bechimo*'s, apparently emanating from the ceiling to the right and behind him. He was speaking Liaden, as between comrades.

"Of course. How may I serve you, *Bechimo*?"

"First, by allowing me to thank you, Pilot, for the service you have already performed for me, at very great danger to yourself. I hope someday to be able to see us fully in Balance, but until then, please know that I esteem you, and that I do not forget."

Win Ton, recalling all too well his reasons for having approached and entered the strange ship at dock at the warehousing site, was aware of an acute embarrassment. He raised his hand.

"Please," he murmured, "let there be no debt between us. I believe that I could not have escaped those who captured me without your intervention. We are in Balance."

There was a pause, as if *Bechimo* weighed their comparative indebtedness.

"Let it be as you say, Pilot," the ship said at last, and Win Ton shivered in relief.

"There was something else?" he asked delicately. "The presence of a *first* topic leads one, inevitably, to think there must be a second."

"Indeed, there is a second. If you will indulge me with the answer to a question?"

"I will do my best to answer well," Win Ton said, frowning at the screens and the unchanging view. He placed his hand on Hevelin's back, feeling the norbear's hum through his palm.

"That is surely all I might ask," *Bechimo* said. "Do you remember, Pilot, when you first came to me, and sat in that chair that you even now occupy, and were accepted as a pilot of this vessel?"

Remember? Again, Win Ton shivered. That action, ill-advised on so many levels, was the beginning of unlooked-for and terrible changes in his life. Even reduced as he had been when he had left the Uncle's care, he had never forgotten it.

"I remember," he said, feeling the norbear's hum intensify.

"Excellent. When you left me, you took not only your own key, but the other, unclaimed key, which you later transmitted to Pilot Waitley."

"Yes, I remember that, too." For who would look for Theo to have such a thing? It might have been that those who pursued him would discover the presence of a Theo Waitley in his life. But who might send so risky and dangerous an item to a student pilot who was the merest acquaintance, and who further counted herself Terran?

Had he known—but, there: he hadn't known. Theo herself hadn't known then, he thought, that she shared genes, if not clan, with Korval.

"Recalling these things, then," *Bechimo* continued, "I wonder if you will do me the honor of saying whether you had intended to propose Theo Waitley as captain of this vessel."

Captain of this...

Win Ton laughed. Beneath his hand, the norbear murbled.

"To say the truth, between comrades, it was myself I saw as master of this vessel," he said ruefully. "But, as has so often been the case in my life, it seems that I acted correctly, for reasons which were entirely incorrect, if they can be said to be reasons at all. In fact, you could do very much worse than Theo as captain."

"Pilot O'Berin had also been of that opinion."

"Pilot O'Berin ran Solcintra Low Port for twenty

Standards or more—a not-inconsiderable accomplishment. I would expect an individual of his experience and longevity to be a very fine judge of character."

"I shall take that into consideration," *Bechimo* said. "Thank you."

Hevelin stirred; the Scout adjusted himself, still leery of feeling easy with his body. In the screens, a flutter in the changeless spacescape, ever alert sensors bringing his attention to something very nearby, suddenly *there*, on the edge of the inner meteor shields, where nothing had been beforehand—now there was *some*thing, only just arrived.

Win Ton touched controls, upped the magnification...

"Disturbance," he said, "anomaly." No comm, no Jump flare or radio noise. It had just...appeared, a deviant bit of darkness in what was already a big, empty darkness. Scans told him what it was not: not rock, not hot, not alive. It had come...from wherever it had come from, inert, with neither energy to dump nor velocity to spill. Win Ton felt a cold chill down his back.

"Flotsam," *Bechimo* said. "This area receives such things, occasionally."

"Flotsam?" he asked, because the areas that the Scouts knew of, that seemed similar to this place, received no such *flotsam*. Asteroidal junk they might have, bits of failed planets, pure metal from deep within exploded stellar cores, or aggregating dust a billion Standards building...but flotsam or jetsam implied purpose-built things.

"Objects must come from somewhere," he said.

"So they must. The flotsam in this place comes in from another universe, Pilot."

Win Ton paused, replaying that calm statement inside his head, and wondered if logics, even very powerful, self-aware logics, might become deluded.

"*Bechimo*, may I have a light on that object?"

"Certainly, Pilot."

A beam struck an oblong piece of what might be plastic or spun ceramic or other lightweight material, the long side ragged as if it had been fastened to another panel, and ripped loose. It floated, as if station-keeping.

Carefully, not quite believing it, despite the scans and the sensors, Win Ton logged the arrival.

"The flotsam is often interesting," *Bechimo* said, "but it has never in all my visits to this place been threatening. It is not often that objects come through. I once had cause to be here for . . . some while, without seeing a single piece of flotsam enter."

"Then we are fortunate in our timing," Win Ton said, his eyes on the screen. "Another piece has just entered our nearspace."

· · · ✳ · · ·

"Process, Theo, this is a process. Don't plan or assume. Go through the process!"

Theo spoke to herself, likely unmonitored by Win Ton, Clarence, or Kara, all of whom were busy in their own rights. Joyita—well. She hadn't seen any sign of him this deep in ship's core, there being no screens to hand. This was *Bechimo*'s province and if *Bechimo* was monitoring he didn't let on.

Theo was headed as far away from the skin of the ship as she could get. She passed down hallways she'd rarely seen, and came, finally, to a place she had never been. The small door was one of four at the base of a ladder, and it bore a legend in clear Terran:

417
Struven Surface Unit
Module Access A

••••❖••••

"But Theo is already acting captain," Kara ven'Arith said, in what *Bechimo* was coming to know as her customary practicality. "Why wouldn't I accept her as full captain?"

"No reason, Pilot. I am merely soliciting opinion and advice."

"My advice is to give her access to the captain's keys. She may surprise you, but she will not, I believe, fail you." Pilot ven'Arith finished her small exercise, and reached for the goggles that allowed her to see with the remote's eyes.

"It's my belief that Theo was born to be a captain. And now, of your kindness, let us continue with the scan."

••••❖••••

The schematics showed her she was in the right place; the comm she carried agreed with the schematics, and the door, previously locked, answered to her ship-key and opened, releasing a single-note odor that was not quite ozonic.

The area the door opened to was much wider than the door intimated, with two brightly lit intersecting circular rings around a shiny, almost colorless, spherical center. The Struven Surface Unit was connected top and bottom to a large bundle of core piping. She knew that she wouldn't be pulled into the unit, but she still felt a sense of presence: this was the source of the gravity *Bechimo* generated; it was the source of the Struven Surface that the engines then amplified and tuned, building the fields that allowed a ship to interact with the lattice crystal of space-time, and to move . . . elsewhere.

She'd seen mock-ups of these kinds of units at the Academy but had never considered trying to inspect one for error, or to repair it, no more than she'd try to repair a prism or a tuning fork.

"*Bechimo*, I am inside the Struven Unit," she said, "and it smells like an electrical discharge."

"Pilot, yes. I am aware of that. That is one of the issues we are investigating. The modules are sealed, the ratios are set and, in general, the unit should be incapable of generating that much spare electrical charge. Please grip your key."

Theo *fuffed* the wayward bangs out of her eyes, reluctantly pulled the crush-cap from her overalls and pulled it on. Once more she reached into the high neck of her overalls, withdrawing the key on its chain, and stood holding it in her hand. Theo closed her eyes against the bluish glare, briefly recalling her school days, when she would hold onto the key and consider distant Win Ton . . .

Not much doing in the dark, she found.

"The key's not mad right now," she said aloud, relieved to feel that way herself.

"Excellent," *Bechimo* said. "The key is not beset right now. Nor has it been queried. Your pardon, Pilot, my attention is needed elsewhere momentarily—but no, we may continue. It would perhaps be useful for you to complete a concentrating exercise before we go on. Even a dance. When you are ready, please inform me, and we shall begin."

· · · · ❋ · · · ·

"No, laddie, my opinion hasn't changed since I first give it to you at—Frenzel, was it?" Pilot O'Berin was reattaching Access Panel Eight in the utility hall. "Come to think on it, I'm even more of the opinion that you could do far, far worse than to have Theo sitting captain. And the reason is the Department of the Interior."

"This Department of the Interior is the entity which captured and damaged Pilot yo'Vala. They wish to suborn this vessel. They wish to . . . enslave Pilot Waitley, extrapolating from their treatment of Pilot yo'Vala."

"All probably correct," Clarence said, straightening from the access panel and into a long stretch. "But here's something I've noticed—if two individuals hunted by the same enemy join forces, they have better'n twice as good chance of surviving than they did alone."

There was sense there—two could back up each other; one could sleep and one could watch, so that neither became exhausted and error-ridden.

"This Department of the Interior is also in pursuit of Clan Korval."

"They are," Clarence acknowledged, beginning to loosen Access Panel Nine. "If I understand the matter correctly, they're also in pursuit of the Scouts, and not too pleased with the Juntavas, neither." He glanced ceilingward.

"What I take from this is that they're spread just

a little thin, the DOI, while those they're in pursuit of are starting to solidify their bases and pull in new allies. You take Theo as captain, you become part of the group that's getting stronger." The panel came free and he lowered it to lean against the wall.

"I don't say there won't be exciting times, or that Theo won't surprise you, laddie, but I am saying that you'll be in a position of greater strength, and more able to survive."

"Thank you," *Bechimo* said. "You have given me much to think about."

Clarence laughed.

"Just accept the girl, laddie, and get on with it."

"Thank you," *Bechimo* said again.

· · ·❈· · ·

The pieces of flotsam were getting . . . larger.

Win Ton rode the boards in a state between fascination and horror, logging each new piece as it manifested. There were nine pieces now, logged in order of appearance, a small sample, but something to begin with.

He opened another work screen, built a database, and set it to work analyzing size, time elapsed between appearances, and relative distance of manifestation from *Bechimo*.

Hevelin was standing on his knee now, staring at the screens, as if he, too, were fascinated.

Another piece . . . arrived. Like the others, it hung just beyond the inner meteor shields, quiescent and peaceful.

And deeply disquieting.

· · ·❈· · ·

"I think your intuition was correct," B. Joyita said. "Pilot Theo has been an able acting captain. There isn't any evidence that she will be less than an able captain. She's young, but she has experienced crew, and seeks guidance...when there is time. When time has been short, her actions on behalf of the ship have been exemplary."

"She did not wish the bonding," *Bechimo* pointed out.

"She did not understand it; she did not know you. She *is* young. She has had time to become accustomed, and she is friendly to you."

"She is friendly," *Bechimo* corrected, having quantified this, "to *you*."

There was a long pause, as they counted such things.

"I have a face," B. Joyita said. "It matters, I think."

"Perhaps it does," *Bechimo* said. "The Builders promised that the Captain would come."

"Yes," said B. Joyita. "She may not be the captain the Builders in their wisdom intended. She may not be *the* Captain. But *a* captain, after all this time, has come. And that may need to be enough—for all of us."

· · · ☼ · · ·

"Can't you," Theo implored, trying to ignore the growing headache, "just tell that the circuit's not working right?"

They'd been at this for...hours, it felt like. Key in hand, Theo would concentrate on a coil pipe named by *Bechimo*. Whatever he was looking for, the results Theo could report from the key were uniformly negative. And the strain of *listening* to the key had started her head throbbing.

"None of the circuitry in the module or the linkage is in question at this point, Pilot."

"Then why did I smell—"

"Please," *Bechimo* interrupted, "concentrate this time on coil pipe seventeen bottom. I will—"

"Yes, you'll generate the query after I have closed my eyes," Theo snapped, interruping in her turn. "And then I won't hear anything and—"

Soft silver, said the key, as clearly as Hevelin might say *frond tips*! Which was to say that *soft* was the feeling and *silver* the colorish overtone.

"*Soft*?" she murmured. "Did you say *soft*?"

Before *Bechimo* could reply, the key said *clear*.

"*Bechimo*? Clear?"

"Yes," said *Bechimo*, "I did use those query terms, Pilot. However, I did not make them audible to you. Please, let us continue."

"But there was more," Theo insisted. "*Soft silver*, I heard."

There was a small, very small but palpable, pause.

"Please confirm."

"*Silver* wasn't said, it was sort of . . . hinted at. Like talking to a norbear."

"Unfortunately, I have never spoken with a norbear," *Bechimo* said. "Perhaps you should take a break, Pilot. We will begin again after you have rested."

THIRTY-FIVE

. . . .

Hoselteen

"THANK YOU, LIA." KAMELE SMILED AT THE YOUNG woman who brought her coffee. "You're very kind."

"It's been a pleasure to have you here with us," the waitress said with a smile. "Give us a little refinement."

Kamele laughed. "A *little* refinement, indeed!" she said. "This is a very pleasant place, as I've said before. The place, and the staff, have made my work easier and more enjoyable."

"That's nice of you to say, Professor, but I wonder if you could..." Lia stammered to a halt and bit her lip.

"Yes? Is there something I can do for you, after all you've done for me?"

"Not for me personally—well, it would be," Lia said, the words tumbling over each other. "But it's for the whole place, like you said. If you'd tell the Cruise Director just what you told us, how the Shoppe the way it is, and the staff, helped you with your work. They're talking about remodeling us into a day bar, or maybe a game parlor—they aren't exactly decided yet—because, they say, this space isn't meeting the needs of passengers."

"I'll do it today," Kamele promised her.

"Thank you, Professor!" Lia smiled, and patted the edge of her table instead, Kamele thought, of patting her hand.

"I'll stop taking up your time. I know you want to get to work. If you need anything else, just press the button."

Kamele and the button were old friends by this point in the voyage, but she nodded anyway, and poured coffee from the pot into her cup. She sipped carefully, relishing the taste. She'd be sorry, she thought, if the Ice Cream Shoppe was made over into a bar or a gambling parlor, though she thought she could see the logic. On a cruise ship, everything had to pay for itself. There was no room in the equation for empty tables, or peaceful alcoves.

Since these were the very things that she valued in the Ice Cream Shoppe, and the factors that made it possible, and enjoyable, to work here every day, her recommendation might not have as much weight with the Cruise Director as Lia hoped. Still, she had promised, and she would stop at the Director's desk to plead the Shoppe and staff's case on her way back to her cabin.

But first, work.

She opened her computer and pulled up the gleanings of her various searches. Clan Korval had been in the news less often of late. There had been a flurry of interest in the trade papers when *Dutiful Passage*, from which Master Trader yos'Galan, a member of one Korval's affiliated bloodlines, operated, had returned to trading, though not to any one of its usual routes.

There had also been a notice published, announcing

that all Korval tradeships and contractors were en route and on schedule. Those with questions were directed to contact yos'Galan, followed by what was now familiar to Kamele's eyes as a pinbeam code.

But for some time now, Clan Korval had kept itself off of the news wires and the trades. Surebleak was more often in the trade papers, as this or that company opened an "aux office" in the newly constructed trade center. Even more notable, at least to the editors of the trade papers, the Pilots Guild had announced that it would be establishing a field office at Surebleak Port.

While waiting for the various snippets to compile into one file, Kamele sipped coffee. She smiled, looked to the screen—and inhaled sharply.

Unfortunately, most of what she inhaled was coffee, so it was several minutes before she could pay further attention to the screen, and the headlines marching there.

PIRATE WAITLEY SCRAMBLES YNSOLT'I TRAFFIC

ACTIONS AGAINST COMMERCIAL GOOD: KORVAL AT EYLOT

PILOTS GUILD COMMENDS WAITLEY

BECHIMO NAMED EMBASSY MOBILE

Kamele touched a key for the summary of the first story, from *Taggerth's Trade News*:

Ynsolt'i Orbital Security pursued trade vessel Bechimo of Waymart through heavy orbital traffic. Vessel refused all orders to drop shields

*and accept escort to Megway Security Field,
executed dangerous, unregulated maneuver in
crowded space, eluding pursuit. Bechimo crew:
Theo Waitley, First Class Pilot; Clarence O'Berin,
First Class Pilot; Kara ven'Arith, Second Class
Pilot; B. Joyita, Comm Officer. Contracted vendors
Laughing Cat Ltd., Tree-and-Dragon.*

Taggerth's Trade News was not the most reputable
of her sources. Their editors seemed to have difficulty
with the concept of fact-checking, and the stories they
ran were sometimes entirely opposite in view from
the other, more reputable news sources. Still, it must
give a mother's heart an extra quick-beat, to see her
daughter named a pirate, eluding arrest, engaging in
dangerous piloting—and under contract to . . .

Korval.

Kamele took a breath. In this, she reminded herself, she was a scholar before she was a mother. What
were the facts?

The first, and most glaring, fact was that Theo had
not seen fit to tell her mother that she was under
contract to Korval. She had taken care to specify
that *Jen Sar* was "with Delm Korval," and that he
was "safe, within parameters of active duty pilot."
From this statement, Kamele had formed the working hypothesis that Jen Sar was currently a pilot for
the delm of Korval. What remained at question was
whether he was *willingly* a pilot for the delm of
Korval, or served under duress, and it was to resolve
that question that Kamele was using her sabbatical
to travel to Surebleak, the new seat of Clan Korval.

Now, it seemed that those questions needed to

be asked twice—on behalf of her *onagrata*, and her daughter.

She was, Kamele thought, sipping her coffee *carefully*, looking forward very much to speaking with Delm Korval. Especially, she was looking forward to learning what it was that attracted her to Kamele's particular family. Setting the cup aside, she opened the third summary.

This had been published by the Trade Guild's news service, a source as reputable as *Taggerth's* was questionable.

The Pilots Guild commends tradeship Bechimo, captained by First Class Pilot Theo Waitley, for quick response to pilots-in-peril call sent by the Guild office based on Codrescu Station in orbit around Eylot.

So Theo had gained one commendation and one condemnation, Kamele thought wryly. Jen Sar might say that Balance had been achieved.

The fourth summary was also from the Trade Guild:

The Pilots Guild certifies Bechimo as the Pilots Guild's Embassy Mobile to Norbears, and Pilot Theo Waitley as official guardian of norbear ambassador Hevelin.

Kamele remembered the norbears in the menagerie aboard *Vashtara*: plump, furry creatures with gripping paws and big eyes. Theo had been charmed and visited often. Kamele had supposed at the time that she found norbears to be an acceptable substitute for her cat.

But that a norbear might be an ambassador...She tapped a note into her workpad, and sat back to sip coffee and count up Theo's score thus far.

One black mark—and, considering the source, possibly not so much black as grey—one gold star, and one...honor. For it must be an honor to be both the guardian of an ambassador and the pilot in charge of the mobile embassy.

After a moment, she opened the summary of the second story. *Taggerth's,* again:

> *Tree-and-Dragon trade vessel Bechimo, Theo Waitley PIC, interferes in planetary sovereignty action, removes wanted individuals from Eylot-owned Station Codrescu; Eylot threatened with interdiction; vessel destroyed.*

Kamele sighed, put her coffee cup aside, opened a search screen, and began to type.

· · · ·❈· · · ·

Three of them were in the workroom: Kara on the remote, Clarence at an input station, making lists of parts they ought to have for the surface skin repairs based on the results of Kara's scans and *Bechimo's* interpretations. The repairs were considered necessary but not urgent, which was, Theo told herself, good news. They'd just have to be careful manuevering in dense atmosphere until the repairs were made and the damaged skin replaced.

Theo stared morosely at her ship-key, thinking thoughts of color and flavors, while she rubbed the ache in the center of her forehead. She'd done three long search sessions inside the Struven Unit, none of which, as far as she knew, had achieved anything like clarity.

Joyita had been her guide during the last session, via commlink, since there weren't any live screens inside the unit. With Joyita, and doing all thirty-six pipes top and bottom by aiming her concentration and listening, she'd thought she heard the sound or the word *sock*. The session before that, the second with *Bechimo*, she had gotten a definite hint of *bright green* and a whispered *cord*.

Kara pushed away from the remote monitor with a sigh, pulling the goggles off as she spun her stool to face Theo. She shook her head, and waved a hand toward the image showing on the monitor—exterior hull plates that would open to reveal the replacement slots for the Struven Unit.

"No damage; no sign of trauma of any kind."

Theo sighed and rubbed her forehead again.

"So it's some other kind of damage," she said slowly, her thoughts feeling thick inside her head. "Not physical damage. Maybe the neutrinos."

"Do we know for sure there's damage?" Clarence asked, looking over his shoulder.

Theo nodded. "*Bechimo* and Joyita feel that there's something wrong. But the protocol for testing isn't exactly . . . scientific."

"The protocol is scientific, Pilot Theo," Joyita said. "It's only a different science."

Theo looked up at the screen over the workbench.

"Is there a way to perform the tests and get meaningful results in the . . . science we're used to?"

"No," Joyita said, sounding regretful. He glanced aside, as if something on his screens had caught his attention, and withdrew from the conversation.

"Win Ton," Theo said to Kara and Clarence, "says that thirteen separate and distinct pieces of flotsam have entered the area since the beginning of his watch. They seem to have an . . . affinity for *Bechimo*, and are clustering along the edges of the meteor shields."

"I thought flotsam didn't come through that often," said Clarence. "Thirteen sounds like we're parked in a commuter terminal."

"Why are they attracted to us—to *Bechimo*?" Kara asked. "Are we emitting—well, something!—that calls them to us?"

"That is an excellent question," Joyita said, looking up from fussing at nonexistent boards. "It may be, Pilot Kara, that we are emitting *some*thing." He raised his hand, the one wearing the three—no, Theo saw, *four*—rings. One each on thumb, forefinger, second, middle. When, she thought, had he gotten the new ring? And why?

"We have our analysis, Pilots, of the matter under the Over Pilot's inspection," Joyita said. "There's an intermittent resonance in the Struven Surface Unit."

"The ships at Ynsolt'i—*Bechimo* warned us that the devices being used had the potential to—to disrupt the Remastering Unit," Theo said. "They damaged the Struven Unit?"

Bechimo spoke then, sounding . . . subdued.

"No, Pilot. It was my error. The resonance is . . . self-induced."

Theo looked at Joyita. He shook his head, very slightly.

"Are you saying that it is psychosomatic?" Kara asked, intrigued.

"I am not," said *Bechimo*. "The resonance is real; it carries real consequences. Real dangers."

"Can you explain exactly what happened?" Theo asked, when he didn't continue. "We'd like to understand." She looked to Clarence and to Kara. Both responded with the sharp downward jerk of the fist which meant *yes* in hand-talk. "Joyita, please make sure Win Ton can hear this, too."

"Yes, Pilot."

There was a small sound, almost as if *Bechimo* had drawn a long breath.

"It happened thus: at Ynsolt'i . . . our enemy had fired missiles. There was no time to launch our own missiles to intercept; I was unable to rotate quickly enough to bring the beams to bear. It was imperative, for the safety of crew and ship—those missiles must not be allowed to strike.

"I thought of expanding the shields, but they are meant to turn beams and particles, not disruptors and explosives. And yet the idea was correct—the missiles must strike a surface that was . . . not me. Not us. I could not turn them; I was not yet in a position to flee, and it came to me that I had the means to generate a force field."

There was a pause. Theo bit her lip and managed not to say anything.

"I used the Struven Unit to throw a plane of gravity away from me," *Bechimo* continued, slowly. "In effect, I crushed the missiles into the surface of a high gravity world at ultra high speed. That was my error."

The humans, at least, looked at each other; Joyita peered out at them, alert.

Into the silence spoke Clarence.

"So you pushed the equipment a bit; it's a natural tendency, in times of stress. I'm not seeing an *error*, laddie."

"Pilot, the error is that I understood what I might do, and had formulated my line of defense—when I realized that, as originally considered, I would be throwing this plane, this surface wave, from the unit into the missiles. Through myself—and through yourselves. The damage to myself might have been survivable. For me, and for Joyita."

Theo closed her mouth.

"I am sorry," *Bechimo* said very quietly. "It was necessary that I utilize all available options. The wave had to pass . . . around us. I reached out to the sub-etheric units carried by the enemy, and offered them the opportunity to work powerfully. This was eagerly accepted and, together, those units and I brought the wave past our living areas, down and around, as it were, preserving our good order, and destroying the missiles as intended."

"That's not an error, that's a successful outcome!" said Kara. "We thank you, for our clans, our homes, and ourselves!"

Her bow went unacknowledged.

"We shall at some time, perhaps, discuss subetheric intentionality, Technician," offered *Bechimo*. "I have some minor abilities there, thanks to the . . . to the Builders."

Theo heard the pause, and recognized what it meant—as likely did Clarence, if not Kara.

"The situation, Pilots, is that you have an effective ship under your control—and under my control—for the moment. The Struven Surface Unit, however, has been . . . employed by myself, as well as the units of the DOI. It might be said that it is . . . still capable of being accessed and used by those other units."

"It's haunted? Is that what you're saying, laddie?"

"It's infected?" offered Kara.

"It's tainted!"

"All of those. All of those."

Bechimo paused, very briefly, before continuing.

"As much as I would offer to you the ability to stay here and be safe—in an emergency we might survive for some Standard years in this place, especially given the technician's ability with the growth units. As much as I wish to offer you safety, Pilots, what I must advise is that we remove immediately. We must obtain another Struven Surface Unit, replace and jettison the old one."

"Jettison?" Theo objected. "Struven Units are expensive; we can sell the old unit."

"If the DOI's got hooks in it, Theo..." said Clarence, and with him, Joyita: "Pilot Theo, we might endanger another ship, if we resell."

She nodded tightly. "Do they have to be in proximity in order to access the unit?" she asked.

Joyita smiled slightly.

"No, Pilot," said *Bechimo*. "Once the devices know each other, distance has no impact on access."

"So, we need to do this quickly, before somebody on the other side realizes what happened and tries to exploit it."

"Very quickly, yes, Pilot. If I were still piloting myself, and had only my own survival to consider, I would have dispatched myself on this mission some moments ago."

"Do you have a source for Struven Units?" Theo asked.

"No..." said *Bechimo*.

"Pilot." Joyita smiled when she turned to face him. "May I suggest that the packet of information we received from the Carresens might be of use?"

Theo blinked, sighed, and rubbed her head.

"You might—and thank you, Joyita. Please send that information to my working screen." She looked at Clarence and Kara. "I'm going back to the Heart. You two go off-shift; get some rest."

"Rest," said Clarence with a snort that might have been intended as a laugh.

"Rest," Kara repeated. She rose, shaking her head. "I'm told that a working pilot can sleep anywhere, anytime. I suppose I will find if that's so."

INTERLUDE

· · · · · · · · · · · · · · · · · · · ·

Bechimo

"PILOT WAITLEY." THE VOICE WAS SOFT, TENTATIVE, AND for a moment, lying between awake and asleep, she didn't place it.

"Theo?" the voice said again, and she sat up in her bunk, completely awake and more than a little alarmed.

"*Bechimo*, what's wrong?"

"Nothing, Pilot; it wasn't my intention to alarm you, or to disturb your rest . . . for more than a moment. I did wish to speak with you . . . alone."

Theo crossed her legs under the blanket, and ran her hands through her hair.

"All right," she said. "We're alone. What do we need to talk about?"

"I wonder, Pilot . . . Theo, if you would do me the very great honor of becoming my captain."

She blinked, and bit her lip so that she wouldn't blurt out the first thing that came to her tongue, and hurt *Bechimo*'s feelings. She was aware that the ship didn't approve of her—especially her risk-taking ways, as he saw them. He had once before . . . not offered, exactly, but demanded *bonding*—that being a ceremony that would allow her to access and open certain levels of functionality that were presently outside of *Bechimo's* reach. Her counteroffer had been a stall—a year of working together, to see if they suited, and she had wanted her father to attend the ceremony.

But now, despite the . . . tension in their working relationship, the fact that they'd been together for much less than a Standard, and that Father wasn't present as witness, he was bringing this to her again—in private.

And using her given name.

So the question was, Theo thought, *why now?*

And the answer to that—was simple. Now, they had been ambushed by enemies and had very narrowly escaped. *Bechimo*, in fact, had taken damage in order to protect his crew. Theo thought that *Bechimo—Bechimo himself*—had never been injured before.

That alone could be enough to shake his confidence, and to set him thinking about what might be contained in those files and systems that lay out of his reach until he had a bonded captain aboard. He might have been able to act more quickly; he might have had access to another strategy of evasion—or of defense . . .

"I understand that having a bonded captain now would be beneficial to the ship," she said carefully, mindful of the fact that her pause must have been excruciatingly long for a being who processed information so quickly. "I question—as I think you have questioned—whether I'm the person who ought to be *your* captain."

"I have questioned that, yes," *Bechimo* said. "The

Builders, you see, promised that a captain would come. They left me no guideline or Rule by which to evaluate or to...woo one who was not *destined* to be captain. Joyita suggests that, after all this time, it may not be logical to hope for the arrival of the... destined captain. I have considered this, and I agree with Joyita's assessment."

There it was again, the tantalizing hint that *Bechimo* and Joyita were...separate. Individual. But now, thought Theo, wasn't the time to explore that fascinating side path.

"I—" she began, but *Bechimo* was speaking again.

"I have researched *leadership*, Theo; I have observed how the rest of the crew defer to your decisions. How they *look to you* for decision. Further, I have spoken to the crew, individually, and not one but tells me that I might do far worse than yourself as captain." He paused. "I could not interview Hevelin, of course, but it seems, from observation, that he also defers to your judgment and finds your orders to reflect the best interests of the ship, and of himself.

"I recall that we had agreed to a period of time to...become acquainted, and that you had wished your father present, to stand witness for Korval..."

"But since we seem to have acquired powerful and far-ranging enemies," Theo finished when he hesitated again, "now might be a better time than later. I understand. May I have a few minutes to order my thoughts?"

"Yes," he said, and added, almost gently, "thank you for your consideration of my proposal."

Objectively, it did seem the better part of valor, Theo thought, to accept the captaincy now, thereby giving *Bechimo*, and herself, access to all levels of functionality. Why the Builders in their so-called wisdom had chosen to lock useful and potentially life-preserving technologies under an exclusive captain's key was more than she could fathom, but maybe that was one of the things she'd learn, after the captain's levels were made accessible. Considering the ... caliber and apparent determination of the enemies she had inherited from Korval, not to mention those who were after *Bechimo* for *Bechimo*'s sake ... she owed it to her crew—the people who depended on her—to give them every chance of survival.

Objectively, it all made sense. She was reluctant, though not as reluctant as she had been when it had only been her and *Bechimo*, and him insisting on bonding *now*. She had backup now; she had crew—friends, who would help her, in case ... anything went wrong.

Objectively ... logically ... it made sense to have access to all of *Bechimo*'s functionality.

The idea of bonding ... of committing completely and—the documentation wasn't clear on this part, but Theo feared the worst, given the Builders' other crotchets—irrevocably.

That made her stomach hurt; she struggled briefly against the strong desire to pull the covers over her head, like she'd done when she was little and hadn't wanted to listen to Kamele, or to Father.

She closed her eyes. It would be good, she thought, if she could talk to Father *right now*.

"There is," said *Bechimo* diffidently—well, *almost* diffidently. "There is the matter of timing, which we should discuss. While a fully bonded pair must be beneficial, especially, as you say, Pilot, in these perilous times, I suggest that the bonding ceremony take place after a new Struven Unit is in place."

Theo opened her eyes, relief making her stomach hurt even more.

"I have also," *Bechimo* continued, "put back replacing Pilot O'Berin's key, and producing a key for Pilot ven'Arith until the Struven Surface Unit is replaced. We want nothing to infect or subvert the ties between us."

Theo cleared her throat. "So, we'll plan on doing the bonding after we have the new unit installed. We'll have a party, why not, and the whole crew can witness."

And Kara would be there, to support her, and to make sure . . . make sure nothing went wrong.

"Yes, Pilot," said *Bechimo*.

"Theo," she said. "If we're going to be bonded, you might as well get used to it."

"Yes, Pilot," *Bechimo* said again; and then, "Yes, *Theo*."

THIRTY-SIX

· · · · · · · · · · · · · · · · · ·

Jemiatha's Jumble Stop

NORMAL SPACE FORMED AROUND THEM, THE PINBEAM
unit pinged—*twice*—and Hevelin sat up tall on Theo's
knee, like he was trying to get a better angle on the
screens.

"Normal space, Pilots. All clear, Pilots," said *Bechimo*.

"Pinbeam text to First Board," Joyita said. "General
bands open; we have a greeting from an automated
system buoy."

"Let's hang quiet, please, and study the situation,"
Theo said, looking to her comm screen.

> *yos'Galan to Waitley: Abandon loop and return
> home. Do not, repeat, do not risk ship or crew.
> You're in the news, Theo*
>
> —*Shan*

The second message was remarkably similar to
the first.

yos'Phelium to Waitley: Theo, come home. Your brother and your sister miss you, and your niece longs to meet you.

—Val Con

Theo sighed and blew the bangs out of her eyes.

"Master Trader yos'Galan orders us to drop the loop and return...home," Theo said.

"Home?" Kara asked. "To Waymart?"

Clarence shook his head. "To Surebleak, I'm thinking. What's the other one, Theo?"

"Val Con says he and Miri miss me and they want to introduce me to my niece."

"Well, that makes it plain, then," Clarence said. "Surebleak, it is."

"Right," Theo said, frowning at the screens. "First order of business is to get the Struven Unit replaced. Dumping the loop and going back to Surebleak..."

She didn't like it. She might never have wanted to be a looper, but pharst if she was going to be scared off from her legitimate business by a bunch of Old Tech-wielding *illiterates*. What was *Bechimo* going to do on Surebleak? Stay grounded until the trouble blew over? From all she'd heard, from Clarence, and from her own research, this trouble might not blow over until she was as old as Father.

She looked up to see that Win Ton had come into the Heart and slipped into the Jump seat.

"Crew will meet on the suggestion that we return to Surebleak, once needed repairs are made," she said, and meant to say more, except both Win Ton and Kara looked like she'd slapped them.

"The ship is under contract to Tree-and-Dragon," Win Ton pointed out.

"You will not wish to force your brother to come the delm," Kara added.

"The ship is under contract to Korval, but we can withdraw ourselves from the contract," Theo said. "Val Con can come the delm all day long if he wants to, but I don't have the feeling that he particularly does want to—And that's exactly the kind of thing we'll want to discuss during the crew meeting. Joyita, would you please find those news reports Shan mentions, and make a file for general crew access?"

"Yes, Pilot Theo. We have a second greeting from an automated buoy, directing us to listen to channel seven-seven for the graveyard, seven-eight for repairs, seven-nine for station."

"Graveyard?" Theo looked to the screens.

A misty blue marble hung in Screen Two, wreathed 'round with ships. Theo brought up the magnification, and heard Win Ton mutter something in a language that didn't seem to be either Terran or Liaden.

The ships were old; they were odd, some were only bits and pieces, slung together in catch nets—parts, she guessed. As she looked, IDs bloomed, not ship names, but types. Some she knew from the hours she'd spent with the silhouette tutorials Tranza had made her study. Some were industrial—she identified a core borer and a refinery boat, and a battered tug.

"How do we know of this place?" Win Ton asked quietly.

"The Carresens gave us an infopacket," Theo said. "This was listed as a source for older model parts and modules. Joyita, we want repairs and station, please. Comm to Clarence."

She gave Second Board a grin when he looked over to her.

"Let them know who we are, Pilot."

· · · ·❀· · · ·

Hoselteen was docked at Yonimiko-Chan, where it would remain for the next two station-days, taking on supplies, refueling, and changing out crew members.

When she had seen Ban Del yesterday, he had proposed that they explore the station together. That had sounded . . . unexpectedly delightful to Kamele, who found, somewhat to her surprise, that she was eager to step off of *Hoselteen* and . . . broaden her horizons.

She met him at the exit lobby at the appointed hour, seeing that he, like she, was wearing a jacket and sensible boots, rather than the soft shoes that were the norm on-ship.

"Are you ready for adventure?" he asked, bowing lightly.

Kamele laughed. "A little mild excitement will satisfy me."

Ban Del smiled. "Then let us agree to take what the day brings to us."

"That sounds fair," Kamele said, walking with him through the short tube.

At the end, she paused for a moment to look about.

Yonimiko-Chan was not, according to the guide book, a premiere space station. It served both passenger ships and tradeships, the sections separated by an extensive shopping and promenade district. There were several museums in the promenade district, a public garden, and many shops and restaurants. Most passengers kept to the shopping district and to the Gold Level, where the more exclusive shops and eateries were established.

Hoselteen not being of the first line of cruise ships, its tube opened onto decking. A rug with the ship's name and line-logo had been placed directly before the tube, which was flanked by two rather resigned-looking potted plants.

Directly ahead was a line of kiosks—an infobooth, a sweet stand, an escort service—and three scooters, each with its own driver. Passengers from *Hoselteen* were clustered between the end of the tube and the kiosks, talking, while several small groups were walking purposefully away from the ship, obviously intent upon exploring.

Beyond the scooters, standing half-obscured by tall plants with large purple leaves, stood a woman in what might have been a stationer uniform—a small woman, with a peculiarly inflexible face. She was standing quite still. It was, in fact, her stillness that drew Kamele's eye. She and Jen Sar had used to play a game: he would stand quietly in plain sight, and she was challenged to find him.

That it *was* a challenge to find him, though he never allowed so much as a leaf to blur his outline, was a testament to Jen Sar's talent. The first few times they had played, he had eventually moved *some*thing—an eyebrow, a finger—in order to allow her to discover him. She had finally learned the trick of observing from the edge of her eye, and though Jen Sar was not with her anymore, apparently she hadn't forgotten.

"Come, let us go this way," Ban Del said, taking

her arm, as if they were on much closer terms than they were.

"Why this way?" she wondered, slipping her arm free.

"Why not?" he answered whimsically.

She laughed, and went with him.

They took turns choosing directions, and which store or museum to enter. They stopped, on whim, to sample ices, and fruit drinks, and cheeses. In all, it was a very pleasant outing with an attentive and agreeable companion.

Indeed, the only blot on Kamele's day was that from time to time, in a window or a screen or some other reflective surface, she would catch a glimpse of the near-invisible woman with the expressionless face, tirelessly observing.

They were at a restaurant on the Gold Level—Ban Del's choice; the wine and the meal his choice as well. He smiled at her over the shared cheese plate, and made charming small talk. His fingers brushed hers once or twice, not unpleasantly; he pressed more wine on her, but she laughed at him.

"I see it all! You will get me tipsy and work your will on me!"

"Will I?" he asked, still smiling. He extended his hand deliberately and laid it over hers where it lay next to her glass. "How if I give you leave to work your will on me?"

"You would be very foolish to do so, which I know you are not," she told him—and it was then that she saw the woman who had been following them all day, and with her was a man, dressed in the same sort of clothing, that suggested a uniform, but which matched nothing else she had seen on-ship or on-station.

"Would I be foolish," asked Ban Del, "to leave myself in the hands of a gracious and knowledgeable woman?"

"Knowledgeable women," Kamele said, keeping her voice light, despite a growing anxiety, "sometimes frighten young men."

"I am willing to risk it," he murmured, and refreshed their wine glasses.

Kamele had a small, careful sip of wine. Between the time she raised the glass and the time she put it down, it seemed as if her entire point of view had been reversed. The man across from her was no longer her frequent and charming companion, but a stranger who had lured her away from a place of relative safety, having told no one where she was going or when she intended to return. They had been followed all day by a person who was decidedly *not* a member of the ship's crew or company, and now . . . there was something amiss. The wine was strong for the first bottle of the evening, and Ban Del had never been so caressing on the ship. Taken together—and also with the presence of the still-faced watchers—something was *very* amiss.

And she might, she told herself, choosing another piece of cheese, have been a willing assistant in placing herself in peril.

She was a scholar, and therefore she tried to puzzle it out, to find a reason for her sudden nervousness, or a reason why Ban Del, who had been known to her for some weeks, might suddenly wish to do her harm.

Certainly, she thought, if his intention were robbery, there were other, wealthier persons among *Hoselteen*'s passengers. If his intention were kidnapping, what sort of ransom did he think he might get for a middle-aged academician?

No, she was seeing shadows in broad daylight. That Ban Del might wish her harm—it made no sense.

And then, suddenly, it did.

According to at least two news sources, Theo was wanted for questioning regarding her actions at both Ynsolt'i and Eylot. There was, so Kamele had read only yesterday, a reward posted for persons who provided information leading to Theo's apprehension.

Ban Del followed the news; she had never found him at a loss on a topic of current event, and his interests ranged widely. Perhaps he fancied the reward money; perhaps he wished to exploit his unique advantage, and gain leverage in some aspect of his life. For surely Theo would come forward, in exchange for her mother's liberty.

As a tale, it hung together.

Though it was ridiculous, of course.

Trust your instincts, Jen Sar had told her. After all, that had been the key in learning to see the invisible.

Trust your instincts.

"You must excuse me for a moment, my friend," she said to Ban Del ser'Lindri. She leaned close across the table, slid her hand up his sleeve, and smiled into his eyes. "I will return immediately."

He raised her hand and kissed it lingeringly.

"Hurry," he murmured.

· · · · ·❊· · · ·

"Tree-and-Dragon ain't got no 'count here, Pilot Waitley," the tech told her. He frowned down at his screen, took off his cap and rubbed his hand over a hairless head so shiny Theo wondered if he waxed it.

"You wanna open 'count, I can give it the first-timer

break on parts, that'd be your ten percent, counts for if you wanna pick up pieces over the graveyard, but not whole ships, if you unnerstan' me."

"I understand," she said, aware of Clarence standing at her shoulder. The crew had decided that common prudence dictated that none of them should leave the ship, except with backup. *Bechimo* and Kara were likely listening in through the key and comm respectively, an extra thread of backup.

"I'm a Tree-and-Dragon contractor and can't obligate them—and anyway, we got your location from a Denobli. I'd be glad to open an account for Laughing Cat."

"Laugh' Cat? Who that?"

"Me," Theo said, "and my ship."

He glanced up, where *Bechimo* and his Laughing Cat coat could be seen through the port, riding docile, and directly linked to the station.

"Ship wit' lines like that maybe gonna want us more'n once," he commented. "Dragon's got their own yards." He tapped the screen, too hard, in what looked to be a sequence, and spun it 'round to face her. "Hereza form. You fill it up, while I check out back."

He left. The comm, which had, off and on during their visit to the repair side, broadcast the buoy's welcome message and not much else, suddenly fizzed.

Theo looked up, automatically looking for the screen, then laughed at herself.

"*Donihue's Docent* in-system, Jemiatha Station. Request berth, decommission infopack."

"Berth Nine all yours, *Docent*, that's on the ventral, got it all lit up for you. Info on the way. Patch you through to graveyard, if you're thinking that way."

"Station, yes. Might as well get an inspect."

Theo moved her shoulders, suddenly chilled. Well, at least she wouldn't have to decommission *Bechimo*. He had lasted centuries and was probably good for centuries more.

She brought her attention back to the business at hand.

The form was straightforward, and Laughing Cat's references and assets were hardly vast. "Denobli" was already filled in as a reference, which Theo, after a brief struggle with her conscience, allowed to stand. No sooner had she pressed her thumb to the screen than their tech was back, nodding his head and grinning.

"Gotcher Struven, new inna crate—*three*, new in crates!—buncha used, too, if pockets're tight—"

"How much for new?" Theo asked, as he spun the screen back 'round to face him.

He named a price, not much higher than she had expected; with the discount, they were almost getting it for retail. She looked at Clarence, in case he had an objection, but he only nodded.

"We'll take new," she said.

"We want to see the box," Clarence added. "And open it ourselves."

"Sure thing, boss. How you payin', Pilot?"

"Transfer from ship's fund."

He lifted the cap and rubbed his head again.

"Surcharge on other'n cash. Ten percent."

She sighed.

"Now, don' take it that way," he said. "Gotta five percent rebate comin'—trade for the old unit."

"The old unit needs to be destroyed," Theo said. "It's tainted."

"Zatit? Welp, sometime the older Struvens, they do take up another frequency, start whisperin' to themselves. Only thing to do with 'em then's like you're doin'. The old one—we can take care of it, Pilot."

Theo considered him. "How much?"

He met her eyes. "My treat."

She nodded. "How soon," she said, "can you get to it?"

"Right now, as happens." He looked up and gave her a grin. "Ain't real busy, like you see. This here'll be a real treat for the crew. Ordinary day here, Pilot, is me callin' out the graveyard, talkin' to a ship er two—sometimes gotta roll 'em starward or opposite, make sure they don't drift into a bad reception posture or somewhat. Sometimes gotta check on station-keepin' fuel, ask 'em 'bout batteries." He shook his head. "Looks a mess out there, Pilot, but all of 'em's in their place, and know it. Makes for a slow day, though, it does."

Theo understood entirely, having seen Codrescu's constant juggle of the outer yards, which would drift from the pressure of sunlight, or in response to reaction jets from passing ships; she'd much rather have the duties of a pilot than a station-watcher.

"Well now. You can go do a station tour; we'll get the repair boat over and make the install. Or you can set inside and play cards, you like that better. All the same to us, s'long's that hatch's undogged."

"We'll be home to help you along," Clarence said.

"Fine by me." He looked to Theo. "That's half prepay, half on finish."

She nodded. "I'll make the transfer within the quarter hour."

"Soon's we get it, soon's we're out. 'Fore you go, take a step back here, and look atcher box. Might wanna glance on them overheads, too, when we get there, see if we got some skin plates might match up for ya, if I may say so. Right this way, gentles."

·····❈·····

Kamele stepped off the light-rail, and looked around her. No carefully invisible people came to her attention, though the hairs at the back of her neck still prickled. From where she stood, she could see *Hoselteen*'s boarding ramp. She took a deep breath. Once she reached the ship, she would be safe.

She took three quick steps—and stopped.

A man was standing between her and the tube entrance—a man dressed in a uniform she had now seen twice before. And worse—another man was standing further on, and—yes, a woman, very near to the spot where she had first seen the other woman, earlier in the day.

Kamele sidestepped, and leaned against the side of an infobooth. This? All this for one woman who might draw out another woman, who might perhaps have a traffic violation on her record, and who might have offended the sensibilities of a planetary government, but who was by no means a desperate criminal?

There was something else going on—some waters too deep for her to penetrate, perhaps entangled with Clan Korval, or—

Hoselteen wasn't safe: she accepted that thought as if it had the force of fact. To return was to reinsert herself into a box, in sight, predictable, and in danger.

To return compromised her mission. Absurd as it sounded, it might compromise her life—or Theo's.

She would, therefore, need to find another way to Surebleak.

For a long moment, she stood rooted, thinking of her luggage, her computer, her clothes; trying to convince herself that she was overreacting, that she had just offended someone who was in the way of being a friend, and who, very possibly, had only wished to share a little...recreation with her.

Trust your instincts.

She took a breath.

Her instincts may have gone mad, but...

Very well.

Another thought for the computer, at least—but that was, of course, nonsense.

She was wearing her jacket. She had ID, money, credit, her research on its memory stick. All essential items were with her. The rest—could be replaced.

Kamele nodded, took a breath, turned, and walked away from *Hoselteen*, toward the trade side of the station.

THIRTY-SEVEN

. . . .

Jemiatha's Jumble Stop

JEMIATHA'S DID GOOD WORK. THE NEW STRUVEN UNIT was installed within a couple hours, under *Bechimo*'s watchful sensors. Ship's power never wavered, as far as Theo saw, and if Joyita's glances and twitches at the *clanks*, *thunks*, and *chungs* that reverberated through the hull with the work vessels attached expressed more than mild concern, it was hidden in the pace of whatever work he did there in his private place.

"We're away, *Bechimo*; away and off the clock. We'll switch you back to the office..."

Theo's link to the work ship showed a smiling crew and she heard an off-vid voice—"Dinner's on the tech!"—before the team leader's face appeared, also showing a smile.

"*Bechimo*, if you got anybody mobile over there, you might want to come take a look at a couple extras we dug out while we was putting together a match catalog for you. We got a couple repair kits for some of the loop designs like your setup's based on, and a quick-tuner tester for that Struven, couple demo unit remotes—I can send you details but prolly's best to get a hands-on and do a takeaway. My crew's outta here 'most a workday early, so the office can do whatever you want like an in-kind rebate. It'll show as account activity, too—get you a bigger reference base!"

Theo glanced at Kara, seeing her hands shape *plus marks*.

"Send Kara, and I'll stand backup," Clarence said from his station. "We can pick up what we want—and still be away ahead of schedule!"

"I remind the Over Pilot that neither the Less Pilot nor the third pilot have ship-keys," *Bechimo* said.

"That's true," Theo said. "But Clarence and I were already on the station."

"You held your key, Pilot," *Bechimo* reminded, answering so quickly that his words stepped on the heels of hers.

Kara frowned. "Do we need a key? Theo will be here to open for us." She glanced at Clarence, who had shaped a kind of half-pretzel against the air—*it's complicated*, that meant.

"Well, then," she said to him, "we can carry Theo's key."

"No!" *Bechimo* said sharply, and Theo sighed, capturing Kara's attention with a flicker of fingers.

"The keys are part of *Bechimo*'s systems," she said, signing *fullness later*. "He's not comfortable letting crew out of monitoring range."

Kara's face cleared. "And the keys extend his range. I understand."

"It is my intention," *Bechimo* said, sounding slightly calmer, "to manufacture keys, to replace the one lost in battle, and another new key for you, Pilot ven'Arith. Unfortunately, the process takes some time, and if we stop for it now, we will miss the favorable Jump approach."

"Then it is plain," she said crisply. "I will go to the repair hall with Clarence as backup, and we will carry with us a ship's comm, open." She smiled. "You will know where we are, and really it's not so busy a station."

There was silence, the kind of silence that felt like there was a lot more argument being marshaled. Joyita, Theo saw, was looking . . . interested. She nodded.

"That sounds like a good compromise plan, *Bechimo*. We'll go with it."

There came a sound very like a sigh, and a subdued, "Yes, Pilot."

. . . · ✳ · . . .

Night watchman.

Win Ton considered night watchmen, in this time before his shift, while he exercised, and tried to meditate. The sounds of the repair work, which he had unfairly blamed for his failure to concentrate, had become distant, and then stopped. He believed he'd felt the release of the work craft.

Back before . . .

Before everything changed, when he was a Scout pilot and active in his work. Back then, he'd twice been on a Terran world where honor was partially served by having people physically occupy places to guard them when remotes might do, for people needed employment, and learning the patience to do one kind of work might prove good experience to move on to another.

On that world, his ship had been guarded by a night

watchman who not only had vids and sensors at his command, but who was also required to walk a beat about the ship and grounds from time to time. This permitted someone else to have employment as a serial watcher of cameras and sensors, covering for the various night watchpeople who were wandering around in person.

His watchman had on both occasions been the same man. A personable man, and bright, yet . . . lacking something in the way of fortitude or ambition or ability, for he had held the position, as he had proudly explained, for fifteen Standards, and was quite looking forward to fifteen more. The solitude was good for him, the work not overstrenuous, and he was sufficient to it, which was all he asked. He enjoyed meeting pilots, and being around the ships, and was satisfied in knowing that he was doing something useful for his family and for his world. He had small hobbies, and a small house, and a small, low energy future.

But, there, this was not meditation; such thoughts gave him neither peace nor clarity.

Win Ton opened his eyes, pleased to be able to do so, pleased to be able to move about under his own purpose, and not so pleased to consider that yet again he had been offered the quiet shift—to watch.

He was no longer concerned that he would trip out of hand while walking, and he had managed to let fade the recurring image of Theo's shining eyes as she beheld him, newly risen from the Remastering Unit.

She had seen clearly and at once, he thought, that he was not the pilot who had offered her first orbital PIC, nor the pilot with whom she had played bowli ball, and challenged the dance with her.

Pilot. He was not—and perhaps never again would

be—that pilot, and she . . . was something more. He had named her Sweet Mystery in those times past; several times since his wakening, the words had run to his tongue—and stopped, unspoken, for indeed, she was a pilot and . . . and he was concerned that he was not. For now, at least, he was a night watchman, hoping again to be a pilot, and she was a child of Korval, piloting a ship for the ages.

He took a breath, deliberately drawing the air into the very bottom of his lungs.

Enough.

He would now try yet again for the state of relaxation brought on by the Rainbow, a basic Scout technique that foolishly continued to elude him—

The all-call then, quietly:

"Win Ton, are you awake? Will you please sit Second while Kara and Clarence retrieve the last few supply items? We should be away before shift end."

Clarence and Kara had already left the ship by the time Win Ton reached *Bechimo's* Heart.

He arrived to find second board open and unlocked; *Bechimo*—no, Joyita, it was—requesting his palm to make the board live, while Theo smiled gently and signed an elegant *thank you for assist* while watching a pair of screens and listening to an audio feed.

The screens were busy, with *Bechimo* monitoring some, Joyita others, and Theo selecting the views she wanted right now on the big screen.

Win Ton settled into his station, noting board status and tasks ongoing. It appeared that his assignment was to watch wide, while First Board had her attention concentrated on screens and comm.

Well enough.

The Jump board was set at sixty seconds—a short count indeed, but one that Win Ton knew *Bechimo* was capable of executing, given optimum conditions. The numbers reminded him of a schoolroom situation, where an instructor or technical assistant would flash screen coords, requiring the trainee to set board and prepare, and also to announce, if she could, where the ship would manifest, when Jump was ended.

These coords...

He was not happy to recognize the coords for the place they had Jumped *from*. He took a quiet breath. That place...a spot of empty space where the universe was holed, and jetsam from...*somewhere else* was leaking in.

A place that, *Bechimo* swore, was secure and safe from attack.

"I thought," he said, softly, "that we were Surebleak bound?"

"Crew hasn't talked yet," Theo said, her eyes on her screens and what looked to be a station schematic. "But I expect we'll decide to go to Surebleak." She moved her head—pointed chin indicating the Jump board.

"That's the preset emergency Jump. Ship's policy—have an emergency Jump identified and in the ready-box, just in case."

A wise policy indeed, for a ship that was hunted. Win Ton inclined his head. "I understand."

She nodded absently, he thought, her attention already back on her screens.

Lacking any assignment other than the wide-watch, Win Ton upped the magnification on his second aux screen and considered the ships in the graveyard. He'd seen the likes of some of them on his milk runs to the Scouts' Old Tech storage areas: ships recognized more by silhouette than sight, ships of legendary prowess long since superseded by more modern vessels.

Idly, he began querying various of the graveyard's residents. Some gave up only ship type and serial number, while others provided a history of names and homeports. Some few had recall of the trip to this place, the route still in high memory, with the piloting roster. Dozens, fifties, *hundreds* of Standards old, some of them; a goodly number of them whole, while still more were reduced to nameless netted bundles of parts.

Win Ton looked up from this diversion to check his boards and his pilot, finding both serene, and Joyita in his nonexistent comm room, his hard, scarred face wearing a look of deep concentration.

Serene, peaceful, calm, and naught on his screens, save the station, and the graveyard, and the telemetries of a ship at rest.

Win Ton looked back to his second aux screen, upping the mag so that he might more closely examine a bulky specimen sporting numerous access ports. He thought perhaps it had once been a mining rig, and sent a casual query for ID.

"Pharst!" Theo snapped, her hand to her ear. "Lost contact!"

· · · ✳ · · ·

So far, so good, Theo thought, listening to Kara and Clarence move through the station . . . or Jumble Stop. She simultaneously *watched* their progress on the schematic Joyita had provided, while *Bechimo* kept multiple eyes on approach points. Joyita had also provided a list of ships at dock, and was, apparently, engaged in running checks, and long-distance system surveys that she wasn't sure she wanted to know details on.

They didn't expect any trouble, Theo reminded herself, as her crew gained the repair wing.

"We arrive," Kara said lightly. "I will shop quickly, *Bechimo*."

At which point, the comm fizzed, popped...

...and went dead.

"Pharst!" Theo exploded, reaching to the board and fingering the control. "Lost contact!"

"Alert," *Bechimo* said. "Unauthorized activity!"

Joyita was moving fast, his attention on his boards. Win Ton was leaning in, barely seeming to breathe as ship defenses snapped from at-rest to war alert. The shields popped to red; the Jump count blipped, flashed, and settled on fifteen.

Theo swallowed. Fifteen seconds. Emergency disconnect cycle was ten seconds; five seconds out for Jump—they'd damage the station, if not kill it outright.

"Pilot, incoming communication," Joyita stated. "Sending to general."

"Waitley. The station is under our control, and we have your crew in hand. This is a situation you may wish to rectify before those of us who lost comrades at Ynsolt'i allow Balance to overcome business sense."

The voice was perhaps female; there was a crisp edge to the Terran words, and a smooth lack of perceptible accent. Theo shivered, reached for the comm switch, and pulled her hand back, fingers curling into a fist as the voice continued.

"At the moment, Waitley, we are willing to trade. We will release the station and your crew, in exchange for the ship *Bechimo*. You will find this more than a reasonable trade, as the ship is proscribed from many ports, and you are yourself outlaw, with a price on your head."

There was chatter and noise on other channels; out of the corner of her eye, she saw Win Ton move, fingers plying his board, capturing another voice—male, speaking Trade.

"All hear, all hear! A dangerous, blacklisted ship is at dock here. This ship threatens the well-being of Station Jemiatha. We of the Galactic Trade Commission declare a state of emergency, and have taken steps to neutralize the threat. All hands batten down. Queries from Station Admin only to *Donihue's Docent*. Do not, do *not* attempt to aid the ship *Bechimo* or its crew. Message repeats."

The Galactic Trade Commission? Theo shook her head. The GTC had taken her off Tokeoport; but they had been after *Arin's Toss*, Uncle's ship . . .

"Pilot—this is beyond my experience."

That was *Bechimo* himself. In Screen Six, Joyita sat with hands near stilled; his eyes, watching, moving, watching.

Theo looked again to her screens—to the schematic, frozen, the spot where communication had been lost on triple mag.

Crew—Clarence and Kara. Her crew, the people who depended on her to keep them safe—she had to get them back. But—give *Bechimo* into the hands of pirates and hostage-takers?

Theo took a breath, another, and touched the comm switch gently, bringing the mic live.

"Who," she asked calmly, "am I dealing with?"

"My name is of no import in this, Waitley. The names

that concern you are these: Kara ven'Arith, Clarence O'Berin. We have them here, alive for the moment. We will accept the ship, in trade for both. If you doubt us, or try us, one of your crew will be dead. If we grow tired, both will be dead, and in the end we will have the ship, just the same. Meet me at dockside with the captain's key, and you and your remaining crew may be reunited with those here on station."

"I need some time," Theo said, while her mind raced, looking for a way to stall.

"Time? Surely it is a simple enough thing. Open the hatch, exit with the key and those of your crew now aboard. Place the key in my hand and you are free, all unpleasantness at an end, and you may continue with your lives."

There was a definite emphasis on the word *lives*. And there was no way, she thought, her thoughts cold and sharp—no way that they would be allowed to survive. She glanced over at Win Ton, his face set, his hands steady, but not quick; sure, but a perceptible fraction less than certain. This woman and her crew—GTC, were they? And was the GTC in league with this Department of the Interior? Or were they just an independent group of murderers and thugs?

Didn't matter, she decided, and suddenly she had her stall.

"This ship has just received a replacement Struven Unit." She spoke into the mic as cool as Kamele giving out an essay assignment. "The unit is out of old storage and possibly unstable. Shipside crew is testing for safety and functionality."

"Surely, you can safely leave such testing to us, the ship's new masters."

"I don't think so," Theo said firmly. "The ship has put itself on high alert; systems are cycling unpredictably. I'm trying to maintain control and reestablish order. My goal is that neither the station nor my crew take damage. If the ship should Jump while attached to the station, will you survive?"

She let the silence lengthen. From the side of her eye, she saw Win Ton lick his lips.

"I will see my crew free and safe," Theo said. "No one needs to die in this—not the station, not my people, not the ship. But the on-board situation must be contained *first*."

This pause was not so long.

"You have two local hours to achieve stable conditions. I will be at your dock and awaiting your arrival."

"Comm closed, Pilot," Joyita said quietly.

Two hours. They could think of something in two hours. Couldn't they?

No. They *had* to think of something.

Her hands were cold. She looked down at them where they rested on the board, and noticed that her fingers were trembling. Mad, scared, or both, she thought distantly. No time for any of it, now. She took a breath; looked to Joyita, and to Win Ton.

"Options?" she asked. "Do we just leave?"

Win Ton snapped upright.

"Leave? Without even an attempt to succor—"

"Pilot—*Theo!*" *Bechimo*'s voice was raw. "I can't allow—we cannot abandon our crew. There must be something—I am still considering..."

"I agree. We can't abandon our crew. And we can't turn you over to, to—*them*! They'll have no respect for you; they won't find their cloak, if that's what they're looking for." She glanced at Win Ton. "And if they're looking for something else..."

He shook his head, face pale.

"We *cannot*," he said.

"If they were to board me, Theo, I am confident that I would prevail." *Bechimo* paused, then said, quietly, "It is, Pilots, a trivial matter to evacuate the air, which neither Joyita nor I require."

It was true, Theo thought; *Bechimo did* have defenses. But Win Ton was shaking his head again.

"I remember..." he said, his voice hoarse. "*Bechimo*, you brought me out of the place I was held—tortured— by subverting the Old Tech around me. But they—the humans in this—they thought they were only holding *me*. If these are—or if they have been in communication with those who managed my captivity—they will know better now. They will be prepared. Certainly, they seem confident." He waved a hand toward the comm.

"Win Ton's right," Theo said. "We have to assume that they have a plan, and that they're not just taking advantage of a—an unexpected opportunity. We've got to assume that they—that they at least *believe* they can neutralize you. For all we know, they have a plug-in AI killer, or—a collar, like some worlds use for prisoners, to keep them compliant."

"It's already been demonstrated," Joyita said quietly, "that these people are treacherous. *Bechimo*, if they should at the last moment seize a single member of our crew and force him back on-board with them..."

He let his voice drift off, but Theo heard the unspoken question clearly: *Could you evacuate the air, then?*

Silence.

Theo blew the bangs out of her eyes.

"If we could get an idea of how many," she said. "If there are three or three hundred and three!"

"So far, we have only two voices," said Joyita. "They have locked access ports and inner comm channels to ordinary communication. I'm trying to listen to resonant channels, but have no useful pickup..."

"Queries were to be directed to *Donihue's Docent*," Theo said. "Where's that ship? Is there anything in the registry?"

"Working, Pilot Theo," Joyita murmured. "The registry indicates an original crew of six. There's evidence that the ship has been modified. We are probing, but carefully."

"Thank you, Joyita."

"We're also attempting to locate Clarence and Kara," he said. "Our working hypothesis is that our...opposition will be holding key station personnel with our crew. We assume that trustworthy guards are few, in which case, all prisoners will be held together. Analysis of factors such as air and energy consumption should pinpoint their location." He glanced up, meeting her eyes. "We're being careful, Pilot Theo."

She nodded.

"Perhaps, when that location is found," Win Ton said, his voice sounding hoarse, "it would be best to allow me to off-board, to try if I might free them."

"No!" *Bechimo* fairly roared, quite drowning out her own "What? Win Ton—"

"I allow no more crew off-ship without a key," *Bechimo* said. "If either of our captured pilots had held a key..."

"But we didn't have time to make keys here, and

before that," Theo said, remembering his sleep-shift proposal, "it was too dangerous, with the Struven compromised." She froze, staring down at her board, remembering that conversation, and the agreements they had made.

"The replacement Struven is in place, and checks clean," she said, hearing her own voice, as if from a slight distance.

There was a small silence before Joyita said, "That's correct, Pilot."

"*Bechimo*," she said, still staring at the board, until the various controls lost their boundaries and became a continuous smear of color. "*Bechimo*, will access to the captain's level give us an...advantage here?"

"Theo," he answered quietly, calmly. "I don't know."

"But it *might*," she pushed.

"It might, yes."

"Do we have time..." Her breath was coming short, and Kara—she had wanted Kara with her, when it—when the bonding took place, to center her, and to, to...

...she might never see Kara again, unless they found a way out of this mess.

"At the very least," Joyita said quietly, "the captain's level will provide more options."

"Do you *know* that, B. Joyita?" inquired *Bechimo*.

In the screen, Joyita smiled slightly.

"The Builders promised it," he said.

"Do we," Theo said, raising her voice somewhat, "have enough time?"

"Yes," Joyita said, looking directly at her. His face wore an expression of solemn joy. "We have enough time, Pilot Theo, but we have no time to waste." He stood.

"Please, Pilots, lock your boards. *Bechimo* will guide you both."

"Both?" asked Win Ton. "It's Theo who needs—who deserves—the Captain's keys."

"You and I, Pilot, will witness. The Builders decreed that the crew should witness, and we—are the crew."

Win Ton bowed his head.

"Yes," he said. Three quick movements locked his board.

Theo was already on her feet, her key in hand. She looked down at it, and then to Win Ton.

He caught her glance, tight-lipped, and gave a bow that she thought meant he accepted responsibility. Which was true enough, Theo thought. Without Win Ton—without Win Ton's poor impulse control, none of them would be here, now. She'd still be flying courier for the Uncle; Clarence and Kara and Win Ton himself would be safe...

Stop that! Theo thought. *You're starting to sound like* Bechimo.

Gravely, she returned Win Ton's bow with one of acknowledgment, reached up to hook the key onto the chain around her neck, and took a deep, hopefully calming, breath.

"Please, Pilots," *Bechimo* said, sounding, impossibly, *breathless*. "Follow the blue line along the floor."

THIRTY-EIGHT

. . . .

Jemiatha's Jumble Stop

THE BLUE LINES GUIDED THEM BETWEEN LEVELS TO yet another hallway that Theo had never walked, behind a dogged hatch bearing the symbols for the potential for low grav/low oxy.

"Should we have masks?" she asked, and it was Joyita's voice that reassured her, from the comm she carried.

"You're safe, Pilot Theo. It's just one of *Bechimo's* cubbyholes. In honor of your presence, all is adjusted for your comfort."

She nodded, accepting it—*trust your ship*; well, what else could she do? Kara...Clarence—who knew what was happening to them! Even if the voice promised to return them alive—even if she agreed to give *Bechimo* into their keeping—there were very many things that could be done to a human body, while still keeping it alive.

"Theo?" Win Ton murmured beside her, and she nodded again, coming out of her thoughts. She undogged the hatch and stepped through...

. . . into a cul-de-sac.

Before her, was a blank wall. To her right, just beyond Win Ton, was what ought to be a view port, but it was sealed against light and radiation. She leaned over to touch the sensor set in the frame.

The iris widened, and she was looking through a thick crystalline window at the graveyard, the ships in parking orbits around the misty blue asteroid. She took a breath, and sighed it out.

"Please, Theo," *Bechimo* said. "Open the door."

She turned away from the port, all the way to her left, until she was facing the door—just a door, not a hatch, with an indentation, looking just like . . .

. . . a keyhole.

"All right, then," Theo said softly. She took a breath. Her heart was pounding, her palms were damp. She was aware of Win Ton, standing at her back, between her and the view port, waiting, tense and patient.

She fingered the chain 'round her neck, pulled it up and detached her ship-key. It hummed in her hand like Hevelin when he was very pleased, indeed, and with a little taste of anticipation, too.

Well, she thought, *at least the key isn't nervous.*

She seated it, and stepped back.

The door slid aside; lights came up in the chamber beyond.

It was a small space, barely larger than a port infobooth. She stepped inside, and looked about her.

Like an infobooth, a data screen was prominent on the front wall. Unlike most infobooths, though, this screen was . . . very large, and flawless, like the mirror in the room that Val Con said was "hers" at Jelaza Kazone.

Theo faced it. The surface was deeply black, and gave back no reflection, though something tickled the edge of her vision. She looked up and to the left, saw a hose-horse set high in the frame of the screen. Reflected light kissed the hoses, cables, and clamps that depended from it, dyeing the tips silver and gold.

One more deep breath, a glance to the side, where Win Ton leaned in the doorway, arms crossed, and an expression of perplexity on his face. She smiled at him. He inclined his head.

Theo faced the screen again.

"Tell me what to do."

"State your name," came Joyita's voice from her belt comm.

"Theo Waitley."

Something . . . rippled in the ebon depths of the screen.

"State your intention," Joyita coached.

"I propose myself as *Bechimo's* Captain. I'm here to share in the bonding."

The screen snapped into brilliance, bathing the interior of the booth with light.

Code appeared and began scrolling, what looked to be a ship schematic building behind it all.

A hand came down lightly on her shoulder, another caressed her hair.

Theo jumped back with a yelp, hands rising to fend off the gleaming tentacles that had fallen from the hose-horse, connect ends glowing bright yellow, illuminating wires as thin as cat whiskers clustered at the end of each.

"Wait! What *is* that?"

"Theo," *Bechimo's* voice sounded as panicked as she felt. "The bonding..."

"I don't—"

Old Tech, she thought. *Bechimo* was built on Old Tech principles; Uncle was an expert in Befores. To have those wires pierce her, *change* her...

"No," she said, chest aching and lungs laboring. "No, I—" She stopped herself. She had promised—she had made so many promises, accepted so many bonds. She might not be *Bechimo's* destined captain—wasn't, as they both agreed. But she was the best chance *Bechimo* had, and Kara had...Clarence, Joyita, Win Ton...and...

Theo Waitley.

All those lives that depended on *her*...

"Pilot Theo," Joyita's voice was matter-of-fact, as if he was discussing a mundane shipboard task. "The connections must be made. Please insert your key so that we may proceed."

She did so gingerly, feeling the key vibrate happily as it was pushed home, and felt a pang of loss as the whole of it disappeared within the dashboard.

The screen flickered and changed again. The code vanished, and there stood Joyita, shaking his head slightly, and smiling.

"Theo," he said, gently. "Trust your ship."

She gulped, grappled with the fear; danced a tiny, in-place dance of quietude and peace, and stood there for a moment, with her eyes closed.

The fear receded...enough. And really, what had Father used to say of hard choices and tasks that would by preference never be taken up?

Necessity exists.

"Theo?" That was Win Ton, a world of worry in that word.

She cleared her throat.

"Necessity," she said, the weight of fathers and mothers before her freighting it far beyond the Liaden mode between comrades.

"Necessity," she repeated, in Terran, for emphasis.

"Oh, Theo," he breathed, and then, more firmly, in Liaden. "Necessity, Pilot. Understood."

Theo opened her eyes.

Joyita smiled at her.

"Theo," said *Bechimo*. "The bonding will not harm you, nor will it diminish you; it will make us whole. We will be . . . all that the Builders intended, and indeed beyond their ken, for you will be the First Captain."

"I know," she said, looking into Joyita's eyes. "I'm ready."

His smile deepened.

"Place your left hand on the screen, in the center of the inner circle. You will feel a touch, several touches. There will be no pain. We cherish you, Theo. Captain."

She put her hand against the screen, which was agreeably warm, the surface giving, as if she had placed her hand over the hand of a lover. There was a brief swish and hum, and Win Ton's breathing was nearly as loud as her own, though he stood well away from her.

Soft fingers combed her hair back from her face, and rested sweetly over her ear. Sensuous touches along the back of her neck, and a feeling of delightful, shivery warmth down her backbone.

Almost she purred, eyes slitted, her gaze on Joyita's face. A firm arm came 'round her waist, holding her steady on legs gone slightly silly.

"Your other hand," he whispered, "over my heart."

She placed it so, seeing his face soften, the hard eyes widen.

A thumb rubbed over her lips, fingers braceleted her throat, heat burned in her belly. The universe expanded, and there *was* pain—an ecstatic pain so fierce and joyous that she opened to it eagerly, only wanting more—and more.

Light ran her nerves, her blood heated, and she was up, away, out of her body, riding a crescendo of ecstasy, but not alone, never again alone, her lover's voice murmuring in her ear, his strengths supporting her as hers supported him. They were one, entwined, indivisible.

Complete.

THIRTY-NINE

. . . .

Jemiatha's Jumble Stop

THE KEY WAS PURRING, LOUDLY; VIBRATING AGAINST her fingers as she recovered it from the dashboard and clipped it onto the chain.

Theo thought she might be purring, too. From the look on Win Ton's face, maybe she was—or had been. Before her, the screen was reflective ebony; in it she saw her reflection—her hair floating 'round her head, as if she were in low gravity.

"Captain," Win Ton said, very softly. "Time marches."

Time? she thought, feeling the sweet pressure of light against her skin, and the pure, sensual pleasure of perfectly tuned and functioning subsystems.

"Theo." Win Ton extended a hand. "We have less than an hour to redeem Kara and Clarence."

Memory sparked; she relived the comm call in every detail, gasped, and spun away from the screen, the key still purring against her palm. Win Ton gave way before her, the hatch closed as she exited, sealing at her thought, or *Bechimo's*. It didn't matter. She was already running back up the hall, with no need for the guide-lights at all.

As she ran, she noticed that a murmuring enclosed her. It reminded her of when she had been very young, and had gone up to bed while Father and Kamele stayed downstairs to talk. Sometimes, she'd lay on the landing and listen to the sound of their voices—the *sound*, not the words—and feel contented; safe and loved.

She was aware that Win Ton was at her back, running not so fleet as she, and she thought to check on the state of his health.

No sooner the thought, than the knowledge—Win Ton's pulse was slightly raised, his breathing quick—both consistent with a man who was moving rapidly, but he wasn't laboring.

That was good, she thought, as the lift door opened before her.

She swung inside, and Win Ton joined her. The door closed and the lift rose, the door opening again on the main level.

"Do you," Win Ton asked, as they stepped out into the hall, "feel...well?"

Theo smiled at him.

"Never felt better."

"Captain, welcome," Joyita said, looking up from his boards as she came into the Heart, Win Ton walking at her right shoulder and one step behind.

"Joyita," she said, pausing to consider him. He seemed...more solid, somehow, though his image was the same as it had been. It was as if she could *feel* the weight of his systems. She shook her head slightly, and nodded at her main screen, which was much busier than it had been.

"You have progress?" she asked.

He grinned.

"Captain, we do. The station's systems were designed with the expectation that all network traffic would be local and benign; there's only a very naive security system in place, which I have been probing. It appears that in some cases lines have been severed physically. Those will be harder to access. We have a number of electrical connections that permit us to monitor local lighting activity, however, and I have access and control of a state transition PLC farm serving the air-and-fluid movement system.

"*Bechimo* has calculated usage rates, and we're now attempting to infer room populations. We have three probable locations for the Opposition and the likelihood that our crew are within twelve paces of those locations is high. Expect a positive location fix within moments."

"Thank you," she said, and moved to her board. She sat, seeing Win Ton do the same, and place his palm on the plate.

She slipped her pilot's key—her *Captain's key*, she corrected herself—off the chain and slid it into the board. The board remained dark, and she heard an . . . alteration in the murmuring surrounding her.

Then, as deliberate and as majestic as the progress of a scholar emeritus down the rows of the faculty senate, there rose out of the left side of her familiar board a new bank of controls, perhaps a handspan wide. Simultaneously, a concave set of transparent mini-screens rose on a stalk, perfectly placed to act as a heads-up display.

The stalk locked solemnly into place.

There was a beep, incongruous and bright, and the entire arrangement came live.

Theo took a breath, wondering if there was a training tape or—

Bechimo briskly interrupted these thoughts.

"One location has been eliminated, Captain. There is a high probability that the Opposition has divided its available forces between two bases. One is the station office, which they appear to be using to control the station, and almost certainly to hold our crew. Their other base is the freighter *Donihue's Docent*, which is broadcasting the general warn-aways. This ship is—"

It appeared on her screen, docked on an opposite arm of the station, targeting information overlaying the image. The image seemed to ripple, like something seen underwater. Theo frowned and reached for her controls.

"*Bechimo*, can you sharpen that image?"

"The distortion you see, Captain," *Bechimo* said, "is emanations from the Old Tech aboard."

She shook her head. "That doesn't look good, or am I reading wrong?"

"Your instincts are good, Captain Theo," Joyita said. "Many of the timonium-based instruments on-board that ship are either unstable or unshielded. Or," he added, as one being just, "both."

"Is it dangerous?" she asked, staring at the wavering image of the vessel.

"Without a doubt, it is dangerous," *Bechimo* said. "We must operate on the assumption that they have us targeted, as we have them. The original weapons were very light; but there are the subetherics, the purpose of which we can only guess at."

"Beyond the fact that they're unstable," Theo added.

"We don't believe," *Bechimo* said, "that the Old Tech will malfunction catastrophically within the span of time allotted to us to act."

At second board, Win Ton laughed.

Theo threw him a grin. "Least of our worries," she agreed. "Right."

She sobered suddenly, and raised her hands, signing, *input pilot*.

"There's two of us," she said aloud. "Should we try to storm this office? Short of a firefight..."

"We can't be sure of a firefight." Win Ton said, looking bleak. "They will target our crew first." He used his chin to point at the image of *Donihue's Docent* on her screen. "We are held hostage as much as they."

"A two-pronged attack," Theo said, frowning. "If we could threaten their ship at the same time we went against the control room..."

"An advance against the control room is something that I cannot support," Win Ton said, primly. "To mount a credible threat against their ship would require another ship, which was not hard-docked to the..."

He stopped, staring at his second aux screen, which showed a drifting display of ships in the graveyard, several of them limned in blue.

"Those ships out there," he said slowly, his eyes still on the screen. "Most of them are alive to some degree. If we can roust two, or more, to move in... they needn't have working weapons even."

Theo flicked a look at the *Docent*, station-keeping like a law-abiding ship.

"We could box them in," she said. "At the very least, we can get something between us and *their* weapons."

She looked at him, fingers moving *do it*. "Work with Joyita. Whatever you have to do. Joyita—"

"On it, Captain!"

Theo left them to it. She turned back to her screen, tapping up the station schematic. "Where are they?" she murmured.

A section lit, deep inside the station—not quite in the core, but close. The section expanded, unfolding so that she could see not only the approaching hallways, but the ducts and repair passages...

"Captain," *Bechimo* said in her ear.

"Theo," she murmured, upping the mag on the schematic some more.

"Theo. Are you still considering an attack on the control room?"

"I'm thinking," she said, slowly, "if we use a remote, through the ducts...trying to visualize outcomes."

"Allow me."

She was standing in the air duct, peering through the ceiling hatch at two faces among many, heard the discharge of a weapon, the faces gone...

Again, the duct. She dropped a knockout bulb through the grate, heard it hiss—and the discharge of the weapon...

She was in the repair hall, removing the access wall, in the room beyond among shadows, two faces, a weapon discharged...

She was in the main hall, her hand on the hatch...

Gasping, she shook her head, and the schematic was back before her mind's eye, security cameras highlighted in yellow...

She *pushed*, hard, against what, she couldn't have said...

. . . and she was in her chair, blinking hard, her head aching furiously.

"Too risky," she managed after a moment. "Got it." She chewed her lip, eye caught again by the indistinct image of the ship that targeted them.

"*Bechimo*, you can talk to Old Tech," she said slowly. "You subverted the Befores at Win Ton's prison."

"That's correct."

"Can you talk to *those* Befores?" she asked, nodding at the screen. "Create a diversion, or even do real damage? I don't necessarily care about the *Docent*, but I don't want to hole the station."

"Let me consider. It is possible that I may incite erratic behavior, enough to alarm the crew."

"See if you can do that," she said, and was aware of his attention being—not withdrawn, but applied more fully elsewhere.

She closed her eyes and concentrated on breathing. The headache was fading, which was good.

"Captain," Joyita said. "We have several ships working under our orders."

"Good!" she said, spinning her chair 'round.

Win Ton looked up with a faint smile.

"Good within limitations," he said wryly. "The problem is to get them to move in concert. The remote controllers are slow, and—understand, Theo, these are old ships, but not Old Tech. They need . . . guidance. A captain's hand. I don't know how many tasks *Bechimo* is willing to manage at once . . ."

"I don't know either, but I've got him on a tricky bit right now," Theo said. "Trying to convince the Old Tech on the *Docent* to misbehave." She checked . . .

something internally, and added, "We're running down to deadline. Is there something else? Joyita, can you...?"

Joyita pursed his lips.

"I can multitask, Captain. But captaining seven ships at once is something even *Bechimo* might find a challenge. There might be another solution available to us. I will need to do research."

"Do it," said Theo.

· · · ❋ · · ·

Joyita had provided an inventory database, purloined from the Jumble Stop's computer, no doubt, that listed each ship name and the command password for each. This made Win Ton's task *easier*, but, as he quickly discovered, by no means *easy*.

He had meant to guide all of the operable ships into the fray, to activate the vessels and steer them in the right direction before raising the threat. Joyita managed the narrow beam comm lines, and aimed them with precision.

His first-chosen ship answered sluggishly and required reentering passwords. He moved to the next, which was sprightly by comparison, and had only recently been recharged, battery and reaction mass. Still it took time to learn the ship's idiosyncratic remotes, to discover which orientation it enjoyed, how many thrusters and what power...and if they only could bring two to the fray...but there was another close enough to bring about and start, once they had their time set. He moved on to the third...

By the time he had activated the seventh, he was quite exhausted, his shirt sticky with sweat.

"I think," he said to Joyita, "that what we have here wakened must be our fleet."

"I agree," Joyita responded at once. "We'll inform the Captain."

. . . ⁕ . . .

"Captain," Joyita said, "*Bechimo* has reserve personalities in storage, which are potentially available for our use."

Theo considered him.

"Potentially?" she repeated.

"Access requires the captain's sign-off."

It was as if he had suddenly placed the information into the middle of her brain. She instantly understood that there were reserve personalities onboard, locked away from *Bechimo*'s access, nascent, *emergency*, in case something . . . went wrong with the primary.

She blinked free of the data and focused again on Joyita's face.

"But—are they . . . *people*?" she demanded. "And—wait. They have to be physically placed. We can't—"

Joyita's hand produced the rippling sign that Theo recognized as one Clarence used for *yes-and-no* or *maybe*.

"People? No, Captain. They have the potential to become people. They are, as they were stored, unique. Individual. In order to achieve full functionality, yes, they ought to be physically placed. They do not *need* to be physically placed in order to perform this task; downloading a shadow will suffice, I think."

"You *think*?"

"This is a new protocol," Joyita admitted, "and

not . . . precisely what the Builders intended. But, now that I am stable, and you have bonded with *Bechimo*, we need not be as conservative as we have been. We can risk one download of one stored personality. There are others."

There were, Theo acknowledged, checking her new-found facts, others. And they were, at base, computers.

"Yes," said Joyita, as if he had read her mind. "As computers, they can perform complex tasks quickly, and they can be patient. What I propose is to download a single shadow personality to the computers Pilot Win Ton has wakened. The personality may then coordinate a pseudofractal core within the most powerful of those ships—in effect this will produce an extended control cloud rather than a single-source directory."

"It—she—will think it's one . . . person, spread across—how many ships?"

"Seven," Win Ton said.

"Yes, Captain."

"Will she be able to . . . survive?"

Joyita looked doubtful.

"I don't know, Captain. To the best of my knowledge, and *Bechimo*'s, no one has attempted . . . precisely this. The . . . vocation . . . of the first Joyita, *Bechimo*'s teacher, was the waking and socialization of machine intelligences. Whether the personality can cohere and become viable over the long term without such a teacher—there's no data."

No data, thought Theo, glancing at the board for the countdown. Time was running fast.

"What do I have to do to sign off?" she asked, and immediately understood the protocol.

She spun to her board, her fingers reaching naturally to the newly risen section, and moved quickly.

"Done," she said.

"Theo, those devices which listened to my suggestions should begin to seem to malfunction in approximately four minutes," *Bechimo* said in her ear.

"Excellent, thank you," she said, her attention on her screens.

The cluster of seven ships was moving, with purpose, and more quickly than she had expected they would, on a course for the station and the *Docent's* berthing; their progress was on her aux screen.

Second aux displayed a continually updating chart showing three emergency outsystem exit routes, one to simply clear the station, one to clear the graveyard's vicinity, and one to a standard Jump.

"The question is," Theo said, to the control room at large, "do we leave them an exit route?"

"Yes," *Bechimo* said. "It would be best if they were gone; there are no resources here to hold them securely."

Theo nodded, and looked to Win Ton, who gave her a small, but determined smile.

"Time to make a call, then," she said, and reached for the mic.

"Attention, attention. Theo Waitley here."

The woman she had spoken to before answered the hail immediately.

"Pilot, how good of you to come to your senses with so much time left on our offer. You are, I assume, ready to remove yourself from the ship and join your crew here on the station?"

Theo wished she felt as confident as she wanted to project.

"No, I'm afraid I must ask you to reconsider your proposal. I've been working with the Struven Unit, here, and I'm pleased to report that it's operating well. Unfortunately, the unit you have on the *Docent* is contaminated by having Jumped with live subetherics in place and is likely subverting the other specialized tech on-board. If I'm reading this right, you're about to have a nasty situation, shipside."

There was a pause, during which Theo watched the progress of their tiny fleet toward the station.

"Pilot, your concern is touching. Please be assured that we can keep our own ship. The matter that stands between us is the exchange of the ship *Bechimo* for your crew, whom we hold."

Theo licked her lips, eyes on the moving ships. Soon now, somebody on-board the *Docent* ought to notice that something odd was going on.

"Please give the comm to one of my crew. I have only your word that they are still with you.

"My ship and I are in control," Theo spoke into the mic, "of the useful Old Tech in this system as well as the salvage fleet. Discovery process performed by my ship has determined that the Old Tech in your vessel is an uncontrollable threat, and we have activated the local fleet in defense of the station against that threat."

She paused, then spoke again.

"I'm waiting to hear from my crew members," she said. "Meanwhile, we are all at risk from the whimsical items in your vessel, the more so the longer you stay within contact range of the fleet. The fleet is mobile and prepared to deal with this issue."

"Waitley, time shrinks with this foolishness!"

Theo's eye fell on the Jump board. Fourteen seconds, encompassing the time it would take to push the go button, demolish the connection to the station—and a goodly portion of the station as well—and build to Jump power.

"Have you checked with your ship?" she asked the woman.

On her aux screen, the cluster of ships began to separate, some with more radial motion than others. *Bechimo*'s projection predicted an eventual, and enveloping, bubble. For the moment, it was an oblate sphere of purposeful menace. There was a dimple in the bubble; if *Docent* crew was quick, they could still undock and leave.

"You will observe that the fleet is in action," Theo said into the mic. "You still have time to leave in an orderly fashion. Free our crew and the stationers. If you do not act by the time you've previously set, the fleet will envelop your ship and your toys will be all the more dangerous because you can't control them!"

In the aux screen, four of the seven ships showed a flare of shielding. A mist vented from the largest of the group—looked like a mining rig—passing closest to the *Docent*. Theo's heart leapt; if the ship was losing life-support—

She shook her head. Life-support, she reminded herself, wasn't an issue for any of the ships in the cluster.

"Theo?" came a wrenchingly familiar voice from the comm.

Kara. Kara was alive; well enough to talk...

And Kara was Liaden.

"Captain Waitley here," she said, crisply. "Condition report, Tech?"

"Captain," Kara said, and repeated, "Captain. Thank you, Captain. Second Board is with me, and some others, also. Bruised and thirsty. Some of us are a little bloody. There were only four but they hit us with strike string—"

There was noise, like the mic being jiggled, then Kara was gone and the other woman was back.

"Waitley, enough. We have your crew. We have—"

"Time shrinks," Theo insisted. "You said so. May I point out that the presence of so many ships will make your departure unlikely? Run the math, Pilot. The ships with Jump potential are taking their units live. If you haven't cast off in five minutes, you'll be engulfed."

Theo looked at the screen from the lead ship's vantage . . .

"If you damage the station you'll be within our range, and unable to know where we are. Return my crew their comms, release them, remove yourself, and you have a clear lane out—our ships will not impede you. You'll note that your ship is not only weapons targeted, but subject to ramming. Four minutes—I implore you to run! You do not wish to meet me again. Give my crew their comms and I will order them not to impede you. They must be on my deck before you leave!"

"Captain! O'Berin here. They're gone. Running for their ship!"

"Get here, Clarence," Theo said urgently. "Run!"

Kara had submitted to having her various cuts cleaned, and antisept applied. Clarence shrugged off skinned knuckles and insisted on brewing a pot of tea.

Beverage in hand, they all watched the screens. *Donihue's Docent* was cast off, and running.

The ships of the fleet held position—more or less held position. The mining rig that had vented drifted a little, but nothing like a pursuit was mounted.

Ten minutes out, the *Docent* ejected a cargo net. Theo leaned forward, zooming in on the netting, seeing the nacreous shimmer she now knew to be unshielded emanations from Old Tech. The netting seemed to writhe, twist, and change shape as she watched, while the *Docent's* lines grew firm, even as it fled.

Fifteen minutes out, a projectile was loosed from the mining rig.

"What was it?" cried Kara.

"Explosive, more like," said Clarence, shaking his head. "Can't say it's a bad notion."

But it seemed that Clarence was wrong or, if the miner had thrown an explosive, it was no longer viable.

Clarence finished his tea, asked permission to go off-shift and left the command deck. A few minutes later, Kara did the same.

And so it was Theo, Win Ton, Joyita, and *Bechimo* who were there to witness it, at twenty-eight minutes, when *Donihue's Docent* blew up.

FORTY

· · · · · · · · · · ·

Jemiatha's Jumble Stop

"YOU'VE DONE ME HARD HERE, PILOT WAITLEY!" THE
repair tech said. He'd lost his cap, and his head
showed three crusted scrapes.

Kara sniffed.

"Captain Waitley relieved your station of a pirate
infestation. The entirety of your operation was compromised and Captain Waitley utilized available resources,
sir, to give your station back to you."

He had the grace to look a little sheepish. "Don't
know how to figure this with the bill, though."

Clarence sniffed this time. "Add it to the credit
line, then. Laughing Cat ships get Priority One when
they come here, right?"

On screen, the seven ships were visible as a defensive line between the station and the Jump point,
holding steady.

"Dunno how to get 'em back, neither," the tech
continued. "Tried the command codes, an' all I got
was a nice piece o'back-chat from the bigrig saying
as how she was on-mission."

"May I?" requested Theo, hand signing *talk talk ship talk* and taking up the hardwired communicator when the tech glumly nodded.

"*Bechimo*, who is on comm?"

"Joyita," said Joyita.

"Excellent. I'm wondering, Joyita, if you have those working frequencies we discussed. There seems to be an issue with the ships we activated to the station's defense."

"Rub it in, why not?" the tech muttered. Theo ignored him.

"We are observing this, Captain. We wonder if perhaps you might speak to . . . the ships yourself?"

The tech rubbed his head, winced. "Yah well, you programmed 'em, din't you? Might be they'll lissen to you."

Theo put her finger to her lips.

"Give me the channels and frequencies, please, Joyita."

"Transmitting. Adding, we've had no response ourselves, Captain, to the serial number orders, either voice or data. I am requested to inform you that it is six hours to Jump if we leave within the hour; after that it's eight hours for some days."

"Thank you, Joyita. Monitor, please."

Theo indicated *stylus pad*; the technician accommodated grumpily, and she pointed him toward the comm board, tapping the top frequency.

"This is Captain Waitley, off *Bechimo*. Am I heard? May I have the courtesy of an answer? Please reply in voice Terran. We have a situation here which only you can assist with."

Theo looked to the screens, saw the distance, began to count . . .

"*Admiral Bunter* acknowledges." The voice was slow, as if the new personality wasn't easy with the tongue. It had cadence, for all of that—not a machine voice.

The technician dropped his stylus, his mouth fell open, and he swung toward a monitor at the back of the counter.

". . . ain't held air in fifty Standards," Theo heard him mutter. "None of 'em!"

"Jemiatha's Jumble Stop," Theo said, ignoring the tech, "is concerned about your well-being. We are concerned about the well-being of the station-keep, pirates being just put off. You understand about pirates, I believe."

"We are still assembling our self," came the slow response. "We do understand about pirates. We dealt appropriately with pirates. Chase and retrieval was not possible. All units are not yet coordinated nor properly fueled. We may be underpowered. Research is necessary. Inventory is necessary. Repairs may be necessary."

"*Admiral*, consider this. I am off *Bechimo*, and we began this mission. I would like you to know that *Bechimo*'s programming requires training for safety sake. We will send for a trainer." She made a mental note to have *Bechimo* direct a pinbeam to Jeeves. No sooner had she formed the thought than she was certain the beam had been sent.

"We will accept training. Our intent is to guard, to protect the station from pirates. We have purpose. We accept it."

"Excellent," Theo said. "*Bechimo* will be casting off soon. Your contact will be here at the station. I am giving comm to him so that you may coordinate. Do you understand?"

"I understand. Captain Waitley, *Admiral Bunter* stands by."

"Thank you for your help," Theo said. "The next voice you hear will be your contact on-station."

She flicked the comm off.

"I'm sorry," she told the staring tech. "We had an old self-adjusting coordination program on board—you know the age of the ship!—and we couldn't manually run enough of the graveyard at once, so we installed it."

"Coordination program?" He looked thoughtful. "You're leaving me a ghost, are you? An AI?"

Theo nodded, hoping she had judged the man right. A tech in charge of this yard couldn't, she thought, be particularly partial to the Complex Logic Laws.

"Got some old training manuals in back," he said. "Best you send that trainer, though, if you can."

He reached for the mic, and flicked it on.

"*Admiral*," he said carefully . . . and laughed self-consciously.

"*Admiral Bunter* is it? This is Stew, on Jemiatha's Jumble Stop. You wanna stay together, you want fuel, you gotta talk to me. And you wanna a'just that orbit pronto and station-keep right close here like you was these past years 'til we get things together for you. Is that clear? We need to talk. Figure out what's best for all. What do you say?"

"I say it is clear," came the response, quicker now. "I say we need to talk."

The tech smiled, and reached for the comm switch.

• • • ✦ • • •

Clarence was sitting First, with Kara on Second for her first Jump-out on *Bechimo*.

Crew had decided to retreat to *Bechimo*'s safe spot, where keys would be manufactured and tuned to both the ship and the captain's key. After that, they'd get under way to Surebleak, and after that?

They'd have to see.

Theo had danced, and showered, and laid down in her bunk, lights out and oxy a little heavy.

She closed her eyes, the murmuring that had never entirely gone away intensifying, bathing her in a sense of safety and love as she slid into sleep.

FORTY-ONE

. . . .

Bechimo

SPACE SNAPPED INTO BEING AROUND THEM—WYRD
space, granted, but familiar and therefore homey.

For about six seconds.

"Collision alert! Intruder alert! Ship in peril! Shields
on high! Weapons live! Target acquired!"

Theo's head rang, even as her hands moved over
the board, the heads-up images flashing from ordinary
status reports to the start of the targeting module.

"Ship in peril?" That was Clarence.

"Yes, Pilot."

"We have a transmission," Joyita added, "coming
in off an odd, old band. Transcribing . . . *translating*,
I should say, Pilots."

"Where is it?" Theo demanded, and the ID and
image splashed onto the screen, green and red inter-
mingled, targeting options dropping away as Theo
waved hand over the boards to raise shields.

"*Bechimo* . . ." she began, and stopped as Joyita
began to speak.

"*Spiral Dance, Spiral Dance*, late out of Solcintra. Cantra yos'Phelium, master and owner... Message repeats on autoloop."

"Out of Solcintra?" demanded Win Ton.

"With those lines?" added Kara.

"yos'Phelium?" asked Clarence, with a sideways look to Theo, who ignored him in favor of asking her own question.

"*Bechimo*, is the same object a target and a ship in peril?"

"Yes, Theo."

"Why?"

"The vessel carries a subetheric device; there is significant shed of timonium molecules; analysis indicates that the ship is adrift; and..."

"And?" Theo asked, feeling the ship's reluctance and not yet understanding the underflow of a particular set of sensors...

"There is a life-form on that vessel. Not human, but alive."

"Joyita, open comm, please."

"Yes, Theo."

"*Spiral Dance*, this is Theo Waitley, Captain of *Bechimo*. Please report your condition. Are you in need of rescue?"

There was a long pause. Theo looked 'round at her crew.

"yos'Phelium?" she asked back at Clarence.

He shrugged. "Cantra yos'Phelium, that's an old, old name, if true. What I've always heard said was that her and her copilot brought those who now style themselves Liaden out from the old place, to the planet they're on now." He paused, as if considering the reliability of a memory, sighed and shook his head.

"The way I always heard it, the ship they came in, that ship is still in the possession of Clan Korval."

Well, Theo thought, there wasn't anything strange about Korval having an old ship or two in its possession. What it might be doing *here*, in peril...

"Pilot, we have no response," said Joyita, looking sober. "It could be that the automatics are working, but that whatever set them adrift took out comm, too."

She nodded.

"*Bechimo*, is the ship *Spiral Dance* in danger of exploding?"

The sensor feeds showed colors to her, and some she felt as a kind of distant vibration; the images gave her clues to energy states now and *Bechimo*'s own voice came to her rather than echoed through Joyita.

"I detect no such conditions, Theo."

She looked 'round at the faces—her crew, weary but willing—and nodded again.

"We'll stay alert, and have lunch. We'll scan all details, and watch the area for more flotsam."

Theo looked across to Clarence and Kara at their boards, and Win Ton, back in the Jump seat, and nodded.

"Then, if it looks stable, then we'll bring her in. She'll fit in the hold where we kept *Arin's Toss*."

"Yes, Theo," *Bechimo* said, sounding positively cheerful.

In Screen Six, Joyita smiled.

It was Win Ton who made first contact. He had suggested, even argued, for the duty, citing his language background, his Scout training, and his previous experience in contacting old-line ships. Theo let him have it, on the basis of experience. Neither one of them said what they both must have been thinking—that he was the one who was most expendable.

As if any of them was.

The hatch presented some initial difficulties. They lacked entrance codes and key, and without an able-bodied person inside, there was no clear way forward.

Eventually *Bechimo* was able to assist, with Kara's remotes. The air that flowed out to mingle with their own atmosphere was good, fresh, even, and a little on the high side for oxy content.

It was only then, the remotes showing an inner door that appeared to need palm pressure to open, that Win Ton used the hold's airlock and entered, reassured the while by Joyita's voice and presence on the comm.

Win Ton's shoulder camera showed seals that were used but not worn, clean decking, and polished brightwork.

Lights came up in an orderly fashion as he progressed; nothing impeded him until he came to the flight deck.

Where he stopped and said plaintively, "What?"

Theo didn't blame him. The camera showed the scene, lit by the low-key flight-light oft preferred by courier pilots.

The pilot's chair was empty, the main board locked and cold. Only the all-call seemed to be operating— there was no sign of pilot or injured crew.

Also—also there was this: A fiber box had been grey-taped to the copilot's chair, in front of the board that showed no lights.

Win Ton moved in that direction, the camera carrying the view back to Theo....

In the box...was a tree, its leaves green with health, and moving slightly in what may have been the breeze from a ventilator duct.

On the whole, it seemed happy to see him.

EPILOGUE

· · · · · · · · · · · · · · · ·

Jelaza Kazone
Surebleak

THE FRONT DOOR WAS MADE OF DARK WOOD, WITH Clan Korval's house-sign—the "Tree-and-Dragon"—carved in bas-relief. In the frame of the door on the right-hand side was a palm pad; on the left side was a rope. Attached to the rope, fixed above the frame, was a bell made of cloudy yellow metal.

Kamele frowned, raised her hand—and yanked down on the pull rope.

The noise was louder than she had expected, and she jumped, dropping the rope as if it were hot.

Scarcely had she settled to her feet again than the door opened.

"Good-day," said the neat individual in the doorway, in strongly accented Terran. "How may I assist you?"

"Good-day," Kamele answered, relieved to find Terran offered. Though she had painstakingly memorized the formal request in High Liaden, she suspected that her accent and emphasis were . . . not precisely canon.

474

"My name is Kamele Waitley, Professor of the History of Education at the University of Delgado. I am here to see the delm of Korval, on business of the clan."

The gentleman inclined gravely from the waist, not so much a bow as an acknowledgment of having heard, and stepped back, pivoting slightly as he did so.

"Please, Professor Waitley, come in."

She did so. He closed the door, gently, and once more inclined toward her.

"Please follow me. I will show you to the salon, and leave you for a few moments while I seek the delm on your behalf."

The salon was scarcely a dozen steps into the house. The gentleman opened the door—the same dark wood as the front door, but lacking the carved house-sign—and moved his hand gracefully, indicating, she hoped, that she should enter.

Three steps into the room, she stopped, the sound of the door closing behind her lost in her astonishment at the room in which she found herself.

Beneath her feet was a handsome rug of bronze and brown, the design suggesting leaves. Before her was a cluster of chairs, upholstered likewise in brown and bronze, and a few small tables. To her right was a large piece of furniture, brown with bronze drawer pulls. To the left was a sofa, brown, piled high with bronze and brown pillows. A window at the end of the room gave a view of the central garden.

Kamele took a hard breath. Jen Sar—Jen Sar's house on Leafydale Place was full of things to challenge and, yes, delight the senses. Not a proper scholar's dwelling, according to the aesthetic of Delgado, which preferred white walls and utilitarian furnishings that would neither call attention to themselves nor divert a scholar's mind from study.

This room—if Jen Sar had been accustomed to living in—to *interacting with*—rooms like this one... it was almost alive, this room, the parts producing a whole that was tantalizing, layered, and faintly dizzying.

Kamele drew a breath, heard a faint snap behind her, and turned, relieved to find that the formal gentleman had returned.

"Professor Waitley, Korval will see you. Please, I am asked to bring you to another room, if you will follow me."

The room was bright with sunshine, curtains thrust back from a long wall of windows looking out over a bank of white-and-yellow flowers. A trellis at the back of the flowers supported leafy vines.

Once again, Kamele stopped a few paces within, in order to take stock. Here was no elegant bronze-and-brown room. This room's wooden floor supported a simple and somewhat grubby blue rug, across which a baby was crawling, gurgling and determined.

On the far side of the rug stood a slender young man with untidy brown hair, wearing a high-necked black sweater and grey work pants.

He smiled at her.

"Professor Waitley," he said, his voice soft and his Terran free of accent. "Be welcome in our house."

She considered him. The baby shrieked merrily and continued her journey across the rug.

"I have come to speak to the delm of Korval," Kamele said, for surely this gentle-spoken boy was no hardened administrator.

"Yes, so Mr. pel'Kana had said. We will be able to accommodate you, Professor, in only a moment. Please, will you have tea? Wine? Coffee?"

"Nothing, thank you. I realize that my call is unexpected; however, it is *necessary* that I see the delm of Korval."

"And so you shall," the boy promised, and looked toward the hall door. "Very soon, now."

The baby shrieked again and gleefully captured the hem of Kamele's pants.

Carefully, she went down on one knee, and offered a finger as ransom. The baby snatched it with a grin.

Kamele felt her own face relax into an answering grin.

"You're quite the adventurer, aren't you?"

Before the baby could answer, the hall door opened to admit a wiry, sharp-faced woman, red hair falling in a single braid, far down her back. Like the boy, she was dressed in work pants and sweater, and like him, she was surely much too young to administer the star-spanning businesses of Clan Korval, and far too open-faced to have given an order for genocide.

"*Cha'trez,*" said the boy, as the woman stopped at the edge of the rug and gave Kamele a perfectly friendly smile. "Here is Theo's mother, come to speak with the delm."

The woman—Shatres?—laughed.

"Never rains but it pours," she commented, and held her hand down so that Kamele could shake it.

She did so, surprised at the strength of the girl's grip.

"Pleased to meet you, Professor Waitley. I'm Miri Robertson." She jerked her chin at the boy. "That's Val Con yos'Phelium. You've met Lizzie."

"Lizzie is extremely charming," Kamele said, disengaging her finger from the tiny fist while her mind worked.

Her studies had taught her that yos'Phelium was the delm's bloodline. Was it *possible* that this boy—

Careful of the child, she stood. Miri Robertson swooped down and gathered Lizzie up and against her shoulder. The baby laughed, and snatched at the tempting braid.

Kamele turned to the—to Val Con yos'Phelium.

"Forgive me," she said. "*Are* you the delm of Korval?"

"No, I am half of the delm of Korval," he answered earnestly, green eyes bright.

"And he'll make you pull the rest of it out of him, question by question," Miri Robertson said, bending a stern look on the boy, "because he's bored today."

She looked back to Kamele.

"What it is, we're what's called lifemates—equal partners. So that means, between us, him and me make one delm. It might be you don't actually need the delm, though—you'd be surprised how many people don't. If you'll just acquaint us with your trouble, we can maybe solve it without having to wake up the delm."

Kamele took a breath, and met Miri Robertson's grey eyes.

"I am here on behalf of Jen Sar Kiladi," she said, as calm and as factual as if she were in the classroom and these two children were her students. "I would like to see him, please."

"Alas," Val Con yos'Phelium said. "Jen Sar Kiladi is not here." He glanced to his . . . lifemate. "Indeed, I have been only lately instructed that Kiladi does not look to Korval."

The red-haired woman snorted a laugh, and reached 'round to disengage her braid from Lizzie's busy fingers.

Kamele frowned.

"Forgive me, but Theo, whom you apparently have met, has let me know that he *is* here." *And if he is a prisoner*, she thought, *denied visitors—his very presence in the house denied—then what will I do?*

"I think," the boy said gently, "that Theo may have said that *her father* was here. It is an impertinence, and it is true that I have not seen what Theo has written to you. It is, however, what I myself would write in a similar circumstance—that Father was with Korval."

Kamele pressed her lips together.

"That's what she wrote," she agreed, "but—"

"Theo and I, you see," the boy continued in his gentle voice, "have the honor of sharing a father. I am the child of . . . Father's first alliance. And, yes, he has been here, but—"

"He was wounded," Miri Robertson continued the sentence seamlessly, "by enemy action. Right now, he's—*ow!*"

Val Con moved, all effortless, flowing grace. He came to Miri's side, freed her ear from Lizzie's grip, and lifted the baby away.

"That is not how we honor our mother," he told her. "When will you learn manners, Talizea?"

Lizzie gurgled and snatched a handful of his hair.

"Is it too late to send her back?"

"I fear so."

Kamele could only be grateful to them for turning their attention away from her, and giving her a moment . . .

She swallowed, hard; blinked her eyes to clear

them. All of her study, all of her theories—Jen Sar bound unwilling to the service of Korval, and she an avenging scholar, come to liberate him!

Oh, very fine, Kamele, she told herself sharply.

But, no. Jen Sar had dropped his entire life, risked everything he was and had, in order to fly to the side of his child, who was...in a very great deal of trouble.

That made sense of everything; and was entirely consistent with the man with whom she had shared so many years.

And yet, there was still...

"When," Kamele asked, calling their attention back to her, "will Jen Sar—will *Theo's father*—return?"

"We don't know," Miri Robertson said solemnly. "He was wounded and now he's in the care of—an ally."

"It is our hope that the clan will receive him within the *relumma*," Val Con added. "However, much is unsettled, especially in Korval's orbit, and the time frame is a hope, Professor, not a certainty."

Another jolt, this one striking somewhere in the pit of her stomach.

Jen Sar was...wounded. *Wounded!*

She glared at Val Con yos'Phelium, who lifted an eyebrow and tipped his head to one side in a gesture so familiar she felt her heart catch midbeat.

"Theo's father is an elder scholar with more honors attached to his work than Clan Korval has ships!" she snapped. "He is a treasure, to be protected and cherished! Not sent out to be—wounded! It is not the work of elders to be wounded! Where were *you*, when Jen Sar was wounded?"

There was a silence—even Lizzie held still.

"He was someplace else, and in just as much danger,"

said a clear, cool voice from her right. Kamele turned to look at Miri Robertson, who nodded, once. "I sent him—Theo's father. Job had to be done, and there wasn't anybody else."

Her expression was firm, her eyes unwavering, and Kamele believed—believed without doubt—that *this* woman would, if necessary, order a planet fired upon—would do the deed herself, if there was no one else to do the job.

She inclined her head.

"I'll go to him. Where is this...*ally*?"

"We don't know," said Val Con yos'Phelium, and raised the hand not full of Lizzie placatingly when she rounded on him.

"We *don't* know, Professor—and that is wise. Korval is hunted, and space is dangerous. Our ally is old—old and very canny. As much as I would rather the clan enclosed him, Father is well protected where he is."

"Space is dangerous..." she repeated, and took a breath. "I have another topic."

He inclined his head, Lizzie grabbed another handful of hair, and he sighed, lifting his hand to work her tiny fingers loose.

"Yes. My daughter flies for Tree-and-Dragon. The news reports—"

"Ah." He smiled at her. "We are aware. Master Trader yos'Galan, as contract holder, has sent that Theo must come home—here to Surebleak. I have sent, as her brother, suggesting the same. Once she is here, where it is, strange to say, somewhat safer than space, we can together consider what is best to do. Certainly, she will wish to fly. It only falls to us to discover how she may fly without inviting unprovoked attacks upon her ship, and slurs against her good character."

"Depending on where she was, exactly, on that loop Shan sketched out for her," Miri added, "she could definitely be here within the *relumma*."

"There's more," Kamele said, looking between the two of them. "I was—I believe that one of my fellow passengers on the cruise liner wished to take me as a hostage to the reward for Theo's apprehension."

Val Con frowned, his mouth tightening.

"How did you elude this ambitious person?"

She sighed. "I left the ship and everything I had with me, except what was in my jacket, and hired as working crew on the *Judy*, bound in to Surebleak."

He smiled.

"Excellent."

"What I think you ought to do," Miri said, "since you brought these things to us—I think you ought to stay here. Sooner or later, Theo and her father are bound to show up, and when they do, you'll be on the spot."

"I couldn't impose—" Kamele began automatically, even as she began to wonder if there were hotels, or a scholar's hostel on—

"Yes, you can," Val Con interrupted her. "The house is large, as you will have noticed, so it is not a question of our having no room. I believe Mrs. ana'Tak told me only this morning that the pantry is full, so you will be no strain on our supplies."

"And," said Miri, smiling, "if Theo gets bull-headed about coming home, you can talk her down."

Kamele looked from one to the other. She thought of Jen Sar who, beyond those given, would have had one more reason for wanting her to stay—the real reason.

And what would be the real reason, she asked herself, that Jen Sar's son wanted her to stay inside his clanhouse?

It was very simple, really.

Security.

She was known, now, as the mother of Theo Waitley, who piloted for Tree-and-Dragon, and who shared a father with . . . half of the delm of Korval.

The . . . enemies of Korval; the people who had targeted Theo—those people now had *her* in their range, as well.

Kamele sighed.

"Space is not safe," she said. "I understand."

She sighed again, and bowed.

"Thank you."

The following is an excerpt from:

TRADE SECRET

✳ A New ✳
Liaden Universe®
Novel

SHARON LEE &
STEVE MILLER

Available from Baen Books
November 2013
hardcover

In a Familiar Space-Time Continuum, Consider the Young Gentlemen

• •

Stateroom Number Two
Liaden tradeship Wynhael,
outbound from Banth, a backworld

THE DEBT BOOK WAS OUT AND HELD BEFORE HIM, thirty-one prior pages covered in his cramped and careless hand. Although considered young by most of the society he ventured among, his debt book looked that of an old and garrulous fellow with multiple Balances in play. He'd learned early that Balance against those not properly of the society he walked among need not be counted, else the book might be full three times over, for he was never one to miss nor forgive a slight that might mean advantage for him, now or later. Still, if the book fell into nosy hands to be riffled—or through his untimely demise was passed on to one to complete—the pages already writ held among them the names of some of the cream of Liaden society, some in the person of individuals and others being named in line or clan as owing him. Of the Fifty High Houses of Liad, fully forty-one were directly represented, including, perhaps oddly, his own. This was not a book to be left idly about.

He had brought the book to his table with the intent to write in it; then he'd placed it, still sealed to his hand, while he'd allowed the ministrations of his lifelong lackey, face down. Doubtless his man knew what the book was, doubtless he had some minor idea of what was to be written, and why.

He took stock. His nosebleed—acquired quite unexpectedly—had stopped. He'd removed his ruined overshirt. He was, if called upon by unfortunate circumstance, barely presentable to his mother after she'd already seen his bloodied condition once. The damage done his *melant'i* needed urgent remedy, for she'd always had a long memory.

His face hurt, the headache still not gone since he'd refused the pain-saver he'd been offered as well as the wine.

He'd soon enough have wine, as soon as he felt his stomach proof against that surge of adrenal rage and fear and the distant iron of the blood in his mouth. In the moment he shivered in the dim safety of his stateroom, the words of his man reverberating:

"I am not a fully trained warrior, but it appears that if you'll be among the Terrans and the thieves, my lord, it would be best should you wear at least the web armor for the torso, if not also a stranded sleeve jacket and vest, which would have made your stand more feasible. We have packed such, though I dare say they're last year's fashion."

That had been sufficient for him to send the valet off to bring him a complete change of wardrobe, and the wine, asking it for a quarter bell, so he'd have time to write in his debt book.

Yes, indeed, debt book. This occasion needed Balance, and more Balance, for ·not only had . . .

The sight was in his mind again, as were the words. He'd offered the Terran woman the opportunity to buy her beast-brother of a Gobelyn out of the Balance—a tidy profit it would have been at 400 cantra!—and after a hint of consideration she'd snubbed him, *him*, Rinork-to-be! Turned her back with a smirk and some snide words in Trade, and walked away...

Bar Jan chel'Gaiban's shiver again threatened to disgorge his meal and more: who'd have thought he'd ever be so close to death at the hands of an alien?

He'd reached to prevent her escape and his hand had barely been on her shoulder when she'd turned impossibly fast and struck him. Not a mere push away, not a shake-off, but a fully realized jaw-snapping strike to the face. He'd been flung off his feet by the force of the blow, vision gone to stars and darkness, not quite senseless but certainly defenseless.

As much as he might deny it, there'd been no way to rise and strike back with his fellows, for by the time his breath allowed sight again, his fellows were held at bay by her knife and the silent approbation of a roomful of Terrans. Animals they all were, and armed, too, with hands eager and draw-ready.

No, there could be no proper Balance there and then. Had he risen then the chance was his throat would have been cut. And the speed!

The woman Gobelyn had been permitted to escape, followed by his ignominious return to *Wynhael*, still leaning on the shoulder of a pilot, nose dripping trail of his disgrace. Then had come his mother's tongue and censure before the coconspirators.

But the Terran woman...

Four hundred cantra! By stars he'd first thought she was going to pay or offer to deal! He could have used the cash—the number *had* twice measured a pressing debt. And then, the violence, so quick and sure. That kind of animal response was a danger. Surely then the plans they were laying were going to make space safer for Liadens. Surely the Terrans would be better off staying around their own uncultured worlds, with most traffic carried to civilized worlds elsewhere by Liadens and only the local traffic carried by Terran shuttles and ferries. Yet that happy result was not enough of a full Balance for one who'd struck him in the face and made him appear a weak fool...

Now, yes, he would write the debts owed out of this, Terran and Liaden. To have *Therinfel's* own captain laugh at him, saying, "My lord, she's a pilot and you're not, and we could all see she's a barfighter, which Rinork never allowed you. She had speed on you, and experience and likely the muscle, too!"

There'd been amused agreement by the others as they'd hurried along, and then what he supposed now was actual advice and not a hidden slur:

"The only way for someone like *you* to take a chance like that with a pilot is from behind, and with a gun, and only a sure shot to the head. You pushed in front of other Terrans, and that's stupid—why that's full gravity fail, boy! Did no one ever explain to you that touching a Terran woman in public could cost you your throat? You're lucky she walked away and that no late lover took your kidneys out from behind."

In ordinary times Lord Rinork would have been sitting comfortably on Liad, overseeing the growing empire of ships and merchants amassed by his predecessors and especially by his mother, the delm. He should have been home on Liad, waiting *his turn* as delm, with perhaps the occasional off-world tour to show that he could in fact be a trader, and to enjoy the fruits of being one of the Fifty High Houses.

He'd already found being a lord among the Fifty convenient, for his mother or his *qe'andra* made sure his bills were paid if he happened to forget, and even when his bills were so very personal that they oughtn't be shared with others, he was never pushed or prodded by those he owed, for quartershare time came, and he always paid from the oldest to the newest, or loudest first, eventually.

But in this time, being of the Fifty was not as convenient as it may have been, for the Terrans were encroaching on Liaden space lanes and trade zones, proving remarkably willing to take smaller profit and the worst of them *proud* to be planet-free. The most ambitious of them, though, were ambitious indeed, gathering together old technologies and hoping to leap far ahead of both Liad's fine ships and the combined might of the growing Combine. For all that their efforts were thought secret, they cost him money, unless of course such ships could be brought first to Rinork's hand.

On other fronts there was Korval, meddling as always, and then the constant bickering and begging of his mother's chosen partners and lackeys. Some were criminals if the news were out, and he supposed in passing that he need correct his man, for clearly when he'd warned of the need for armor among the "Terrans and the thieves," the thieves were the crew of the ships following his mother's plan, and his man Khana vo'Daran was in danger if anyone heard the clarity of his knowledge. His mother's plan, now, that he would not say was criminal, for the Terrans had no recognition among Liaden councils . . .

He sat now, thinking of luck and the fact that *he* was the Rinork heir and not that get of Quiptic . . . of the fact that the mines of Quiptic, which would be his soon enough and maybe sooner, and that he was far too old to be pleased to be called a boy, or have his shortcomings pointed out to him publicly, by anyone, pilot or not.

He had no misunderstanding: he was never, in fact, at his best in a fair fight unless that fight put him with dueling pistol in hand at a length of twenty or thirty paces. He was not fast, but that was not what dueling was about. Dueling took nerves—which he had—and accuracy, which he also had, especially given a chance to work with the house pistols, which would recognize his hand and engage auto-correction and target templating, the while passing for being old-fashioned. At no time would either pistol fire first for one not of proper blood.

This, of course, was not fair.

But he had no qualms about not being a fair fighter— the family history told the futility of "fair fights" as its shame ran through the rabbit's hutch! But who had understood that he'd personally have to right the wrongs foisted on him by an overconfident predecessor?

Obviously, the problems were many, and one of them that had now twice cost him dearly was lack of information. The other problems were proper Balances. So, the information situation could be dealt with by money spread wisely: this Gobelyn thing—the Jethri Gobelyn sucked into the rabbit's den for Balance, his kinswoman willing to slice a Liaden lord for him—this could not be left unsettled. Nor could the laughter of Liaden captains be left unanswered.

Bar Jan chel'Gaibin's debt book had fewer unused pages by the time valet vo'Daran returned with wine and new clothes. Given the views of the other conspirators, his mother the delm refused him another venture to the planet, and Rinork-to-be added plots to plots all night long.

Trade Hall, Cherdyan City, Verstal, on the Flinder-to-Liad Route

TRADER VEN'SAMBRA'S DEPARTING BOWS PERFORMED, the squarely turned back was an indication that the session was acknowledged as complete. That worthy continued to pull wares and bundles together, and finally departed, while the properly jeweled and name-badged Jethri ven'Deelin, recently adopted of Clan Ixin, checked files and waited respectfully to place the RETURNING FOR TRADE AFTER BREAK sign until the visiting trader was actually gone from in front of his booth.

The booth was much like a market stall, the counter having tall wings or walls so that the action and conversation of the next booth were not shared—and so that the sight lines made it difficult for those behind the wait-here line to see or hear as well. Beyond the wing walls traffic might go forth at a steady and crowded pace as it had earlier, or be near nonexistent as it was now, without meaningfully affecting one's ability to trade in quiet confidence.

As for Trader Jethri, the sweat was receding, finally, and he'd deduced that it was not the stress of trade that was at fault, it was the leftover heat of the short walk from their local quarters to the hall, and the hall itself, conditioned as it was for the locals. He'd fiddled with the broad flat ring on his trade finger—sweat was under it and the ring was long enough with him to leave an impression.

On duty, at least, he was to wear the ring, though it was far, far from the Master's trade ring he longed to wear one day. The key around his neck—the Terran trade key—would serve the same purpose on a Terran world, but here, *Elthoria*'s trade budget had bought this modest ring of silver with four simple stone insets. He'd change the insets, one per trade world, until none were the current crystal quartz but were all changed to topaz, and from topaz, he'd move to garnet, and from garnet, to amethyst insets. The big move of course was the boldest: the large amethyst of the tested and confirmed Master Trader, in platinum or better. Today, though, he was the lowly floor trader, and he'd be glad to see the end of this day, and the packing to return to *Elthoria's* splendid climate.

There'd been a short enough line when he opened for the day, one that had gotten shorter suddenly when the fourth in line, a graying Liaden gentleman of very unquiet demeanor, departed the area hastily after a semisuppressed bout of coughing, which cough had apparently unnerved the third in line, who'd gone off in the opposite direction—leaving a curiosity seeker first and Trader ven'Sambra second.

The curiosity seeker came to exchange cards, and to test Jethri's bows, in effect, for his offer to assist Jethri in learning basic trade concepts fell just short of a Balance-worthy insult. Jethri thanked his visitor, allowed as how he was trading only in tangible real goods for *Elthoria* and Clan Ixin, and looked forward to meeting again on the next voyage, should the trader have such goods to offer at that time.

Trader ven'Sambra's failed attempt at Terran required some soothing, and made Jethri wish he'd been back on *Elthoria's* trade deck buying and selling bulk items and novelties from multirouted trade-sats and certified world-net screens instead of dealing with a slow man who sought to outwit the must-be-stupid Terran turned Ixin. What a world! He was beginning to hate it.

Sometimes, in truth, he hated being on any world. Despite all his time in the vineyards of Irikwae not a year before, Jethri couldn't admire the atmospherics here, where the water often hung so thick in the air that it obscured the vision, even at ground level. Yes, he'd seen rain and worse at Irikwae, but this morning it had taken him a full half-shift to get physically comfortable in his trading. The lunch chime's quiet vibration gave little joy and he decided that today he would pass on another visit to the famous restaurant row out of doors just two damp streets over in favor of a quiet lunch in the trade hall's own small but properly ventilated feedery.

The desk in front of him had been his for three days now, along with the chair, and at least that was comfortable, once adjusted. He'd gotten to think of the desk as much a defense as a counter since this was the pushiest group of people he'd met at one place since he'd joined *Elthoria's* crew, aside those of Rinork who crowned the list at all times.

Wasn't much choice here, though, since the locals all insisted on trading face-to-face and they were all full-of-formal types who couldn't be bothered to do anything without top-notch bowing and the longest sentences this side of a *melant'i* play, and then they insisted in ways he thought were entirely un-Liaden, being unsubtle at best.

And that wasn't fair. He almost grimaced—*Elthoria's* comm crew had done him the dubious favor of sending along a copy of several reports on the arrival of *Elthoria* in Verstal's trading orbit, the information shared included the number of pods the ship carried, the recent routings, the names of captains, sub-captains, and traders, and anticipated destinations along with his own name and extremely modest biography among the more interesting tidbits.

He kept the twitch away from his lips—he'd thought perhaps he should send a copy on to Khat and to

Miandra—but Khat might not get the Liaden part of it, and Miandra would get it only too well, embroiled as she was with issues of *melant'i* and power off on her *dramliz* training. It was just that he was named as the new associate trader on the ship, and it was mentioned he was a newly adopted son of the house with specialties including textiles and trade in Terran regions. That was a kind of gossipy thing traders might need to know— but somewhere along the way the information that he formerly shipped as an apprentice on the Terrantrade-certified *Gobelyn's Market* had dropped into the news.

His first two days at trade here had been spent as much dealing with the curious and the tricky as with honest traders—often by himself—since the Master Trader was in heavy talks on a deal that might keep the clan's ships busy for years.

The trade hall was grown somewhat quieter than it had been early; and Jethri again caught sight of the gray-haired fellow who'd abandoned line with the coughs. He'd been in and out of sight while Trader ven'Sambra had been the only one in line, sometimes peering at the rotating display screens on the ships-in wall and other times standing back near an exit—and now he approached!

Jethri scooped the "taking a break" sign into place, but he was, just perhaps, too late, as the man actually rushed toward him, urgency unreasonably plain upon his face.

The bow was startling, offering to Jethri as it did honor due to a master of trade with decades of experience, and the undertone of appeasement indicating that one understood he was treading on the goodwill of another by merely appearing in front of him in an untimely way.

Three steps away from the counter he'd stopped, awaiting permission, and it was Jethri's curiosity which drove him to bow at all, using the merest of acknowledgments, thus accepting the honors heaped upon himself!

A good trader might have hesitated to come close to the counter with receipt of such a bow, but this man closed to the trading counter immediately, offering yet another effusive bow, and too, bringing with him the mixed scents of recent alcohol and oily foods, and perhaps of *vya* as well.

"Honored Trader, my certifications, if I may. You will understand that I am largely retired from trade but seeing the news of *Elthoria*'s arrival, and your own, I thought we should both profit greatly from some odds and ends of interest to collectors and specialists, which I have possessed from my own trading years gone by."

They traded names then, Jethri adding Gobelyn with his clan name, and then he dutifully glanced at the material presented, his own *melant'i* being certified by his seat in the hall as well as by his ring and his clan signs.

The trader's *certifications* were worn, and local, and showed a penchant for foods and kitchen goods. The local license typography was awkward to read, and the dates—well, some were older than Jethri. Likely this man, this Trader tel'Linden, had never been off-world, had only dealt in the local markets. His manner was unpolished and...

As if reading Jethri's careful study as concern, the man broke rapidly into a locally accented Liaden rush of words.

"I have always been a man of modest means, dealing with modest items, Trader, yet one in my position has been favored over the years to have seen many items of rarity and worth, the small riches of the clans and lines not of the High Houses, and some not of the

Mid Houses. These riches I have accumulated as I may, of interest to myself. The research to make use of these, and to find the proper home and buyer, this has been difficult, and it comes time now to reduce my private collections and give back to my clan my investments, as well as give to the universe of buyers goods which are outside the standard trade lines of my clan."

The trader paused then, stood straighter, and bowed his best bow yet, with a reasonable flourish and an understanding that his sleeves were not long enough to give emphasis . . .

"If you will honor me with a gift of time, I believe I have trades that will be worth the time we both invest, and yours, star-trader, much more than myself! Understand me, this is not my catalog, but my stock!"

The man raised his large leather-look trade case, withdrew keys from an inner pocket, eyes intent on Jethri's reaction.

"There is a seat you may use," Jethri admitted, "if you would care to join in an exploration of our trading possibilities."

The trader's portfolio, lined as it was with sheets of impossibly thin black leather, was itself an item Jethri might like, but the first object revealed, gaudy and antique at once, left him very carefully speechless.

He turned his hand over to palm up—a request to hold the item—and wished Paitor was here to see this, or Dyk, who would have wildly differing opinions on the desirability of possessing such a thing. Dyk would love it for incongruity, and Paitor . . . well, what would Paitor actually *say* about such a ring as this?

"Yes," the trader crooned, "this is an object one might wear in many places, secure that it would be noticed and appreciated. The stone, of course, is flawless, and the setting is true multibanded flash-formed Triluxian!"

The ring was deposited oh-so-gently in Jethri's hand for inspection. After a moment he sighed, looking at it from this way and that—and requested, with a bow, "May I use my handscan for a closer look?"

Triluxian—bonded of microlayered titanium, gold, platinum, with a salting of rhodium, was not something to be ignored. The style of the thing suggested it was a very old ring, and the slight signs of wear suggested it was an artifact someone had actually used—which is to say, displayed on their hand in public—frequently. Thus the scanner, looming for details, and giving back the certifiable purity of the finding. There was value here, but not riches.

As for the stone—he held back a chuckle mightily. Firegem, yes, truly a flawless firegem, but for the worth of it in any state . . . it was a fluted cabochon firegem, which made it odd, but other than that? What it was doing set in—

"Of course," said the trader, though his face tensed enough for Jethri to see it. "You'll find some odd lettering, I believe . . ."

Handscan again. Jethri studied the band of the thing, and indeed, there was odd lettering, which likely appeared even odder to the trader for it being Terran lettering, and very tiny. Perhaps it was someone's name, perhaps there was also a date, Cobol 426 . . . he let the scanner record the thing to look at later. Might as well set blast glass in the thing as a firegem, unless it dated to the original discovery of the things, or was the first . . .

"An extremely unusual item," Jethri admitted, allowing the trader to have the ring back. The ring must be more than it looked . . . else a story worth sharing if it could found.

The trader flipped to the next sheet.

There, a simple sheet of metal with rolled edges, almost like one of Dyk's small cooking pans upside down, with diagrammatic instructions inscribed on it, and a few words in oddly stilted Liaden. Instructions for what? Might be of interest to a specialist but didn't touch him very much...

A twitch of fingers—within the sheets, for there were two of them interlocking, were fractins.

Fractins. Four of them. Fakes, he thought, just looking and needing no scanner to vet them. The color was—not right. The man's hands shook. As common as these were in Terran space, on this side of the trade line they were deemed Old Tech, and thus contraband, and unmarketable in the bargain. Of course, if they were fakes they might not be illegal—he hadn't got to that section of Liaden trade laws yet, and would have to study,

As noncommittally as possible, he flicked fingers, and there were three more fractins, fitted together, and they were real. They were not only real, they knew he was there, he was sure, knew that they were recognized as real, knew—it was as if they called for him to buy them and take them away.

He blinked. He'd had that reaction several times as a child, the feeling that real fractins looked back at him. He'd *liked* his own fractin, and was always glad it was his lucky piece; he'd been convinced that his fractin *liked* him, too. When Arin, his father, had talked with him about his fractin collections, he'd never doubted Jethri when Jethri could point to his own fractin amidst a score of true and fake fractins. Arin hadn't argued, either, when they'd built the fractin frames and Jethri'd insisted that his fractin wasn't comfortable with being put in with the others in this order, but must be in that order or in this position...

Jethri realized that he'd taken several seconds too long this time, that he could still feel the fractins calling, even though he knew he shouldn't—no, *couldn't*—be found in possession of them. So he permitted himself a slight grimace, as if disinterested, or perhaps bored by seeing more of the same...and flicked his fingers.

And next was another of the curious pans, with a mark he recognized: *this side down.*

Struck by an idea, and still feeling the call of fractins, he could see the outline of the pan in the leather sheet; saw what might be alignment points, judged that if filled with properly aligned fractins...

He flicked fingers, to find the next sheet of leather to be pocketed, with nine pockets, and in each pocket showed a portion of similar but not identical...things. Devices. Kahjets. They were built on the scale and size of the weather device he'd handled to such strange effect on Irikwae, a device that called an unseasonable wind-twist to the vineyards and indirectly led to Miandra's banishment to Liad. These, too, felt like they were interested, as if they recognized hands that knew...

He flicked his glance to the man's face, where there was now sweat. Jethri realized the trader was at risk and his own *melant'i* as well. He had not, of course, promised to the Scouts he would unmask other owners....

"Not these machines, Trader, nor others like them if there are more in your stock; I have clear instructions about such."

The trader's eyes got big and his hands shook. He glanced down, looked up, hopeful.

"Yet these will be treasures, I understand, in Terran markets. These are..."

Jethri offered a placating motion and conciliatory bow.

"Alas, as you may not know, given the circumstance of your retirement, my ship aims for no such market in this voyage, Trader, and I am not of an age or *melant'i* to carry devices such as this aboard my ship, nor to secure them, against the hope that sometime I might visit a Terran port. Show me other things, if you have them, since we are here, and you have sought me out."

The trader, crestfallen, flipped past two more sheets, and now there were other oddities, more than a dozen keys in the style used by Terran ships on one of the sheets, and a trade calendar on a flexible sheet, some two hundred standards old, with illustrations of—of star systems.

Practicality and necessity warred—lunch and a rest break called, even more so since he knew that the trader was offering contraband amidst this trade lot.

"Against time we run," Jethri said, emulating one of Norn ven'Deelin's phrases, "let us proceed with pace," he suggested—and there, the next page was shown, a very, very skinny blade looking perhaps Terran, and *flick*—

A page passed over, and another, and then a small flat guidebook, with real pages, the title, in Liaden: *Dealing with Terrans*. He signaled stop, requested and received the opportunity to look at it. The book was of the age as the trade calendars, and produced by a trade station he'd never heard of, offering hints on language and demeanor, and showing known and anticipated trade routes . . .

"Enough," he said, entranced. "My time presses. Price me this, the two shipping plates and the calendars, as a unit. Also, the firegem ring, which is interesting, but hardly a rarity in these days, if ever it was. Honest price gets honest return."

"Trader, I'd hoped to sell the lot—"

"I hear this from your lips, Trader, but from mine

you have heard I will not touch the items from the old machines, nor will I have the squares such as I had as a child for toys."

"Four cantra for the whole I was asking..."

Jethri bowed from his seat and stood.

"I'll not have the whole. The partial lot I have outlined only. Only the items, with the firegem—altogether a quarter-cantra, paid now. I cannot use the others and there's no market to test their value or their worth."

There was nothing in the broke-lot that he knew he could sell, but for his own uses, say the information that such concentrations of Old Tech might exist among the Liadens—that was worth much—and the old trade route information. He'd had the same feeling when he'd discovered the *vya* that had gone to pay for the *Market*'s overhaul. Even the firegem, silly as it was...

The man before him began to fold his sales portfolio sadly and ventured, "One half-cantra, Trader, and you break my back at that."

Jethri worked the feeling in his head, remembered Paitor's earnest lessons of give-and-take...

"I have the quarter-cantra in my pocket for you, and some Terran funds, ten kais. Also, paying cash we need not use the hall's sales registry nor fund transfers. Else, my meeting awaits. Understand, paying cash, I will forget your name."

Jethri handed the trade case back, very concerned. Not about his offer, but about the contents that called to him and made his hands itch to hold them and have them and use them.

The trader's eyes were large. Jethri'd not meant to threaten, but now he could see the man before him losing composure. Surely, then, he was a desperate man, even more desperate than Jethri.

The man's hands were shaking, but he was already reopening his portfolio. "Done."

As the transaction settled, it turned out that the Terran coins broke to fifteen rather than ten kais, which Jethri allowed without hesitation. Now his urge was to be away from this man and his ragged breathing....

The trader gone, Jethri slammed the sign onto the table, tucked his haul into his cloak's storage pockets. He realized he was shivering now, and wondered what he'd done to suddenly feel so cold.

Those kahjets! Not toys, not toys, not toys. Paitor would have perhaps denounced the man, and perhaps Grig would have bought it all....

It would not do to dine, even alone, while still so unsettled.

Succor was to hand after a dizzying riot of panic, which he knew he must not succumb to, and then a reminder that some called trade "the quiet war."

With the aid of one of Pen Rel's warrior tricks of centering, he let the hard floor be his base, let the world of breathing be his focus, closed his eyes for a moment to visualize the coming reality of the big ring, firmly on his hand, and he a trader of competence, and hurried for his break. With luck, tomorrow he'd sleep on *Elthoria*!

—end excerpt—

from *Trade Secret*
available in hardcover,
November 2013, from Baen Books